Son of Rhubarb

H. Allen Smith

SON OF
RHUBARB

Illustrated by Leo Hershfield

TRIDENT PRESS New York 1967

Library of Congress Catalog Card Number: 67-16405

Published simultaneously in the United States
and Canada by Trident Press, a division of Simon & Schuster, Inc.,
630 Fifth Avenue, New York, N.Y. 10020.

PRINTED IN THE UNITED STATES OF AMERICA

Other books by H. Allen Smith

ROBERT GAIR: A STUDY
MR. KLEIN'S KAMPF
LOW MAN ON A TOTEM POLE
LIFE IN A PUTTY KNIFE FACTORY
LOST IN THE HORSE LATITUDES
DESERT ISLAND DECAMERON
RHUBARB
LO, THE FORMER EGYPTIAN
LARKS IN THE POPCORN
WE WENT THATAWAY
LOW AND INSIDE (WITH IRA L. SMITH)
PEOPLE NAMED SMITH
THREE MEN ON THIRD (WITH IRA L. SMITH)
MISTER ZIP
SMITH'S LONDON JOURNAL
THE COMPLEAT PRACTICAL JOKER
THE WORLD, THE FLESH, AND H. ALLEN SMITH
THE REBEL YELL
THE AGE OF THE TAIL
WRITE ME A POEM, BABY
THE PIG IN THE BARBER SHOP
DON'T GET PERCONEL WITH A CHICKEN
WAIKIKI BEACHNIK
LET THE CRABGRASS GROW
HOW TO WRITE WITHOUT KNOWING NOTHING
TO HELL IN A HANDBASKET
TWO-THIRDS OF A COCONUT TREE
A SHORT HISTORY OF FINGERS
POOR H. ALLEN SMITH'S ALMANAC

Son of Rhubarb

⊗⊗ Prelude: End of a Cat

HE chose an enchanting and exotic setting for his departure, and he had deep within him a wildly eager libidinous urge—which some believe to be the best of all urges—as he came to his end.

The flagship *Thaddeus* of the Banner Line had just entered Pago Pago Bay and moved across one of the truly scenic harbors in the South Pacific. The great luxury liner tied up at the Pago Pago docks, within sight of the ramshackle building where Sadie Thompson twitched and wriggled things at the Reverend Mister Davidson, driving him out of his Bible-whacking mind and proving to herself that all men are the same: "PIGS!" So said Sadie.

The *Thaddeus* had been at the wharf no more than half an hour when Eric Yaeger, entranced by the storied, tropical scenes spread out before him, absently let the thin silken leash slip out of his hand. In two minutes Rhubarb was over on the port side of the vessel, perched on the rail, looking across at Rainmaker Mountain and the sprawling waterside structure flaunting the trade name, in huge lettering: "CHICKEN OF THE SEA."

An auxiliary ketch of respectable dimensions moved past the *Thaddeus*, headed for the open sea. Rhubarb glanced down at it and instantly the jog in his tail began to jerk. On the deck of the ketch was a big woolly soft-looking snow-white girl cat. Rhubarb tensed himself. It was a far leap but for reasons of hunger he didn't hesitate. He shot through the air in an arc that would have scored for an Olympic diver; but he had neglected to remember —or did not even know—that he was no longer young, no longer as strong as he once had been when he terrorized dogs, crocodiles, kinkajous, mules, people, and other fearsome beasts. His reflexes had grown sluggish and so he missed the stern of the ketch by two or three feet. He hit the churning water, the violent slapping blow against his belly knocked all the wind out of him, and he was sucked into the swirling wake. A deck steward on the *Thaddeus* had been the only witness and now he raced to starboard and shouted to Eric that Rhubarb had gone overboard. Eric and several others dashed to port; as he ran Eric began divesting himself of clothing, fully intending to dive forty feet into the bay to rescue Rhubarb. But there was no trace of the cat. He was gone.

Thus passed one of the major figures in the whole pantheon of American finance and industry; thus departed one of the most engrossing personalities of his time; thus, with an ameliorating passion enflaming his senses . . . thus died the most celebrated animal of the Twentieth Century. Within a few hours it would be announced in New York that the Stock Exchange would shut down for a day in his memory.

This was the magnificent alley cat, big and rangy and smoke-yellow, that had emerged from a Long Island community to become, first, the house pet of old Thaddeus Banner and, later, his lawful heir. Disgusted with the deplorable and undependable ways of the human species, Thad Banner had willed his fortune and his daffy baseball team, the New York Loons, to the cat. And under the inspiring stewardship of Rhubarb, the inept and wobble-headed Loons, bumbling and fumbling worse than the Brooklyn Dodgers in the time of Babe Herman, somehow came to life and won the World Series from the Philadelphias.

Rhubarb's life story, up to that point—which would certainly seem to be the highest point attainable by a cat—was put in print by one of the most talented litterateurs of the nation, and appeared under the simple but dramatic title, RHUBARB.* The biographer was eminent at home and abroad, a recognized authority on cats, baseball, psychiatry, money, political science, gourmet cooking,

---

* It differs from most great classics in that it cannot be bought anywhere.

ants and bees, Dixieland music, oceanography, horse racing, the theatre, Kelly pool, Washington protocol, poontang, the stock market, cowboys real and imagined, the Jet Set, the sewers of Paris, and people. He carried spear in no man's opera. More than that, he wrote a lyrical and lilting prose that astonished and often stupefied and confused the reading public. Sometimes it was said of him that he spelt good.

It may be surmised that Rhubarb died of sex starvation. This Croesus of Catdom was given everything a cat could possibly want in the way of fine foodstuffs, first-rate creature comforts, expensive people comforts, a miniature swimming pool sans water but always half full of catnip grown in Shropshire, all the sleep he wanted . . . but the one thing was missing. It was sheer oversight. If Eric Yaeger had ever thought that the cat entertained deep yearnings within him, by reason of his being a virtual prisoner for month after month and year after year, that Rhubarb would have taken *anything*—a mildewed grimalkin with cockleburs in her tail—then Eric would have made provisions. But somehow the matter had been overlooked; it may have been that in the back of his mind Eric had a vagrant notion that Rhubarb had gone whizzing past the so-called dangerous age, and was now content to slurp warm milk, commit horrifying mayhem on any living creature that got in his way, and sleep for hours in front of a television set. If that's what Eric thought, he was in error. Rhubarb was, in fact, *fraught all over* with lust, and that fluffy white creature had been his undoing.

Now, on this saddest of sad days at romantic Pago Pago, years had passed since the writing of Rhubarb's biography and things were no longer the same with Banner Enterprises. Things were, in fact, somewhat better. More than somewhat. Rhubarb no longer owned a big league baseball team, but he had become the owner of pretty much everything else. Through the shrewd operations and expert maneuverings of his guardian, Eric Yaeger, and the Executive Committee functioning under the direction of Eric, he had become the J. Paul Getty of cats. His holdings included the Banner Line of thirty-two cruise ships, oil fields and refineries in Oklahoma and California, tin can factories and wolfram mines in Bolivia, the Banner chain of superb resort hotels, a complex of great plants in which computers kept themselves busy manufacturing other computers and, of more recent origin, most of the town

3

of Bannerville in Michigan—seat of the automotive works producing the quality cars, the Tomcat, the Bobcat, the Fiery Pussy, the Red Tabby Runabout, and the luxurious Catillac. Not to be overlooked in this brief inventory are the Banner skyscrapers in San Francisco, Chicago and New York, from which the cat's great empire was directed. Banner Enterprises had, in putting up these tall, graceful structures, inaugurated a new architectural style: the buildings were fabricated of steel and stone and concrete, with only enough glass to fill windows of ordinary size. These Banner skyscrapers were a national sensation, an artistic triumph, and the styling was promptly copied by other great corporations.

Something of Rhubarb's stature in the business world, as well as his standing in public esteem, was contained in a newspaper article written in recent weeks by the sensational young New York reporter Ringo Fox, who strolled the avenues in milk-white oxfords, with certified whooping crane feathers sticking out of his hip pockets. Some New Yorkers deemed him eccentric.

Ringo Fox's article was noteworthy for two reasons: it consisted of a report on two weeks spent constantly in the company of Rhubarb and his entourage, giving him an opportunity to project a fairly accurate portrait of the celebrated tomcat; more than that, it represented the beginning of young Mr. Fox's break with the new order in metropolitan journalism, in which the schematics of makeup and the raw-vital Crisco-assed . . . whomp-whomp-whamp-whamp snuddle gogs were crying out of their shibby-poons ZARP ZARP BeeeeZARP . . . hubby-mummy VA-ROOOOOOOOOOM!!!!!!!!

    crying

        indeed

           for

               the

                    Guuuuu-rooooo

                  proles

                          pussycat life-style wailing in their fright-wiggy stretchy pants proley proley PROLEY Rupture Rupture Ruh-Hup-Choor HOYN-YA! But But But But But Kissa My . . . Precisely!

It was rough going for Ringo Fox, difficult for him to cast aside the chromatic New Dimension; thus far he had been unable to get the whooping crane feathers out of his hip pockets, but he was making progress with his prose. In his portrait of Rhubarb he interpolated little scenes in and around New York and these vignettes served to illustrate the cat's hold on the public imagination. Here are a few of Mr. Fox's bits:

SCENE: *Small section of multi-glandular grandstand at Loonlandia, formerly known as Banner Field. Two frabjous fans are in raw-vital conversation.*

OSWALD: *Hey Ferdie, looka! Inna fiel' box ovah theh. That's him. Useta own the team, useta own this whole ball pock. Man, them was the days! He's the one sole out to this lousy Vladimir Borateen Syndicate. Looka! Good Ole* Rhubarb!

FERDIE: *Sheeeeez! Inna flesh!*

* * *

SCENE: *Beside swimming pool at Westchester Super Scuba Country Club. Two cattypussed pussycats in black decal G-strings. Loll. Lolling. Lolly-woddling.*

KITTEN: *Get a load of him! All that money! Whoooo-eeee! So he takes one drowsy look at my build and then drops off to sleep. This is the first time since I left high school I can't figure out what to do about it.*

CANDY: *You'll figga it out. You'll figga somethin'.*

* * *

SCENE: *Opening night at the opera. Splendidly-caparisoned customers along one of the aisles gawk, hug their Harley-Davidson 74s, center their attention on a non-pussy cat moving slowly along at the end of a leash.*

BABY ROSE JAGGER: *It's him! Isabelle, it's him*—aren't *he* divine! *And the checkbooks!*

ISABELLE JONES: *I mean he's the* beautiful *people! Owns a whole town out there in Michigan. Got a statue of him right in the middle of the town. Sex-eeeee!*

BING KAHN: *Yeh. Called 'em the Loons. 'Member? Them players couldn't get hits less they rubbed the jernt in his tail. Strawdnry!*

UNIDENTIFIED MANBIRD: *What's a god dern cat doin' in this here place of culcher? Ahm a-goin' back tuh Johnson City!*

* * *

SCENE: *Newspaper city room. Reporter at desk typing. Ricky-Ticky-Ticky. City desk man squarges in, stretch pants straining against hawglardy buttocks.*

5

CITY DESK MAN: *You think he's actually the real power behind this merger?*

REPORTER: *Could be.*

CITY DESK MAN: *Don't sit there and tell me he can understand about stock transfers and amortization of bullish upside-down debentures and all that stuff.*

REPORTER: *I wouldn't say he understands it, and I wouldn't say he don't. Just don't forget who he is. Don't forget he happens to be the majority stockholder in this newspaper. You fool around with him and you'll find yourself out scratchin' spit with the rest of the chickens. Just keep it in mind—he's RHUBARB!*

In the splendid suite which Rhubarb had shared with Eric aboard the *Thaddeus*, the dead cat's guardian sat with his head in his hands. Now and then he let his hands drop and said to the carpet that it had been his fault and his alone. The three men in the room with him, three members of the Executive Committee, also were showing signs of profound shock and sadness. But whereas Eric's depression stemmed from the genuine deep affection he had always felt for Rhubarb, the men of the Executive Committee were dissembling. There was no true sadness in them, merely inner wonder and speculation as to what would happen to Banner Enterprises now. A complex question indeed, all things considered.

Ogden Crump, a pudgy, mean, money-hungry genius who knew all there is to know about oilfields and minerals, had to outscore the other Committee members in sentimentalizing his spurious emotions. That was the way of Ogden Crump.

"It's just got to be," he murmured, as though speaking to himself. "There's just *got* to be a place for Rhubarb in Heaven. Ah refuse to sit here and think that our little pal has not been taken directly into the Kingdom of God."

Eric raised his head and stared at Ogden Crump—a man he had never liked, yet a man the others felt was unexpendable in the organization. Eric had to lay one on him.

"Ogden," he said, "I feel low, as low as a man can get. But I have something to say to you. You may know all about depletion allowances and catalytic fragmentation and go-devils and ad valorem and hard-rockers and Protestant ore and silicosis costs and

6

gallows-frames and wiggle-tails, but Ogden, god damn you, you don't know your ass from your eyelid."

It didn't seem to bother Ogden Crump and, wisely, he made no answer. Eric turned and stared out the porthole. He realized that he, too, must concern himself with the future.

"My God," he suddenly burst out, "if I'd only had sense enough to let him go out with the girls! If only he'd left us an heir! Then we could hold things together!"

What Eric didn't know was . . . .

&o& Chapter ONE

EIGHT thousand miles in a northeasterly direction from Pago Pago a girl named Diana Fowler emerged from La Fortaleza after a stroll through four hundred years of history—Puerto Rican history. The weathered and crinkled old buildings at the edge of San Juan Bay have served as the seat of Puerto Rico's government since the middle years of the 16th Century. Within the walls of La Fortaleza are the offices of the Governor, as well as his private chapel and his residence.

Diana Fowler, in addition to being one of New York's top fabric designers, was the somewhat rare kind of person who has a feel for history. It seemed to ascend from the ground, or from the pavement, and flow into her consciousness by a process of osmosis. She could *feel* the procession of the centuries, and sense somehow the presence of the colorful ghosts—at this moment the wraiths of Columbus and Ponce de Leon and men in armor clanking back and forth in these narrow streets of Old San Juan. Diana sauntered along, looking at the faded but still elegant homes with inner patios sometimes visible from the street, and with their wrought-iron gates and their balconies overhanging the sidewalks. The roadway, paved with smooth blue-gray cobblestones, fascinated her as those pavements have fascinated many other travelers.

The stones had served as ballast for scores of Spanish ships in the westward voyages to the Indies, and they were dumped in piles on the waterfront, until someone with an artistic eye came along and said:

"*En mis tiempo patillas las piedras mismo adoquines con vega baja y playa de ponce, tambien de vez luquillo, por que corozal los barranquitas.*" (Oh, look how pretty are these blue dornicks—let us use them for cobblestones in the streets.)

Some argue that they are not stones at all, but rounded castings from the residue of iron furnaces in Spain. A few scholars—members of a historical society dedicated to the belief that Puerto Rico was discovered by Polynesian navigators and that no such person as Christopher Columbus ever existed—hold that the blue-gray cobblestones were lobbed ashore from seaborne catapults during an ancient and obscure war with the Virgin Islands.

But enough of these academic matters, fascinating though they may be. We must hasten back to the side of Miss Diana Fowler, who owns non-technical equipment which far overshadows the blue stones of the pavement. The reference is to her glorious hair, her unforgettable face, and her figure. The hair is rich straw yellow, falls almost to her shoulders, and swirls and tosses with the movement of her head; the face—let it be said that in contour it is pure Garbo, with the added attraction of a twinkly, crinkly little grinnish smile; and the body . . . Good Gracious God! Miss Diana Fowler carried around with her on her travels and in her day-to-day life such a body as would cause grown men to fall to the ground and bite sticks.

There are two segments of this body that seem to stand out more than the others. One segment is on the front, the other is on the back, and each of these segments consists of two equal parts. If there were nothing more to Miss Diana Fowler than these two segments, fore and aft, with all her remaining structure non-existent, she would still have it over almost every other young woman on earth. If you should gather from this that Miss Fowler is breasted superbly and bottomed-beyond-belief, you are close to the truth.

Diana knew what she had. And she knew how to use what she had. It would be unfair to her to say that she was unplucked. She had, indeed, been plucked. Twice, maybe three times. And it would be equally unfair to her to say that she did not enjoy it.

9

She simply came to the conclusion that she had a little something more than most girls, and that she should not slosh it around as if it were water in a two-buck car-wash.

She wore no bra, ever. She owned no girdle. She was splendidly adept in the art of jiggling, a delicate anatomical exercise which, in its purest forms, outranks all the art treasures in the Louvre for grace, beauty, and a propensity for stirring men to their very roots. Beneath her outer garments Diana habitually wore the briefest of briefs, elastic panties so sheer that they could have been sent through the United States mails, first class, for a five-cent stamp. Whenever she walked abroad, whether on Fortaleza in San Juan, Fifth Avenue in Manhattan, or any other place on earth during warmish seasons, male creatures had a tendency to drift in behind her and hold position, sometimes walking great distances out of their way rather than abandon the joy of watching Diana jiggle. Let it be understood, jiggling belongs to the behind. In the forward area, bobbing is the thing. A girl who has learned to synchronize her bobbing with her jiggling is a girl who will likely make a mark in the world.

It is well, too, for us to realize that jiggling can be overdone and *is* overdone by a great many beautiful but uninspired girls. One of these was Marilyn Monroe. She was inclined to roll and rotate and *warble* her hinder parts. She was not, by any means, the founder of the warble-technique, but she brought on a fashion amongst young women with bottoms of a suety composition. During the reign of Miss Monroe as Hollywood's leading sex-wagon, there was an outbreak of butt-warbling in the United States that got clean out of hand and, before long, spread southward through Latin America and eastward to the motherlands. Sociologists tell us that this mass-hysteria (among themselves they referred to it as *ass*-hysteria) led to the frightful outbreak, in the early 1960s, of a disease which struck at the muscles known as the *tensor fascia latae*, the *latissimus dorsi*, and the *gluteus maximus*. These muscles are situated in the middle area of the human body. The sociologists say that the wide incidence of the disease in turn led to an even more fearsome epidemic which manifested itself in certain spastic "dances" designated as the Twist, the Slop, the Frug, the Watusi, the Mashed Potatoes, the Traf, the Mule, the Hully-Gully, the Pigeonwing, the Monkey, the Jerk, the Castle Walk and the Farfel-Farf. It is not necessary that these spin-off symptoms of the plague be described in detail—the world knows about them all too well. The wild and idiotic movements of each variation were known to an earlier generation, who referred to this type of activity as "throwing a fit." Sad as it may seem, it is necessary to say that Miss Marilyn Monroe was unwittingly responsible for turning our most elegant and genteel supper clubs into Holy Roller revival meetings; at the height of the dementia the disease even reached into the White House, where some of the leading people of the land often assembled for the purpose of throwing fits together.

Diana never warbled. She jiggled. She jiggled with all the finesse that a master chef uses in flavoring his finest sauce. She knew that jiggling, if kept under rigid control, is far more provocative than gross and undisciplined warbling. A girl who knows how to maintain that discipline almost persuades the gentlemen who fall into step behind her that she majored in jiggling at college.

Diana had not noticed that the sky was darkening and now a few large drops of rain hit the pavement and in seconds she was standing in a cloudburst. It was a hard, slanting rain and she began running. When she arrived at Calle San José she turned right, ran a few more steps, and entered an establishment called the Small World Bar.

Howard Conley, proprietor of the little saloon, watched her come splashing out of the street and then spoke to Frank Evans, his chunky bar beast. "One scotch on the rocks," Conley ordered and then turning to the girl standing in a puddle of dripwater, he said, "You look like you've already had your chaser, so I'm buying you a hot toddy."

"Very thoughtful of you, Howard," said Diana. "No Midge yet, huh? Listen, Howard, can't the government figure out a warning system of some kind, let the citizens know—set off sirens and ring church bells? I had less than a block to go and before I could make it to the world's smallest grog shop, I was drenched. Where's the drip-dry room?"

"Paradise," said Howard. "That's what we call it. Paradise in the Caribbean." Diana climbed onto a stool between Howard and a striking-looking girl, auburn-haired with delicate, almost classical features, and a torso to go with these things. Howard began a conversation with Frank the bartender and Diana took a sip of her scotch.

"You a friend of Midge McLean?" The auburn-haired girl's voice was pitched low—the particular kind of female voice that some men think sexy; there are other men who consider *all* female voices to be sexy. Her eyes, looking now at Diana, were dark brown and she had eloquent skin.

"Matter of fact," Diana said, "I was supposed to meet her here."

"She'll be here," said the girl. "She's probably holed up somewhere waiting for this rain to stop." She told Diana her name was Muffin and then turned her attention in the other direction. Two men were on stools beside her, and the one farthest from Diana was talking to the other.

"Yes," he said, "I'm a magazine writer out of New York. Gonna do a piece on Doña Felisa."

"I'm from Ohiuh," said the other man, older, paunchy, thinning hair. "Come down for a visit with my sister, Ole Muffin here. She's down here all by herself, but she don't need nobody to look out for her. She's smart as a treeful of owls."

"She's also," said the magazine writer, "one of the most beautiful girls I've seen down here. Or anywhere else."

"Wanna make a play for her?" asked the man from Ohiuh.

"You mean," stammered the New Yorker, taken somewhat aback, "you mean you . . . you wouldn't mind—her brother?"

"Christ no. We got a good understanding between us. She goes her way, I go mine. She does what she wants to do, I do what I want to do. If you don't mind my saying so, we got an intelligent approach to life, me and Ole Muffin. Here, move in here and set with her. I got to stagger over to the travel agency and see about my plane ticket." He gave his sister an indelicate jab in the ribs with his elbow and wagged his head toward the writer. After which he went out into the rain. The magazine writer sat for a spell, cogitating. A most unusual situation. Brother offering up sister to the first guy to come along. He turned and she was sitting looking straight into his face, her lips parted in a smile that illuminated her glistening teeth, her eyes tightening just a trifle. Little tingling things ran up from his heels and twittered over his thighs. All systems were go.

The two now began talking, and Diana eavesdropped shamelessly. The laws that govern human nature dictate that she, **an intensely curious young woman, should hold position and observe** the working out of this little drama. She herself was perplexed, though not as much so as the young man grown radiantly raunchy. He had made his decision and he was beginning to ball the jack.

Diana listened intently as the young man splashed livid language around the premises. His weapons of assault ranged from purple-prose tributes to the young woman's beauty, to eighth-gradey type cracks of the where-have-you-been-all-my-life variety, to the Hard Approach. A whimsical notion entered Diana's mind —that this young fellow had started his magazine writing career on *True Confessions* and made it finally to *Guideposts*. As for the girl Muffin, she played it cool and coy, leading the guy on, plainly enjoying the little game. When he asked her if she'd like to go to dinner with him at the Condado Beach, she began to put on a slight chill.

"If you think I'm a one-night stand," she snapped at him, "then you are Mister Jerk from Jerkville. How much money you got on you? I'm expensive."

Dismay came into the young man's face. This changed the whole picture. He was one of those guys who always said that he'd never pay for it, not even if he could get it in the discount houses. He was upset, and he was miffed with Muffin. More than miffed.

"But," he said, almost whining, "your brother said that I . . ."

"My brother my ass!" Muffin interrupted, her deep sexy voice now modulating into an animal growl. "That wasn't my brother, you puny booby. That was my jack gagger."

"Jack gagger?" the young man repeated, clearly bewildered.

"You call yourself a writer!" she said disdainfully. "Some writer! You couldn't be Mr. Mailer, could you? The lad you talked to, who said he was from Ohio, is my husband. He's my jack gagger. He *pimps* for me. I do hope you know what a pimp is."

The young man turned away, slapped a hand on the bar and spoke bitterly to the ever-present ambience: "God Almighty! Hooked like a sailfish! H. Allen Smith *told* me to look out for this sort of thing! Why, oh why, don't I heed his words? Bartender, my check!" He left the place without ever looking at her again.

Muffin turned to Diana and grinned. "That ought to hold *him* for a while," she said, delivering a friendly pat to Diana's top round. Diana chose not to respond, and didn't look at the girl. At first she thought she had detected an element of warmth and sincerity in this young woman, but how wrong can you get? A prostitute with her own husband for her pimp. Good Godly, young Wadley!

Howard Conley sensed that something was out of plumb and asked Diana to join him at one of the small tables cuddled against the wall to the left of the bar. Howard took considerable pride in the distinction of owning one of the smallest saloons in the Western Hemisphere, not counting the occasional Latin-American cantina no bigger than a two-broom broom closet. His place is patronized almost exclusively by people who have come down from the continental United States and who either live permanently in Puerto Rico or are visiting the island for fun or business or both.

The Small World Bar could almost pass for an outdoor bistro. Two wide doors that give on the street are always open and the space between them is just sufficient to accommodate the jukebox and a cigarette machine. There are two whirlybird fans suspended from the high ceiling and they get a good workout, for in Puerto Rico it is often as hot (and as humid) as a witch's tit. There are several travel posters occupying the available wall space, including one that pleads unaccountably, COME TO DUBLIN. The place is as clean as a hospital room in a clean hospital, and is so compact that any time a customer falls down he is in the toilet.

Diana and Howard were no more than settled at their table when Midge McLean came through the far door and stopped to shake some of the rainwater off. She waved at Diana and started toward the table when she spotted Muffin on the bar stool. Midge stopped and exchanged a few words with the girl and then joined Diana and Howard.

"Anyone for soggy tennis?" she asked, gesturing toward the street. "Sorry I was late, Diana. I thought maybe it would let up. I don't see any sense in wading down to look at the Tapia. Let's just sit here, pretend we've got a log fire going, and lap up the happy stuff. Pierce will meet us for dinner at El Convento."

"That's fine with me," said Diana. She gave Midge a long searching look. There had been something peculiar about that exchange of pleasantries at the bar. Diana had known Midge McLean little more than a week, but they had become warm friends and Midge was being most helpful about Puerto Rican ragstuffs; she had good connections with local designers and stylists, and even knew a few native weavers. She was taller than Diana, of the type called svelte, with black hair that dipped and swirled to her shoulders, a knack for wearing clothes and a somewhat liberal approach to life. Her husband Pierce McLean had a law office in Old San Juan, seemed to be prospering, and they lived in one of the restored colonial houses that have become so popular, and expensive, in recent years.

"Midge," said Diana, "what's with you and Little Miss Muffin up at the bar?"

Midge gave her a lingering amused look, then grinned suddenly at Howard. "You mean," she said, "you don't . . ."

"Hold it Midge," Howard interrupted. Then to Diana, "You don't know about our Muffin?"

"Of course I know," said Diana irritably. "Do you two expatriates think I'm some kind of a Manhattan square? She's a holady who uses her husband for her pimp-boy. God, what people you get in here, Howard!" Howard threw back his head and laughed. Midge did the same. Then Howard called out, "Hey Muff, come over here a minute!"

The beauteous Muffin came tripping from the bar and stood before them.

"Take it off," said Howard.

Off came the smooth and lovely auburn hair, uncovering a neat cap of black curls—a man's hair.

"It's a man!" cried Diana, aghast.

"Certainly," said Howard. "Diana, you are in the presence of our island's leading female impersonator. You ought to catch his act some night at the Papaya Club."

"The cruddy son of a . . ." Diana said, staring into the man's makeup, ". . . he put his hand on the top part of . . . the top part of my bottom when I was sitting next to her, I mean him, at the bar, and thought he was a girl."

So they told her about Muffin, or Muff. He was the star of the floor show at the Papaya Club where he was billed as "Mister Muff." He had come to Puerto Rico about six months ago, unheralded and unheard of and within a week he was performing as a female impersonator.

"Female imp," he said to Diana, still holding his auburn wig. That is the term employed by people in show business for those few remaining men who follow in the toe-dancey tradition of Julian Eltinge and Harry Le Clair.

"Meaning," put in Midge, "the ones who are actually men. The woods are teeming with tried-and-true nances who are wiggling their behinds and trilling soprano on night club floors."

"You're really a male-type man?" Diana asked Mister Muff. For answer he reached into his bosom and brought forth a cigar wrapped in foil. Howard lit it for him.

"I wish," said Diana, "that you'd either put that wig back on or get dressed in your man-clothes. You look a bit grotesque playing it half-and-half. I'd like to see you as a man."

"Come out to my hotel," said Muff, "and I'll accommodate you real quick like."

"You'll always be a sweet and charming lady to me," Diana responded, a grace note of nastiness in her inflection.

"Look, beautiful," said Mister Muff, "this is a stop-gap operation for me. I never stepped on a stage or a night club floor in my life till I got to Puerto Rico. It's a long story. If you're around here tomorrow I'll wear my beanpole britches and take you to lunch and tell you everything."

"I'm out to see the world," said Diana, "and that includes its more sordid aspects, so I'll try to make it."

"Why don't the three of you come on over to my house for lunch?" Midge suggested. "Around half past two?" It was agreed.

"Got an umbrella around here, Howard?" asked Muff, his auburn tresses back in place. Then he lapsed flippantly into fag-talk: "I simply can't dreee-um of allowing this bitchy old rain to wash my makeup off!"

Howard went looking but all he could find was an old newspaper. And so the female imp went loping up the street toward the taxi stand, protecting himself as best he could with a copy of the *Christian Science Monitor* over his head.

Diana now grinned her wry, twisty grin. "You people," she said to Midge and Howard, "sure run a loose little island. Spring another one on me . . . I can take it. No. Tell me first—who was the shill, the goon from Ohiuh?"

"Jack J. Jackson," said Midge. "He's the comic at the Papaya.

They like to come down here sometimes in the afternoon, pick themselves a loud mouth, and give him the business. A tourist gent who's been racked up by those two goes home to Chillicothe with unforgettable golden memories of the moonlit tropical Caribbean."

"Everybody in the place, except the victim, knows what's going on," said Howard. "Unless, of course, some smarty-pants young career girl from the middle of New York City gets roped in."

"I blush," said Diana, hanging her head and putting her thumb in her mouth. She was annoyed with herself. She worked in a business with a high incidence of faggotry and the steady evolving of fresh techniques that would have set old Sappho to gnawing at her own knuckles. She was not a part of this world, and yet she lived in it. She lived also in a period when moral values were changing so rapidly that it took fast people to keep up with the pace. She was well acquainted with such things as the Kitten books and Candy's papa and Fanny Hill and the pervert novels out of Brooklyn and Septic Tank Dramaturgy and the waitresses in high-class supper clubs suspending their naked titties over the coffee cups as if they were expecting the customers to order a dash of mother's milk. For shame! That such things should be!

She was staring out the nearest doorway, looking at the rain, and suddenly she let out a little yip. Midge and Howard turned and saw a cat striding through the downpour, walking a straight line down the middle of the pavement. It is a fact known to cat people that domesticated felines abhor storms of any kind, and abominate rain. In mythology the cat is a symbol of drenching rain, but that doesn't mean the cat has to like it. With the falling of the first drops, presaging a rainstorm or even a mere sprinkle, a cat will gallop for shelter. Diana, who had kept cats in her New York apartment, knew this. Yet here was a large, yellow, gaunt-looking animal marching through a tropical squall, impervious to the soaking he was getting, his tail sticking straight upward as if it were an oriflamme of defiant rebellion against the laws that govern the conduct of cats everywhere.

Diana sensed this defiance, this rebelliousness, immediately. On an impulse she got out of her chair, walked quickly into the street, crept up behind the cat, and suddenly grabbed him. He screeched like a Billingsgate fishwife with the green apple colic. He wrenched and flopped himself from side to side, trying to escape

17

from Diana's grip. His yowl sounded like a hoarse fire-siren. He clawed at his captor, slashing long rents in her sleeves and inflicting a few painful cuts. But Diana held on, and carried the writhing beast back into the bar.

"Howard," she said, panting from the struggle, "hurry and get me something I can use for a leash."

"I'll find you a ball bat," said Howard. "Listen, kid, throw that critter back into the street. He's wild. Look at those red eyes!"

"I'm keeping him," she said firmly, "if I can hold onto him."

Frank Evans came from behind the bar to get a closer look, but he maintained a respectful distance and he had a tendency to jump, as if goosed, each time the cat let go with a snarl or slashed viciously at the atmosphere.

"Looks to me," said Frank, "that his tail has been run over. Something wrong with that tail."

"I want this cat," said Diana, apparently not concerned with run-over tails. "I'll keep him if I have to tie him in a bowknot. I know a little something about cats and this one is special."

"He looks special," said Frank, "and he sure acts special, but my god look at the long claws! And the way that tail jerks! I wouldn't want to take him on as a lap cat."

He's special, Diana repeated to herself, because it's clear that he embodies all the distaste and contempt and hatred that cats entertain toward the human race. No cat has ever really been tamed. They have far more intelligence than people think. They are superb actors. They can *pretend* great affection for human beings, and make it stick, but it is pure play-acting. They pretend love and even admiration for their owners, because it guarantees the groceries, and comfortable sleeping quarters, and generous rubbing beneath the ears, and other pleasant things. But when the chips are down, they'll turn tail and abandon their masters forever, maybe after bloodying them up a bit just for old times' sake.

Howard came in through the far door, somewhat damp. He had run around the corner to a dressmaker's shop and they had scissored off two strips of a red fabric which had the look of close-weave canvas.

Diana knotted the red strips together and asked Howard to close the saloon doors during the operation of getting the leash securely fixed around the cat's neck. He was still snarling and slashing in much the same way that Clyde Beatty's big cats used

18

to go at him, and once Diana slapped him a brisk one across the face, saying, "Hold still, Tiger, or I'll bust your brains out!" That slowed him down, but not much.

He did cease his struggling a couple of minutes later and undertook a careful scrutiny of the long strip of fabric that was holding him prisoner. He reached out and touched it with a paw, almost caressed it. Diana may have misinterpreted his motives—she may have felt that he was preparing to rip hell out of the crimson leash. Just to let him know who was running the show, she gave him another belt across the chops. Then she left Howard's place, hauling and dragging her refractory pet up to the Plaza de Armas. Somehow she got him rammed into a taxi and headed out east for her hotel.

Arriving at the Sheraton she untied the cat—she was now addressing him as Tiger—and sat down to see what might happen. He had simmered down but he appeared to be sulking, and then he grew restless and prowled the edges of the room, looking for a way out. By this time Diana had grown aware of the fact that any jerking of the jog in his tail was an indication of displeasure. She now noted that the tail-jog was static, inert, quiescent. So Diana picked him up and shut him in the bathroom and went downstairs to keep a dinner date with a young man, a Latin lawyer she had met during a dance out at El Conquistador.

The dinner was pleasant enough until the coming of the Moment of Truth. She was fully aware of the fact that the young man's right hand was snaking beneath the tablecloth. Then the hand was on her knee. She gave him a simpering smile, throwing him off guard, and he responded by moving his hand slightly to the north in the direction of pay dirt. He squeezed the delicious flesh in a firm grip just in time to receive the thrust. Diana's own hand had crept under the table, holding her salad fork in a chisel grip, and she brought the sharp tines down hard on the hand of the explorer. He gasped with the pain and his hand came out from under the table, spilling blood on his trousers. He grabbed up a napkin and wrapped it around the hand and without a word to dainty Diana, hurried away.

Diana went on to her room and talked to The Tiger for a while and finally fell asleep, little suspecting that the morrow would bring on events perhaps even more exciting than those of the day just ending.

The Tiger, his red rag leash fastened to a chromium basin leg, slept on the fluffy mat beside the bathtub. Nobody knew it, of course . . . but this was the most comfortable bed he'd ever had.

 # Chapter TWO

BY morning Diana was not too sure of herself, not at all certain that she wanted to keep The Tiger. He came off the bathmat full of fury, snake-mean. He snarled at her and hissed at her and his tail was jerking fitfully. She was convinced that he had the most expressive tail anywhere outside the realm of the rattlesnake and the scorpion. When he was just beginning to work up a pout, The Tiger jerked in a leisurely adagio rhythm. He did not appear, at this point, to be ready to create disaster areas. But if he shifted into a pattern of spasmodic, uneven twitchings, the flags were up—the time had come to man the starboard cannon and prepare to repel boarders. And then, if that tail began to jerk rapidly, like a piece of machinery, he was ready to spill blood.

Diana realized that she would be in trouble if she took this cat back to New York and installed him in her apartment. She would have to keep him locked away in a closet, like a lunatic old aunt, when company came, or delivery people, or repair men; she would have to keep him in solitary when she was off at work.

She went downstairs and got him some liverwurst and milk and wheedled a soup dish out of the waiter. It had never occurred to her last night that The Tiger might have been hungry. He had been. He had been famished. He went at his breakfast like a mad thing. And when he was finished he sat down and quietly washed his face and following that he walked over and rubbed himself against Diana's leg. "Good Lord, Tiger," she said to him, "I do believe you're purring!" And he was.

She went out and had a taxi take her to a pet shop where she told the proprietor she wanted a strong leash for a cat.

"The word is *lead,* madam," said the proprietor.

"The word is *Miss,* Mister," she said.

"A leash," he said, unperturbed, "is for fastening onto a hawk's jess."

"And what," she asked, suspecting the worst, "is a hawk's jess?"

"Something on a hawk to fasten a leash onto," he replied. "Now what you probably need is a harness. You have a strong cat. You want to walk it outdoors. You need a harness with a strong lead. Damn fool people put collars on cats and the cats go out and hang themselves. You'd be amazed the number of cats go out and hang themselves on account of damn fool people."

He fixed her up with the harness and a thin nylon lead which he said would hold an ill-at-ease rhinoceros. When she returned to her room she also had some canned salmon, some hamburger, and more milk.

At this point The Tiger, fairly wallowing in gourmet vittles, must have thought that he had died and gone to heaven. Yet his euphoric mood was due for a sudden, cyclonic change. When she started to fasten the harness on him he went into a rage as wild and as untrammeled as the fight he put up when she snatched him out of the rain. Diana was perplexed, but only for a few moments. The cat broke away from her and ran across the room and flattened himself on top of a pile of red rags. Diana had thrown the dress shop's makeshift leash on the floor and now it came clear to her—The Tiger wanted no part of harness and nylon lead. If he was going to be led around, it would be the red rag thing or nothing. Those tattered crimson strips were his teddy bear, his baby blanket, his chewed-up precious diaper. So Diana shrugged and tied the rag around his neck again and they left the hotel.

Back at the pet shop she told the dyspeptic man that her cat didn't like the harness. He had himself a long look at the shabby red thing tied around The Tiger's neck. The dismay on his face grew deeper and he seemed on the verge of breaking into tears.

"I call this," said Diana, "a *leash*."

"I call it an outrage," exclaimed the man, flinging his arms upward as though appealing to the powers and principalities. "Do me a favor, young woman," he went on, "and don't go out in public with that hideous piece of dry goods attached to your cat. You'll have all the kids in town shagging you up and down the streets and jeering at you. No self-respecting cat would even hang himself with that disreputable rag. Get a cage for him, or a carrier. Don't put him to shame before the whole world."

"He likes this disreputable rag," said Diana, "and he's going to wear it. Now, I could take my money back, or I could buy something else for him. How about cat toys?"

"I don't keep playthings," he said. "Damn fool people buy all these damn fool playthings, it's pure murder—they *murder* their cats!"

"I don't seem to get your message," said Diana.

"Damn fool people buy toys made out of wool," he said. "Cats eat wool. They acquire the wool habit, like say they are wool hopheads. They'll chew a blanket right off a bed. Then they buy toys with feathers on them, and the cats eat the feathers, and die in convulsions. They buy rubber toys, and cats like to eat rubber, and they die screaming and flopping around on the floor. Even cellophane toys—cats like to chew up cellophane and plastic and Christmas tree ornaments, all such as that. They throw fits, jerk a couple of times, and fall over dead. Tell you what, Miss. The only plaything *I* advocate for cats is a mirror. A cat can spend hours looking at itself in a mirror, primping around, and a cat won't eat a mirror."

He took one off a stack and showed it to Diana. She said she'd like to try it out before buying it. He set it on the floor against a wall and Diana picked The Tiger up and put him down in front of it. He seemed rather listless and was gazing sleepily off to the side. Then he swiveled his head around and stared straight into his own face. "YOWRRRRRRRRRRRR!" He leaped backward, away from this ferocious beast, as far as the red leash would permit. As quickly as he could set himself, he spoke a spine-tingling snarl, readied his fangs and went flying through the air, whanging up against the glass of the mirror and knocking it over. He was trying to rip the frame off with his claws when Diana succeeded in pulling him away. The proprietor was already clanging

the gong on the cash register, getting her money for her.

"Lady," he said, handing it to her, "you got a nut for a cat. Get him the hell out of my place and don't bring him back."

"Go take a good look at *yourself* in that mirror," she snapped at him, then grabbed The Tiger off the floor and carried him back to the taxi. The entire episode had been exhausting, a strain on her nerves . . . and there was more to come.

Riding down to Old San Juan he crawled into her lap, purred some more, and went to sleep. At the little plaza they got out of the cab and Diana was digging in her pocketbook to pay the driver when . . . Zing! Zip!

A large black dog had spotted The Tiger and came charging down, shrieking in soprano clef. A mistake on the dog's part. The end of the rag leash was jerked from Diana's hand with all the suddenness a cane pole leaves the hand of a carp fisherman when his worm is hit by a hammerhead shark. The Tiger sprang forward in a high arc, trailing the red cloth behind him so that he had the appearance of a skyrocket in flight. The dog slammed on the brakes and came to a shuddering halt. Something told him he ought to be home in the bosom of his family. This intuitive notion came too late and The Tiger was on his back, chewing ferociously at his withers, digging in and ripping with his claws. The dog howled and screeched for mercy, his eyes bugged out and rolling in fright, and it seems likely he would have been destroyed had it not been for a Puerto Rican boy who came running over from a supermarket on the north side of the plaza; the boy dashed in, grabbed the end of the red leash, and pulled The Tiger off the un-happy dog. He brought the red rag to Diana and she fished into her pocketbook again and gave him a dollar. Then she spoke a few words of appreciation, in mock Spanish, saying she was from Nueva York, that she had come into the plaza for the purpose of mugging some Puerto Ricans, but now because of his act *galante* she had changed her mind and *viva muchacho*. The kid didn't dig a single word of it.

During Diana's little Good Neighbor speech The Tiger had been standing by with an air of boredom, but suddenly he made a fast move and took a couple of swipes at the boy, who lit out in high gear for the supermarket; he had no way of knowing that the cat was special, and that the red rag was never to be touched by anyone except the cat and the cat's owner.

There were half a dozen people in the Small World Bar and Diana had to inspect them all carefully before she was able to spot Mister Muff. Today he was a man—a smallish man, but nonethe-less a man. He had on his britches, which were a gray silk, and a handsome sports shirt of matching quality and color. He was sit-ting at the bar with Howard Conley but at Diana's arrival they moved over to one of the tables.

Diana was ill at ease in the presence of the female imp. It had to do, no doubt, with the striking character of his metamorphosis, and she was a little flustered. "Do you shave your arms?" she blurted. "No," he answered, "do you?"

There was quite a bit of Joe Show Business about him—he was an actory type, working hard at trying to make an impression.

"Look, Mister Muff," Diana said, "you must have a real name. Somehow I don't care much for Muff. What can I call you?"

"Keep calling me Muff," he said, making it sound like an order. "I don't tell anyone my real name."

"My gracious!" Diana exclaimed, feigning alarm. "How the plot does thicken! You must be some kind of an international spy —a small-sized James Bond."

"Don't . . . mention . . . that . . . name . . . in . . . my . . . presence!" It was almost a shout.

"I think," said Howard, "that you two are going to get along beautifully. So I'll leave you for a while. Gotta get to the bank."

Diana and Muff sat for a few minutes, not looking at each other, and then she said, "What's eating you, boy? I keep secrets." During the next half hour she found out about the little man who played girl.

What he told her added up to this:

Muff, he insisted, was not his real name. She had set him back on his heels with her random remark about his being an international spy. He *had* been one. All during his boyhood he had been spy-crazy, with an intense interest in the art of disguise; he had a natural talent for it, amounting almost to genius. He was able to fool the people in his home town, even his own family—fixing himself up variously as an Italian fruit peddler, or a little old lady with bifocals and reticule, or a frowzy-headed schoolboy with freckles and bucked teeth. Then one evening he got himself up in the rig of a high school girl, went to a prom, and was a raging sensation among the concupiscent lads on the stag line. At this point he realized, somewhat regrettably, that he had stumbled on something of importance; he had all the equipment to pass convincingly as an alluringly nubile girl, all except bosom and that was no great problem.

He didn't relish the idea of making a career out of disguising himself as a sexpot, but the ambition to become a spy was strong and he knew the girl-act might serve as his foot-in-the-door. He went to Washington with two fat suitcases, a trunk, and a letter to a congressman. Some conniving and maneuvering followed and in the end this boy—he was scarcely past voting age—was in training for a career as a secret agent. His artistic skill in turning himself into a voluptuous woman, plus his burning eagerness to make a big mark in a world of big men, brought steady advancement. His superiors were well aware of the fact that a sexy woman, in some circumstances, can be a more effective weapon than a stockpile of nuclear bombs. What better, then, than a sexy woman who could turn herself, in short order, into an Italian fruit peddler, or a little old lady, or a buck-toothed schoolboy? He didn't need much anatomical assistance from his superiors, although they did get him a late-model set of breasts that were soft and resilient to the touch, with nipples that popped themselves alert at the slightest pawing.

"Now," Muff said to Diana, "I was on my way. I would have become the greatest secret agent on earth, maybe the greatest in history. But along comes this goddamn James Bond and all the others. Nobody *knew* I was a spy except me and the people I worked for. But something happened inside of me. I got all frustrated. These book-spies and movie-spies and comic-strip-spies got wilder and wilder. Cigarette lighter that drills through steel walls; transistor in the filling of a tooth, sending out a steady stream of signals clear to Murmansk; diddling the dames from pillar to post; knife jumps out of the toe of a shoe and, if not that, out of the heel; attaché case fires shells at the foe; bang every broad that comes along; fire extinguisher in the cufflinks, buttons on the jacket that'll blow up the Alps; shoot and poison and stab and behead and torture and diddle your damn brains out. I tell you, Diana, I got *ashamed* of myself, ashamed of the job I had. I said that if this was the way the business was going, I was getting out of it."

"But *you* didn't have to do all these goofy things?" said Diana.

"That's not the point. You get to be a big legitimate spy and you take a lot of pride in it. You feel *important*. You *are* important. You realize that you might personally mean the difference between war and peace, that you might be the instrument to save civilization. A guy can't get along if he's ashamed of the business he's in. So I walked out. There wasn't any decency in the spying trade any more, the way the idiot public was lapping up this James Bond stuff. Those birds were going around giving everybody karate whacks on the neck, only they had to use their own kind of karate that they learned from snakes; and they were shooting retractable cannon out of their sports cars, and still finding time to yank off girdles in every known hemisphere and all this in the interest of achieving world peace! Get this: one guy had a revolver that was just for his enemies to steal off him—it shot backwards and killed the party that pulled the trigger! Jayzus!"

It turned out, however, that Mister Muff had not given up on espionage altogether. He wandered down to San Juan, lay around on the beach for a couple of weeks, and gave thought to the future. The hell with trying to save a country that would go for these new-style, button-punching, murdering jerks. He already knew that government employment is only one phase of the spying profession. The place to get the money is in industry. Big business is hiring more secret agents and paying them better than all the governments in the world. Why wouldn't Muff, with his flawless sexpot act, be of use to some big corporation?

"I didn't feel at all sure of myself," he said, "but I kept thinking about it, and then I realized that I had to regain my confidence. I had to have some good solid practice. So I got this job at the Papaya Club. Imagine my surprise to find myself a sensation in show business! Still, I had to get closer to people, and that's why I come down here to Howard's some afternoons and fool the tourists. It's all part of the practicing. I'm almost ready now to go back and give it the big try in industry."

"What kind of industry you have in mind?" asked Diana.

"Heavy industry," he said.

Diana sat still a while. She passed a hand across her brow as if she might have a headache. There was a flickering sensation that she wasn't in Puerto Rico at all. These things could all happen, maybe, but not in such rapid succession.

Muff the Master Spy brought her back to reality. "Maybe now," he said, "you'll understand why I don't want anybody to know my real name."

"Do you tell other people about your past, and your plans for the future?"

"Of course not."

"Then why've you told me?"

"Give a guess," he said.

She liked him one moment, and didn't like him the next. She had a distinct feeling that someone had neglected to tighten his nuts and bolts. She hoped this didn't mean salad fork again.

They assembled in the cool patio of the McLean house—Midge and Diana and Howard and Mister Muff and The Tiger. There was a small fountain of handsome mosaic design and much greenery and pinkery surrounding them as they had their open-air lunch.

A man in brick-red slacks and a gay Madras jacket wandered in and Midge, who seemed to know everybody in the Greater, Lesser and Intermediate Antilles, introduced him as Mr. Angus Belasco. He was in his sixties, deeply tanned below a handsome head of silver-white hair and just three months ago he had come to give the island a try as a place of retirement.

"Angus hasn't got to know many people yet," said Midge, "and he gets lonely. He gets so lonely that sometimes he comes around here and spends half a day cooking for us. He's really a whiz in the kitchen. Pull up a chair, Angus."

"I've been out," said Mr. Belasco, "inspecting the world famous population explosion."

"How do you go about that?" Howard wanted to know.

"Just walk around these streets and look at the people," said Mr. Belasco. "This being a place they always talk about, I've been giving a lot of thought to it since I got here. I do believe that I've figured one thing out. You take all this propaganda about birth control pills and contraceptive clinics and Planned Parenthood and pre-marital . . . Oh! Excuse me, young lady!" The apology was directed at Diana.

"Don't mind me," she said. "I use them all when the moon's on the wane. Sail right along with your lecture, Professor."

He gave her a nervous, quizzical glance. These young people today! "Well," he resumed, "all this propaganda spread around the island has had a kind of reverse-english effect on Puerto Rico populationexplosionwise. I have observed this, and reasoned it out. I am one of the aging men who are expelled out of the business and political world and cast into the ashcan. Damn it to hell, we should be consulted! We are the men who . . ." Mr. Belasco's voice was rising and he appeared to be approaching a condition of hysteria. "We are the men who," he repeated, "men who . . . who . . . through long trial and experience have learned to cope with these problems and get them solved and read books on serious subjects while these pipsqueak yahoos in Washington and Wall Street are . . . my God, just look at what I found in the New York *Times!*"

He got out his wallet and extracted a small clipping, and put on his glasses and read it aloud in a voice that was trembling. It was a classified ad, about two inches deep, headed:

WE ARE LOOKING
FOR
RETIRED EXECUTIVES

The body of the ad said in part: "If you have entree to front offices & can talk at arms length to top echelon authorities we can offer you full or part time work that will afford you substantial remuneration with one of the largest *Pest Control* organizations in the world." There were directions on how to proceed for "the dynamic personality who finds being retired leaves a void that must be filled."

Mr. Belasco pounded on the table with his fist. "Throw us to the cockroaches!" he cried. "That's what they want to do! By god I won't let them turn *me* over to the termites!"

It took a little time and a slug of brandy to get him calmed down and after a while Howard suggested that he go on with his dissertation on the population explosion.

He stewed around a bit and then said that the propaganda in the newspapers and on the radio and in the pamphlets had sifted down to the multitudes of the lower classes, the peasantry. These people, Mr. Belasco asserted with great solemnity, had never before paid much attention to sex matters. They attached little importance to it. And now these impoverished peons, he suggested, having learned about sex from the government and from the do-gooders, had begun flogging the sod, thumping the forage in the cow pastures, pounding the moisture out of the rain forests, turning out babies as briskly as the young marrieds of the continental United States were doing it.

"What's the answer?" demanded Mr. Belasco. "Well, my friends, it's not so simple any more, but these people of ours who come in here with their birth control propaganda ought to be stopped. They're only putting ideas into the poor people's heads. The government ought to put a stop to it, and the government ought to put a stop to this god damned insane business of throwing all us mature thinking men to the god damned cockroaches and termites and . . ." He was aflame once again and they let him yell it all out of his system. Diana tried to puzzle him out and soon arrived at a decision: a nut.

Muff had been sitting with his coffee-and-brandy, lazily enjoying everything. Then he noticed The Tiger stretched out on the floor.

"There's something," he said to Diana, "about that cat of yours."

"There's more than something," she replied.

"No, I mean . . . well, I got a feeling . . . look at that tail."

Midge in turn glanced down at the sleeping animal. "He seems," she said, "to have tamed down a lot since you whacked him a couple. You been flogging him into submission out at the hotel? Beating him with chains?"

"Nary another blow struck," said Diana. "All I did was feed

him. The poor guy was starving to death. I gave him two hearty meals and he became my pal. He rubbed against my legs. He purred. He climbed into my lap and went to sleep."

"I'd be careful," put in Howard. "I live surrounded by cats and it's my guess there's a lot of jungle insanity left in this one."

"Oh," said Diana, "I didn't mean that he's become a tame cat. He's just tame toward me." She now told them about the incident in the Plaza de Armas, The Tiger's whirlwind assault on the big black dog.

"He actually tore loose from you and jumped a big dog?" spoke up Howard. "You're not kidding us?"

"Of course not. That big dog will never show his face in public again as long as he lives. At least not in this part of town."

They were all now looking at the cat and Midge and Mr. Belasco were standing up to get a better view. The Tiger's long tail was stretched out on the tiled floor and the double bend, midway of its length, began a series of slight jerks, or twitches.

"Great balls of fire!" cried Midge. "Howard! Look at him! Don't you remember?"

"Rhubarb!" came from Muff. "He's almost exactly like Rhubarb. I saw Rhubarb in person two or three times. So look at this one. He jumps on dogs and chews them up and claws them to ribbons. And . . . he's . . . got . . . that . . . famous . . . jog . . . in . . . his . . . tail!"

"But Midge," Howard interrupted, "Rhubarb's dead. You know that."

"Of course I know it. But I also know, and so do you, that Rhubarb was right here in San Juan just a couple of years ago. Good God, it was more exciting than if the Duke and Duchess of Windsor had brought Gloria Guinness and Frank Sinatra down for a long weekend of churning."

"Churning?" Mr. Belasco repeated.

"Butter-churning," said Midge. "I thought you knew that butter-churning is now the rage among the more mature members of the Jet Set. They sit around in drawing rooms and on terraces and in the better night clubs and even on the beaches and . . . well, they churn."

"What's the point of it?" asked Mr. Belasco, ever on the prowl for knowledge. "Do they really get some butter?"

"No," said Midge. "As I understand it, they have certain rules

31

governing their latest sport. Anybody who gets real butter in his churn is designated a rat fink. The others all sit around flogging their dashers and yelling in rhythm, 'Rat fink! Rat fink! Rat fink!' "

"These," said Mr. Belasco bitterly, "are the people who are running things, these are the people who count, and they want to throw *me* into the ashcan, hand *me* over to the cockroaches. God damn each and every one of them!"

"Hold yourself in, now, Angus," said Midge. "Howard, what do you think? I mean about the cat."

"I think you've got hold of something," said Howard.

"Pardon me to the very core, folks," Diana put in, "but this happens to be *my* cat. Will somebody tell me what you're all talking about?"

And so they told her, and there was a mounting excitement in the air as they talked. A little over two years ago the Banner Line's flagship *Thaddeus* put in at Pier Three, usually called the Tourists' Pier. The arrival of the beautiful ship went almost unnoticed, for Puerto Rico is an island where beautiful ships and elegant yachts are almost as common as tree frogs. Nobody, including the newspaper and radio and television people, knew that the multimillionaire cat was in port. The *Thaddeus* lay serenely at her berth and then, on the second day, all hell and selected portions of purgatory broke loose. Rhubarb had somehow vanished from his ship. His guardian, Eric Yaeger, came storming ashore at the head of a unique organization of thirty men, called The *Thaddeus* Guerrillas. This band of hardy crewmen was maintained aboard the ship for precisely this kind of emergency—the escape of their employer, Rhubarb. They had their own squad room where they trained, and stored their equipment. They hit the shore in steel helmets and heavy boots and they had uniforms for invading jungles, for climbing mountains, and for playing at frogman. They carried nets, coils of rope, traps, snares, and patented pussy lures. Among the last-named were two gorgeous female cats, a fluffy blue Persian and a fawn-colored jezebel of the Siamese family. These two were shampooed with liquid catnip and when they finished leaping up and down and flopping around on the deck they were led forth on long lines by individual guerrillas who kept up a continuous crying of "Rhubarb! Rhubarb! Rhubarb!" And finally, an animal known as The Bloodcat—a ring-tailed civet cat from Arizona, possessed of an acute sense of smell and trained to follow the trail of Rhubarb and Rhubarb only. Eric Yaeger was very proud of The Bloodcat and had supervised its training, but it should be noted that the animal never succeeded in tracking down a single creature except a chipmunk that walked with a limp.

All this activity, plus the full strength of the *policía* of San Juan, scampering and prowling across the face of the city. Radio and television stations filled the air with blatting appeals in English and Spanish, urging the populace of Puerto Rico to join in the search for the wealthy and distinguished stray. The military swung into action, spreading out across an area of forty square miles.

"On the second night," Howard recalled, "the cat was captured. He was sound asleep behind a trash barrel in a passageway just a block from the very building where I live. He was exhausted, played out, didn't have enough strength to try for one bite on the boy who found him—a teen-age kid who spotted Rhubarb lying in the midst of a litter of feathers and chicken bones. The boy simply grabbed him, found a cardboard carton, shoved the *gato rico* into it, and made his way to the Tourists' Pier. He handed the box full of multimillionaire cat over to Eric Yaeger. For this half hour's work young Eduardo Tuerto was rewarded with a one hundred thousand dollar trust fund plus a scholarship giving him four years at Yale." . . . "Now . . . the funny thing about all this, Diana, is the name of the street where the boy found Rhubarb, the same street where I live. Legally it is San Sebastian, but it is often called *La Calle de los Gatos*—The Street of the Cats."

"How did it get *that* name?" Diana asked, all abubble with enthusiasm. "I'd love to have a look at it. Is it far from . . ."

"Back up, baby," Midge interjected. "You're missing the whole point. The hell with The Street of Cats. The important thing is, you've got a tremendous fortune lying right there at your feet. Your Tiger is the son of Rhubarb. Has to be. Can't be any other answer. The same size, the same color, the same fundamental meanness, the same violent animosity toward the entire dog world, *and* . . ." Midge raised an imperious finger for emphasis, ". . . *and* that trick bend in his tail. Diana, you are the owner of Rhubarb's son and heir—you are so incredibly wealthy that you are beginning to smell up my tacky Spanish hacienda."

33

"But how . . ." Diana began, a note of bewilderment in her voice.

"I'll tell you how," volunteered Howard. "That rich cat got away from the ship. I think it's probable that he had a tendency to revert to the status he enjoyed during his youth on Long Island, when he was a genuine alley cat and didn't have two nickels to rub together. He got loose from the ship and some kind of animal instinct led him straight to *La Calle de los Gatos*. God knows how many girl cats he violated before his zing gave out. One thing you can be sure about—that cat right there on the floor is his boy."

Mr. Belasco of the silvery hair got up and walked around and bent over to get a better look at The Tiger. "Don't come too close," warned Diana. "You might get your eyebrows scattered all over the patio." Mr. Belasco went hmmmmm and uhmmmmm and ahhhhh. "This," he said, "is a red-letter day for me if it's all true. I have followed the fantastic career of Rhubarb since old Thad Banner first adopted him and made him his heir. Seems to me I once read a book written about him when he owned that baseball team. Magnificent sort of book. Splendid in every way."

"Who wrote it?" asked Diana.

"Let me see, now," mused Angus Belasco. "Could it have been Fannie Hurst?"

"Never," said Midge. "I know Fannie Hurst. She's always had a house full of feisty little dogs."

"I read that book," put in Howard, "but I can't seem to recall the name of the author. Could have been Steinbeck. No. He's a dog man. Maybe Jack London."

"Another dog man," said Diana, "and anyway Jack London's been dead for years."

"E. Phillips Oppenheim?" suggested Muff.

"I can remember," Mr. Belasco concluded, "that I read it and enjoyed it, but I guess I just didn't notice the name of the party who wrote it. Oh, well, the hell with it."

And the hell with you, Mr. Belasco.

&⊕≥ Chapter THREE

DIANA walked with Howard Conley through *La Calle de los Gatos* and Howard took on the role of tourist guide, pointing out historic buildings, the fine house that Juan Ponce de Leon built, and the statue of Ponce in front of San José Church.

"San José," lectured Howard, "is supposed to be the oldest church *in continuous use* in the western hemisphere. That's the first thing people tell you about it. What bothers me is that qualifying phrase, 'in continuous use.' Makes me think of the ads for television sets back home. The ads yell at you in fat type that the set has a 28-inch screen, and a little asterisk, and down at the bottom in type so small that you need a magnifying glass to read it, it says, 'measured diagonally.' And the tourist hotels, even the big plush resort places, use the same sort of gimmick, big type at the top saying you can have a glorious week, seven full days, in this posh hotel, for only $130. Then the asterisk, and down below in the tiny type, the qualification, '* Rate per person, double occupancy.' This means that if you bring your wife, or somebody else, you get that room for $260. Never $130. If you don't bring a wife or a friend, I suppose you have to shack up with a stranger. What I'm trying to say, Diana, is that you are looking at the oldest church in the western hemisphere, only it ain't."

As they moved on down the street Howard asked her, "Speaking of *old*, do you ever tell your age?"

"Sure," she said, "up to this year. I've leveled off at twenty-seven and I intend to hang around that neighborhood for a while."

"You may age a good deal faster than the rest of us, now that you've got that cat on your hands. If I were you I'd lay in a washtub full of tranquilizers and another one full of Band-Aids."

"I still think," Diana responded, "that you and Midge are wrong, that you're both flitting around from Cloud Nine to Cloud Ten and back."

Howard let it pass, and resumed talking about the statue of Ponce. He said it was bronze and that the history books contend that it was cast from cannon abandoned by British invaders as they fled for their lives.

"The British," Howard added, "say that this is the bloodiest of bloody gawd demn lies."

Howard said that in Spanish times Calle San Sebastian was known as The Street of the Fools. Spanish sailors were given a rugged time on shipboard, being flogged and brigged and starved and compelled to walk long planks unsupported at the far end, and keel-hauled—surely one of the worst punishments ever devised by the human mind. Thus it was that when the Iberian ships came to San Juan there were always a few sailors who made a run for freedom. As sailors go, these worthies left something to be desired in the brain department. Invariably they headed for the same street because there were many little alleyways and crooked passages where they could hide until their individual, personalized hell ships left port. All officers aboard these ships soon found out, of course, about the hiding places, and goon-squads were sent forth, armed with stout clubs, halberds, Toledo machetes, whaling harpoons, bicycle chains, hackbuts, knuckle-dusters, and whatever else was available. These squads simply marched down San Sebastian, and individual *malvados* dropped away from the main formations, entered the side passages and alleyways where they slugged and clubbed and slashed and pulverized and sometimes *bit* the escaped men they always found huddled there. The disgruntled ones, who fled their ships year after year, never learned. They gravitated straight to San Sebastian and hid in the alleys and groveled in corners until the goons come and knocked out their teeth, cracked their skulls, and punted them in the crotch. Thus it came about that San Sebastian was known, throughout that gay and romantic Spanish period, as The Street of the Fools.

All this local history poured out of Howard, who is a studious man, because he felt that Diana should know these things; he was quite positive that she would come into Rhubarb's vast wealth, and this street, being The Tiger's birthplace, ought to hold some sentimental attraction for the New York girl.

Throughout their leisurely stroll up and down the street Diana was conscious of cats. A parked car might have three or four asleep underneath it. Some, wanting warmth, were curled up against walls where the sun hit them. Others wandered in and out of the same passages where the dim-witted sailors once tried to hide themselves.

"How does it happen," asked Diana, "that this street has all these cats and other streets don't seem to have any?"

"Come on, I'll show you," said Howard, and he walked her to a point about midway of the street's length and indicated an old building, the Parvulos School. A hundred years or so ago, give or take a century, the nuns who ran this school somehow developed a special feeling about cats. It was favorable. It was not an official distinguishing mark of their order—the sisters simply went ape for cats. And so there developed a custom whereby, at certain hours of each day, the nuns emerged from the school and scattered food scraps in the street. Cats came, and then more cats, and then committees of cats, and processions of cats, and whole parliaments of cats. Most of them stayed on and called the street their home, and among their descendants was a lady cat . . . a lady cat surely possessed of strong character, good taste, and ennobling hauteur . . . and she became the mother of the cat now known as The Tiger.

Howard did his best to reconstruct the events of that two-night period when Rhubarb had his sex binge in The Street of the Cats. Shortly after it was discovered that the Gaekwar of all Catdom had crept off the *S. S. Thaddeus*, a phone call came to Casa Blanca, official residence of General Walter Wamsutta, commanding the Antilles Forces of the United States Army. Casa Blanca stands at the western end of The Street of the Cats and was built by Ponce de Leon himself, to serve as his family residence in his old age. Certain historians say that Ponce never lived in the house.

37

Other historians say that these historians are not fit to tote guts to a bear. It appears to be a fact that while Casa Blanca was being constructed Ponce de Leon was off playing the fool in Florida, where he was cold-cocked by the Calusa Indians. His fine house has been the residence of the American military commander since 1898.

The phone call to General Wamsutta was from the Governor. He asked that all available troops be turned out to aid in the search for the missing cat. Most of us know that one of the principal elements hammered into all West Point men is the importance of tact and diplomacy in dealing with government officials at home and abroad. When General Wamsutta heard the Governor's words he sputtered a bit and then cried into the phone:

"Christ in the Andes, Excellency! Have you popped your buttons? You got a hell of a nerve to . . ."

"Just a minute, Wamsutta," snapped the Governor. "Please don't go into another one of your tantrums. You are going to turn out your troops to look for that cat. Period. Within minutes you will get your orders from Washington. So get ready for action, and let's not have any goldbricking. Turn out your comic opera army or you'll be jerked out of this soft life you've wangled for yourself here in Paradise."

The Governor banged down his phone. General Wamsutta got up and began pacing the floor. "A cat," he said aloud. "A c-a-t *cat!* That I should build my whole life to such a climax—turning out my troops to look for a god damn cat! Oh, those hopheads in the Pentagon! Oh, those civilian sonsabitches in the Defense Department! Jesus wept! A cat!"

He slumped into a chair and closed his eyes and tried to compose himself, but he could not get the vision of the Pentagon and its people out of his mind. He knew, of course, that the employment of unlawful influence, and the institution of special privilege, and the use of pressures from vested interests, in matters of government . . . he knew that these things have vanished. But only insofar as people are concerned. It becomes a different matter when an emergency involves a cat—a cat that has more money than all the Rockefeller Brothers after they have pooled their resources with Bing Crosby. General Wamsutta realized this, and little groans and whinnies of distress came from his throat as he waited for the call. It came within a few minutes. The man in Washington passed along the order in a cold, peremptory manner, his language formal, precise, beyond misunderstanding. General Wamsutta clicked off the phone, permitted a tortured expression of towering disgust to flicker across his face, and then said, "Some god damn slobbering clerk!"

He picked up the phone again and called Fort Brooke.

"General Wamsutta," he barked. "I want every available man put on the streets of San Juan at once to search for a big yellow cat named Rhubarb. I'm told that this cat can be identified by a jog that he has in his tail. This jog . . ." The General stopped, and listened for a moment. "Good God, man," he suddenly exploded, "don't you know what a jog is? Haven't you ever been on a road? Well, all right. That's what this cat has in his tail. Get those men out immediately or you'll have a jog in *your* tail. I'll be over shortly."

And so the armed forces turned out, and ranged the streets as far as Santurce, and found no cat with a jog in its tail—that windfall being reserved by Fate for young Eduardo Tuerto.

The frenetic activities of Rhubarb during the time he was ashore, enjoying high life, liberty and the pursuit of Latin-hot happiness, will no doubt figure in future histories of Puerto Rico. At this time, however, intimate detail is lacking. Almost nobody saw him in *La Calle de los Gatos*, but the inhabitants of the area still insist that the cat-yowling and the cat-shrieking and the cat-whinnying heard during those two nights were of a more exciting quality than the cat noises available on normal nights. The volume and the tremolo were greater, and it was possible to detect dirty-clarinet notes, and atonality, and Basin Street improvisation, in the sounds that came out of the alleys, stirring the blood of many residents, leading some to flop around like Holy Rollers full of corn-squeezin's.

Still, Rhubarb was seen plain by a congress of several hundred sportsmen assembled in a structure of circular design out toward the International Airport. This was a pit for cockfights, a sport that is both quite legal and quite popular throughout the island. Here, on a Sunday morning, aficionados of the angry rooster were assembled for one of the most important cocking hacks of recent years. This was a grudge match, involving a man named Carlos Oggli from Mayaguez and a man named Robar Bizco of San Juan, sometimes called the King of the Cocking Mains. Carlos Oggli had come on the scene with a gamecock called El Guerrero, a bird as nasty as a barrel of bushmasters. El Guerrero had built himself a large reputation from Mayaguez to Ponce to Guayama in the southern reaches of the island. Having slashed everything to ribbons in his home country, El Guerrero had now been brought north to meet the champion, Señor Bizco's coal-black, vicious, seemingly-indestructible killer called Sizzer Romero. In the folklore of the worldwide cock, black has long denoted a bird of evil, a creature of the devil. Sizzer Romero was all of that. Mean clear through. Some sports writers said that, pound-for-pound, he was the greatest gamecock ever to suit up in steel gaffs. He had made his owner rich and in the doing, he had become something of a national hero. He had been taken once to Honduras to fight the champion of that nation, a blood-spilling lump of sadistic poultry named Señor Cabron. In less than three minutes of action the Honduran champ turned chicken, flew out of the pit, landed on a spectator, and struck the man in the heart with a two-inch gaff. The populace was outraged. Latins are capable of worshiping an animal one moment and beating him to death the next. They seized Señor Cabron, trussed him, and carried him to the nearest courtroom. He was given a swift trial and sentenced to death; the mob then took him to the plaza and hanged him from the limb of an ironwood tree. A deterrent and a warning to all other gamecocks, that any future crimes in this direction would result in swift justice. The mob leaders then proposed that the foreign pig, Sizzer Romero, be accorded the same treatment, but by this time Sizzer Romero and Señor Bizco were approaching the Guatemalan border on a motor scooter.

Now, in the twenty-foot San Juan cockpit, El Guerrero and Sizzer Romero were squared off, and beginning to slash tentatively. The clamor from the circular galleries was so great that the worshipers in a church a block and a half away were unable to hear the words of their padre's sermon. The fans screamed and bellowed and waved sheaves of important money in the air, making wagers back and forth across the arena. Now the action picked up, and the feathers were beginning to fly. And lo, the freewheeling killer from the south had drawn first blood. El Guerrero's followers, who had journeyed north in large numbers, now howled for the immediate death of the black Bizco cock. And as they were howling an object came flying through the air and landed in the middle of the pit. It was a cat, a big snarling yellow

cat. It seized the champion, Sizzer Romero, by the neck. El Guerrero, an astonished bird, rocked back on his gaffs and stared, and he seemed to be saying to himself, "What kind of idiot cockfight do these San Juan nuts put on, in the name of a kindly God?" The yellow cat moved fast, carrying the bird, feinted in one direction, then turned and leaped the barrier, shot up the aisle and out through a gate before any of the fans could get into action. They, like the Mayaguez cock, had been stunned for a minute or two. Now they set up an unearthly howling, crying out, "*Ay bendito!*" and "*Mata al gato!*" and "*El paredon!*" and "*Sawn ah beech!*"

Thus the explanation of the feathers and chicken bones in the alley where the boy found Rhubarb—he was lying asleep surrounded by the mortal remains of a great champion.

Word of the cat's heinous crime spread swiftly across San Juan and its environs. Then came news of the discovery of the cat and the rooster remnants in the alley. The gringo cat that had escaped from the ship had snatched the wonderful, the beautiful, the valiant Sizzer Romero right from the cockpit—an act so frightful, so despicable, so sacrilegious, as to call for immediate retaliation and maybe war. Mobs formed in various localities and they were starting their march to Pier Three and the *Thaddeus* when the Governor hit the phone again.

"Señor Jaeger," he said to Eric, "get that cat away from Puerto Rico, instantly! Get that cat out of Caribbean waters! Keep that cat forever away from Latin-American countries! Go, *hombre*, go!"

They went.

In time the populace cooled off and new champion cocks came out of the provinces. But the fabulous cat Rhubarb had left his mark on the land. It is to be noted that the *puertorriqueños* are an extremely superstitious people, the same as people everywhere. There are said to be more than a hundred thousand spiritualistic mediums functioning on the island, throwing up tidal waves of ectoplasm, eager to put people in touch with their loved ones who have "passed over," or even with celebrities of past eras, such as Christopher Columbus, Juan Ponce de León, Captain Kidd, Alejandro Ramírez, W. C. Fields, José Martí, Simón Bolívar, and . . . well, it is said that there are several dirty-headed old harridans who are able to fetch back the wraith of the immortal murdered cock, Sizzer Romero, and prevail upon him to speak a couple of spiritualistic cock-a-doodle-dos.

Nowadays the superstitious people of Puerto Rico have accorded Rhubarb a firm position in island folklore. It is often told that the big gringo cat, in addition to rapine in depth among his own kind, sired a few offspring out of dogs, produced one out of a feral pig, and one out of a turkey. In some quarters, this is known as a score.

ॐ Chapter FOUR

THE Executive Committee charged with conducting the affairs of the gigantic corporation known as Banner Enterprises was meeting informally in the Fairmont Hotel suite usually occupied in past years by Rhubarb and Eric Yaeger. Eric was present as was Hickey Dolbier and the four other members of the Committee: Simon Horney, specialist in real estate and construction; Carlyle Waterhouse, whose field was transportation; Asa Nutting, real good in arithmetic, and Ogden Crump, a former wheeler-dealer in oil and mining and teen-age girls.

Eric addressed himself to Dolbier, chief counsel for the corporation, a man with the look of a wistful, hung-over chipmunk that has just missed his grab at the last hickory nut. The façade was deceptive; Hickey Dolbier was one of the top corporation lawyers in the land and in his present circumstances he needed to be. He was such a superior corporation lawyer that he hated ever to appear in a courtroom, contending that the courtroom should come to him.

"Hickey," said Eric, "all of us need to remind ourselves of where the corporation stands, and where we as individuals stand. Did you bring that stuff?"

Dolbier riffled two sheets of paper out of his briefcase.

43

"It's all in simple language," he said. "This is how it shapes up. Thad Banner wrote a codicil to his will covering disposal of his estate upon the death of Rhubarb. Let me interpose at this point that Mr. Banner had no idea that his estate would double and then triple and then triple again, on and on. He believed, in fact, that his fortune would be dissipated by the time Rhubarb died. Nevertheless, he made the following proviso: one year from the time of Rhubarb's demise, a third of the estate would be liquidated and the money given to charity. At the end of two years, another third would be liquidated and the proceeds given to charity. The final accounting would come at the end of three years, Eric Yaeger to get one-half of whatever was left, the other half going to the same charity."

"Judas Isss-cariot!" exclaimed Ogden Crump. "We got three lousy years at the hawg trough and then we're out on our butts. What dern charity *gits* all this money?"

Hickey Dolbier permitted himself a slight frown. He never approved the crude ways of the Texan; he never approved the crude ways of anybody, but he had to put up with more than one man's share of boorish behavior. "No specific organization is mentioned by name, Ogden," he said to Crump, "but Mr. Banner made it clear where he wanted his money to go. Rather, where he *didn't* want it to go. This is the way he put it—these are his words."

Dolbier now read:

> *When I speak of charity I mean that the money is to go to sick people, such as drug addicts and boozers and arthritics and people with cancer and broken necks and things like that. The money is to be placed directly into the hands of these sick people, to do with as they please. They will all be free to spend it on themselves. Not one penny is to be contributed toward medical research or any other kind of research. Research is usually conducted by well people, and I don't want a single dollar of my estate to fall into the hands of well people, excepting only in the case of my loyal friend, Eric Yaeger. Well people are not to be trusted. They steal hot stoves . . .*

Dolbier hesitated, cleared his throat, cleared it again, and glanced nervously at Eric, who said, "Come on Hickey, give us that last line. Let's have the snapper." The lawyer ran his tongue across his lips and then read Thaddeus Banner's valedictory to the world: "Balls to well people!"

Eric grinned—he could almost hear old Thad dictating that line.

He spoke again to Lawyer Dolbier: "What's the latest score on cat claimants?"

"It's beginning to taper off," said Dolbier. "There have been something over two thousand and it has cost us a fair amount of money, but my people have been able to handle things. Got one yesterday from New Zealand, with home movies. Out of curiosity I ran the film. The cat was as black . . . as black as the Pit from pole to pole. Invictus. William Ernest Henley. He was filmed indoors, lying on a carpet, gnawing at a large bone . . . the femur of a ram, I should judge. Messy."

"I've had a telegram from a woman in New York," said Eric. "I'm flying there tonight to see Ray Merriman about that sugar cane proposition, and I may call on this dame. Her story interests me and it may interest you guys, too. She says her cat was captured running wild on the streets in San Juan, Puerto Rico. Remember Puerto Rico? About two years ago, when he got loose and ravaged half the town?"

"Will I ever forget it?" spoke up Simon Horney. "I sprained my ankle and fell down and damn near killed myself chasing a cat in an alley and the cat turned out to be a mongoose."

"This lady in New York," said Dolbier, "is no doubt a fraud with a fraudulent cat, the same as all the others. Think again of the ones who have dyed their cats yellow. I almost despair of my own kind. Why must men be so larcenous? Isn't it possible any more for people to lead lives of common decency?"

"Hickey," said Eric, "I'm surprised at you. If a man tried to lead a life of common decency today he would immediately find himself out of step with the rest of the world."

A growl came from Ogden Crump, meant for no one but himself. "Sick people!" he muttered. "Three short years, and out on our butts!"

Diana was sitting in her apartment leafing through a journal whose contents were devoted to the rag trade. The cat was somewhere about, possibly in the kitchen sniffing at things and looking for new devilment to involve himself in. Diana had bought him a sanitary tray made of plastic and costing three dollars; she put a mixture of peat moss and sand in it, but The Tiger wouldn't go near it. She took out the peat moss and sand, and then shredded up the book sections of the Sunday papers, and her cat began using the tray with such zest and avidity that it worried her. At Bloomingdale's she picked up three fluffy bath mats to make a bed for her pet but thus far he had spurned this luxury and chose to sleep on the floor of the bedroom closet.

She looked up from the pages of *L'Officiel*. Her radio was going and she had become suddenly aware of a voice, a resonant, masculine voice with a magnetic quality that made her feel as if she were being drawn across the room.

"I really dislike talking about it," said the voice, "but it's true. I'm not altogether sure that having a breed of chicken named for me is quite flattering. The word *chicken* means several different things nowadays."

"I think it's flattering," came a female voice which Diana recognized as belonging to Martha Deane. "I simply can't wait until I put Bill to work broiling an H. Allen Smith on the outdoor grill."

"Personally," said the magnetic male voice, "I wouldn't be able to eat even a wing from one of them. They are very handsome chickens. But . . ." and he spoke now with an air of resignation, ". . . I suppose that is what they are for in this dog-eat-dog, people-scrozzle-people, chicken-peck-chicken world we live in."

"Just tell me," said Martha Deane, "and we will never cook an H. Allen Smith hen at our house. And if you'll excuse me, now, I must get at this shopping list. We'll be back shortly with more from today's wonderful guest. All of you know about him, but few of you have had the privilege that is mine, the privilege of sitting here across the table from him, in the physical presence of all this warmth and wisdom. He'll be back shortly to tell us of his adventures as a swordsman and of the time he pinked both Errol Flynn and Douglas Fairbanks, Jr., in a single bout with the foils. He has promised to tell us of that sensational night when he broke the bank at Pull-Jerk-&-Holler, the biggest slot machine casino in Las Vegas. He has assured me that he will give us the details of how he drank Jackie Gleason to the floor in one hour and twenty minutes; of his recent accomplishments as a gourmet cook and as a boulevardier on three continents, of how he won the Croix de Guerre four times, of the memorable day when he drove Elizabeth Taylor into the arms of Richard Burton, and of how he is, reluctantly, the author of those literary works appearing under the pseudonym *J. D. Salinger.* This most remarkable of men, this distinguished and charming gentleman, will be with us right to the end today. Now, Macy's!"

How does it happen, Diana thought, that I know so little about this man? I'm sure I heard his name mentioned in San Juan. Have I become so involved with nubby-and-slubby that I'm overlooking some of the better things in life? I wonder how old he is, what he looks like, if he's married. He must be really something. Something special, like The Tiger. She decided she'd ask around. She settled down to await the end of the commercial messages, so she could hear this H. Allen Smith talk some more. But a capricious kismet ordained it otherwise. The doorbell rang and it was the telegram from San Francisco. It read:

MUST ADVISE YOU THAT THERE HAVE BEEN OVER TWO THOUSAND PERSONS LAYING CLAIM TO RHUBARB FORTUNE ON BASIS OF CATS IN THEIR POSSESSION. OUR INVESTIGATORS HAVE PROVED THAT MORE THAN HALF OF THESE CON ARTISTS BAGGED THEIR ALLEY CATS AFTER THE DEATH OF RHUBARB WITH CLEAR INTENTION OF FRAUD AGAINST BANNER ENTERPRISES. ALL OTHER CLAIMANTS HAVE LIKEWISE HAD LARCENOUS INTENTIONS. I WOULD NOT BOTHER GIVING YOUR CLAIM ANY CONSIDERATION EXCEPT THAT I WILL BE IN NEW YORK TOMORROW AND I MAKE A HOBBY OF STUDYING THE CRIMINAL MIND.

YAEGER

When she finished reading it, Diana threw her head back and spoke emotional words at the ceiling. "How . . . snotty . . . can . . . you . . . get!" She read it through again and her anger rose to a roiling fury. This knothead, who had been leeching off an innocent cat for years, was now calling her a crook, a con artist, a criminal. She began framing sentences that she would speak to him, when he came, and they were not ladylike sentences.

She had sent the telegram to him somewhat against her own better judgment. It had been Midge's suggestion, back in San Juan. Now she was sorry she had done it. By her very nature she was a person of fibre, independent and self-reliant. She could stubborn up like a wet rope left out in a blizzard. She had more than enough money to suit her needs for she was paid something over twenty thousand dollars a year at Hershfield & Diamond. Just for playing at nubby-and-slubby. Her world was the world of fabrics, centering around Third Avenue and the Upper Fifties. She was at once a stylist, a designer, a whiz at promotional work, and something of an artist. Her daytime hours were spent up to her jiggler in damasks and linens, matelasse crepes, orlons, dacrons, rovana, flocked papers, velvets, voiles, printed cottons, brocades, chenilles, all manner of drapery materials and woven fabrics used in upholstery. She had done her turn at Parsons and in Paris and she knew her job and felt quite secure in the highly competitive fabric business. There were people around in plenty who had learned that Diana Fowler didn't relish being walked upon. And she didn't really yearn for cat money.

Three days of her vacation remained and so she was at home when Eric Yaeger arrived. She opened the door for him and he swept by her without giving her a second glance—a most unusual performance for Eric. In most circumstances he gave lovely young women second glances; he was, indeed, famous for it.

At the same time Diana was not standing slack-jawed and bug-eyed in the presence of a man as handsome as a movie idol. His charm and bearing had not changed a great deal with the years, but she did not notice it; she contemplated him as if he were a foul mud turtle. From the first instant they faced each other it was clear that these two were ready for total war.

"Okay," he said, glancing around the room. "Where's the cat?"

"Don't *push!*" Diana responded.

He turned and looked her up and down. He still didn't see her for what she was. His difficulty at the moment was his customary dealing-from-strength frame of mind. He had shifted into this no-funny-business gear as he approached her apartment door, and he remained in it now. He was all business.

"Sit down," Diana said, avoiding the "please" and making it sound like an order. "I'll get The Tiger in a moment."

"The Tiger!" Eric repeated acidly. "Look, sister, I actually don't care about seeing your animal. I have a paper here in my pocket for you to sign, and a check for five thousand dollars, which is considerably more than the average we've been . . ."

"Out!" said Diana, rising from her chair. "Get *out!*"

48

Her face was ablaze with anger and Eric stared at her, seeing her for the first time. The rather rare word *muliebral* popped into his mind as suited to this girl, meaning that she was buoyantly overflowing with womanliness and, more than that, there was a strong suggestion of mulishness about her.

"Just a moment, my dear," he said. "Take it easy. Please sit down and tell me the whole story about what happened in . . . where was it? . . . Mexico?" He knew quite well it was not Mexico.

"It was Puerto Rico," she said, "and I am in no mood to talk to you about what happened there, or about anything else. I don't put up with your kind of insolence. I don't want your check, and I don't want any part of your industrial empire or whatever it is."

"Well, then," said Eric, "let me see the cat before I leave."

She hesitated for a bit, then left the room and returned with The Tiger.

"What," Eric demanded, "is that thing you've got tied around his neck?"

"That's his leash," said Diana coldly, "designed for him by one of San Juan's leading couturières."

"She must have been smashed when she . . ." but Eric never finished the sentence. His eye had fallen on The Tiger and his jaw dropped and he leaned forward intently. "Spittin' image!" he said to himself. He felt as if he were looking at a ghost, and the ghost was staring back at him, quizzically, cocking its head to one side.

"Bring him closer," he said to Diana.

"He'd scratch your eyes out," she responded.

At that moment The Tiger moved of his own volition. He pulled on the red rag leash, straining toward Eric. Diana took a couple of faulty steps forward and then Eric reached down and gave the cat a couple of pats on the back. Diana braced herself for the hurricane—but it didn't come. The Tiger glanced up at Eric's face and then suddenly leaped into his lap, purring. And now Eric looked at the long yellow tail and saw the jog in it. His first response was emotional. Flabbergasting! Incredible! The symmetrical disposition of the jog in this cat's tail was precisely the same as that of the jog in Rhubarb's tail. Everything fits! He sat still for a few minutes, striving for corporate calm and objectivity. He tried to apply discursive reasoning to the presence of that Rhubarbian jog. No go. Gregor J. Mendel himself, had anyone told him that a male cat had inherited a jog in his tail from another male cat, would have gone out of his skull and started throwing garden peas all over the Augustinian monastery at Altbrünn. Still, the implications were alarming and Eric shifted back into his cold-turkey frame of mind. Don't let this broad get to you, boy, he told himself; he had known others much like her . . . as hard as granite underneath that beautiful façade. He fancied himself as a man able to make swift and accurate judgments of character. This girl was unleavened bitch. Anyway you arranged the letters, she spelled trouble. He must move cautiously—this cat must never fall into the wrong hands. He began rubbing The Tiger gently under the ears while Diana stood before him, agape at the behavior of her misanthropic pet.

"Miss Fowler," Eric finally said, spacing his words carefully, "this cat appears to like me, and I like this cat. It is obvious to me that he cannot be the son of Rhubarb. Impossible. But I have spent a large part of my adult life in close company with a cat. I say to you quite frankly that I miss that companionship. There are millions of cats all around us, but this one set up an immediate rapport with me, and I with him." He paused to effect a moment of silence before he hit her with the large proposition. Then, "I am prepared to offer you *twenty* thousand dollars for this animal."

Diana gave a mighty jerk on the red leash, removing The Tiger from Eric's lap and sending him sprawling and scrabbling across the floor. She reeled him in as if he were a fish and then picked him up.

"You'll do this ray!" she cried out. "I mean day this roo! Oh damn! You'll rue this day, you conniving fathead! You call *me* a con artist! I told you to get out and I tell you again. Oh—You—Tee, OUT! Move fast or I'll turn The Tiger loose and this time he'll fix you—there won't even be a scalp left to bury! Git! Scat!"

Eric stood up. This girl was insane; he was not so far removed from his days as a sports writer as to low-rate the sum of twenty thousand dollars. But he was forgetting something . . . this dame knew the extent of the Banner fortune. Easy, boy. He took a couple of steps toward the door, then turned back.

"Miss Fowler," he told her, "your cat wouldn't attack me. Never. He *likes* me." He was holding his voice at the level of amiability. "For one thing," he went on, "all cats like me. For another, he's not as ferocious as you think. He's not one-tenth as ferocious as Rhubarb. One night I took Rhubarb to the World's Fair here in New York. He actually tried to get away from me and throw himself onto a life-size mechanical dinosaur. Do you think *this* creature of yours would ever jump a dinosaur?"

"He'll jump *you*, if you don't get moving!" shrilled Diana. "You'll look like . . . like a demolition site in the middle of a depressed area. Get your arrogant hide out of my home!"

"I'm on my way," said Eric with a demoniacal smile. "In parting let me say that I would not deal with you if the very life of Banner Enterprises depended on it. Let me say further that Banner Enterprises is slightly bigger and more important than you and your piddling pursuits."

"To me," Diana replied stingingly, "your precious Banner outfit is the corner delicatessen. Nothing more."

"Hah!" exclaimed Eric. "One final thing: from the looks of this setup it is obvious that you are more than just a bitch—you are a *kept* bitch!"

A sound similar to the cry of an asthmatic embergoose came from Diana's throat. She began dashing about the room as if looking for a poker or a bullwhip or a Three Iron. Eric let himself out of the apartment rather quickly.

Diana scurried into her bedroom and checked the telephone number given her by Midge McLean in San Juan and dialed the office of Jeremy K. Jenkins. After some delay she got through to Mr. Jenkins and when she mentioned Pierce and Midge McLean he said he would see her in two hours.

Fifteen minutes later the doorman phoned and said there was a Mr. Crump from Banner Enterprises asking to see her.

"What does he look like?" Diana wanted to know.

"Middle fifties, medium height, talks like Ladybird, got on a sort of Gunsmoke hat . . . he ain't Cary Grant style like that last one."

"Good. Send him up."

Ogden Crump walked into Diana's presence exuding good cheer, his girl-getter personality turned on, all his inner rheostats and distributors and plug points flashing and sparking and zinging.

"Dawg-gone New York traffic!" he observed, taking off his Laredo hat. "Mr. Yaeger been here already? Too bad. I was hopin' to meet him here but . . . oh, well, nothin' lost. *He* does all the talkin', anyhow."

"He tries to," Diana interjected. "I was able to wedge in a few well-chosen words before he left. Frankly, Mr. Crump, I don't care much for your Mr. Yaeger's manners, methods, ethics, conversation, tailoring, brains, morals, personality . . ."

"Honey chile!" Ogden Crump ejaculated, flinging his lumpy fingers into the air, "what in the name of time come off?"

"Plenty come off," Diana assured him. "But first, please tell me what your connection is with this cruddy Banner outfit."

"I'm a member of the Executive Committee that runs ever'thing. When they write us up on the financial pages they gen'ally refer to us as the *all-parrful* Executive Committe. My department is oil and mining operations but I would much pree-fur . . . I would *pree-fur* to have charge of the stenograffers' pool." He wiggled his eyebrows meaningfully.

Diana forced a smile. She had seen his kind before, many times. Beneath a show of bluster, a pretense of worldliness, Ogden Crump was plainly a country-jake casanova, a chawbacon letch with unruffled gray moss growing around his belly button. Some corporation! she said to herself. Some industrial empire! From what she had seen of the high command thus far, she was convinced that Rhubarb committed suicide in Pago Pago Bay just to get away from it all. But, out of curiosity, she decided to play along a bit. She already sensed the fact that this Crump was lying about meeting Eric Yaeger here. He was up to something. She invited him to have a chair, checked the time, and then stirred up a brace of drinks.

"Eric wanted to talk to you about your tawm cat," said Crump, "and I must admit I been more than a little innarested. Is th' ole boy around?"

Diana left the room and returned immediately with The Tiger. "That's a mighty purty red picket rope you got on 'im," observed Crump, and then he stiffened in his chair and sat like a figure carved from stone, staring straight at the cat. He started to say something, then caught himself and held off for a moment.

"A nice cat," he finally offered, speaking through a dryness that had come in his throat. "A very nice A-Number-One pussy-wussy kitty-cat . . ." (Diana thought: Glory be! We air a-gonna have a lovely admixture of Taixuss twang and baby talk!) "Where was it," Crump went on, "that you found 'im? Porta Ricka?"

"Right, Porta Ricka," said Diana. "There's an idea around that he might be the son of Rhubarb but your insolent Mr. Yaeger has convinced me it isn't true. I'll tell you something, Mr. Crump, I'm real *glad* The Tiger is not going to get involved in the affairs of your company. I simply don't trust your top boy."

"Now," protested Crump, "you looky here, mah little dewberry blossom. You are mistaken. Eric Yaeger is all wool and three foot wide. Course he does try to tell ever'body around him how they oughta run their lives. Sometimes I think God Almighty's over-coat wouldn't make a vest for that Eric. He's nosey—that's what he is. Rides hellity-larrup over ever'body. He's even tried to tell *me* things to do with the bauxite we dig outa the ground in Arkansas. Said I should figure a way to get them pea-sized pisolites offa the vermicular lateritic bauxite that comes outa are mines. Jesus Henry God! The man is a moh-ron! There's times when I'd like to scrape the pea-sized pisolites offa *him!*"

They somehow managed to interrupt this run-down on Eric, and talked some more about The Tiger. Both Diana and Crump were dissembling, out of different motives. Diana knew that Crump was faking—she was correct in her reading of the look on his face when he first saw the cat. He believed without question that The Tiger was Rhubarb's son. Just what he was scheming to do about it she couldn't guess. She had a feeling that he was mak-ing it up as he went along. Crump, on the other hand, had no idea that Diana was putting on an act; he was one of those strange men who believe that attractive and shapely young women melt away in their presence and can be swiftly unfrocked with a juglet of Arpège. Or even witch hazel.

At length Diana excused herself, saying she had to freshen up and leave for an appointment in Rockefeller Center. Crump said he'd be going in that direction and that he'd drop her off. She headed for her bedroom, taking The Tiger with her. The moment she was out of the room Ogden Crump popped to his feet and be-gan prowling. He peered behind furniture and pulled a couple of paintings out and looked at the wall behind them. He *sniffed* all around the room like a dog testing the morning air, and opened a couple of drawers in a desk. Then he seemed to realize that he didn't know what he was looking for, and so he sat down again and pulled an envelope from his inner pocket and got out a ball-point pen. He began making a sketch of the room and the dis-position of its furnishings, and the location of doors and windows.

Twice he got up and tip-toed around and opened doors, peering through them and returning to add more detail to his sketch.

He was on the far side of the room when Diana reappeared. He was standing before a painting of a red barn—clearly a Pennsylvania Dutch barn with its large hex signs—and he was teetering on his heels, pretending to study the detail.

"Looks like in France," he ventured. "A Vander Gog?"

Diana suppressed a smile. "Wrong," she said, "but close. It's a Hugh Troy and it's in Bucks County. Take a close look at it—it doesn't show in the painting, but behind that barn more than thirty people are having an apple-butter boiling." He studied the matter for a few moments, then caught on. "'y god," he said, "Ah *like* you, Goose Fluff!"

They hadn't gone two blocks before he was complaining again about the New York traffic. "Mighty rough goin' in the coulees today," he said. He asked her if she could have suppa with him during his stay in town and she said she might if they could have hog jowls and hominy. "We call 'em hawg *joles* back home," he corrected her. "They make larrupin' good eatin'. Ah expect we can locate some—they say you can find anything you want in New York, you look long enough, but *you cain't find Taixuss!*" She was somewhat relieved to hear this and then told him that she was very busy, getting ready to return to her job. He then probed around about the extent of her fondness for The Tiger. Diana assured him that she was deeply and irrevocably attached to the cat.

"Ah gotta admit," said Crump, "that he looks a mighty good deal like Rhubarb looked, but then so does a whole passel of cats that people been fetchin' in. Ah was real close to Rhubarb—closer than *some* people might think. Ah miss 'im. He was a sort of pal, a buddy, a chum like. Ah have never, muh dear, bin married. Well, Ah take that back—Ah bin married, but divorced ever time. Ah don't mind tellin' you sweet-thang, Ah get lonesome. Ah'd be willin' to taw the line with a nice fat price for 'im. Ah might even go as high as ten thousand dollars."

Unlike her reaction to Eric Yaeger's bargaining, Diana took this one without a flicker of emotion. She still had an urge to find out just how far this implausible man would go in his effort to do whatever he was trying to do.

Arriving at her destination on Sixth Avenue of the Americas, he seized her hand and planted a wet kiss on her knuckles, to the accompaniment of a deep sigh. She crinkled up a smile and closed her eyes for a moment and said to herself, I do believe the old goat wants more than my cat. As she got out of the cab he said to her in a confidential tone: "Watch that tush-hawg Yaeger. He'd steal the pennies off a dead man's ah-lids."

She made her way to one of the high floors in the skyscraper and found the door labeled "Jeremy K. Jenkins." The reception room was plain but neat and a young woman ushered her straightaway into the larger chamber occupied by the lawyer. He was sitting in an old-fashioned swivel chair, at a rolltop desk. He glanced up quizzically and for an instant Diana thought she was in the presence of one of her favorite people—Samuel Pickwick, Esq., G. C. M. P. C., man among men, author of the scholarly work, *Speculations on the Source of the Hampstead Ponds, with some Observations on the Theory of Tittlebats.* He popped to his feet, a small roundish man, and trotted to her side, taking her by the arm and with sweeping courtly gestures, accompanied by old-world bowing, escorted her to a leather chair.

"Please permit me two more minutes with this fiendish bit of parchment that someone has inflicted on me," he begged. "Then I'll be completely at your disposal. You are lovely, my dear. But, then, it is to be expected that Midge would send loveliness. There are periodicals there on the table."

He hurried back to his rolltop and the fiendish parchment and she looked at the magazines. Two copies of the *North American Review*, dated 1828 and 1830, featuring work by Richard Henry Dana, George Bancroft and Daniel Webster. Also the *Dial*, *Godey's Lady's Book*, the *Southern Literary Messenger.* Diana decided she would not attempt to cope, right now, with literature of such quality. Too overpowering, too Kafkaesque, too Kierkegaardy, too ring-a-ding-ding. She looked around the office and noted a glittery chandelier that might have come out of a dining room of the 1880s. In one corner of the room stood a small marble-topped table with a stereoscope lying on it. Elsewhere she noted a gleaming brass cuspidor, a good twelve inches high, a wicker rocking chair and a high-backed sofa which she judged was stuffed with horsehair. In the middle of the room stood a long mission oak table and on it a marble bust of Gladstone or Roger Brooke Taney or someone on that order. There were red velvet drapes at the two windows and big red roses in the Axminster carpeting. Midge McLean had mentioned that Jeremy K. Jenkins was somewhat eccentric in his attire, but nothing had been said about his office decor. Diana now noticed that while Mr. Jenkins had a modern cradle phone at his ancient desk, across the room a crank-box phone was fastened to the wall. She had no doubt that it was connected to the outside world.

Mr. Jenkins finished with his paper work and came over and took a chair facing her. "Please don't feel that you've been snooping on my possessions," he urged. "Everybody does. That's one of the reasons I maintain my office in this style. There's another reason. I'm in honest revolt against the overmodernization of furnishings, both in houses as well as offices. Lloyd Morris wrote in one of his books (and this has been twenty years ago) that the designers of furniture have been flooding us with things which in their unabashed metal nudity resemble agricultural implements taken indoors for protection from the weather. You may also have heard that I am in rebellion against the creeping disease that has afflicted the men's clothing trade. They are backing us into the same corner where the Parisian and Fifth Avenue style-setters have had the women in thrall for years. Men's fashions are now being changed at least once a year, usually in such a manner that tailors can't do a thing with our out-of-date clothing. I simply refuse to hold still for this insufferable swindle, and so I've gone back to the turn of the century for my styles. It costs me far more money than if I went along with the so-called fashion arbiters. This is a modified tailcoat I'm wearing—I have them tailored a half dozen at a time, always in black-and-white checks but of different textiles and weights. I always wear gray derby hats, the square kind, which are made for me in Connecticut—yonder's one on the hall tree. This collar is what you might call a wing collar without wings, and my necktie—well, my dear, please note the width of the knot at the top. A full three inches. It isn't really a tie, it's a stock, of the kind worn by iniquitous dudes and clergymen many years back. For the reason that it could never be tied properly in an average lifetime, the big knot is permanent and the whole rig is hooked together at the back of the collar. A couple of years back I decided I would like to change to the belcher, but then I found that the Hairy Ones of the Hideous Generation have been taking up that kind of neckwear when they

56

take up any at all. And what else, of course, but Congress gaiters?"

Jeremy K. Jenkins elevated his legs and showed them to her. Then he opened his modified tailcoat (four buttons buttoned) and exhibited a heavy gold watch chain, and lifted a big snap-case gold watch from his weskit.

"Feel the heft of it," he urged, putting it into Diana's hand. "You could kill a man with this watch. I believe I am the only man left who carries a snap-case watch bequeathed to him by his grandfather who was—I swear it!—a locomotive engineer."

Diana reflected back to the day in San Juan when Midge McLean had told her about Mr. Jenkins. "The first time you meet him," Midge had said, "you'll probably run from him. You'll think he's a nut. But just keep in mind that underneath all that William McKinley folderol is one of the sharpest lawyers in New York. He's the man for you and the cat."

Up to this time Diana's idea of a great lawyer was a man who glowered and growled and howled at witnesses, and pawed the courtroom floor like a fighting bull, and threatened physical as-

sault on opposing counsel, and put the judge in his place, and gulped down a bottle of poison right in front of the jury to prove that the poison isn't poison. This image didn't square at all with the mild-mannered, gentle, soft-spoken Jeremy K. Jenkins.

She was thoroughly satisfied with him and they got down to a discussion of the paternity litigation she had in mind. And at this point the true character of the Pickwickian lawyer came to the fore. The average attorney of any importance would likely back swiftly away from a proposal that he represent a cat in open court. Not Mr. Jenkins. The moment he heard that he might be counsel to The Tiger, in a proceeding against the far-flung Banner empire, he rubbed his hands together and exclaimed, "Dee-lightful!" Just as if he were Teddy Roosevelt.

He told his secretary to cancel all appointments, put on his square hat, and accompanied Diana to her apartment to have a consultation with his new client.

&⊙% **Chapter FIVE**

JUDGE Ambrose Bippus was receiving in chambers. He sat back
of a long table and stared, with a pained expression, at the group
before him. It was not difficult for Judge Bippus to achieve a
pained expression; Nature had given him a head start over most
people. He was tall and quite bony, with a long face, a long
pointed nose, and eyebrows consisting almost entirely of wild
hairs. He somehow managed to retain the look of a man with a
constant stabbing toothache. That, or a sour stomach.

One of the principal reasons Judge Bippus was a man of myriad
scowls and wincings lay in his distrust of people. He was convinced that only a handful of people in the whole wide world
understood about a woodpecker's hole. And he was certain that
when he tried to explain the joy to be had from a woodpecker's
hole, people lied to him, saying they knew exactly what he was
talking about, whereas in fact they were secretly classifying him
as a nitwit and a nut.

This very morning the Judge had a fine woodpecker's hole
lying on the table near his right hand. Now and then he picked
it up and rubbed his fingers over it. He always kept a woodpecker's hole with him whether at the dining table, on the bench,
or playing knock rummy with his brother-in-law, a failure in

life. It settled his nerves when he handled it, just as the Chinese achieve serenity from their jade fingering-pieces.

A door opened and Judge Bippus glanced up. His scowl deepened.

"You," he said abruptly. "Dill. What are *you* doing here? You still trying to get yourself disbarred? Well, don't stretch your luck."

Eric Yaeger, sitting between Hickey Dolbier and Simon Horney, closed his eyes for a moment and then the name came clear. He turned and looked at the man who had just entered. Orlando Dill, soiled rogue of the New York bar. He looked older, to be sure, than the last time Eric had seen him, but he still had something of that splendid dash and swagger, the handsome profile, the sartorial elegance, the waxed mustache, the various insignia that had made him a legend in courtrooms all over the land.

"Your honor," Orlando Dill spoke, and his voice was as resonant and compelling as ever, "I am here representing a particular client whose name I would prefer not to mention at this time. Let us say that I am here as an observer. And let us say further, for the benefit of your honor, that the low jackals and stinking jackasses of our profession have never succeeded in having me disbarred."

"Don't worry," said Judge Bippus. "You'll make it. Success is written all over your face. Now, let us get on with this affair."

He pawed at some papers, grabbed a couple of feels at the woodpecker's hole, and then resumed: "As I understand it—and I may be clean out of my head—this is a paternity case involving a cat. I am asked to hear evidence and then decide if a certain cat by the name of Tiger is the legitimate offspring of the world-famous cat Rhubarb, deceased. This case presents certain difficulties. Plenty. How, for example, can we ever describe a cat-child as being legitimate? Parent cats do not get married. Therefore, according to human standards, every cat in the world is a bastard." He paused and muttered an aside, "They're worse than bastards, the way they treat woodpeckers!" He glanced at the woodpecker hole on the table and then continued, "I don't want to get into the trial of this action until Monday. I want to get away—I have an important engagement with a copse of coniferous trees up near Katonah."

Jeremy K. Jenkins leaned over and spoke to Diana. Had she

heard the judge make that remark about cats being worse than bastards? She had.

"I don't like it," said Jenkins. "This judge is king of the crackpots." The rotund little lawyer had his face turned to her and she noted the tuft of white hair that seemed to stick straight up like an exclamation point, giving him an elfin look at times, a look of incredulity at others.

"Say it, Mr. Bumble," Diana ordered.

"The law," he responded, "is a ass, a idiot."

Diana laughed out loud, and the Judge frowned in her direction. Then he went on with his somewhat cockeyed exposition of the ground rules.

"The thing I can't get straightened out," he said, "is the identity of the litigants involved. I mean the human litigants. You, Mr. Jenkins, represent the petitioner Diana Fowler. Right?"

"In a sense, I do, your honor," said Mr. Jenkins, rising to his feet. He felt of the huge knot at his throat and then used both hands to flicker out the abbreviated tails of his checkered coat. "My actual client, however, is the cat Tiger, often referred to as *The* Tiger. We are prepared to prove, your honor, that this cat, The Tiger, is the true offspring of the cat tycoon Rhubarb. We intend to show that said cat Tiger is entitled to . . ."

"For God sake, Mr. Jenkins," the Judge interrupted. "Will you please quit all that 'said Rhubarb' legalistic mumbo jumbo and give us some of your flowery talk? I have observed your work several times in the past and I've enjoyed the show you put on, except for one thing. Don't flip your coattails at me—it's a bad habit you've got and it makes me jumpy."

"A thousand pardons, your honor," said Mr. Jenkins. "I had no idea I was flipping them at you. I thought I was flipping them at Mr. Dill back there."

"You flip them at me," called out Orlando Dill, "and you'll get 'em flipped back so fast they'll leave welts."

"You shut up, Dill," ordered the Judge. "I hear any more from you and I'll give Mr. Jenkins the privilege of taking you to pieces, and he's the boy who can do it."

"Thank you so much, your honor," Mr. Jenkins said. "By the way, did I hear you say you had an engagement with a . . ."

"A copse of scorched balsams, Mr. Jenkins."

"You make it sound like an important project, your honor."

"It is *most* important. I've been informed that in one of those balsams there is an Arctic Three-toed woodpecker. Have you ever, Mr. Jenkins, seen an Arctic Three-toed woodpecker?"

"Not to my knowledge, your honor, but I'm certain I would enjoy seeing one."

"There are nine people," said Judge Bippus, "only nine people in the United States who collect them, and you, Mr. Jenkins, are looking at one of the nine."

"Collect what, your honor?"

"Woodpecker holes."

"But what is a . . ." Mr. Jenkins began.

"They go cruck-crick, crick-cruck, y'know," said Judge Bippus.

"The holes?"

"The Arctic Three-toed, Mr. Jenkins. You stalk, you listen, you hear him, you follow that cruck-crick, crick-cruck, and if you are one of the fortunate, there's his hole!"

Almost tenderly the Judge now picked up the wooden object lying on the table.

"This," he lectured, "is a piliated woodpecker's hole, exactly the size of a Ben Franklin half-dollar. You may note that I am of the Antishellac School. I much prefer raw wood and I hold no brief for those collectors who slop shellac all over their holes."

"From this distance," said Lawyer Jenkins, "it appears to have the raw wood around it. The hole, I mean."

"Of course, Mr. Jenkins. Got to have wood around 'em. Hard

to handle, without. Easy to mislay a hole that doesn't have wood around it. Cruck-crick, crick-cruck. Yes, indeed. I have holes created by the hairy woodpecker, the downy, the yellow-shafted, the red-bellied, the Zebra-backed shamshack, this piliated here, and the American Three-toed." The Judge held the woodpecker's hole aloft for all to see, and both pride and euphoria were detectable in his countenance. "And so today," he concluded, "I go forth in quest of the Arctic Three-toed and his Katonah hole."

"I'm sure," said Mr. Jenkins, "that none of us wants to hold you up in such an important undertaking. So far as The Tiger is concerned, he will be happy to . . ."

"What's that? What's that?" The Judge seemed to be emerging from a deep coniferous haze. "What tiger? What tiger are you talking about?"

"The petitioner, your honor," said Mr. Jenkins. "The cat. He will be happy to wait until Monday morning."

"So ordered," sang out the Judge, rising. The others filed out, entering a corridor, and Diana said to Jeremy K. Jenkins, flashing her small enigmatic smile, "I think the Judge is *sweet!*" At that moment she came face to face with Eric Yaeger.

"Miss Fowler," he said, "would you and Mr. Jenkins do us the honor of having lunch with us? We're heading for a nice restaurant, just a block from here."

"I don't care to be seen in your company," Diana declared. "Anywhere. Will you kindly get out of our way?"

He stood glaring at her, not moving from her path.

"So, Miss Pighead," he rapped at her, "you really want to play it rough! That's all right with me. Everything's all right with me because I figure myself to be a most fortunate man."

"In what way, Mr. Yaeger?" Mr. Jenkins inquired, softly and politely.

"I have long considered, Mr. Jenkins, that this cannot be the horrible world that some people think, because I had not had the misfortune to be married to a folk singer. I no longer think that. I now believe that this is a lovely world for the reason that I am not so unfortunate as to be married to this client of yours."

Diana sputtered. She was so angry that she couldn't think of adequate words to use on him. Suddenly she raised her right hand, index and little fingers pointing outward, and she jabbed straight in the direction of Eric's face.

"Miss Fowler!" cried out Mr. Jenkins. "That's a very vulgar thing!"

"Good!" said Diana. "What's it mean?"

"Well," said Mr. Jenkins, "it means . . . it signifies . . ."

Eric Yaeger was now laughing heartily. "I'll tell you what it means," he said. "It means that you are hanging the horns on me, you are calling me the Member from Horncastle. And *that* means, Miss Pighead, that you are telling me my wife is cheating on me."

"Good!" snapped Diana.

"Which is all very interesting," Eric finished, "because I have no wife." With which he turned quickly and walked away.

Eric and three other members of the Executive Committee walked to the restaurant near the courthouse. Two men were missing from the group—Asa Nutting, who said he wanted to go uptown and finish up some long division, and Ogden Crump. Crump had been with them in Judge Bippus's chambers, but he was not with them now.

Nobody had much to say until they had ordered lunch. Then Eric leaned his elbows on the table.

"Does anybody here know what Ogden is up to?" he asked. There were negative responses all around. "Well," Eric went on, "I saw where he went. He ducked through the courtroom and joined Orlando Dill and they scampered down a corridor and vanished. Now, let me explain about Orlando Dill. He was involved in that crazy court proceeding when Myra Banner tried to break Thad Banner's will. Myra and her lawyer, this same Dill, sought to prove that Rhubarb was insane and therefore not entitled to the estate. Dill tried all his pyrotechnics, but this time they failed, and we won the case. We won it because at the last minute we were able to prove that Myra was *not* the daughter of Old Thad. And now we have Orlando again. Apparently he has tied in with Ogden Crump, and that makes two of a kind. I've been suspicious of Ogden for quite a long time. He's been laying back, off the pace, waiting to make his move. He is always and forever working for Number One and it is my guess that Orlando Dill will end up getting reamed."

"Let's tie a can to the son of a bitch," proposed Simon Horney, the hardheaded manipulator of factory sites, oil fields, cattle

64

ranches and skyscrapers. He never believed in fooling around, this Simon Horney.

"I'm for it," put in Hickey Dolbier.

"Me too," said Carlyle Waterhouse, "but it appears to me that this whole proposition is getting pretty complicated. Here is this girl and her funny-paper lawyer, with a cat that could readily pass for Rhubarb's brother. We all know that. We *need* that cat or, as Crump himself put it so delicately, we'll be out on our butts in three years. I think each of us has enough money to last us through the so-called golden years. But I for one just hate to think of putting Banner Enterprises into the hands of other people. We've run things pretty well and we've enjoyed it and seen it grow to fantastic proportions. Now, the way it looks to me, if we win this case, the girl and her cat are out in the cold and we, in the end, are out on our butts. If we lose the case, the girl and the cat take over and we are out on our butts period. I'd like to know what goes."

Hickey Dolbier, the legal wizard for Banner, took over.

"C. W.," he said to Waterhouse, "I wish you wouldn't use such dirty language when you're discussing a matter of this gravity. And I can't say I like your attitude about everything. Admitted, we are up against schemers and plotters. Don't you realize that Eric and I are capable of doing a little scheming and plotting on our own? We have to proceed with extreme caution on account of that Judge. He is considerably more fatuous and foolish than most judges, and you never can hazard a guess as to how such a man will act. Especially in the presence of fatuous and foolish people who sit around grinning and nodding and toadying to him when he's talking about his idiotic woodpecker holes."

"If things are going on," put in Waterhouse, "I think all of us ought to be given a fill-in. We've got to know the score in case we should be called to testify. If it should happen, I want to know why . . ." He cast a defiant look at Hickey Dolbier, ". . . I want to know *why* I'm being thrown out on my butt."

"You'll be briefed in ample time," said Eric, and they bent to their soup. This little matter, Eric told himself, is beginning to shape into a three-way Kilkenny cat-fight.

Ogden Crump and Orlando Dill didn't talk to each other very much in the taxi that took them uptown. In the first place Dill knew from long experience that New York cabdrivers are, by and large, far from the wise and heroic characters they are often made out to be in the public prints. The generality of cabdrivers, in Dill's view, were the same as the generality of all men—bombastic knaves and liars. Moreover, they have ears that are delicately tuned to conversation of an illicit and conspiratorial nature. The second reason for reticence was that neither man trusted the other. Orlando Dill normally enjoyed—even favored—the company of unscrupulous men, but Crump was blessed with far more shining qualities than mere rascality; he was half weasel and half water moccasin, a crossbreed usually associated with success and prosperity. Crump, on the other hand, fell back on the cultural patois of his native heath in warning himself that Orlando Dill couldn't be trusted as fur as a lady could th'ow an elephant . . . against the wind.

They spent two hours in Dill's office in Herald Square and there were moments when the lawyer's faith in his client grew a bit feeble. At one point, for example, Ogden Crump smacked his fat hand on the desk and declared, "If the worst comes to the worst I'll jest th'ow that little gal into the hay and give her a good bait uh poon. That'll fetch 'er round!"

By this time they had become committed, each to the other, and there could be no backing away from their less-than-holy alliance. They discussed several avenues of approach to their problem and as matters moved along, Dill, the Machiavellian schemer, was surprised to find that underneath his new partner's crude and boorish exterior there beat a heart as cunning and as perfidious as his very own.

He was real pleased with this. Theirs might be, Orlando Dill concluded, an effective and profitable partnership.

# 🐾 Chapter SIX

JUDGE Ambrose Bippus came out of chambers and started for the bench, a heavy folder under one arm, a piece of wood in his right hand, and a small leather kit in his left. He was staring at the piece of wood as he walked and when he hit the first step he plunged forward, sprawling himself all over the carpeting. The piece of wood and the leather kit flew in opposite directions as the Judge fell, and the skirts of his robe somehow ballooned upward, covering his head. By the time the court clerk and the court reporter could get to him he was threshing around, snarled inside his own robes, and howling, "Jesus God will somebody get me the hell out of here?"

Hickey Dolbier turned his solemn chipmunk face to Eric. "This," he said, "is going to be an unpleasant day."

"It's already been unpleasant enough for me," Eric observed. His mind was on the unbridled mob scenes he had just witnessed in the corridors outside the courtroom and in the street outside the sedate hall of justice—riotous surging and swirling and cursing and howling, a mad and clamorous montage representing the sensitive news media of New York City engaged in its workaday tasks. Eric could never forget the similar horrors attending the Rhubarb trial, but they were on a lesser projection than this exhibition of the more civilized 1960s. There were now three times as many barbarous participants, walking on each other, shrieking vile names at each other, even throwing punches, male and female, and this canaille of today included the electronic hordes from television, snagging their slithering cables around the necks of the foe, tripping up the newspaper people, bowling over the yammering radio commentators with the red-eyed monsters that served them as cameras. Eric himself had come out of newspapering and public relations, but the stampeding herds of idiot buffalo operating today in the world of communications were somehow beyond his comprehension. Nobody *got* anything. The only news these thundering herds were able to get was the news of thundering herds. A major symptom of the illness was implicit in the frequent bellowing of television and radio reporters, informing the world in hysterical accents that the system was breaking down before their very eyes; their bleatings were much of a pattern—"these people here are acting like hopheads . . . these newspaper people and radio people and television people and heaven knows what else . . . get offa my foot you crummy son of a bitch! . . . they've gone absolutely outa their skulls . . . it's unbelievable, the stark madness . . . stick that camera in front of my face one more time you bastard and you get knocked right on your ass! . . . the utter lunatic *uselessness* of it all . . . hold it! . . . there goes the cat . . . I think . . . ladies and gentlemen, unless I'm mistaken, the cat just went by!" Eric grinned at the egocentrism of the mike-howlers, at their individual inability to realize that *they* themselves were contributing more than their share to the strife and confusion. But, he reflected, such is the course of modern-day journalism and he felt pleased that he was long out of it.

Judge Bippus had finally put himself back together and made it to the bench. Once settled into his chair he glared malevolently upon the people spread out before him. "I was tripped," he said. "Somebody tripped me. Dill! Where were you when it happened?"

"Please, your honor," Dill responded in a hurt voice. "I was standing right at this spot, showing my respect for this most honorable court. Judge, I wouldn't trip you up for anything on earth."

"Except money," snapped the Judge. His attention now focused on the table where Diana sat with Jeremy K. Jenkins. "What in the name of God is that?" demanded His Honor, pointing.

"This is the cat," said Mr. Jenkins, waving in a courtly manner at the cage standing before him—a wire cage draped with some kind of cheesecloth so that the occupant could not be seen clearly. "This, your honor," said Mr. Jenkins, "is The Tiger—gallant son of Rhubarb."

"Objection!" cried Orlando Dill.

"Stay out of this, Dill," ordered Judge Bippus. "You're not even a part of this litigation. Now, before we get into the matter at issue, I wish to make a report to those of you who were with me in chambers yesterday. Here. Look at *this!*" He picked up the wooden thing and held it high and moved it back and forth so all could contemplate its beauty.

"This hole," he went on, tenderly inserting a finger through the aperture, "this hole, my children, was pecked out by an Arctic Three-toed woodpecker, a bird that may have flown all the way down to Katonah from Alaska or Baffin Bay. Let me explain to you how we operate, we who are in the woodpecker-hole game. Several months ago I read in the newspapers that the country house of a gentleman named Gripcrupper Garity, choreographer for the Bedford Village Ballet Company, had been destroyed by fire. It was mentioned in passing that a small grove of imported balsam trees had been swept by the fire. This *meant* something to me. I happen to know that the . . ."

The court clerk eased up alongside the Judge and began whispering to him.

"Judge," he said, "you forget what you're here faw?"

"What are you talking about, Harry?"

"The paterniddy suit. The cat case."

"Go back to your desk, Harry, and sit down, and don't interrupt me again or you'll find yourself collecting parking fines over in Traffic Court. You want to lose your position in this court, with its atmosphere of dignity, and get yourself exiled to Siberia, just interrupt me one more time when I'm talking about Arctic Three-toeds."

Harry went back to his desk. Miss Higgins, the court reporter who sat nearby, heard him say in a low voice, "Digniddy my bare ass!" and she recorded the words on her stenotype before she realized it was not an official declaration.

"Now," the Judge resumed, "I know that Arctic Three-toeds are difficult to come by because it is their habit to build their nests in balsam and spruce trees *that have been burned over*. Big old ugly black things, standing maybe thirty feet high, but that's the way the Arctic Three-toed likes it. Now, there is one more . . ."

"Your honor," Eric Yaeger was on his feet. "I would like to call your attention to the fact that several of us here have the burden of running one of the largest corporations in the country. If it please the court, could we get down to the trial of this case?"

"Who the devil are you?" the Judge inquired.

"My name is Eric Yaeger and I am theoretically the head of Banner Enterprises. We are men with large responsibilities and . . ."

"I don't care," the Judge broke him off, "if you are theoretically the head of the Democratic County Committee. I don't care if you are the Chief Justice of the United States Supreme Court, the Pope of Rome or Perry Mason. Nobody interrupts *me*. One more interruption and I'm going to have people thrown into the street in wholesale lots. Now, if you please, I'll get on with this other matter. I want to explain that the Arctic Three-toed has only three toes, as against four toes on most woodpeckers. That makes it difficult for him to cling to the burnt bark while he's doing his pecking. So Nature has given him a set of stiff tail feathers with sharp spines on them, and he fastens these spines into the bark to serve as a purchase, or prop . . . here, like this . . ."

Judge Bippus stood up, moved away from his chair, and turned himself sideways. He held both hands level with his shoulders and formed the thumbs and the index and middle fingers into claws. "Our bird takes hold this way," he said, jabbing the claws forward, "and then he sort of rams his tail feathers into the bark, like this." He jerked his pelvis to the front in the manner of a burlesque queen executing a hard bump, crying out at the same instant, "Cruck-crick, crick-cruck!" Nobody dared laugh but there were probably damp underthings in various parts of the room.

The Judge resumed his chair and pulled some papers out of his portfolio. "This," he said, "is the transcript of the case in which an attempt was made to override the will of Thaddeus Banner, deceased. You are all familiar with that case, I presume. It was tried before my old friend Judge Phidias Loudermilk, a paragon of judicial wisdom and virtue. Judge Loudermilk manages to get a lot of fun out of his trials simply by changing a few of the rules of procedure. I have decided to give his methods a try in this case, if there is no objection, and I'd *rather* not hear any. Any squawks? No? Then I am ready. You may proceed, Mr. Jenkins."

The trial began with the testimony of a deck steward from the *S. S. Thaddeus*, the only witness to Rhubarb's high dive into the water of Pago Pago Bay. Following that there was the reading of depositions from several residents of Puerto Rico, describing the manner in which Diana Fowler had grabbed the cat off the rainy street. Judge Bippus appeared to be paying no attention to this part of the proceedings. He opened his leather kit and got out an agate-tipped burnishing tool and a pair of calipers and began fussing with his woodpecker hole. At one point he interrupted the proceedings, held the calipers aloft, and told the spectators: "Some of you would probably enjoy knowing that these are *not* hermaphrodite calipers, and if they *were* hermaphrodite calipers, they would *not* be used for measuring hermaphrodites." He flung back his skinny head and cackled with laughter. "Laugh it up, folks," he ordered. "Let's make this a *fun* trial, the way old Phidias Loudermilk would do it!"

As soon as the depositions were out of the way, the Judge put down his tools and his hole and motioned to Mr. Jenkins.

"Clare Boothe Morse to the stand," Mr. Jenkins called out.

She came forward, a henhussy in her middle forties, shaped somewhat like a thick Letter S as a consequence of upper frontal stick-out and lower rear protrusion. If it were possible to persuade Miss Morse to join the stylites, go into the Syrian desert and sit on a pillar for six or eight months without eating anything but rock salt, she might come out of the experience more reasonably shaped. This condition she would greatly enjoy, for she nursed a deep-seated urge to have pleasurable traffic with men. Any men.

She stated her name and address and described herself as conductor of a column in the *Nine Lives Journal*.

"I am employed," she said, "by the finest and most dependable cat publication in the country and my column, *The Cat House*, is far and away the most widely read column on cats anywhere in the world."

"A lie!"

The half cry, half cackle, came from a voice among the spectators. An old man stood up and began waving a heavy cane in the air. "Your honor," he yelled, "that despicable fat-pratt on the

witness stand is a dirty liar!"

"And who are you?" inquired the Judge. "Please identify your-self. And holler louder so all may hear."

"I am Samuel McMurtrie McNabb," the old man cackled. "I am editor of *The Cat Gazette*. I have been this nation's foremost authority on cats through three generations of cats. *I*, Samuel McMurtrie McNabb, by god, *I* am the author of the most widely read cat column on earth! *Pussy Preferred*—that's the name of my column and . . ."

"Now you listen to me, Sam McNabb!" the S-shaped woman in the witness chair suddenly bellowed. "You took over that miserable column when your staff witch Clarissa Wood caught the distemper and began frothing at the mouth right at her nasty lying typewriter. Sam McNabb, you are a rat fink dirty poop to come in here and try to challenge my superiority."

"Your honor," came Mr. McNabb's indignant voice, "I refuse to stand here and let myself be insulted by this dog-sodden woman. She doesn't . . ."

"Excuse me one moment, Mr. McNabb," the Judge called out. "How can anyone be *dog*-sodden?"

"This female monstrosity can, your honor," Mr. McNabb responded. "She's the type that could be *anything*-sodden! She doesn't know any more about cats than I know about how to teach an armadillo to darn socks. It is pretty well known in the cat world, your honor, that this woman *keeps dogs*." Mr. McNabb spoke the last two words as if he were accusing Miss Clare Boothe Morse of sucking duck eggs stolen from the A & P.

"Hold it," the Judge ordered. "This is all very interesting but things are getting mixed up. Let's go it one at a time. You can have your chance in the hot seat later, Mr. McNabb. And after that you two can peck each other to shreds. Cruck-crick, crick-cruck! Let's get moving!"

"Miss Morse," said Jeremy Jenkins, "could you tell us some more about this Clarissa Wood? Wasn't she the same person who testified as a cat expert in the Rhubarb trial?"

"She *lied* herself blue in the face at the Rhubarb trial, counselor. She made up a lot of things about cats that a dog wouldn't eat for breakfast. She . . ."

"There she goes on dogs, Judge!" cried Mr. McNabb, but Miss Morse was not to be stopped. "Clarissa Wood," she went on, "was a witness for that guy Yaeger over there! She was a witness for the dirty capitalists!"

"Get *that*, your honor!" came the shrill cry from the back of the room and Samuel McMurtrie McNabb was on his feet again, flailing his cane wildly and endangering the skulls of everyone within his reach. "Out of her own mouth, Judge, she's convicted herself. Not only a dog-nuzzler—she's a Commie! Have her searched, your honor, she's probably got her card on her somewhere."

Miss Morse squared her jaw, arose from the witness chair, and took a few steps forward, wagging a bulky handbag back and forth in a menacing manner.

"Wup, wup, wup, wup!" Judge Bippus called out. "Back in the chair, Miss Morse. Heel, girl!" She hesitated, then turned and lashed at the Judge: "Don't you ever say 'heel' to me, Mister—that's for dogs!"

"You're for dogs!" bellowed Mr. McNabb. "Search the Commie, Judge!"

Jeremy K. Jenkins whispered to Diana: "I feel as if I'd like to invoke cloture." And Diana replied: "Whatever it is, invoke it. I'm beginning to enjoy this. At any moment, now, that door at the back is going to open and through it will come Stan Laurel and Oliver Hardy."

Miss Morse had returned to the witness chair. "I'm perfectly willing to be searched," she told the Judge, "provided it is done by that man over there." She pointed to Harry the court clerk. Harry was a stockily-built man with the appearance of some virility. Some—but not much. A little would go a long way with Clare Boothe Morse.

"God fabbid!" Harry protested. He shuddered and turned his face away from her gaze, which was confected of fondness and lunatic passion. "Judge!" he almost bawled. "Look at 'er! She's *simperin'!*"

"What's the matter with you, Harry?" asked the Judge. "You afraid to take this charming woman into my chamber and take her clothes off and search her real thoroughly? You afraid? Huh, Harry?"

"Judge," said Harry, "I wooden take that woman's clothes off if she was Zazz Gabor. I don't like her disposition."

"Miss Morse," said Judge Bippus, "I'm really not interested in whether you are a Communist or not. But come on—tell me."

"I take the Fifth," Miss Morse proclaimed, and this brought Samuel McMurtrie McNabb into cane-swinging action again.

"Jail 'er, Judge!" he cried. "Send 'er up the river!"

Judge Bippus appeared to be losing his patience. "Mr. Bailiff," he called out, "if that old man gets up and hollers and swings that cane one more time, I want you to seize him and lead him out of this room and chain him to that railing at the far end of the corridor."

"Where'll I get the chain, Judge?" asked the bailiff.

The Judge clapped a bony hand to his forehead. "Heaven help us one and all!" he groaned. "Is it up to me to do *everything* around here? What the hell kind of a bailiff are you, anyway, that you don't have a chain?"

"I just didn't bring none . . . today . . . Judge."

Mr. McNabb was not intimidated. "You throw *me* in chains," he whickered, "you try to chain *me* up to anything, and I'll get you impeached and unfrocked and degaveled—that long snout of yours will be yanked away from the public trough, if I . . ."

The witness now let go again. "Chain him up, Judge!" she clamored. "Chain him up by the neck! And if you don't get back to my testimony, I'll walk out of here *and I'll write a column about you!*"

Judge Bippus was furiously fingering his woodpecker hole.

"Yes, your honor," interposed Jeremy Jenkins, "I agree with the witness that we should get on with the case. May I inquire what all this cat-industry quarreling has to do with the paternity issue that brought us here?"

"Credibility of the witness, I suppose," said the Judge, "and good clean fun. Aren't you enjoying yourself, Mr. Jenkins? Is your pussycat getting restless?"

"Our pussycat," the lawyer replied, "is the only sensible creature present in this courtroom right now. He is sound asleep. Couldn't we let these two cat journalists claw at each other out in the street?"

"Just one minute," Clare Boothe Morse interjected. "I'm not finished with that frightful Clarissa Wood creature. I have very important evidence to submit to the court. Clarissa Wood is as crooked as a dog's . . . I mean a cat's hind leg. She sits at home claiming she has an acute case of agranulocytosis and maybe a hair ball in her stummick. She's faking. She is the mastermind back of these new experiments where they cut open the cats and put little dynamos in them and then turn on the juice and make the poor pussies jump around like crickets. Those scientists are torturing cats the same way they always have, except that now they put these little dynamos inside their heads and turn on the juice."

"Not dynamos," came from Orlando Dill. "Electrodes. They put electrodes in their brains."

Judge Bippus returned to the fray. "Who asked for your opinion, Dill? he inquired. "If this lady says those cats have dynamos in their heads, then they have dynamos in their heads. I told you to stay out of this. You are not even an attorney of record, so sit down and keep your trap shut or you might get a swift kick in the lower jowls."

"Your honor," Dill went on, maintaining his aplomb, "I now wish to become an attorney of record, representing the interests of Mr. Ogden Crump. My client is not here at the moment, but he'll be here. In due course I intend to present a whangdoodle of a petition, a bill of particulars, transcripts galore, depositions from Puerto Rico, quitclaim deeds, subpoenas duces tecum, pussycat affidavits, equities of redemption, chattel mortgages on cat magazines, grand jury true bills, a book that has got all about the law in it, traffic summonses . . . in short, your honor, if we're going to crazy it up, I want to play." Then, to the witness, "Out of that chair, Fatso!"

Clare Boothe Morse scorched Orlando Dill with a lengthy glare, started to say something, changed her mind, and left the stand.

Judge Bippus addressed himself to Dill. "Tell me something, counsel," he said and his attitude was almost friendly, "you used the word *whangdoodle* in that nice little speech. Is that a legal term?"

"Indeed it is, your honor."

"Cite your authority."

"Biggerstaff versus Keller, 1926, revised statutes State of Idaho, Section 192, revised downward, see also Code Napoleon, has to do with estoppel out of wedlock, your honor."

"Very good, Dill," said Judge Bippus. "I knew the citations— just slipped my mind. Now, since we'll be wanting another witness, I have a splendid idea. One of the most interesting phases of the Rhubarb trial was the appearance of a Man-in-the-Street on the witness stand. Most revealing, very illuminating. Let's do it again. Mr. Bailiff, while we have a ten-minute recess, so everybody can go to the can, I want you to go out in the street and fetch back the first person you lay eyes on. Ten-minute recess," he concluded, banging the gavel.

As the people in the courtroom began making their way to the corridors, Eric approached Diana. He was wearing a small grin and in his hand he had a tiny bit of white cloth attached to a lollypop stick.

"Flag of truce," he said. "Let's have an armistice . . . I want to talk to you."

She brushed past him without a reply, headed for the door. He stared after her as she marched away, her chin held high, and her lovely jiggle going. Jeremy K. Jenkins looked at Eric and smiled a smile of commiseration. The little lawyer tried to think of that Chinese word that described the look on the younger man's face. Yentz? Oh no, that was Yiddish. Then he got it. Yen.

⚙️ Chapter SEVEN

AS court resumed the bailiff had not yet returned with his Man-in-the-Street. Judge Bippus spoke to Orlando Dill, asking him to be a bit more explicit about his involvement in the case. "I don't like you, Dill," said the Judge, "but I must confess I'm pleased that you're here—you always seem to add a certain verve to things."

"Thank you, your honor," said the debonair lawyer. "All I can say at this time is that I represent Mr. Ogden Crump. We will clarify our position a bit later. It is my hope to blow everything sky high and startle the entire nation."

"Splendid!" exclaimed the Judge.

There was a commotion at the rear entrance as the bailiff came in dragging a young woman. She was fighting him every step of the way, flailing at his face when she could get her arms free, kicking him vigorously in the shins and biting at his arms. They hit the floor together three times before he could get her to the gate in the railing.

Judge Bippus contemplated this scene with a morose expression. "Mr. Bailiff," he called out, "I told you to get a *man* in the street."

"No you didn't," puffed the bailiff. "You told me to grab the first party I seen, and this here is it. Hold still you god damn bitch!" The young woman stepped up the pace, giving forth Comanche yells, and her frenzied battering of her male opponent had something contagious in it, for suddenly another female figure crossed the aisle, a second avenging Fury in the person of Miss Clare Boothe Morse. She leaped upon her tribal enemy, Samuel McMurtrie McNabb, and began trying to jerk out his chin whiskers. The eminent editor in turn flung her off and began to clonk her on the head with his cane; this diversion was so brisk that the other two, the bailiff and the female whirlwind, ceased their own battle and gave their attention to the journalistic combatants. And Jeremy K. Jenkins spoke above the uproar, addressing himself to Diana: "There is something sweet and tender in the rapport that exists between mature people who enjoy the same interests in life—such as an interest in cats. My! Look at them go!"

Miss Morse finally settled on retreat, for her noggin was lumpy and aching. She went back across the aisle, waving a handful of McNabb whiskers triumphantly above her head. This was the signal for the other Amazon to go back into battle, but before she could whirl around, the bailiff was on her, pinioning her arms and giving her his knee in the backside—over and over, whumpety, whumpety, whump.

"Young woman," Judge Bippus called out to her, "stop all that silly prancing around!"

"Prancing!" she cried derisively. "*Prancing* he calls it! Who the hella you?"

"I'm the Judge of this court."

"I don't keh if you're G. Edgar Hoover. Get this clunk offa me before I give him one in the crotch that'll send 'im clean to th' ceilin'!"

Diana now surprised everyone by leaving her chair and going to the rescue of the damsel-from-the-street. She told the bailiff to go find himself a game of dominoes, and then gentled the girl up to the witness stand. This unexpected intervention twung the heartstrings of everyone present except Eric Yaeger, who muttered bitterly: "Mean women always stick together."

Harry the clerk faced the quiescent girl and said, "Raise yer right hand." She ignored him and turned to Judge Bippus.

"You a *real* Judge?" she asked him. He smiled down at her.

"Oyer," he said, "terminer, special sessions, domestic, juvenile, traffic, appellate, District, State Supreme—anything you got in the way of judging, my dear, I'll judge it."

"Well then, whozz th' idea draggin' me offa the streets like I'm some kinda comma crim'nel?"

"You are to be a witness in this case, young woman. What's that you got on your face? I mean all that paint?"

"You mean my cosmeddics?"

"No, I mean whatever it is that makes you look like a circus clown."

"You don't look so hot yourself, Long Nose. Come on, get it over with. I want outa here."

Orlando Dill arose to his feet and informed the court that if there were no piddling objections from opposing counsel, he would question the witness.

"Tell us your name," he said to the girl, playing it suave, piling the sex into his voice.

"Tell us yours," she snapped back at him. "You some kinda fuzz? Some kinda plainclothes creep? Some kinda spy that come in outa the cool?"

"You are very comical," said Orlando. "Are you comical like this among your vast circle of devoted friends?"

Before she could respond Judge Bippus leaned forward and stared at her.

"Young lady," he said in an austere tone, "are you chewing gum?"

"Certnee."

"Well, remove it from your mouth this instant. Nobody comes in here and violates the dignity of this court. Get rid of that gum!"

"Where you want me to put it?"

"I don't care where you put it. Put it behind your ear. Put it on the end of your nose. Just get it out of your mouth."

With considerable dramatic delicacy she removed the wad of gum and then, uttering a quiet but colorful curse, she flung it onto the courtroom floor.

"Free country!" she exclaimed, speaking to the courtroom in general. "Alla time sayin' FREE COUNTRY! How'd I ever get inta this schemozzle? Self-respectin', decent girl ain't even allowed to chomp on a little piece gum, take the tarder offa her teeth."

Judge Bippus leaned forward again but this time his words were for the court clerk.

"Hey, Harry," he said, "guess where I picked up *that* one? The Judge in Divorce Court, on TV. He's always making insolent witnesses take the chewing gum out. Good idea. I think I'll use it from now on. Damn good Judge, by the way." He turned back to the witness. "Now, state your name."

"Ring three times and ast for Gertrude," she said.

"Last name, too," said the Judge.

"Boxholder."

"Proceed with the questioning of this witness, Mr. Dill."

"What business are you in?" Dill asked.

"I ain't in any business. What business *you* in?"

"I'm asking the questions, Miss Boxholder. You keep making snotty remarks and you're going to find your . . . uh . . . your left pectoralis protrusion caught in a wringer."

"What's a wringer?"

Orlando Dill flung his hands heavenward. "Oh God," he cried in a semblance of deep anguish. "Please, Judge, let's throw this broad out of here and get down to cats."

The Judge was fingering his woodpecker hole. "I don't know about that, Dill," he said. "I find this witness quite interesting. We have more or less established her as the typical New Yorker, even as the typical American. She represents the whole wide inspiring triumph of our species. Let me have another crack at her." The girl turned and looked wide-eyed at him. He picked up the woodpecker's hole and extended it toward her.

"Do you know what this is?" he asked.

She gazed at it a long moment, as if she suspected trickery. "Certnee," she finally ventured. "It's a hole in a piece wood."

"Any idea how it got there—the hole?"

"You could have made it with your . . ." She started to say nose, but thought better of it. "You tell me," she said.

"This hole," declaimed the Judge, poking his forefinger through it for emphasis, "this hole was made in a fire-charred balsam tree by an Arctic Three-toed woodpecker. This hole is worth perhaps twenty thousand dollars."

"You mean," she said, "just the *hole* part?"

"Just the hole part," the Judge repeated. "Plus the wood that's around it, to hold the hole together."

"Twenty thousand bucks, you say? Sheeez! That's what I call an expensive hole. Who'd you say made it?"

"Arctic Three-toed woodpecker."

She thought a while, then tried to repeat the words to herself. "Three-toed Artie Woodpegger," she mumbled. "Sounds like that goon I useta know from Philly." Then to the Judge: "Was this Three-toed party from Philly?"

"He is a woodpecker, my child," said the Judge. "A bird. A bird with a black body and a yellow head. He finds a charred tree and he begins pecking on it and pecking on it till he gets a hole like this, and then he pecks downward and makes a little room inside the burnt tree—a little bedroom, you might say—and then he climbs in and lives there."

Miss Gertrude Boxholder looked at Judge Bippus a long time.

"You say you're a Judge?" she asked. "You send people up the river? You put people in the chair, and like that?"

"That's right, my dear."

"Goodbye," she announced. "I've had enough. Outa my way, you squares!" As she strode toward the door she looked over at the bailiff. "And *you*," she warned, "stay in your place unless you want me to take one foot and make you into a harem-type younick." And so, warbling vigorously as she walked, there departed from our scene . . . One Of Us: Ring three times and ast for Gertrude.

As she galumphed along the corridor outside she passed a man who was hurrying toward the courtroom, carrying a large square-shaped wicker cage, or basket. She couldn't tell what was in it, but she assumed it to be another woodpegger. Artie Three-toed.

Ogden Crump carried the container on into the courtroom and put it on the table in front of Orlando Dill. Then, before taking his seat, he turned and bestowed a rather special sneer on Eric Yaeger and his associates. It was the kind of sneer favored by horse-toothed villains in the old silent movies; on the face of Mr. Crump it was not too effective . . . in fact Eric was under the impression that Mr. Crump had a shred of inferior beef stuck between his teeth and was trying desperately to suck it out.

Judge Bippus contemplated the wicker cage at some length.

"Dill," he spoke sharply, "are you by any chance having wine brought into this courtroom?"

"Oh, no, your honor!"

"Then what is in that basket, a picnic lunch?"

"In this *cage*," said Dill, "is the closest consanguineous relative of the cat occupying that wire cage on the table in front of the funny-looking little man, what's his name? Jenkins. Your honor, we have here the mother of The Tiger. My client, Mr. Crump, is the *owner* of this mother cat, whose name is Maria—with a trill on the 'r' your honor. We intend to prove . . ."

"If the court please," interjected Jeremy Jenkins, who was not one whit perturbed by the reference to himself as funny-looking, "this is a paternity suit, not a maternity case. We have here a feeble attempt to confuse the issue. There is no logical reason why another cat should be brought into this affair."

"Oh, there isn't!" exclaimed Dill. "Well, just wait a while, Mister Edward the Seventh, and you'll find out!"

"I appreciate the compliment," said Mr. Jenkins with a polite bow, "coming as it does from the King of the Mods."

"The court feels," put in Judge Bippus, "that we have about reached the saturation point in cats, and we are slowly being stomped to death by great floundering herds of lawyers. Be damned if I ever saw such a case. I think we're about ready for an adjournment. Will counsel please approach the bench?"

Jeremy Jenkins, Orlando Dill, and Hickey Dolbier stepped forward.

"We are making *some* progress," the Judge said to them, speaking in a low and confidential tone. "But not much. There isn't enough *meat* showing up to suit me. This being a paternity case, we've got to take up the business of blood samples. So I want all three of you to do your best to get some blood and have it analyzed and all that frolic and foofaraw."

"But Judge," spoke up Dolbier, "how are *we* going to get a blood sample when we don't even have a cat? Our cat is at the bottom of Pago Pago Bay."

"That's *your* problem," said the Judge. "I'll make it a little easier for you. I'll adjourn the trial till Wednesday, to give you an extra day. Okay? Crick-cruck?"

Dolbier said nothing, but simply pressed the palm of his hand against his brow. Dill, however, responded. "Crick-cruck, your honor," he said, trying to make it sound cheerful and woodpeckery. He would not be cheerful long. He had just arrived back at the counsel table when a little old woman with celluloid grapes on her hat, a bushel of lace at her throat, bifocals perched on her nose and a fat reticule in her right hand, came tripping out of the spectators' section. She had a wry senior-citizen kind of grin on her face and she went straight up to Orlando Dill. *Whong!* Before he realized what was happening she had swung the reticule, bringing it down on the top of his head. It was loaded, apparently, with two or three brickbats and the lawyer crumpled to the floor, quite unconscious. Everyone in the room seemed to freeze as the little old lady thrust the reticule above her head and cried in a high stridulent voice: *"Damn the torpedoes!"* Before anyone could make a move she scampered through the gate, up the aisle, and out the door.

Judge Bippus sat immobile, staring straight ahead, as if he had just eaten a platter of mescal buttons. Finally he began thumping the side of his head as if he were trying to get water out of his ear. He turned slightly and looked at the sprawled form of the fallen Dill. Ogden Crump and the bailiff were flicking cold water into the lawyer's face.

The Judge swiveled around and looked at Harry, the court clerk.

"Harry," he said, "damndest bunch of weirdies I've ever seen in a single courtroom. You enjoying it?"

"Tell you the honest truth, Judge," said Harry, "I ain't had as much fun since the day my grandma fell off the Willemsburg bridge."

"I think," concluded the Judge, "that we'd better adjourn this Mack Sennett wingding till tomorrow. Give people a chance to bind up their wounds."

🐾 Chapter EIGHT

STRUGGLING through the corybantic discothèque in the corridor where the gooks of the news media were patiently gathering their items, Eric tried to break away from two journalists who had him by the coat and, being already aware of the fact that one pocket was gone from the same jacket, he was about to clout a couple of Fourth Estaters in the teeth. He twisted himself around, fist cocked, to discover that one of the characters attached to his coattail was Miss Fowler. Her corn-yellow hair was in wild disarray and she had a look of desperation in her eyes. The instant, however, that she recognized Eric, she let go her hold.

"I got lost . . . from Mr. Jenkins," she panted. "I was . . . I was going down . . . saw this coattail . . . made a grab . . . if I'd known it was . . . known it was you . . . I'd have gladly suffered . . . trampled to death."

Eric shucked off his other hitchhiker, a bearded reporter who looked as if his neck hair might be growing all the way down to his coccyx, and then seized hold of Diana and hustled her along through the mob.

Somehow he managed to get her to the door and into the courtroom where press accommodations were restricted to a mere fifty reporters. At the head of the aisle Diana paused to have a try at rearranging her hair.

"That, out there," said Eric, gesturing toward the corridor, "that's what is called Freedom of the Press. It's sacred. If old John Peter Zenger could have a look at it, he'd start throwing up."

"It's pretty wild," Diana agreed, plying her comb and forgetting, for the moment, that she despised this man.

"I've got something to show you," Eric pressed on. He took some papers from his pocket and began unfolding them. "Friend of mine at an ad agency," he said, "snaffled them from an account executive who's working up a new Puerto Rico campaign. It's all based on this trial. It's to be splashed in the newspapers and magazines and on the air only if *you* win the case."

Her curiosity was aroused and she took the papers and began looking through them while Eric continued with his explanatory notes.

The advertising agency had come up with a fresh method for luring tourists to Puerto Rico. Two elements were involved in its conception—the sensational cat paternity case, and the moral temper of the American people. It scarcely needs mentioning that literature in all its aspects, including even display advertising, had become somewhat more liberal and more lively. Shapely girls were appearing in ads either naked or half-naked. Titties were IN, and bottoms à GoGo. The new novels were generally peppered throughout with words and phrases that would have got François Rabelais a slap in the face; and the sanctified act of love was being described in print in such great detail that it was becoming a ridiculous function—comic, foolish-looking, animalistic and herky-jerk. This state of affairs was, of course, to be deplored, and *is* deplored here. Yet, who is to cast aspersion on the advertising warlocks for carrying out a procedure that has long been standard in their profession, namely—they dropped a gimmick down the well to see if anyone would salute it, and what came up was the following inspired display ad:

As he watched her reading the lines of the ad, Eric grinned, anticipating a burst of laughter from her. It never came, and his grin vanished when she thrust the papers back into his hands. She was once again her cross-grained, pigheaded self.

"We are not amused," she said imperiously. "Our sides remain unsplit. Our risibles survive untitillated. Kindly keep your distance, you vulgar thing!"

The language was grandiloquent and the delivery was seventh-grade elocution, yet Eric knew that she meant it. For a while he had felt that he was making progress, but now the anger was rising inside him again.

"Woman," he said to her, "you are sodden in ignorance and hardened in sin. I give up on you. I am now of the opinion that one wild escapade with you would be the equivalent of spending an entire winter on the outskirts of International Falls, Minnesota."

"I stamp my foot at you!" she said, stamping it, and then she flounced off to join Mr. Jenkins at their table.

"Go thread your needles!" Eric called after her and he too marched forward and settled into his chair beside Hickey Dolbier. His mind was still on the way she looked when she was combing her hair and there was a scowl on his face as black as a bucket of stove polish. He was furious with himself for letting her get the hooks into him. She was unalloyed chippy, he assured himself, and it was nothing more than her physical equipment that had gathered him in. But no! He had not been gathered in! He set to work getting her out of his thoughts.

Judge Bippus was on the bench, his long nose poked into some papers he was signing. Why was it, Eric asked himself, that jurists who were involved in cat cases enjoyed conducting cat trials with little or no regard for the established rules of procedure?

Eric's pleasant reverie was interrupted by the voice of Judge Bippus.

"First lawyer with his hand up gets to call the first witness!" the Judge sang out. He had not altered course. He was still playing it by ear, and for kicks. Jeremy Jenkins uttered a mild protest, contending that he was entitled to finish with all his witnesses before anyone else got a chance.

"Not the way I run things," snapped Judge Bippus. "Mr. Dolbier had his hand up first, so we may proceed. By the way, Mr. Dolbier, did anyone ever tell you that you look like a sickly carp?"

"Oh, thank you, your honor," said Hickey Dolbier, forcing a sickly carplike smile. "That is very nice of you, and I appreciate it, coming as it does from a man with a face that could be used by the Con Ed people as a jackhammer. In fact, your honor, if I may say so, you've got the snout of an Australian bandicoot."

The Judge merely smiled down at the lawyer, and nodded his head in gratitude—a true bird lover. Eric, however, was quite astonished at Dolbier's departure from his customary rectitude.

"One moment, your honor," spoke up Clarence Dill. "You haven't asked about the reports on the blood samples."

"Right!" exclaimed the Judge. "Anybody with blood sample stuff bring it forward." Dill went to the bench and handed over an envelope and behind him came Mr. Jenkins, also with an envelope.

"What about you, Mr. Dolbier?" asked the Judge.

"Your honor," Dolbier responded, "please remember that we have no cat and therefore, at the moment, we have no blood test. However, very shortly we will be able to hand you a report on *our* cat."

"What cat is that?" inquired the Judge. "I see Dill's wicker thing with the female cat in it. I see Mr. Jenkins's chickenwire cage with that Tiger cat in it. Nothing whatever on your table, Mr. Carp . . . I mean Mr. Dolbier."

"Please bear with us, Judge Bandicoot," said Dolbier. "We will have a delightful surprise for our opponents shortly. May we call our witness now?"

"Cruck-crick, crick-cruck . . . let's get going!"

Back in his chair Orlando Dill said to Ogden Crump: "One of these days I'm going out and find me an Arctic Three-toed . . . see if he actually talks that way . . . see if he says it . . . and if he does, I intend to *kill* the bastard . . . sure as God made big green apples."

"Little green apples," Crump corrected him.

"Melvin Markle to the stand," said Dolbier. A seedy-looking middle-aged man came forward, was sworn, and climbed into the witness chair. He identified himself as the proprietor of a small pet shop near Nutley, New Jersey.

"Did you ever work for a pet shop in New York City?" asked Dolbier. "A pet shop called Cat Heaven?"

"Yehr," said Melvin Markle.

"In the course of your employment there, did you ever have occasion to meet, or see, a man named Thaddeus Banner?"

"Yehr."

"Tell us the circumstances of your meeting with Thaddeus Banner."

"Tell you the what?"

"The circum . . . the way you happened to meet him."

"Why dint yuh say so? Well, this Ole Banner he come in the store and he had this big cat. Yella. Had a crooked tail. This Ole Banner says his cat has got a bad case of the shoulder trembles and he thinks it comes from an overdose of sassatate. General purpose sassatate I mean. So the boss takes the cat in and says he'll give him some tests and cure him of them trembles. He only trembled in one shoulder, like this." Melvin Markle of Nutley began twitching his left shoulder but it was a twitch, and could never have been construed as a tremble.

"You a hophead?" Judge Bippus interposed. "Quit that damn shaking."

"You want the truth, don't yuh?" said Markle, sorely wounded.

"Now," said Dolbier, "was the cat cured?"

"Yehr," said Melvin Markle. "He was cured of the shoulder trembles but then he got the twitches and jerks in that crooked tail. The boss was all upset, because he said Ole Banner was rich and rotten mean, but he called up Ole Banner and told him about the tail, and Ole Banner says screw the tail . . . scuze me . . . that this cat was *born* with a shaky tail. So Ole Banner come and got the cat and took him home and that's that."

"Mr. Markle," said Dolbier, "did you recently come over to New York to see me and Mr. Yaeger here about that yellow cat?"

"Sure. I knew who that cat was, all the time. I seen in the newspapers about this trial, they even got it in the newspapers over in Jersey, and it was something about Ole Banner's cat Rhubarb, and I had some papers about that cat I figured somebody might wanna look at, and maybe give me a little something, like money."

"Hold it!" yelled Orlando Dill. "Did these crooks pay you to give them some papers concerning the Banner cat?"

"Yehr," said Markle. "You don't think I go around doin' good samaritans and gettin' cold-cocked on street corners, do yuh? I'm human like ever'body else, includin' you. What you got them pointy things on the enda your whiskers faw?"

"Kindly leave my whiskers out of this," barked Dill. "Now, Mr. Markle, please tell the court just how much bribe money these people paid you to give them the Rhubarb papers."

Melvin Markle glanced at Dolbier, who nodded assent.

"They give me gasoline money from Nutley to here," said Markle, "and toll money for the tunnel, two ways, goin' and comin', and lunch money, and a ticket to a picture show for when court lets out, and on toppa all that they promised to buy six hammisters from my store."

"You mean to say that's *all* they gave you?" Dill demanded.

"Good Lord, ain't that a God's plenty?"

Dolbier now intervened. "Melvin," he said, "you can tell Mr. Dill how you happened to be in possession of the Rhubarb papers."

"I didn't even know," said the witness, "that they was any blood things mixed up in them papers. When I got let go by Cat Heaven, I remembered about Rhubarb and I took them papers out of the files because I wanted to have me a souvenir of him. He was owner of the Loons. I'd a lot ruther have the club owner's personal papers than a baseball autographed by some ole wore-out shortstop."

"Why?" asked Dolbier.

"Because I was one of the biggest fans the New York Loons ever had. I just *loved* that ball team. And then when Ole Banner died and left the team to his cat, I remembered, and I was proud to think that I once shoved some green pills down that cat's throat. I useta feel that I was sorta related someway to the owner of them wonderful Loons. Oh, how I useta enjoy seein' them Loon-Goons lose! That's what we young fellas called them—Loon-Goons."

"You were a big fan," interrupted Orlando Dill, "and yet you enjoyed seeing them lose?"

"Sure. Oney squares likes to see their team win. You gotta have somebody to swear at. When your team loses, you don't swear at the other team. You don't swear at the team that beat them. You swear at *them*. That time the Loon-Goons won the World Series I was so upset I broke out all over and threw up and went to bed for three days."

"Your honor," Dill addressed the Judge, "I would like to move that all this witness's testimony be stricken on the grounds that he is two bricks shy of a load. I further propose that he be stripped of his picture show ticket and escorted out of the City of New York."

"You are miffed, Dill," spoke up Dolbier, "because you thought you were going to catch us in a big blackmail scheme."

"Wait a minute," said Judge Bippus, "I want to ask this witness something. Mr. Markle, don't you pay a bit of attention to those men out there. They are lawyers, and lawyers are a dime a dozen. Now, I have been trying to total up what you got in the way of a payoff. I don't seem to arrive at any reasonable figure. How much did they give you for gasoline?"

"Buck fifty," said Markle.

"God what cheapskates!" cried Dill.

"I got it all added up myself," said Markle. "They give me a buck even for my lunch money and . . ."

"Great day in the mawnin'!" came from Dill, who was pretending to pull out gobs of his own hair. "A dollar for lunch! From one of the richest corporations in the world! Shame on you, you stingy-guts!"

"Dill," said Dolbier with a smirk, "calm the pointy things on your mustache. A moment ago you were virtually accusing us of giving him a majority stock interest in Banner. What a poor loser you are!"

Judge Bippus whacked his gavel. "I still," he complained, "I still haven't got what I wanted about this man's profit out of the whole deal."

"Oh," said the witness, "you mean the profit on the hammisters? I make me twenny cents on each one, and six times twenny is a buck fifty. So . . ."

"I give up!" shouted Dill. "Your honor, I repeat, this witness couldn't locate his crotch with both hands if his jockstrap was on fire. Can't we get on to more important things?"

"Dill," replied the Judge, "I *like* this witness and the way he comports himself on the stand. He has good manners, which is more than I can say for you. But I suppose we ought to move along."

Melvin Markle left the stand, his face wreathed in a goopy smile. As he made his way toward the exit, he stopped beside Orlando Dill, bent down and said: "Nobody ast me, but the picture show is *Hercules Vi'lates Frankenstime's Aunt Sarah.* Scary, I hear."

Dill stood up, pointed dramatically toward the rear doorway, and bawled: "GO!"

Jeremy K. Jenkins now addressed the court. "I didn't get a single opportunity to cross-examine the last witness," he said.

"What did you want to ask him?" inquired the Judge.

"Oh, nothing in particular. My client, Miss Fowler, advised me that she enjoys hearing him talk, and I felt that since we don't have anything better to do, we could just let him run on about his hammisters and his jockstrap and his picture show ticket until time for adjournment."

"Mr. Jenkins," the Judge spoke sharply, "are you by any chance trying to be sarcastic?"

"Certainly not."

"Okay. Now, there's one thing been overlooked here. All this insane talk about the Rhubarb papers and we don't even know what's in them. Enlighten us, please, Mr. Dolbier."

"Here in my hand," said the Banner lawyer, "is the most significant piece of evidence yet to be brought into this case. It will, if you'll pardon the vulgarism, it will bust things wide open. We have here an authenticated laboratory report on a blood sampling taken from the cat Rhubarb. The veterinarian at Cat Heaven thought that the Banner cat was suffering from an infection, so he took the blood sampling and had it analyzed. We believe that the lab report will prove that this young woman's cat, yclept The Tiger, could not be the offspring of Rhubarb. And as for that she-cat that Dill has in his wine basket over there—that is the biggest absurdity yet. With all due respect to learned counsel, meaning Mr. Dill, everybody knows that he is a trickster, a shyster, and a *gonof!*"

"Come outside and say that!" roared Dill.

"Later!" ordered the Judge. "Mr. Dolbier, bring that blood thing up to me, so I can keep them all together. And Dill, I want you to quit grandstanding—quit threatening people you couldn't lick if you had a Scout axe in each hand. You got a witness for us, Dill?"

Orlando Dill turned his pointy whiskers toward the spectators, spotted his man, and said, "We call Desmond Slattery to the stand."

A tall strikingly-handsome man wearing lean-legged pants, a corduroy jacket in gaudy purple, a blue-and-white ascot that looked as if it had been knotted by a backward Brownie, and a green leather hat of the type favored by Robin Hood and his merry men, emerged from the spectators' section and strode forward. The moment he was sworn Judge Bippus spoke.

"Who's your tailor?" he asked.

"I select my own things," said Desmond Slattery.

"Are you chewing gum?"

"No, your honor. I kicked the gum habit during the Coolidge Administration."

"Then take off that idiotic hat," the Judge commanded. "You raised in a barn?" It was becoming apparent that the Judge didn't cotton to this witness. Slattery snatched his Nottinghamshire hat from his head and flashed his white teeth at Judge Bippus.

"What business are you in?" asked Dill.

"I am a gentleman adventurer," said the witness. "I am also a soldier of fortune. I have been called the King of the Crickets, as well as the Napoleon of the British Honduran Bee Trade. I was once a method calf-roper as well as an avant-garde pharmacist's mate. At the present time, however, my sole driving passion is worm painting."

Judge Bippus leaned forward. "Worm painting?" he said. "You mean you paint worms?"

"In a manner of speaking, yes, your honor."

"Dill," said the Judge, "aren't you the one who complained about the mentality of that New Jersey fellow? And you bring *this* in here!"

"Your honor," said Dill, "please bear with us. Mr. Slattery has not even begun to state his qualifications. He is really one of the rare men of this world. He is an authority on ants, on tropical birds, on rodents, on crickets, on vermin, on woodchucks, and almost alone among men he is the champion and defender of the man-eating shark and the much put-upon domestic cockroach. He is vice president of the James Sterling Moran Spasm-Throwers Club. He is here, however, as an acknowledged authority on cats."

"Acknowledged by whom?" asked the Judge.

"By H. Allen Smith," answered Dill.

"Oh," said Judge Bippus, deeply impressed. "That makes it different. Proceed."

"Now, Mr. Slattery," Dill addressed the witness, "please tell us if you have had a chance to investigate the ..."

"Hold it a second," interrupted the Judge. "Mr. Slattery, I'm still interested in the fact that you are a worm painter?"

"I believe I am the best," said Slattery. "That is, my worms are the best."

Judge Bippus gave him a long puzzled stare.

"I don't really paint worms," Slattery went on. "I put the paint on the worms, but the worms ..."

"You put paint on the worms," Judge Bippus broke in, "and yet you sit there and tell me that you don't really paint the worms. What do you call putting paint on the worms if it is not *painting* the worms?"

"I'll try to clear it up for you, your honor. Some time back I heard of a group of intellectuals in San Francisco who had taken up worm painting. A worm painter spreads his canvas on the floor, or on a table. Then he takes his worms and ..."

"*His* worms?" came from the Judge.

"Let's say," continued Slattery, "that he has provided himself with some worms. He also has provided himself with six or eight small cans of paint. He dips the worms one at a time in the paint and then drops them on the canvas. Paint contains volatile sassatate and volatile sassatate smarts, if you are a worm, so the worms crawl about at an abnormal rate of speed, leaving trails of paint—reds and blues and purples and pinks and so on. After a while the worms are snatched from the canvas, with padded tweezers, and the worm painting is finished. I have heard that they are bringing as much as two thousand dollars per canvas in San Francisco." The witness paused and then sang, "High on a hill—it calls to me."

Judge Bippus waggled his head around and rolled his eyes toward the ceiling, pretending to be losing his mind. "And you, yourself," he said to Slattery, "you do this sort of thing with worms?"

"Indeed I do, your honor," said Slattery, eyeing Judge Bippus with sudden interest. "Do you collect paintings, sir?"

"God no," said the Judge. "This is what I collect." He held up the Arctic Three-toed woodpecker's hole. "What do you suppose this is, Mr. Slattery? You'd never guess in a million years."

"I would say," replied Slattery, "that it's an Arctic Three-toed woodpecker hole sectioned out of a charred balsam."

The Judge was astounded. He all but fell out of his chair.

"Mr. Slattery," he said, "I would like to tell you that you are a man who knows his way about. I would like very much to look at some of your worm paintings."

"*Me siempre et tu pueblo,*" said Slattery, adding, "That means my house is your house."

"It does not!" Diana Fowler cried out impulsively.

"Young lady," the Judge said sternly, "let us have no more unseemly interruptions. Whatever Mr. Slattery says it means, that is what it means. No smarter man ever sat in that witness chair than Mr. Slattery. Proceed with the questioning, Dill, and treat this witness like a gentleman."

"Have you, Mr. Slattery," said Dill, "ever seen the female cat Maria, belonging to my client Mr. Crump?"

"I have seen the female cat that is occupying the wicker cage in front of you, counselor. I didn't know her first name."

"Have you ever seen the cat known as The Tiger—the one now occupying the cage in front of Mr. Jenkins and the young lady?"

Slattery said he had prevailed upon Mr. Jenkins, before court opened, to let him have a close look at the cat from Puerto Rico.

Diana, whose interest in the proceedings had been, up to this time, one of amused indifference, made herself heard again. "You said you were a reporter!" she shouted at the witness. "And you flirted with me to try to *prove* you were a reporter. You should be exposed as a liar and a cheat and a man who tortures worms!"

Desmond Slattery merely smiled down at her, unaffected by her indignant outburst.

"Miss Fowler," said Judge Bippus, "you have used some strong names and made some strong accusations against a man who has impressed the court as being an upstanding citizen, an outstanding scholar, a dedicated friend to worms and woodpeckers and all other manner of birds and beasts and creepythings. I want you, right this minute, to stand up and apologize to Mr. Slattery."

Diana got to her feet, faced Slattery, and almost spat at him: "Cruck-crick, crick-cruck!"

"Is that your apology?" asked the Judge.

"It is."

"Accepted," said Desmond Slattery.

"And I," declared Judge Bippus, "think it was very nicely put. This psychopathic ward is adjourned until ten o'clock tomorrow morning."

❧ Chapter NINE

THURSDAY morning . . .

"Mr. Slattery," said Judge Bippus as soon as he got settled in his chair, "I tossed around in bed for a long time last night. I suppose I couldn't get to sleep on account of the tremendous responsibility weighing upon me in this important and difficult case. Then I got to thinking about worm painting."

"I'm sure *that* put you to sleep quick enough, Judge!" sang out Hickey Dolbier who seemed, as the trial went on, to shuck off more and more of his ultraconservative character.

Judge Bippus ignored the chief counsel for Banner Enterprises while Orlando Dill took hold of a hardcover law book, preparing to throw it at Dolbier's head. Then he changed his mind. "Too early in the day," he mumbled.

"For one thing," the Judge continued, "you didn't make it clear yesterday what kind of worms you use in worm painting."

"The common earthworm," said Slattery. "A terrestrial oligochaet. When I was a boy around Wichita, Kansas, we called them fishin' worms. The ordinary variety was designed by Nature to fit almost exactly on a fishin' hook. There are, however, much larger terrestrial oligochaets. There are some in South America over six feet long. Too big for worm painting."

"How about murals?" suggested the Judge.

"Yes, I suppose you could do murals with them, your honor, if you had a real big postoffice. No. The postoffice would have to be turned over on its side. All but insuperable problem, Judge. Now, let's consider for a moment the Giant Gippsland worm which expands to better than seven feet in length when he is angry. This is the time when he discharges his coelomic fluid—when he is deeply bugged."

"Bugged?" put in Judge Bippus. "A seven-foot worm is bugged?"

"Right, your honor. All earthworms, no matter what size, discharge coelomic fluid when they are hopping mad. I have a theory that when a worm is dipped into paint, he gets as mad as a wet hen. He gets . . ."

Judge Bippus was frowning in bewilderment. "Mr. Slattery," he suggested, "please talk a little slower. I have a feeling that I'm picking up some static. Diathermy thing going somewhere around here."

"He gets irritated," Slattery went on, "and he exudes coelomic fluid to beat hell. This fluid mixes with the paint and enhances the depth of the colors in the same way that monnyum sodium glugginate enhances the flavor of food. I try to keep all my worms in a state of anger. When I get enough worm paintings finished, I'm going to prevail upon Huntington Hartford to let me have a one-man, eighty-worm show, and I'm going to advertise my painting as unequalled anywhere in the land—the finest work of The Angry Young Worms."

"Crump," said Orlando Dill to his client, keeping his voice low, "if I had played my cards right, a long time ago, I could have got a job hustling garbage in the Sanitation Department. Nice pleasant, clean, fragrant outdoor work with the assurance of a pension—and I could have avoided all this."

"Orlando," Ogden Crump whispered back, "you're just makin' a joke. You're as calm as the wotter in a hoss trough."

"Incidentally, your honor," Slattery continued on the witness stand, "my own worms are night crawlers shipped in dry ice from my home town, Wichita. Judge, a worm that has spent a whole day in dry ice and is then dipped in paint, that worm becomes an *active* worm. He will do some routine crawling, but he will also give little hops and jerks and flopovers, creating a remarkable effect on canvas, an effect those San Francisco worms have never been able to achieve. Matter of fact, your honor, if . . ."

Judge Bippus broke in again, interrupting this highly competent, relevant and material testimony.

"One thing that occurred to me in bed last night," he said, "was the idea of using woolly worms. Sort of got their own brushes on them."

"Ah!" said Desmond Slattery, "but that, your honor, would never do. It would throw worm painting into the Honey Hollow Swamp Fever school, and *that* I wouldn't wish on the lowliest worm in all Christendom."

"*If* the court please," came the despairing voice of Hickey Dolbier, "are the nation's night crawlers putting in a claim against the estate of Rhubarb? Are the fishin' worms destined to take over Banner Enterprises? In the name of Sweet Christ, Judge, will you please get us back on cats!"

"In my own time, Dolbier," barked the Judge. "Now, Mr. Slattery, I want you to know that in my considered judgment, you know *everything*. I have never seen such a man! Where do you acquire this vast fund of information? You must read a lot of books."

"Oh, no, your honor. Never. You never get nothing out of no books that is worth the powder to blow it up with almost. I get most of my knowledge by hanging out in bars on West Forty-ninth Street. That's the place to go if you want to smart up, Judge."

"On what subjects, Mr. Slattery, other than worms I mean."

"Anything and everything. Like last night I heard two gentlemen, one of them a raging faggot, talking in one of the bars. The straight guy asked the gay one a question that had never occurred to me. He said, 'Listen, Josephine, suppose a fellow got a hankering to become one of you—a homo. How would he go about it?' So the fag says . . ."

"Mr. Slattery," said Judge Bippus, "you are getting me even more confused than I was when you were talking about your worms. But go right ahead—I love the sound of your voice."

"Well, your honor, this Nellie tells the straight guy that if he wanted to become a queer, he should start out sort of easy—pick his boy and *try it first on a Platonic level*. Such alliances, the

99

fag says, usually work into the genuine thing and turn out to be real sweet."

Diana felt that she was beginning to secrete coelomic fluid. "This," she said to Jeremy Jenkins, "is getting too weighty for me. Let's call off the whole thing. Withdraw the suit. These people are all off their rockers. Woodpecker holes and hammisters, Loon-Goons and Giant Gippslands, hermaphrodite calipers and hopping fishworms, the King of the Crickets, the Queen of West Forty-ninth, and now the Platonic Homosexuals. Mr. Jenkins, I want to take my cat and go home."

"Let's wait just a while longer," Mr. Jenkins urged her. "Things will probably get worse, and you wouldn't want to miss out on anything." She nodded and her attorney made a request of the court. Might he ask the witness a couple of questions? Of course he could.

"Mr. Slattery," he inquired, "what have you learned about *cats* in your saloons?"

"Which kind of cats, counselor? There are two kinds—cat cats and musician cats."

"Cat cats, Mr. Slattery."

"The cat," said Slattery, speaking with an air of authority, "is very likely the missing link that science has been seeking all these years. He is the link between the brontosaurs and mankind. A brontosaur is as dumb as they come, while a cat ranks very high in intelligence. Cats talk. Did you know, your honor, that there is a dictionary of cat talk?"

"Mr. Slattery, you astonish me more and more. Where can I get a copy?"

"I'll try to find one for you. I have, at home, a dictionary on hen talk, and a treatise on the language of the stork. Storks talk to each other by clapping their bills together. A certain number of claps means a certain thing, like time to eat, time to sleep, time to copulate, time to . . ."

"Time to deliver babies to people!" cried out Judge Bippus. He then aimed his bandicoot beak at the ceiling and went, "Haw haw haw haw haw! Deliver babies to people!"

"God's teeth!" groaned Orlando Dill.

"Keep talking, Mr. Slattery," ordered the Judge.

"Now, your honor," said the witness, "there has been a lot of tongue-wagging about the jogs in the tails of the two cats involved in this case. I would like to inform the court that cats *talk* with their tails. That is . . ."

"So do people—women people!" announced Orlando Dill.

"Dill," growled the Judge, "I will not permit improprieties in this courtroom. Do not be vulgar in my presence or you will get your ass kicked clear up between your shoulderblades. Understand?" Dill grinned.

"Cats learn rapidly," Slattery resumed. "Did you ever turpentine a cat, Judge?"

"No," said the Judge. "I wouldn't know how to go about it."

"I will forbear entering into the details, your honor. But a cat can be made to shudder all over if a jug of turpentine is brought into his presence. It is necessary, however, to give the cat a good turpentining first. He will shudder at jugs the rest of his life. Jugs of anything. Empty jugs."

"Your honor," spoke up Mr. Jenkins, "we have at last got back to cats, but the emphasis now seems to be moving toward turpentine. I would like this witness to give us his learned interpretation of the tail jogs."

"Rhubarb," said Slattery, "had a jog in his tail. This Tiger cat has a jog in his tail. As the great philosophers have said, *Pot hock, ergo et tu propter hock.* The one is from the other out of. The Tiger is indubitably the son of Rhubarb."

Hickey Dolbier pulled himself wearily out of his chair.

"*Poppycock, ergo potluck, et tu possum poop!*" he asserted. "Your honor, at this point I want to get into the record the precise position we of Banner Enterprises take in this matter. This young lady's cat is *not* the offspring of Rhubarb. A cat with a jog in his tail cannot pass that jog along to his son. Jogs in the tails of cats are sustained by accident, such as a door being slammed on the tail, creating a sort of double bend. We of Banner have been looking around the cat world lately and we have found many cats with jogs in their tails."

"You of Banner, as you put it," interposed Orlando Dill, "have jogs in your noggins."

"I know where you've got a jog," snapped Dolbier.

"If I am thinking what you are thinking," responded Dill with a cavalier bow, "then I must deny the imputation, and add only that I wish I *did* have such a jog, if only a slight one."

"Come on," said Diana, tugging at Jeremy Jenkins's arm. "Bring the cat. I've had it."

"Hold it, my child. This exchange of pleasantries shouldn't last long."

"Furthermore, Dill," said Dolbier, "on the basis of your reputation for total depravity, I wouldn't put it past you . . . I wouldn't be at all surprised to hear that you've been out slamming doors on cat tails, trying to get the jog you think you need in this case."

Desmond Slattery, striving to get back into the picture, spoke loudly from the witness chair.

"I told you," he said, "that cats talk with their tails. So, a cat with a jog in his tail has what amounts to a lisp in his voice."

"You mean a lisp in his tail, don't you?" suggested the Judge.

"You hit it right on the nose, your honor."

Hickey Dolbier, showing signs of gaseous distress, almost yelled at the witness: "A lisp in his tail! Did you get *that* from your Platonic pansies?"

"Sir," said Slattery, bristling, "you are a bowlegged crud!"

"Bowlegged cruds yet!" yipped Diana. "Add bowlegged cruds to our shopping list!"

Desmond Slattery was not finished. He directed a long and juicy Bronx cheer at counsel, sweeping his head from left to right to take in everyone in front of him.

"You are all a bunch of ignorant churls," he said, "and that includes you, Dill. I'm getting out of this snake pit."

"I feel like going with you," spoke up Judge Bippus.

"So do I!" cried Diana.

"I insist, however," Slattery went on, "on finishing my testimony. The jog in the tail of a cat is the same as a lisp. What the cat has is an *impediment* in his tail. It is my understanding that a lisp, or an impediment, in human speech is hereditary. *Propter et tu hick* . . . I mean, wherefore, The Tiger is the son of Rhubarb."

"Your honor," said Hickey Dolbier. "This man is getting more ridiculous every minute he is on the stand. *He* ought to be turpentined out of here."

"You," Slattery said to Dolbier, "I ignore. I am finished with my testimony." He directed his next remark at Orlando Dill, whose witness he had been. "I'm sorry," he said, "that I had to testify to something that might be of benefit to you. I know all about you. I have seen the dossier on you up at the Bar Association. It states quite clearly that you sucked your thumb until you were twenty-seven years old, and that you've never yet learned to wave bye-bye."

"GO DIP YOUR WORMS!" bellowed Dill.

"Just one moment," Hickey Dolbier put in. "One more question, Slattery. How much did Orlando Dill and Ogden Crump pay you to come in here and testify to all this tail-jog guff?"

"They gave me taxi money, two ways, comin' and goin'," said Slattery. "They gave me lunch money, one buck, and specified pork subgum chop suey. They gave me a pair of freebies to a motion picture, *Hercules Violates Frankenstein's Aunt Sarah*. And they promised to buy one of my worm paintings."

"Provided," spoke up Eric, "it is a still-life seascape." Eric whispered something to Dolbier, who turned from the witness and gave Ogden Crump a long hard glare.

"Crump," he said, "you have been dismissed from Banner Enterprises. After you got your walking papers, you cleaned out your desk and departed with your tail between your legs."

"No doubt with a couple of jogs in it," murmured Eric.

"You, Ogden Crump," Dolbier went on, "are well aware of the fact that Banner Enterprises has a financial interest in this picture, *Hercules Violates Frankenstein's Aunt Sarah*. It now appears that you purloined some of the free passes we had around our New York office, and that you used at least one of the stolen tickets to pay for the false testimony we have just heard. Deny it if you dare, Crump!"

Ogden Crump came to his feet, fury showing in his face.

"Dolbier," he said, "Ah'll not deny it. Ah had a suspicion that this Slattery maverick would turn out bad for us. Ah gave him a ticket to your flea-bit movie as a kind of punishment. He told the truth only one time—when he said that a cat can inherit a tail-jog from its father. The rest of the time he was snotty to mah esteemed counsel. Ah think the court oughta assign a bailiff to *drag* this Slattery into the theater and *force* him to look at your miserable picture."

"Crump, you ticket thief," Dolbier came back, "did you ever look at your neck in the mirror? It was designed by a Wise Providence to accommodate the hangman's noose. That is all I have to say, your honor."

"Mr. Slattery," said Judge Bippus, "thank you for your enlightened testimony. You may step down now, but before you go I have a suggestion to make. Would you like to join me tonight on West Forty-ninth and hit some of the spots with me? I'd enjoy meeting some of your Platonic friends, and maybe we could have a look at your worms."

"Well, your honor," Slattery answered with a smile, "it would mean missing *Hercules Violates Frankenstein's Aunt Sarah*."

"Oh, come on," wheedled Judge Bippus. "I want to meet those Nellyfags."

"I'm willing to make the scene, Ole Hippus-Bippus," said Slattery.

"Twenty-three skidoodle, then!" said the Judge, and Slattery returned to the spectators' section.

To the stand, at the behest of Orlando Dill, now came a young man of brownish skin, lank black hair made shiny through the use of cooking oil, and little twitchings here and there. He said his name was Pedro y Gonzalez y Zapata.

"What is your business or occupation?" asked Dill.

"I om hunkie," said the young man.

"You are a junkie—a drug addict?"

"Sí."

"Did you ever meet a young man from Puerto Rico named Eduardo Tuerto?"

"Oh, sí. Him woss Yell fella."

"You mean he was from Yale University?"

"Sí. Yell fella."

"Did you attend a party for junkies about a year ago in a Riverside Drive apartment when this Eduardo Tuerto was present?"

"Sí, Señor. Tuerto. Iss fonny name. Mins in Espanish, have only one eye. Him has two eye."

"Was this the same night that somebody in that apartment strangled Eduardo Tuerto?"

"Sí. But nobody see. Comes many fuzz, but nobody see."

"Was Eduardo Tuerto a mainliner?" asked Dill.

"Oh, sí!" exclaimed the young man. Then, making gestures as if he were giving himself an injection in the arm, he added, "Yell fella squirt *heroina*. All peoples squirt squirt."

"Now Pedro," Dill resumed with the witness, "before this Eduardo did much squirt squirt, what did he tell you?"

"Yell fella sayze . . ." Pedro began, but Dill interrupted him.

"Listen kid," said the lawyer, "ease up on that dialect—you don't handle it very well, and you're not getting through to people."

"Yes, sir," said Pedro, and lapsing into comprehensible English, he delivered the following story:

Eduardo Tuerto told Pedro about the reward he received for capturing the rich cat in San Juan. He told it in precise detail because it was a great and glowing moment in his life. There had been a second cat present in that alleyway; this second cat had much the same coloration as the rich cat, and was snuggling up to the rich cat. More than that, Eduardo told Pedro that he *knew* the second cat—a female coquette belonging to the wife of the barber Hernando Ramirez.

When Pedro was finished, Orlando Dill addressed the court.

"This is conclusive proof," he said, "that the female cat now belonging to Mr. Crump is the true mother of the male cat called The Tiger. Anybody who knows anything at all about cats knows that those two, in that alleyway, had been indulging in sexual congress just before that boy Eduardo came upon the scene."

"Dill," spoke up Judge Bippus, "you are being illogical. When I was attending Harvard College I once woke up in a dark alleyway and three young women—all with the look of having been dipped in Mr. Slattery's worm paint—were sprawled all over me. I didn't indulge in sexual congress with those young women. At least I have no memory of it. Certainly not *all* of them."

"I've not finished," said Dill. "We have here a deposition from the barber Ramirez, and one from his wife. They swear that their female cat, María, gave birth to four kittens just sixty-three days after the cat Rhubarb was captured in that alley. And they swear further that one of María's litter was a male kitten with a jog in its tail. *There*, by god!"

Jeremy Jenkins spoke to Diana. "Mr. Dill," he said, "makes it sound quite convincing."

"I've reached the point," Diana replied, "where I don't believe anything about this mess I've got myself in. I'd like to go home and get back to my job."

"Settle down, my dear," said Mr. Jenkins, "and let me play a small card of my own and see what happens." He asked the court's permission to call a witness, permission was granted, and he said, "Is Mr. H. Allen Smith present?"

𝕾𝕺𝕾 *Chapter* TEN

AN excited murmuring was heard in the courtroom. Heads were turned this way and that. And then a suave and soigné gentleman arose from his seat and came forward. Well set up, hair graying slightly at the temples, skin glowing with suntan, tiny wrinkles of the kind that bespeak vigor and virility, tailoring and haberdashery showing the unmistakable stamp of Savile Row—a man's man, a woman's man.

Striding with a pantherine yet masculine grace, his every movement suggesting animal strength coupled with Nureyevian fluency, the witness made his way to the stand. He stated his name and gave as his address, "The world, sir."

Every eye in the courtroom was on this galvanic personality.

"Mr. Smith," came the first question from Jeremy K. Jenkins, "what does the H. stand for in your name?"

Silence from the witness, with just a suggestion of tightening about the eyes.

"Tell us, Mr. Smith," Mr. Jenkins continued hastily, aware that he had blundered, "what is your studied opinion of the relationship between all the cats involved in this litigation?"

"The cat called The Tiger," said Mr. Smith, speaking in a well-modulated, mellifluous tone that brought fluttering to female hearts throughout the room, "is the true son of the cat Rhubarb. The cat known as María is quite conclusively *not* the mother of the cat called The Tiger."

"Thank you, Mr. Smith!" Mr. Jenkins said with an air of finality.

"Yes," echoed the Judge, "thank you, Mr. Smith, for your very wise opinion. You have made my task less onerous."

Mr. Smith nodded courteously, permitted a wisp of a smile to flicker across his lips, got out of the chair and walked toward the exit, passing alongside Orlando Dill, who lay forward, stretched on the table, his hands clasped to his head, moaning like a beast caught in a steel trap.

When the magnetic presence of the last witness was gone from the room Judge Bippus ordered Orlando Dill to straighten up in his chair and act like a grown man.

"I almost sympathize with you," the Judge said, "because Mr. Smith really broke it off in you. Now, I think we've had enough evidence. I don't understand why someone didn't think of bringing H. Allen Smith in at the very beginning. Would have saved a lot of time. On the other hand, we wouldn't have had all this fun. I note but one further item on the agenda. We have had all this talk about the jog in the tail of the deceased cat Rhubarb, and in the tail of the Puerto Rican cat Tiger. It occurred to me a few minutes ago that I have not yet had a look at this seemingly significant jog. Mr. Jenkins, will you please remove the cat from its cage and bring it to the bench?"

Diana jumped to her feet. "You'd better not, your honor," she cautioned. "He can get pretty wild."

"Please, Miss Fowler," the Judge responded, "we are all grown up, mature people, lovers of nature, never frightened of small domesticated animals. I'll have the bailiff handle this. Mr. Bailiff, remove the cat from the cage in front of Mr. Jenkins and bring him up so I can inspect his tail jogging."

The bailiff, a man who lived in the eastern arrondissement of Greenwich Village and considered all cats to be creatures straight out of hell, bent upon sucking the life's breath from babes in their cribs, assumed the look of a man about to break down and cry. He approached the counsel table with faltering step, and cast one final appealing look in the direction of the Judge, but there was no reprieve. He stood as far back from the wire cage as was possible,

bending forward and stretching out his right arm, and suddenly he flipped open the cage door.

A yellow streak shot across the table just as yellow cats zip blindingly across the screen in Disney cartoons. The Tiger landed twenty feet from his cage, pivoted, crouched for another leap, and said, "Rrrrr-owrrrr!" This time he jumped in an arc that cleared his own table, landing on the table occupied by Orlando Dill, Ogden Crump, and María. The Tiger uttered a few more cat shrieks and yowls, reared up on his hind legs, and began slashing madly at the wicker cage. "God damn you!" roared Orlando Dill, "that's your *mother*, you god damn idiot! Fog off! FOG OFF!" The lawyer reached forward to try for a grab at The Tiger but he was far too dilatory. The cat was all over him, ripping his face, slashing his jacket, and Diana told people later that she clearly saw The Tiger take at least one bite at the pointy mustache.

Women were screaming among the spectators; the bailiff, fearing some vague kind of cat revenge, decided he had to go to the men's room hurriedly; the Judge was beginning to pound with his gavel and bawl for order; and Eric Yaeger was trying to decide if he should make a stab at containing the cat, or simply let nature take its course. He sat almost transfixed, staring at the berserk animal. "Just like his old man!" he said.

Over in the press section Gerard Robinett of the Liverpool *Daily Liverpudlian* turned to Miss Pamela Swilley of the London *Gazette.*

"Rawther unusual case," he said.

"Raw-*ther*," agreed Miss Swilley.

Nearby, forgetting himself in the excitement, Ringo Fox, the people's choice for Number One Journalist of the day, cried out, "Scatty wah . . . whamp whamp . . . hubby-mummy BeeeeZARP! Get me to the scene ON TIME!"

Diana was on her feet and yelling, "Baby, come back! Tiger! Come back here!" But The Tiger was too occupied with the public shredding of Orlando Dill. The lawyer managed, in the end, to knock the yellow tornado back onto the table, whereupon The Tiger renewed his assault on the wicker cage, creating noises like a hot silo full of Rupununi jaguars, chewing at the wicker, slashing at it, sending splinters flying over the floor.

The uproar grew more frenzied. Suddenly the door at the rear of the courtroom opened a bit and a head appeared, a head topped by a green leather hat.

"Citoyens!" the head yelled. "Blood samples are a lot of bushwah!" It was Desmond Slattery, the worm painter. Nobody heard him and he was gone as quickly as he had come.

By this time The Tiger had clawed open one whole side of the wicker cage and out came María moving at a respectable speed— the speed of greased lightning. It quickly became clear, if anyone had doubted it, that The Tiger was bent on annihilating the cat that had been presented to the court as his mother; he was not trying to liberate her—his aim was to do her in. She took off like a skyrocket, jumping to a moulding above a window, and from that point made it to a perch on top of a portrait of Martin Van Buren.

The Tiger eyed her position carefully, went into another crouch, wiggling his behind as he set his rear claws for the leap; then he hesitated, and turned to see what in hell all the loud pounding was about—the measured thumping of the Judge's gavel accompanied by his honor's hoarse cries for order. The Tiger turned quickly and sprang through the air, hitting the Bible used for oath-taking and knocking it from the shelf beside the witness stand —sending the Good Book cat-west-and-crooked a distance of thirty feet. Now the noisy gavel-pounding man-creature was just above him, and The Tiger leaped again, but his trajectory was faulty, assuming that he was trying to reach the Judge. He came skidding onto the desk alongside an untidy-looking piece of wood with a hole in it. Judge Bippus staggered backward, threw his gavel at the yellow demon, missed by a yard and a half, and began howling for help. He had just brought his forearms up to protect his face from the imminent onslaught, when the cat changed his objective. He saw the piece of wood. He *glared* at it . . . and fresh horror flooded over the Judge's face.

"Get him away!" he shrieked. "Don't let him touch it! Somebody grab him! Oh my God, my precious toe-threed Arkick! Garrote him! Bailiff! SHOOT THE SON OF A BITCH!"

The cat slowly extended his right paw and touched the piece of wood. He pawed it gently and cocked his head a trifle, staring at it. Then he began to purr and before the astonished eyes of the Judge, he stretched out on the desk and began to *nuzzle* the woodpecker's hole.

Judge Bippus stood as if in a trance. Then he took a few steps forward.

"Look at him!" he called out to the spectators, who had almost recovered from the excitement. "Just look at the little bugger! He likes my woodpecker hole!"

With that the Judge reached out and placed his hand on the cat's head. He stroked The Tiger. He talked softly to him.

"You sweet little thing, you!" he said. "You smart little kitty cat!" Then he raised his eyes and looked at the courtroom.

"Let's adjourn," he said, "until ten o'clock tomorrow morning. At that time I'll announce my decision."

Down below Orlando Dill had his head in his hands once again, and he was groaning under the duress of the double disaster that had hit him—the testimony of H. Allen Smith and the wild and ferocious attack by the hellcat from the Caribbean. Suddenly the lawyer straightened up in his chair, dabbed a couple of times at his cuts, and then announced to the whole wide world:

"Orlando Dill never gives up! I have just begun to fight!"

⟨⋄⟩ Chapter ELEVEN

ALL were present for the payoff on Friday morning. Orlando Dill wore a couple of strips of adhesive tape on his face but he seemed to be in good spirits. The Judge hadn't come out of chambers yet, so Eric Yaeger walked over to the counsel table where Diana was sitting with Jeremy K. Jenkins. Diana glanced up at them and then quickly averted her eyes.

"Hey," said Eric, "don't be like that. People are not supposed to get mad at one another in courtroom things of this nature. Only things of a rape and robbery and murder nature."

"This," said Diana, still not looking at him, "is *attempted* rape and robbery and murder. Get lost."

"I knew," Eric pressed on, "I knew that he was old Rhubarb's baby—I knew it for certain when he got loose yesterday and tried to pulverize the whole courthouse. I wanted to . . ."

"Beat it," said Diana.

"I wanted to let you know," Eric persisted, "that I'm willing to throw in the towel. There's no reason why you . . ."

Diana looked at him now. "Hit the turnpike!" she snapped. Growling noises came out of him and he walked back to his chair. He was in a state of confusion brought on by what he thought might add up to divided loyalties, or something on that order. He had a very large obligation to Banner Enterprises, to the people who directed Banner Enterprises, and to the tens of thousands who gained their livelihood from Banner Enterprises. He also had an obligation to himself. All during the progress of this litigation, if it could be called progress, he had grown increasingly uncertain about where he stood—if he stood anywhere. As of this day, the only thing he seemed to be clear about was his deepening and inescapable fascination for this girl. He tried to tell himself again that it was snake-fascination, but he knew it wasn't so.

Judge Bippus came through the door. Once in his chair he looked out over the courtroom as though to check who was present. Everyone was present.

Poised, impeccable and charming, H. Allen Smith now stood up and in that compelling voice asked the Judge if he might come forward.

"By all means," the Judge assured him and Mr. Smith walked to a position before the bench while women spectators sighed and breathed heavily and fought off spells of dizziness.

"Your honor," said Mr. Smith, "I have had an opportunity to examine the transcript of your preliminary meeting in chambers, and I find you are quoted as follows: 'According to human standards, every cat in the world is a bastard.' Now, your honor, I wish to challenge that judgment. The petitioning cat in this case, The Tiger, is a native of Puerto Rico. There is a law on that island, enacted under the dominant Popular Democratic Party, which declares every child to be legitimate, regardless of parentage. It is required that every child be registered under the names of both parents so that there shall be no taint of bastardy. There is a popular axiom in Puerto Rico, your honor, which goes: *No hay hijo sin padre*, and means, 'There is no son without a father.' That axiom is an echo of the island's law. That is all, your honor."

Down below Eric Yaeger murmured: "What a brain!"

Ogden Crump thought: "There's an hombre with savvy!"

Diana Fowler said in a whisper: "How can I arrange to meet him?"

Simon Horney pondered: "Why haven't they given him a ticker tape parade?"

And Judge Bippus spoke to the witness: "Thank you so much, Mr. Smith. It has been a pleasure to have you here. Before you go, may I ask you a question? What does the H. in your name stand for?"

The celebrated author, explorer, swordsman, raconteur, gourmet, yachtsman, lothario and windmill-fixer, gazed steadily at the Judge, not answering.

"Excuse me for asking," Judge Bippus apologized, recognizing that he had been indiscreet. He thought: "Now I'll be able to tell my grandchildren that I exchanged views with him."

"Your honor," Mr. Smith said, "there is one more thing. Whenever anyone says 'Scat!' to a cat, the cat never scats. Nobody has ever seen a cat scat, except my friend Desmond Slattery. He tells me that a cat scats only in privacy; a cat doesn't even want other cats to witness him in the act of scatting. Mr. Slattery tells me that when he had the good fortune to observe a cat scatting, it was done two-and-a-half feet in the air. I simply thought the court would like to know this."

The Judge was fumbling at his chin, frowning in concentration. He wasn't at all sure he had it right.

"I want you to know," he said to the witness, "that I almost never say 'Scat!' to a cat or to anybody else."

"Quite wise, your honor, and commendable." Mr. Smith returned to the spectators' section.

"If everyone is ready," the Judge now announced, "I shall proceed. One: I find first of all that the cat brought here by Ogden Crump and Orlando Dill is not the mother of the petitioning cat. I have private information that this cat, known here as María, was snatched out of an alley in the Throgs Neck section of the Bronx, and her true name is Mildred, or Millie.

"Point Two: I find that the cat . . ." He was interrupted by an indignant yelp from Orlando Dill. "You call yourself a judge?" the lawyer bellowed through his adhesive decorations. "I know what you are! You are a ward-heeling tool of the interests! I charge that you are in the pay of Banner Enterprises. Why don't you do the decent thing and resign and go off somewhere and collect turkey holes!"

The Judge pointed a finger at the bailiff, then made a flapping gesture with his hand, meaning "Out!"

Ogden Crump leaped to his feet and began sputtering out unintelligible Texas noises.

"Out!" yelled the Judge. "Both of you—OUT!"

"Not quite yet, Judge!" Crump insisted. "Ah've got one more thing to say. You know god dern well that the last will and testament of Thaddeus Banner was the product of a diseased mind, a lunatic. Now it is bein' proposed here that this tremendous corporation be turned over lock, stock and barrel, to *another cat!* Good God, Judge, just consider this for a moment. There are six members of the Executive Committee. Ah'm the only one of the six with the guts to stand up and say that it is a cryin' shame that the six men who have contributed long hard work, and given of their special skills and talents, that these men are to be thrown out on their . . . on the seat of their pants. Ah'd be happy to see the other five drop dead this instant, but *Ah'm* not gonna surrender without a fight!"

Hickey Dolbier came out of his chair. "Ogden," he said, "why don't you shut your big gassy mouth and get out of here. Go back to Corpus. I told you already that you are not a part of our organization any more. You have been fired. Go get yourself a job Avon-calling from door to door."

"I'll Avon-call you!" screeched Crump, and charged across the floor, planting a hard right on the chipmunk chin of Dolbier, who dropped like a stunned ox. Eric leaped in and belted Crump in the teeth, sending him to the floor. Crump had the hardihood of Texas blood in him, and now this hardihood was dribbling over his chin. He looked up from the floor and announced: "Yaeger, you have just signed your own death warnt. Ah knew you had it in for me that day you told me Ah didn't know my ass from my eyelid. Ah'm gonna *ruin* you!"

Judge Bippus called out from the bench: "If you gentlemen are all finished with your little diversions, I would like to continue." They got Dolbier back into his chair and Crump was able to struggle to his feet unaided. He and Orlando Dill, carrying the wounds of the vanquished, made their way out of the room, and Judge Bippus continued with his decision:

"Point Two: I find that the cat brought here by the petitioner, Miss Diana Fowler, is by dint of a jog in his tail and the testimony of H. Allen Smith, plus the fact that he, the cat Tiger, has Type-A Prime blood, which is the same rather rare blood type of the cat Rhubarb . . . that this cat, The Tiger, is the *legitimate* son of the celebrated cat Rhubarb, deceased. Hold it now. There's some more.

"Point Three: It is my observation that there exists some kind of antipathy, even bad blood, between the petitioner, Miss Fowler, and the executives of Banner Enterprises. For this reason I hesitate to pass final judgment on disposition of the Banner estate. I feel that the cleavage of the parties might easily be brought to an end if we could find some way to bring them into closer association. Accordingly, I am going to grant custody of the cat for one month to Miss Fowler. For the second month, Mr. Yaeger will have custody. Then back to Miss Fowler, and back again to Mr. Yaeger. At the end of four months we should know a good deal more than we do now, as concerns the attitudes and feelings between Miss Fowler and the corporation, between the corporation and the cat, and between Miss Fowler and Mr. Yaeger. I will expect the principals to return here four months from this date, at which time I will hear a report on what has transpired in the period just prescribed."

The Judge looked out over the room.

"That's it," he said. "Any more squawks, any more squabbling, any more punches in the nose? All right then, kiddies, school is out. It has really been a *fun* trial. Cruck-crick, crick-cruck!"

As Judge Bippus left the bench, woodpecker hole in hand, Diana grabbed up the cage containing the victor and said to Jeremy K. Jenkins, "Let's get out of here. I want to get home."

"We'll be two hours running the press gauntlet," said the lawyer. "And it'll be like this, for you, from now on."

Hickey Dolbier, an elder in his church, a member of the American Committee to Fight Pornography, a man who thought of Cotton Mather as a heroic figure in history, was stuffing papers in his briefcase.

"Eric," he said, as he clicked the snap on the case, "I had no idea open court could be so much fun."

"You may get some more of it before we're finished," Eric answered. And they went out to square off with Journalism.

❀❀ Chapter TWELVE

"WHEN Ah come up to twelve years of age," said Ogden Crump, "mah Mama made me promise to read somethin' in th' Scriptures ever day of mah life. Then she made me promise Ah wouldn't ever touch the ole red disturbance."

"What in God's name is that?" asked Orlando Dill.

"The ole red-eye," replied Crump, hoisting his glass high. "Ah always figgered she meant the puhticular brand of heifer pee that was available for drinkin' purposes around Corpus in them days. It wasn't any problem to keep the pledge then. That stuff would've growed hawns on a muley cow. Ah've kep' mah promise pretty well. Ah manage to read a little from the Scriptures ever day— maybe only a couple or three words—but that's enough to validate the contract, you might say. Oh, sure, Ah miss once in a while— like when Ah wake up with the black whibbies."

Dill glanced quizzically at the highball in Crump's fist. They were in the Texan's suite at the St. Regis and at one side of the elegant sitting room stood a small bar of such exquisite design that it looked as if it might have been made from peachblow porcelain. The bar was well stocked with the ole red disturbance, plus an adequate quantity of the ole white disturbance.

"Times change," said Crump, reading his friend's thoughts.

"And locations change. A promise made in Texas more'n fawty years ago don't necessarily hold good in New York City as of today. Even the Cath'lics have got around to this way of thinkin'." He paused and took a long swig of his drink. "Then," he resumed, "they was a third promise Ah made to mah Mama. Never commit adultry. That one had me upset for a sight of years."

"I should think so," agreed Dill, an adulterer of some consequence as adulterers go.

"Solved the god dern problem," Crump continued, "by just settin' down and thinkin' it out. One day Ah got holt of a big dictionary and looked it up in it, and it said you had to be married to commit adultry. It says that. In the book. Adultry is only allowed between people who ain't married. When you do it the other way, that's fornication. Between the two of them Ah prefer fornication because that means neither one of you has to be married. Fornication don't sound so all-farred sinful the way adultry sounds. Ah reckon that's why Ah was always gettin' divorced so much because, like the fella says, Ah sho like that stuff."

"You mean," suggested Dill, "you sho *used* to like it. Don't try to let on to me that you're Mister Whirlwind, that you can handle it any more."

"Ah can handle it," said Crump stiffly, "and Ah can do more'n handle it."

"So, what about your promise to your Mama?"

"First," said Crump, "Ah just tried to keep myself unmarried and only fornicate. Ah tried to play it honest. Ah studied out, by the rules, that if Ah was married Ah couldn't commit adultry with a girl even if she was single; and if Ah was unmarried, Ah couldn't commit adultry with a woman that was married. You know as well as Ah do that a man gets strong notions about women that're married, but who are frisky-pantsed anyhow, and in spite of it. Well, whenever Ah got the itch to wrassle down a married lady, Ah'd take up the old-time Mormon religion on a sort of try-out basis. Ah'd say to mahself, 'Them old-time Mormons had a pretty good idea goin' for them. Maybe Ah'd oughta give it a try.' So, just before bangin' a married lady, Ah'd haul off and say grace, like this, 'We thank thee Moroni and Joe Smith and Urm and Thumb for the bounty of this we are about to do.'"

"Ogden," said Orlando Dill, who was working on his third double-scotch, "you ought to have been a lawyer. You have the true legal attitude, and your ethics are in place. Loophole Crump—that's what they'd call you. Tell me something—did the Mormons actually say grace the way you said it?"

"Nawp. Ah made it up. That's one of the nice things about mah lifelong religion. You don't say prayers that were written out ten thousand years ago. Some of these religions, the people set down to supper and they say the same words over that they been sayin' since they was little bitty ole kids. No imagination. In mah religion we give the head of the house some room to work in. Mah Daddy never said grace the same way twicet in his whole life. He ad-libbed it. He was the best god damn grace ad-libber in Nueces County. He could knock it off in two words, or he could sprangle it out and put in the rousements till the meat got cold."

The two men moved over to the bar and Crump freshened the drinks with heady lacings of light tan disturbance. Dill glanced at his watch.

"Your dame is due any minute now," he said, "so let's get it all clear. We are partners in this thing right up to the end whether we get possession of that cat or hornswoggle 'em some other way. Right? I get one-third of everything, no matter how much, and no matter where it comes from. We'd better have a paper between us."

"Texans," said Crump, somewhat resentfully, "don't ordinary need to have a paper."

"Ah ain't no Texan," Dill answered, mimicking Crump's cultural accents. "Now, let's get to scheming. If there's one thing I enjoy it's scheming—firkytootling around. When I set to work on a proposition, all the rules go out the window. I think I'll start off by crashing that party Yaeger's giving tomorrow. You want to try it with me?"

"Ah'd ruther take a hawg to a hoedown," Crump answered pettishly. "Did you find out if that Fowler piece and her cat are gonna be there?"

"All I know is that she's been invited, and so has Grandpappy Jenkins, square hat, topknot, checkered coat, and all. It's a sort of no-hard-feelings get together."

"Watch your step with that Fowler dame," warned Crump, employing an unnatural paternal air. "It don't pay to mix business and poon."

"I find the exact opposite to be true," said the lawyer and before

Crump could give him an argument, their attention was attracted by a slight but alien noise. They both turned from the bar and looked across the room. A closet door was slowly opening. As they stared, the door was suddenly flung wide and a figure leaped into the room and came flying at them.

Dill flung up his hands and his drink splashed over the bar, the wall, the carpet and Crump.

"Grab 'er, Ogden!" he yelled.

Whong!

The loaded reticule hit Dill a glancing blow on the head just as Crump jumped toward the grim-lipped little old lady who had celluloid grapes on her hat. Crump gave her a mighty shove with both hands and she went reeling halfway across the room. Then, with her hat wildly askew, she raised the reticule above her head and cried out, "*Fifty-four forty or fight!*" In a twinkling she was at the entrance door and out. Gone.

"God in heaven!" wailed Orlando Dill. "Who *is* that monster? What's she got against me? How the hell did she get in here?" He was clasping both hands to his head—an attitude that was becoming almost routine with him in recent days. Crump got a cold towel and put it on the knot that had risen out of a flattish plain, like the volcanic mountain of Paracutín that found itself standing suddenly in a Mexican cornfield. The Texan was clucking over Dill, mother-henning him, and the lawyer was eyeing him with a suspicious air.

The clout had been a vigorous one but, as noted, the little old lady's marksmanship had been slightly off. "At least," said Dill, one hand clamped over his knot, "at least this time she didn't cold-cock me. God's teeth, but that aches!" Still grasping his contusion, he made his way to the bar and replaced the drink he had scattered wholesale over the room.

"One thing you can say for the ole red disturbance," said Crump, trying to sound vibrantly sympathetic, "is that it numbs up your head like novocaine."

"Thanks, gobs," growled Dill, who was neither mollified nor amused. "It hasn't numbed up *my* head. What I need is some airplane glue to sniff. Now, look here Ogden. This is your suite. I assume you pay good money for it. Why the hell aren't you on the phone to the house dick? You seem to be accepting this whole thing in a rather cavalier manner. The people downstairs could grab Whistler's Clobbering Mother in a matter of seconds. These clonks on the head are growing just a bit tiresome."

The door buzzer sounded and Crump moved to answer it. "Don't for Christ's sweet sake open it!" Dill called out in a hoarse whisper. "It's Mother Machree with her carpetbag again!"

"Who's there?" Crump spoke, and a soft feminine voice responded. He pulled the door open, revealing a young woman for whom the word *gorgeous* was probably coined.

"You must be Señora Kockamaney," said Crump, a bit of a stammer in his voice.

"No, señor," said the young woman in a slow, throaty voice, which set Crump's middle-aged gonads to thumping and vibrating. "But please," she begged, "sayze it more better *Señorita*. Señorita Tornillo. No more Señora. Did I no tell you on the telephone I am divorce lady now? You are Meestaire Grump?"

"Step right in, Señorita!" Crump ejaculated, coming suddenly to life. Orlando Dill had been sitting on a sofa, staring at this vision, but now he got to his feet and the girl *flowed* toward him. She had superb auburn hair and dark brown eyes and her every movement was music. Dill, a veteran of amorous engagements beyond the numerical reach of IBM, began to tremble slightly as she came up to him. If she noticed it, she didn't let on.

"This," said Crump, "is mah young lady!" He appeared to place a slight emphasis on the Texas pronoun *mah*.

"We've been waiting for you, my dear," said Dill, bending to kiss her hand. Then he elevated the same hand as if he were preparing to lead her into a stately toe-pointing minuet, and escorted her to a large chair.

"The shade of that blue," he said, indicating the street dress she was wearing, "plus the delicate beauty—the heady effervescence—of she who occupies it, these things put me in mind of the indigo bunting—surely one of the loveliest and happiest of our feathered friends." He gave one pointy end of his mustache a deft twirl.

"Our feathered friends!" grumbled Crump, wrinkling his nose at Dill's grandiose maneuvers. If anyone was going to get a crack at this girl, he, Ogden Crump, would be the favored party. He was the one she had telephoned. He was the one whose hotel suite she had come to visit. Crump placed himself directly in front of her chair and essayed a rather cumbersome bow of the type he had observed in costume movies, extending his left hand outward as if he were grasping a tricorn hat.

"Now, mah little roadrunner," he said gently, "Ah want you to . . ."

"Hold it, Oggie," Dill interrupted, employing a nickname that Crump despised. "Why in the name of God are you calling this enchanting creature a roadrunner?"

"A roadrunner happens to be one of *mah* feathered friends," Crump responded with considerable belligerence.

"But," argued Dill with juridical placidity, "a *roadrunner* of all things! I've seen a roadrunner. Ugly as sin. Looks like a bilious buzzard. Audubon himself turned his face away and shuddered the first time he saw a roadrunner."

"Now, just one dern minute!" protested Crump. "You're goin' just a little too far. You're a churn-headed New Yorker, Dill, and you've never seen a roadrunner runnin' alongside of a road. They's not a purtier sight to be seen in Taixuss."

"I might agree to that last observation," said Dill, "but I would call attention to the fact that when you refer to this ravishing young lady as a roadrunner, it has a most unpleasant connotation —I get the impression that you are calling her a streetwalker who works out in the country, a sort of fast-traveling hooker. You get what I mean, Ogden?"

"Dill," said Crump, a note of threat in his tone, "you had better get shet of that phony lawyer manner of yours, quit showin' off, if you wanna go to the bridge with me. Just keep in mind that Ah'm the one hired you. You got no compeltry over me!"

"You're right, Ogden," Dill replied amiably. "Whatever compeltry is, I've got none of it over you. I apologize." Then he muttered the word *compeltry* to himself a couple of times. It was not strange that he had never heard it before. *Compeltry* is a word invented in Texas for the use of Texans; its meaning is not known in other parts of the world, nor is its meaning known in Texas. Nevertheless, Orlando Dill had a definite feeling that he had some compeltry over Ogden Crump. Plenty compeltry.

"Now, Señorita, mah little roadrunner," Crump said, speaking in a mildly defiant tone, then continuing unctuously, "please tell this man here, this lawyer, all about the ranch, and how you . . ."

"Yes, indeed," Dill interjected, moving over and seating himself on the arm of the girl's chair, seizing her hand and gazing raptly into her eyes. "Please, little bunting, tell me about it."

Señorita Tornillo launched into a spell of coughing, making it necessary for her to withdraw her hand from Dill's grasp. She hastily extracted a small handkerchief from her handbag and placed it over her mouth. At the same time she bent forward, hiding her face, and when she straightened up there were tears in her eyes. Dill quickly whipped out his own handkerchief and began dabbing gently at the girl's cheeks.

"On second thought," Crump now intoned, trying to get command of things, "Ah think Ah'd better do the preliminary talkin' mahself. Orlando, god damn it, will you please pay attention to this! It's important! We got that cat to deal with!"

"You have already told me the ranch story," said Dill, who was clearly under a double emotional strain—one facet induced by continuing draughts of alcohol and the other by stirrings of rank lechery. "But go ahead if you feel like it," he added. He hadn't taken his eyes away from the girl's face and she was clearly enjoying it all.

"This little lady," Crump began, "called me up on the phone yesterday and told me about this ranch of one hundred seventy thousand acres she used to own in God's Own Glorious Private Estate, Taixuss. West Taixuss, to be exact. Out around the Big Bend country."

"Ogden," Dill put in, "this lovely girl is a Mexican. How'd she happen to own a ranch of that size in the United States of Texas?"

"She was married to a character named Petticoats Kockamaney. Everybody called him that because he couldn't never keep his mind offa petticoats."

"His real name," spoke up the Señorita, "is Clyde. Clyde Kockamaney. What a bom! Always he pushes up the petticoat!"

"You mean, of course, *your* petticoat," said Dill.

"Oh, no, Señor! He pushes up petticoats worldwide."

"Señorita," Dill went on, "one thing, please. It is my impression that stylish ladies do not often wear petticoats anymore. Have petticoats become stylish in Texas?"

"In Texas," she told him, "wears the girls petticoats only so my hosbon can push up. All places goes my bom hosbon, wears the girls petticoats. Feelty marrana peegs!"

"Orlando," Crump remonstrated, "will you please leave me continue? The thing is, this rich jerk Kockamaney—you've heard the name, big in chili powder—this Petticoats Kockamaney pushed up more petticoats than our young friend here thought was proper, and she divorced him a year or so ago, and she got the whole blamed ranch as a settlement."

"Where's the old petticoat-pusher now, little bobolink?" Dill inquired.

"Ah," sighed Señorita Tornillo, "it is a badness. Clyde is fall down dronk in Ail Paso, in San Tonio, in Dollis, Hoosten, Longtree, any place peoples got whiskey. Dronk, dronk, dronk from drinking up. No more even pushes the petticoats."

"Very sad," observed Dill. He himself was getting somewhat dronk from drinking up, but he did not feel at all averse to pushing up a petticoat here and there, if he could locate the handle. He was trying to hit upon some way of suggesting a bit of petticoat-pushing when Señorita Tornillo stood up and asked if she might have a moment to powder her nose. Crump pointed the way to the baño through the bedroom. She picked up her handbag and turned suddenly to confront Dill, who was still seated. Without warning she kicked him—a sharp, stinging kick direct to the shin. Then she hurried out of the room, leaving the lawyer gasping with pain, his eyes bugging out in astonishment, clutching at his latest raging wound with both hands.

"Crump, you vicious bastard!" Dill finally howled through his accretion of misery, "you are a Jonah to me. You've got a Lone Star hex on me. Up to the time I got involved with you, women just flopped over backwards and pushed up their own petticoats for me. Now they push dents in my skull and try to kick my shinbone off. I'm beginning to think . . ."

"Calm down, Orlando," urged Crump. "This dame sold her ranch to Banner. Ah understand they want to put in some kind of a big resort down there. Anyway, she now thinks that Banner diddled her out of her cattle spread, and there's somethin' about a gold mine mixed up in it . . ."

The entrance buzzer sounded again. "Man the barricades!" cried the distrait Dill. "Old Lady Overkill is back for sure this time! I'm getting out of this House of Usher! Let the god damn place crumble and fall into the tarn!"

Crump eased open the door that gave on the corridor. It was another girl, very beautiful and consummately Latin. She flashed white teeth at Crump in a dazzling smile.

"I," she said, "am Señorita Tornillo. You are Meestaire Crump?"

"But," said Meestaire Crump, thoroughly befogged, "Señorita Tornillo is already here."

"Yes," said the dark beauty, "I am now already here."

"Señorita Tornillo," Crump persisted, "is takin' . . . is chalkin' 'er nose in mah bathroom. In yonder. You are not Señorita Tornillo."

"Eeeee-yay!" cried the girl. "Somebody is personify me? Some woman say she is me? But I do not . . ."

"Come on in sweetheart!" Dill called out. "Maybe we can use one more Señorita."

Crump and the girl advanced into the room just as the bedroom door opened. Out came a man, a handsome smallish man with dark curly hair, wearing nothing but his socks and a pair of chartreuse underpants.

"Permit me to introduce myself, gentlemen," he said, starting toward them. Then he saw the girl. "Oh!" he exclaimed. "One moment." And he hurried back into the bedroom. He returned immediately wearing Crump's bathrobe. From the moment of his first appearance in the doorway, both Dill and Crump had been tongue-tied. What had begun as a secretive business conference was fast taking on the appearance of rehearsal time at the Ed Sullivan Show. The Swiss bell-ringers would be bouncing out of the wings at any moment.

"Where's the girl at?" Crump finally managed to blurt at the strange man. "Where's Señorita Tornillo?"

"I am still here," spoke up the young woman who had just recently appeared.

The man now smiled and said: "I am . . . I mean, I *was*, the Señorita. The first one. I have just made a quick change in your bathroom. Also, Mr. Dill, I was the old woman with the reticule, both in the courtroom and in this room. Had you going for a while, didn't I?"

"Why, you insufferable . . ." Dill snarled, taking a couple of steps toward the man. Then a thought appeared to cross his mind and he halted his threatening advance. "You are that girl? Impossible!" He walked up to the man, took him by the shoulders, and stared intently into his face. "Well, I'll be damned," he said. "I believe you *were* the girl. Talk fast, you bastard, because I'm going to raise knots on *your* head that'll stay in place for the rest of your miserable life. Talk!"

"Please," said the man, apparently unperturbed. "I had to convince you, Mr. Dill. I had to sell myself, to demonstrate how expert I am at my job. Please, all of you, sit down. This," he said, smiling at the girl, "is of course the real Señorita Tornillo. My name is Muff—at least you may call me that. I have been known as 'Mister Muff' on the stage, but the stage is not my calling. I am a spy, an agent trained in all phases of espionage."

"So, what are you doin' in mah place?" demanded Crump. "What's the idea snoopin' around here, hidin' in mah closet, kickin' mah guests? Ah ought to bust your haid wide open!"

Mister Muff raised a hand in remonstrance. "Watch your temper, Mr. Crump," he said. "I'm an operative with a genius for being thorough. I know all about you. I know all about Mr. Dill here. And I know all about the Señorita and her ranch." He paused, and fixed his eyes on the Señorita's face. "I said," he told her, "that I know *all* about you. Everything. So let us sit down and have a drink and be friendly together. I am dealing myself in, and there are things to be done. We can . . ."

"And I," said Orlando Dill commandingly, "am calling your bluff, Hawkshaw. You talk in very expensive terms. You know all about me? Like what?"

"Oh, for openers," said Muff airily, "let's mention the Clements affair, and possibly the case of Mrs. Florence Forbush, and . . ."

"Forbush!" Dill exploded. "That two-titted sow! Let's get on," he added quickly, "with our discussion."

"And let's keep in mind," continued Muff, smiling broadly, "that just minutes ago I was someone's sweet little indigo bunting, and someone else's charming roadrunner."

"First of all," Ogden Crump spoke complainingly, "Ah wanna know how you got in mah rooms here, and how you know all this stuff about everbody, and how you can dress up like a dame so good you can fool two sharp fellas like Orlando and I, and how you . . ."

"Mr. Crump," said Muff, "I am a spy, turned detective. I combine the best features of the two professions. I have methods at my command that would set you to mumbling to yourself in dark corners. Would you enjoy having me speak of Albert Apple, the Corpus Christi gunslinger, and certain transactions you . . ."

"What's your proposition?" Crump interposed.

"Let me begin," said Muff, "by telling you that I have a personal acquaintance in this town with a girl named Diana Fowler. I was with her in Puerto Rico, by pure chance, at the time she came into possession of a certain cat. I was the person who first detected the strong physical resemblance between her cat and the multimillionaire cat Rhubarb. Miss Fowler does not know that I am at present in New York."

Orlando Dill, who had sobered appreciably in the last ten minutes, studied Mister Muff with a speculative eye.

"Does Miss Fowler know," he asked, "how you look when you're dressed as a girl?"

"She does."

"Does she know how you look when you're an old woman going around knocking lawyers in the head?"

"She was there the day I clobbered you in the courtroom."

"You stinking bastard. And she knows how you look as a man, as you look right now?"

"Yes."

"Tell me this. Can you fix yourself up as an attractive woman, slightly younger than myself—that is, a youngish woman with poise and physical charm, and a sort of aristocratic way?"

"Mr. Dill," said the spy-detective, "I can disguise myself as Mrs. Florence Forbush if necessary, and I can do it so well I think I could lure you once again to her mattress—or at least to the very brink of her mattress."

"God forbid!" exclaimed Dill. "And now, I think we are in business. Tell us, Señorita, about the gold mine."

"First," interposed Muff, "let me acquaint the Señorita with the fact that I am the person who got in touch with her in San Antonio. My dear, I am a first cousin of your former husband Clyde Kockamaney. I was born in Menard County, Texas. I may as well tell all of you my real name. It is Millard Muffgainer. Not at all good for the spy trade, and even less so for show biz."

"I don't care for Millard," said Dill, "but Muffgainer I like."

❡❡ Chapter THIRTEEN

IN the Banner Manhattan town house, Doom was writing a book. In the years of his close association with the richest and most celebrated animal in the world, he had met whole battalions of bubble-headed people who were writing books, or talking about books they planned to write.

Fame attracts fame, of course, and Rhubarb was a world celebrity of special character and drew to his presence a rabble consisting largely of terminal-stage actors and actresses, industrial giants with the kindly disposition of the jungle python (and its wisdom), death-rattle songbirds out of the superior supper clubs, great statesmen publicly acclaimed for their genius at eye-gouging, urban renewal whorehouse madams, avaricious testimonial-liars out of baseball and other areas of splendid sportsmanship, spastic butt-grinders from the Jet Set, fluff-and-thistledown dancers from England and Russia, vividly homosexual social historians, famous out-loud readers of factory-processed news scripts on the television networks, folk singers sought by the police, and so on and on . . . until one wonders how our small world has ever managed to produce such an array of glamor and talent and probity, such shining exemplars of the Good Life and the True.

Many of these characters who gravitated in the rich cat's direction had written their books, or spoke often and feelingly of work in progress, making special mention of how much fun it was . . . and so easy. When Doom made it known that he was going to set down his own life story, Eric Yaeger told him the truth about those other people and their authoring—how in almost every case there was a little mole-type guy with dandruff on his coat collar, wearing thick-lensed glasses, living on gray hamburgers, sitting in a grubby little room doing the actual writing . . . and making a good deal of it up, for want of sufficient factual material worth putting on paper. This little man's prodigal dishonesty was justifiable in a way, because the true facts of the life story he was ghosting were usually dreary beyond all belief and pompous beyond all credibility.

"And furthermore, Doom," said Eric, "these little ghosty-guys have now reached a point of perfection in their work where they deliberately misspell words and commit handsome grammatical errors and compose clumsy sentences—all to make the book sound authentic, all to make it sound as if it were written by the oaf or oafess whose name would appear on the cover. Now, do you want to get mixed up in such a swindle?"

"Yehr," said Doom quickly, and then caught himself, and changed it to, "I certny do not! I'm gonna write my own life story, ever damn word of it. I don't need no little mole. What you don't know is I been readin'. Books. Hard tops. I can write as gooda book as a lot of these jokers . . . all that killin' and screwin' and kids on motorsackels poppin' them capsools. No, sir, Eric, I'm writin' my own stuff." In that final word Doom unwittingly accredited himself firmly to the literary establishment; the best of professional writers always refer to their stuff as stuff.

So Doom was writing his book. Rather, he was dictating his book into a tape recorder, set up in the library of the house where Thaddeus Banner had lived and died. He had given the typewriter a try, but that proved hopeless, and then he went at it with pencil and ruled legal pads, but his predicates were all out of plumb and his sentences turned into snaky, snarly things that never seemed able to find an ending for themselves. Doom had heard that some of the highly-esteemed authors he had met used tape recorders to compose their best-sellers, usually explaining, "I seem to talk more cogentwise and dramaddic than to put it down in plain words on paper like."

Several months had elapsed since Rhubarb's death in Pago Pago Bay when, on a sloppy, slushy afternoon, Doom lugged his new tape recorder into the Banner house and dictated the first words of his book, which were: "My Exciting Life With My Pal Rhubarb a book by Joseph Collaboletta." He played this line back, and the lyric quality of the twelve words stunned him with their beauty, but Willy Bodfish flung a critical harpoon and told him he oughtn't to use his real name, because nobody knew him by any name other than Doom.

"It's too short, Willy," complained Doom. "You can't have a book that oney says 'by Doom.' My God that would practicly be illiderate. Wait a second. Maybe I got it. When I first started bookin' around Times Square, that's when I got the name of Doom—it was after Eric give me the wonderful name of The Doomsday Bookie. That's it!"

He got the machine going again, and erased the beginning line on the tape—a procedure that took him almost an hour. He didn't seem able to grasp the directions for erasing and seldom bothered about it, which may well turn out to be living literature's gain, and one cheerful moment for posterity during the sad and woeful time when posterity is trying to struggle up from the ashes. At last Doom was able to start anew, as follows: "Lemmy see now how did I say it before My Exciting Life With My Pal Rhubarb a book by The Doomsday Bookie."

In the succeeding two weeks of creative struggle, he had filled one three-inch reel of tape. Now his immense body, weighing a trifle over three hundred pounds, was wallowed down in Thad Banner's black leather chair, microphone in hand, and a vacant look in the eyes. Doom didn't know it but he was deep in what literary people call a writer's slump. A fresh reel was on the machine and he had made several attempts to get back into the lovely rhythms that mean so much to a writer—but the phrases he spoke were somehow wooden and devoid of any intelligence.

Willy Bodish, still majordomo of the Banner house as he had been in the time Old Thad was stomping and ranting and cussing around the place, came into the library with a bottle of beer in his hand.

"You still stuck?" he inquired timidly. He already knew that one should tread softly and speak in whispers when dealing with an author, especially an author in a slump.

"God damn it," Doom responded, "long as you got to come yellin' and rampagin' in here, botherin' me right when things was about to straighten theirself out, then go out and get me one of them beers. Jesus Christ Almighty!" Willy brought another bottle and Doom tipped his head back and took a long gulp. Then he went back into his dream world.

"It's none uh mah business," Willy persisted, risking his life, "but Ah was wonderin' ef you put in about that time ole Rhubob nilly scratched mah eyes outa mah haid. That was aftuh Ah boilt mah britches in catnip soup so's he'd be fremmly wiv me."

Doom turned a choleric eye on the brisk little Negro, pressing his lips together and shaking his head slowly from side to side.

"Willy," he said, "how many times I told you to quit talkin' like that? Don't never say things like 'nilly' and 'haid' and 'fremmly.' My God! These is new times we're livin' in. You ain't allowed to talk like that any more. You keep it up and somebody's gonna beat your head clean offa your neck."

"It's still onclear to me," Willy objected. "What'm Ah suppose to say whin Ah wanna say 'fremmly'?"

"Friendly," said Doom. "Friendly. Friendly. *Friendly*."

"Okay, fremmly," agreed Willy. He got up and shuffled back toward the kitchen—yes, *shuffled*—and in leaving, murmured, "Ah still woosh sometimes Ah was livin' back in th' olding time when Mistuh Thad war alive an' kickin' mah black pickaninny ass all ovah this house. Ah could at *lease* talk Tessus-talk lak that Mistuh Crump he talk."

Doom heard the parting words and shook his head in despair over Willy's ignorant condition. He finished his beer and sat motionless for a long while, striving for the serenity of a balanced perception. He had, by no means, unslumped himself; if anything he was worse off than ever. He thought of giving up for the day, of getting out of the chair and going to the kitchen for the other half of that apple pie. Then a sense of discipline, so essential to the craft of writing, took possession of him and he decided on a new course. He was a man with a certain depth to him; he was, in a sense, a thinking animal, and he was cognizant of this fact, to a degree. He decided to think. He thought back to the words he had already spoken into the recorder, and this transported him back in time to that magical day when he, Joseph Collaboletta, personally and alone and single-by-god-handedly, you might say, when he, The Doomsday Bookie, had put an alley cat on top of the world. "No other man," Doom said half aloud, "can make that statement."

It was true. The fat bookie was responsible, more than anyone else, for the beginning of the Rhubarbian Saga, one of the great romantic episodes of American history. The fictional heroes of Horatio Alger, Jr., and the true-life protagonists in Dale Carnegie's world were craven and inept slugabeds alongside the towering figure of the multimillionaire cat. Up from the alleys of Jackson Heights to the very pinnacle of world power—that had been the course of Rhubarb, all because of Doom's inspired activities on a snowy night in Times Square.

He had been an improvident dealer in two-dollar bets when the cops deprived him of his livelihood, advising him that if they ever caught him making book again they would pound his ears level with his sideburns.

Hours of the deepest despair followed for the big man. And now, sitting in Old Thad Banner's fine chair in Old Thad Banner's fine house, he remembered, as he often remembered, the words and music that came out of the little radio in his hotel room on that wet afternoon. He had been lying on the bed, desperately trying to figure an angle that would get him some groceries. What came out of the radio was a jingle sung by a male quartet to the tune of "Smiles." It went:

> *There are scalps that itch like blazes,*
> *There are scalps that burn like mad,*
> *There are scalps that steal away the hair roots*
> *As the porpoise steals away the shad,*
> *There are scalps that have a tender sur-fuss,*
> *Where the dandruff gets beneath the hide,*
> *But the scalp that's free of all these ailments,*
> *Is the scalp wet with Ban-ner-ide!*

Then came the voice of an announcer, shouting the merits of Banneride in straight deafening prose, and concluding with an offer—if any purchaser should be dissatisfied, his dealer would gladly, willingly, even eagerly, asking no questions, give him *double* his money back.

Doom was a rigidly honest man within reason and functioned

strictly under the National Business Ethic. He heard the radio message in midafternoon. By evening he had visited most of the drugstores in the Times Square sector, telling startled clerks and managers, "I ain't satisfied with this moose pee you call scalp erl." He was not being dishonest—he actually *wasn't* satisfied with the moose pee. When he finally returned to his hotel he was holding a profit on the operation of eight dollars and twenty-eight cents.

Something over a hundred years ago there was published a scholarly yet readable book called *Extraordinary Popular Delusions and the Madness of Crowds,* demonstrating with great incontrovertibility that the human race, up to that time in history, had dedicated itself to staggering stupidities, one piled upon another, in all climes and in all classes. Anyone who has observed the more recent scene with care knows that *homo sapiens* and his helpmeet have deteriorated and gone steadily downhill since the publication of that book; far more rocks are being thrown today per capita than in the halcyon times of the Old Stone Age, and it takes very little urging in the Twentieth Century to set the sheep to blatting in mad togetherness. The seemingly unimportant little act of larceny by The Doomsday Bookie set off just such a scramble. Word spread quickly that a person could actually get double his money back if he talked tough to the drugstore people, and the fever spread—mobs were soon standing in line at the drugstores throughout the length and breadth of our sovereign land, clamoring for a dollar and thirty-eight cents in exchange for a partly-filled bottle of scalp juice that cost sixty-nine cents. And getting it.

The Banneride Corporation might possibly have survived this disaster, but it didn't, for the reason that Old Thad Banner blamed the entire affair on the American public, an ethnic group which he already despised. The irascible old man paraphrased Commodore Vanderbilt, declaring unequivocally, "Screw the public!" and wrote a new will, bequeathing his remaining money and his baseball team to his cat.

Every time Doom thought of his own part in this historic episode he seemed to take on new spirit and energy. So now he grabbed up his microphone, grat his teeth, shook his head vigorously and renewed the dictation of his autobiography, speaking as follows:

This is gonna be about Them. I seen them last night. Mister

Dillon of all people he was there but without no big hat on. He wasn't the marshal. He was a G-man. And he went after these here big ants with a poop gun like they used in the war in Korear and Vit Nam and like all that, hold it on one fella's shoulder and shoot it off in all them jungle trees but Mister Dillon he goes after Them with it. That was the name of them. Them. The big ants. That was the name of the picksha, too. Just Them. It's got Mister Dillon in it without that big ungodly hat on his head and without Miss Kitty and Doc and shooting a poop gun over another G-man's shoulder. At these big ants.

Oh, them was the glory days, when we had Rhubarb right here in this house and Polly Pinckley lived next door and Eric was bangin' her and didn't care who knowed it and . . . god damn it the hell . . .

Well, so these ants, they get inaggulated some way by the atom bombs, like everbody else, it's out there where the desert is with rattlesnakes and cactruss with pricks on, and they grow up to be eight or ten feet long, mean as a snake, they go around in the night and grab a-hold of people and eat them right down to the bone, scare the daylights outa you—all they need in this picksha to turn your hair white is Charles Laughtman with a hunch on his back. I'd hate to think there was real ants like that, runnin' around in the night, bigger than dynersours with claws on all their feet.

There's this girl Jone something, I don't remember seein' her before in pickshas and she is a girl scientist that knows all about bugs and her granfodda is the world's best bug scientist, and they go out there to see the best way to kill these godawful big ants, and the old man, the granfodda, says there is two queens got loose from the tribe, and we got to find them and kill them because they will breed up and we will have all these big ants runnin' all over the earth and eatin' people right down to the bone and in nine months there won't be any people left.

If I may return to the subjeck of the glory days of Rhubarb and I, and the time we win the World Series by leaving the Loons rub him on the crooked part of his tail, it was about then, but wait a minute there is more about Mister Dillon. Sugar. I forgot about the sugar. Them ants they like sugar. They tear down a whole freight train fulla sugar. When they get upset they make a squeakin' noise like a bunch of birds that have gone out of their head. So Mister Dillon he gets out there—I'm tellin' you my gentile reader it's a howl to see him without that big hat on and with a suit of reggula clothes on. But he's as tall as he is in Dodge, and this broad that's a scientist takes a long time gettin' around to it, givin' him the old come-on, because her main interest in life is bugs—I wouldn't want to have a daughter that was a girl bug scientist, would you?—and one of these ant queens is . . .

I interrupt to make a pernt. It is the bounding duty of a writer like I to write his life story by tellin' the absolute truth about everthing he does so the gentile reader will know what kind of a guy he is, so that is what I am doon, tellin' everthing I did and do and this was what I seen last night on Channel Five at ten-twenty p.m. Well, they blow up this ship and kill one of the loose queens and then a drunk out there in Los Angeles he sees them in this big cement ditch that's got cement walls with holes in it like caves, and that's where the other queen had gone, and some of her ant guards, but first they et up this drunk bones and all and didn't leave a thing but his bottle layin' there. So they send for Mister Dillon and all the others and jeeps fulla soldiers and fire-throwers and somebody says there is forty thousand miles of sewers under this town of Los Angeles and for Christ sake don't put no gas in there as it will kill ever single person in the town, and they agree that this would probly be bad for the country, so they have to go in there with poop guns and these hoses with fire shootin' outa them and . . .

A door opened and Eric Yaeger came into the room, followed by Simon Horney. Their entrance startled Doom and he flung the microphone down into his lap as if he had been caught *flagrante delicto* with a lively broad. He started to get out of the chair.

"Sit still a few minutes, Doom," Eric ordered. "Simon, go on out in the kitchen and get Willy to fix you a drink or some coffee while I tell Doom about his new job. Then we can talk gold mine."

"Eric," said Doom, speaking with the animation characteristic of an author who has just composed a series of soul-shattering sentences, "you want to listen how far I got with my life story?"

"Not right now, Doom. I think you're going to have to give up your book. You've got to go back to cat-guarding. I haven't worked it out with Miss Fowler yet but . . ."

"Give up my book!" Doom exclaimed, rising slightly in his chair. "Godamighty, Eric, you know what you're askin'? I *can't* give it up. I have poured too much of my innermost life's blood into it. A man ain't able to just stop a big projeck like this like as if it was a subway local."

"Now, Doom, you haven't even got two three-inch reels dictated yet. You want to know the truth? Go ahead and finish your book and have it published and then the critics will belt you all over the place and call you an ignoramus and a goon and they'll say you got a slopjar mind, and it'll make you so unhappy they'll have to put you on sedatives and tranquilizers from morning to night."

"Not if it's good, Eric. Not if it's as good as it is. You ain't even listened to it, Eric. It's got my life's blood poured into it with plenty of action and I ain't hardly got warmed up."

"Doom," Eric persisted, "I want you to take charge of Miss Fowler's cat, The Tiger. After all, don't forget that you loved old Rhubarb like he was your own son. And The Tiger is Rhubarb's own son. No question about it. Rhubarb would *want* you to do this for him. You haven't even seen The Tiger yet, but he's the real thing, just like his father. Now. Look at it this way. You become The Tiger's bodyguard and a whole new series of adventures will open up for you. That'll make your book twice as good as it would be otherwise. You might even be able to write *two* books."

"Sheez!" said Doom, thoughtfully.

"You'll be The Tiger's constant attendant during the weeks when I have him. I hope that Miss Fowler will agree to let you be his bodyguard during the periods when she has his custody."

"Oh, Eric, I hope so. You know how I was about Rhubarb—couldn't hardly stand to be away from him a single day. Maybe I should go over and talk to that broad . . . to Miss Fowler, and turn on the ole charm."

"No," said Eric. "Just put that tape recorder away for the time being, and don't go around composing your book in your mind, or you'll get run over or walk into a lake or something. Now, get lost for a while—I've got important business with Simon. It looks as if we may all be heading out for Texas."

"Texas?" Doom repeated. "Did you say Texas? Oh, God help us all! I've hearda that place!"

⚙️ Chapter FOURTEEN

A modest bash was being held to celebrate the conclusion of The Tiger's paternity trial. It was the first party ever attended by the Caribbean-born heir to the Rhubarb riches, and it was to be carried out in an atmosphere of secrecy; Eric concluded that everyone involved would welcome, for a change, an escape from the clamor and disorder that would almost certainly attend the party if the press were invited.

But these were the times of The Leak, the era of leaks from the State Department, seepage from the White House, droolings from the Kremlin. In the case of The Tiger's little party, the news got around by virtue of a leak the size of the leak that started the Johnstown Flood, a leak as big as the leak that leaked on Noah. Accordingly . . .

Warner Crockley, the celebrated television newscaster, clawed his way along the sidewalk in front of the Banner house, microphone clutched in his sweaty hand and a somewhat incoherent babble coming from his mouth. Crockley was up to it; he had been through this sort of thing before. Many times. There were at least fifty cops on his side of the street and he was surrounded by well over two hundred intelligent, brawling, well-read, snarling, idealistic, name-calling members of the metropolitan press engaged again in the business of gathering an item.

"Surely this takes you back," proclaimed Warner Crockley to his worldwide audience, "back to that distant day when we first learned that another cat, a cat named Rhubarb, had . . . get outa my way you cheap NBC bastard or I'll flog your god damn head off with this mike . . . when the ladies and gentlemen of the press assembled on this very spot, drawn by the inexorable . . . officer! you there, cop! will you get this son of a bitchin' NBC jerk away from me—he's tryin' to strangle me with that wire! . . . ladies and gentlemen, please excuse the needless confusion that is going on here, the raucous yelling of these miserable people who have never learned how to behave in public, in the final analysis this is really just another hard-core assignment and should be taken in stride, with . . . No! I won't move, you god damn Gowanus roughneck, and if you wave that camera in my face one more time you're gonna get it rammed down your cruddy throat! . . . most of these people, ladies and gentlemen, behave as if they had never been on a news assignment before, and it is really disgraceful, and something ought to be . . . Jeeeeeeeeeeeeeeeeeezus!"

Inside the house Eric stepped up to the front windows where Doom had been standing, watching the mad brawling mob.

"Looka them riffraffs," Doom observed. "Puts me in mind of all them college pupils that're always spittin' on flags and throwin' rocks at liberries on the TV, down in them South American countries and Japan and all over the world and Alabammer and also down South in Los Angeles."

"Don't speak so harshly of these people," urged Eric. "If you asked them why they are behaving this way, they would say they are only doing their job. Some of the most famous byline writers in the country are out there—look, Considine just went down! I think that was Earl Wilson that got him!—and keep in mind, too, Doom, that we of Banner Enterprises are locked in mortal combat with many of our competitors, and we are not above indulging in a bit of industrial in-fighting from time to time, but only when it is necessary, meaning every hour on the hour."

"You mean you slug and elbow and kick each other in the crotch like these kerrickters?"

"Only, well, only allegorically."

"Allegorically," Doom repeated. "Oh what a glory word! I think I'll use it in my book about my life's story if I ever take up writin' it again."

137

"It's all yours," said Eric, and then stiffened to attention. A small car had come down the street, preceded by two motorcycle cops who were trying to carve out a passageway through the crowd. Arriving opposite the Banner door, the car stopped and Jeremy K. Jenkins got out. The portly little lawyer's feet had no more than hit the pavement when his square derby hat was knocked off and a microphone shaped like a billy club got him in the side of the neck. Mr. Jenkins fought back with his right arm while helping Miss Diana Fowler out of the car with his left. Miss Fowler had something in her arms, something that brought a swelling roar from the mob. A cat. A long-legged yellow cat enmeshed in a welter of red rags. The two motorcycle cops had dismounted and abandoned their metal steeds, which were promptly knocked off their stands and trampled by teeth-grating journalists. The two officers were joined by several patrolmen who moved in from the far side of the street, and a wedge was driven through the howling crowd and the forest of waving hardware. Many small cuts and second-degree contusions were inflicted in this progress, and there was a great effort on the part of the more enterprising reporters to snatch The Tiger from Diana's arms.

One large lady, a society reporter whose frontal landscape looked as formidable as the underside of a Swiss cow at the approach of eventide, was making a frenzied effort to get her hands on The Tiger—for what purpose it was difficult to fathom. She might have made it, save for the fact that a pair of hands came up from the maelstrom and fastened themselves clamplike around her face, closing off her breathing. The large lady began kicking in every direction, or trying to kick, though there was not much room for it, and at length she succeeded in dragging the alien hands away from her face. Having regained speech, she gasped out, "Don't . . . shove you . . . bitch . . . double dare . . . I'm-you-tell-he-can-take . . . and furthermore, god damn your black heart, I'll sue you for every . . . you wait till you see . . . gallstones . . . kingdom come . . . chewed out . . . and THIS for you!" She swung, and missed whatever she was swinging at, and her arm struck Diana on the shoulder. Diana struggled around to face the hysterical society reporter, her chin jutting forward, and yelled, "Frug off! Frug the hell off, you nasty woman, or I'll stomp you back into the dirt!"

At the window Eric turned to Doom and said: "Hey. How about that? That's our gal!"

The slow-moving wedge was now arriving at the Banner doorway, already guarded by half a dozen cops. Diana and her cat and her lawyer were swept into the house while great groans and yowls of frustration arose in the street.

Eric was in the foyer to greet his guests, but his mood had undergone a swift change, and he performed the rite with an air of disapproval.

He glowered at Diana. "Why in the name of God did you have to shriek at the press like a fishwife?" he demanded. "A fine way to begin your career in big business!"

"Come, Mr. Jenkins," said Diana, nastily. "Let's get out of this majestic presence. Back into the mob for us, Tiger."

She had a hand on the doorknob when Eric reached her, gushing apologies, trying to explain that the wild disorder in the street had put him out of sorts, that he didn't mean to be rude.

"It would be better for all concerned," snapped Diana, "if you managed to keep your big mouth shut."

"Now, now, Diana," cautioned Jeremy K. Jenkins, "Mr. Yaeger has apologized. You can see that he's under a strain. Let's go on inside and enjoy the party."

They moved into the drawing room where a dozen men and a few women were standing in small knots, drinking and chattering. Eric called out a covering introduction and Diana smiled prettily and nodded and held The Tiger up for all to see. She noted the presence of Judge Bippus and Hickey Dolbier and Desmond Slattery.

"My dear Miss Fowler," said Eric, in a subdued voice, "I simply don't understand why you brought him here with that horrible red rag tied around his neck. One thing you've got to learn, my dear. The Tiger is not just a cat. He stands as the symbol, the talismanic image, of Banner Enterprises. You know about images, don't you, Miss Fowler? You must have a few of them in the dirty red rag trade."

"I know," Diana spoke with actressy asperity, "that you take some kind of pleasure in badgering me. It's my guess that you've got a streak of queer in you. You'd better lay off. I didn't bring The Tiger in the cage because he wouldn't get into the cage. He *wants* to have this red rag around his neck. He insists on it. He won't move out of my apartment unless he has this red rag with him."

"May I suggest," said Eric archly, "out of a somewhat extensive experience in nursemaiding a famous cat, that you might try putting the red rag inside a nice cage, and letting him have it for his traveling companion, without fastening it like a . . . like a . . . like a god damn flaming albatross around his neck? In time we might wean him away from it. Would I be offending you by making such an obvious and sensible recommendation?"

"You would," said Diana.

"What an interesting proposition," mused Jeremy Jenkins, his little white tuft of hair seeming to stiffen with the thought. "Weaning a creature from an old red rag. I'd like to be in on it, Diana." He was obviously quite eager to effect better relations between these two.

The uproar in the street outside suddenly approached a new crescendo and Eric stepped quickly toward the front door. Mr. Jenkins seized this opportunity to chide Diana gently concerning her behavior. "You must remember," he said, "that the real genius behind Banner Enterprises is this young man. The cat Rhubarb was the owner, but the cat Rhubarb never made a business or financial decision in his life, nor will The Tiger ever be called upon to make such decisions. Sometimes we might be inclined to overlook the true importance of Mr. Yaeger. In the end analysis, he runs the corporation. He is somewhat more than consort to a cat. You should try to give him a little more respect, my dear."

"Gladly," agreed Diana. "But I'm entitled to a little more respect myself. He may bludgeon down some of these other people, but I don't bludgeon very easily. I'll do my best, Mr. Jenkins."

Eric by now had snatched two more guests from the clutches of the throng outside. One was Orlando Dill, who paused in the foyer to adjust his necktie, which had been yanked around to a point beneath his left ear. At his side was an attractive woman, attractive in spite of an overload of cosmetics, a blonde with high-piled hair, clad in an afternoon dress cut provocatively low in front. Eric brought the two forward and Orlando was the very quintessence of drawing-room urbanity as he greeted Diana and Mr. Jenkins. Then he introduced his companion.

"This," he said, a prideful smile crossing his face, "is my dear sister Araminta Waggoner, who has come all the way from Texas to pay me one of her distressingly infrequent visits."

Simon Horney, the Banner real estate manipulator, was standing nearby talking with a couple of Wall Street men, and at the sound of the word "Texas" he glanced around. Eric Yaeger also seemed to tighten a bit when Orlando Dill spoke of Texas.

"Araminta," Orlando continued, "lives in a little Texas town out in the cow country, a town named Menard. She grew up with cattle and horses and cowboys and hound dogs and mules and wildcats and possum, and so what do we have? Here she is in New York begging me to let her meet the famous Tiger of Old San Juan."

Now Araminta spoke for the first time: "Ah been readin' bout The Tiguh in the Taixuss papuhs. Ah been *so* fass-nated! Speshly with mah big brothuh Awlando aw-ull involved like he was. Please, Mizz Fowluh, moughten Ah jes' touch that lil ole sweet thang?"

"What lil ole sweet thang?" Diana countered, a chill in her voice. She didn't like Orlando Dill and that dislike extended to all members of his tribe.

"That ole sweet Tiguh cat yonda."

Araminta took a step forward and placed her hand on The Tiger's head. She withdrew the hand promptly. The Tiger had been half asleep, else his aim would have been better—his swipe merely nicked her on the thumb.

"Mah sakes!" Araminta cried in crinoline alarm. "Awlando, you sutteny was rat when you said he had speerit."

At the edge of this little group stood Willy Bodfish, wearing a white jacket and carrying a tray of drinks. He was looking at Araminta, his eyes showing a lot of white. Suddenly he moved on toward the other side of the room where Doom was in conversation with Samuel McMurtrie McNabb, world authority on cats.

"Doom," Willy said in a half whisper, "Ah woosh you'd go ovuh yonda and listen to that lady talk, the one that's with Mistuh Eric and them. Mah goodness, Ah nevuh . . ."

"Don't bother me, Willy," said Doom. "Dr. McNabb here is tellin' me all about cats and vacuum cleaners. If that Tiger ever comes here to live, I don't ever want you runnin' no vacuum cleaners in the same room with him. Cats hate vacuum cleaners, don't they Doc?"

"Indeed they do," said Dr. McNabb. "Deathly afraid of them. And another thing. A cat does not like music. Music made by human beings. One should never sing, or even hum, or play violins, or pianos, or radio music, or television music, whenever a cat is within earshot. Never take a cat to a parade. Maddening! I was once at a big house party and the people had a beautiful blue persian. A man named Louis Armstrong, a musician I heard, was at this party, and he suddenly reached into his pocket and pulled out a large white handkerchief, and that blue persian threw up right on the carpet. That cat seemed to sense that music was coming, and it was."

Across the room Eric suggested that Orlando Dill and his sister get acquainted with the other guests while he took Diana on a tour of the premises. At this moment Simon Horney came strolling along and Eric stopped him.

"Come into the Trophy Room in about ten minutes," said Eric. "Got a matter to discuss with you. Won't take long."

With The Tiger still lying somnolent in her arms, Diana went along with Eric. They visited the library and Eric showed her Doom's tape recorder and described the fat man's struggles with his autobiography. They played back just a few sentences, to get the flavor, and the lines seemed to concern a queen being trapped beneath the city of Los Angeles and some sort of plot was afoot to asphyxiate everyone in the town. They moved along to the dining room where several men from the catering service were fussing over a splendid buffet. The bar was in operation at one end of the room, and the thirty-foot dining table was crowded with comestibles, including three smoked turkeys, three bulging hams, platters of cold cuts, cheeses from four European countries, and a vast variety of tidbits and confections. At the center of all this stood a colossal mound of frilled and frizzed gelatin, of a greenish color, almost two feet high, a gourmet creation of stone crab in aspic—the masterwork of Pierre Ecrevisse, who stood proudly behind it in his tall white hat, his heavy black mustache bristling with warmth and happiness.

After a look at the kitchen, where three more men and a young woman were at work, Eric escorted Diana to the second floor and the Trophy Room. Here were collected the belongings of Rhubarb, and Eric knew intimately the history of every article in the room, for he had been closely associated, one way or another, with everything Rhubarb possessed. First of all there was the wooden boxlike trap which Eric had used to capture the untamed cat that distant day in Jackson Heights—a trap made of tough wood to withstand the primordial fury of the animal—and still inside the box, the six golf balls and six tennis balls that had been used for bait.

There were five silver cages, and one gold-plated carrier. There were half a dozen custom-built scratching posts, plus dozens of playthings, though Eric admitted to Diana that Rhubarb had little use for conventional toys, much preferring the exercise and amusement he sometimes got from chewing on living dogs. In one corner of the Trophy Room was a gorgeous Oriental cushion, four feet in diameter, covered with velvet in brilliant colors, with matching plumage taken from the Asiatic Mandarin duck, the whole being stuffed with down from young virginal ducks of the same breed.

"He never used it," Eric said, grinning. "He wouldn't go near it even when the Japanese Ambassador brought it into the house as a gift from Hirohito. Put The Tiger on it and see what happens."

Diana removed the red leash and dropped her cat onto the

sumptuous cushion. The Tiger sniffed at the velvet and the duck feathers and hopped quickly off the thing. Then he made a bee-line for another object across the room—the famous sanitary tray which Clarissa Wood, who then conducted the "Pussy Preferred" column in *The Cat Gazette*, had designed especially for Rhubarb. Miss Wood engaged artists from the Walt Disney studios to help her with details of the tray and it was then constructed from bits of semiprecious stones such as chalcedony and zircon and jade and opal, by a craftsman formerly with Tiffany's. Then Clarissa Wood had a carload of special sand sent up from Daytona Beach for use in the tray; when all was in readiness, Rhubarb had been intro-duced to it and Eric stood by, positive that the cat would scorn such a garishly superb convenience. Rhubarb, however, gloried in it and there were even times when Eric thought he was overdoing in the use of it.

The Tiger strode uninvited to the middle of the glittering tray, scooped himself a neat hole in the Daytona sand, and perched himself over it. For the first time since she had walked into the house, Diana let herself go and almost bent double with laughter.

"We'll have to get them to run up a duplicate for your apart-ment," Eric said, and just then Simon Horney walked into the room.

"Please stay with us for a few minutes," Eric said to Diana. "I think you might want to hear this. Now Simon, give us the dirt on this ranch with the mysterious gold mine."

Simon Horney, a man seventy-six inches in length, each inch having the look of morose dissatisfaction with life on this planet, possessed nevertheless a dry wit and a delicate sense of humor. The difficulty with such people is that one never is certain when the wit is sarcasm or the sarcasm humor or the humor a disguise for slow-wick fury. In that part of the financial world devoted to large real estate operations, Simon Horney was accorded great respect and looked upon as a man not to be pushed.

"I got involved in this Texas ranch proposition," he began, "quite by accident. Ogden Crump, that scurvy fink, asked me to go on a fishing trip with him down there. Crump's religion, as we all know by this time, is lying and cheating. We went down to Del Rio and hired a Cessna four-seater and flew to a little mining town on the Mexican side of the Rio Grande. I did all the fishing and Crump spent his time flying around the area looking for what he really came after. I caught a barrel of catfish out of the Rio Grande and Crump explored for gopher-rock."

"Gopher-rock," Eric interrupted, speaking to Diana, "is ground into a fine powder and treated with iodized talc and soapstone. It is then spread out in enormous flats and gusts of Texas natural gas are blown across the surface, and out of this process comes . . . guess what?"

"Feen-a-mint?" suggested Diana.

"Come on, now. We're dealing with one of the most stirring developments in the romance of modern chemistry. From gopher-rock comes the miracle chemical, sassatate. Go ahead, Simon."

"Wait!" cried Diana, clutching at her bosom and permitting a look of wild wonderment to cross her pretty face. "Please, sir, tell me, what does this miracle chemical do? This sassatate?"

"We use it," Eric said, retaining his solemn manner, "in the treatment of the steel that goes into our automobiles. We use it in conjunction with a silicate called diatomaceous earth, mixed with radioactive sawdust to create the only surefire method of ridding the world of cockroaches. A lowly clerk in a hardware store in Lake Jackson, Texas, made the key discovery for us—found that all we need do is persuade cockroaches to walk through the silicate-sawdust-sassatate compound. Sprinkle it around the floor, the cockroach walks through it, and it cuts his feet to ribbons. Hurts like the very devil. If he can walk at all, he goes limping off to the swamps and sits around trying to invent some kind of tennis shoes that'll protect . . ."

"For Christ's sake, Eric," Simon Horney intervened, "knock it off, will you? Let me get on with this story. You can explain sassatate-sawdust versus the cockroach some other time, 'neath a Texas moon, probably. Now. Let me finish up the gopher-rock angle and have done with it. Crump found no gopher-rock, but he got interested in some fluorspar mining operations in the region east of the Big Bend Country. Now, fluorspar . . ."

"Simon," Eric interrupted, "I'm sure Miss Fowler is not much interested in the workings of the fluorspar trade. Can't we get to the ranch part?"

"A big Texan named Morgan Heath took me on a jeep tour of the Big Bend National Park," said Horney, "and told me how the tourist business down there is increasing year by year, and how there is a shortage of good tourist hotels. I suggested that a big luxury-type dude ranch might be the thing, and Heath told me about the Bowlared Ranch, one hundred and seventy thousand acres, set in the middle of a region known as the Doodah Desert. Crump was still down at . . ."

From up front came a wild cheering, a roar that unquestionably came from the crowd in the street. Eric hurried out of the room and down a hallway to a front window, Diana and Simon Horney right behind him. They peered into the street just in time to see H. Allen Smith making his way through the throng. He needed no police escort, for the people of the newspapers and television and radio made a path for him, whooping their lungs out, waving their arms and jumping up and down in their enthusiasm for this man, who had once been one of them. He smiled as he moved toward the front door, lifting a hand in greeting now and then when he recognized someone he had known in his earlier career.

"Look at him!" Eric breathed. "Just *look* at him! The poise, the self-possession, the consummate grace under pressure!"

Diana grabbed Eric and pulled him around and spoke to him in a schoolteacherish way. "You listen to me," she observed. "This is about the third or fourth time I've observed you making reverent obeisance in this guy's direction. He's not all *that* magnificent. Listen, boy, you happen to have a few good points going for *you*. I don't know this H. Allen Smith, but if I had to make a choice, I'd choose you. So quit making nance noises whenever he comes around."

Eric stood frozen with astonishment. Great God, this beautiful woman had just made love talk to him! Or what sounded a good deal like love talk. What for *her* must have been at least *like* talk. For an instant he thought of sweeping her into his arms and giving her a kiss that she'd remember for at least twenty-six weeks, with options.

Instead, he simply put a hand on her arm and said, "Sometimes, not too often, but sometimes, you can be real sweet. Almost human."

She dazzled him with her smile, and they went back to the Trophy Room.

ᘓᕷᔆ Chapter FIFTEEN

AS they reentered the room Diana thought she detected a slight movement. She walked over to a door, stood looking at it for a moment, then jerked it open. It gave on a small closet and standing inside this closet was Orlando Dill's sister, Araminta Waggoner. She was bent slightly at the waist, a golf club in her hands, and her eyes fastened on an imaginary ball at her feet.

When Diana flung open the door Araminta straightened up, a look of mild surprise on her face.

"*Fo-uh!*" she shouted.

She glanced flittingly from Diana to Horney to Eric. "Mah gracious goodness!" she exclaimed. "Yawl scared me a little! Ah was jes' practicin' up on mah aye-yut arn. Jes' noseyin' aroun' like a lil ole Taixuss girl lookin' ovuh how you Eastunuhs live, an' saw this peachy setta clubs in heah, an' Ah jes' dee-cided to swang a few in th' san' trap. That ole doah musta blowed shut!"

"Quite a trick you got there," observed Simon Horney, "slashing out of a sand trap in total darkness. I have trouble doing it in broad daylight."

Araminta Waggoner giggled and gurgled and made an aw-shucks-an'-lan'-sakes gesture with her hand, then exclaimed, "You funny ole man you! Ah couldn't help it if that ole doah blowed shut!"

Then she suddenly jumped as if a ghost had goosed her, and went tripping out of the room, permitting her hinder parts to warble zestfully. Diana kept those hinder parts under careful observation until they were no longer visible, and thin wrinkles appeared on her forehead. Her period of heavy meditation lasted only a few moments and then she moved the thin wrinkles down to her mouth and grinned her little grin.

"Eric," Simon Horney finally spoke, "I have been working with you for quite a few years, and scarcely a day has ever gone by without some kind of a little surprise, but this one, opening a closet door and finding a woman engaged in shooting out of a pitch black bunker, by god Eric, this one takes the cake."

"Oh, I don't know," Eric responded, grinning slyly, "there've been a lot of others, such as the time that . . . Hey. What about this painted creature? What's Orlando trying to . . ."

"Let's go ahead with the ranch story," interposed Diana with great complacency in the light of what had just happened. "I'll tell you about the charming female golfer. I know about her."

"I'm dying," said Eric, "to have just a little bit of light shed on things. Go ahead, Simon."

"The ranch," said Horney, "belonged to a fellow named Kockamaney, the last surviving member of a family that made millions out of chili powder. This Kockamaney lad is no teen-ager, but I hear he acts like one—playboy of the western world, a ne'er-do-well scraped off the bottom of the barrel. The ranch was for years the Kockamaney family seat, but this bird changed it into a combination country club and nuthouse, bringing in young girls from Dallas and San Antonio and jazz bands and keeping things in a whirl right around the clock. Then this Kockamaney character met a Mexican girl, came from a good family down in Torreon, and married her. Within six months she had had enough of his insanities, and she divorced him. A judge in another county gave the Mexican girl the ranch by way of alimony. So it was this Torreon girl who was in charge when I arrived at the ranch. She's a real beauty and belongs rightly in the ballrooms of Mexico City instead of on a bone-dry West Texas ranch. She had been trying to keep the place going but her former husband had let it fall to pieces, and so she was receptive when I told her what I had in mind—a wonderful dude ranch, part of the Banner chain of resort hotels. We made a deal. Acting on behalf of Rhubarb, and the Executive Committee of Banner Enterprises, I bought the ranch. And I put this big guy Morgan Heath, a mining engineer by profession, in temporary charge of the ranch, which is known as the Bowlared."

There was a knock at the door and Willy Bodfish stuck his head in, saying somebody in Mitchee-gan wanted Eric on the foam. He left the room for a few minutes and when he came back spoke sententiously to Simon Horney: "That was Gloke Hooma in Bannerville. He says they've got the Fer-de-lance ready to roll. Tell you about it later." Then smilingly to Diana: "I'll tell you, too, cat lady."

"Miss Fowler," said Simon Horney, "I've gone into a lot of detail about this ranch proposition because I felt you ought to know about it. There have been some strange developments in the last few days. I've had our security people working around the clock on it. The Mexican girl, Señorita Tornillo, is now in New York and she seems to have a good deal of Latin fire in her eye. Someone has told her that a famous lost gold mine has finally been traced to the Bowlared Ranch. Whoever it was who gave her the tip said it was the Lost Nigger Mine. People have been searching for that mine since the 1880s, believing that it is one of the richest gold mines on earth. The only rocks ever brought out of it assayed eighty thousand dollars to the ton. Good Lord! This is almost unbelievable! At the famous Homestead Mine they figured that if their ore assayed twelve dollars a ton, it could be profitable. The Señorita apparently knows all about this, and she thinks I rooked her. She thinks that we knew about the gold mine all along. I'd like to advise you, Miss Fowler, that a Mexican señorita rooked once is formidable. A Mexican señorita rooked twice on the same proposition will start carrying daggers in her socks."

"I think," Eric spoke up, "that we'd better get down to Texas, and in a hurry. We ought to have The Tiger along, so you'd better come with us, Diana. This gold mine may, in a manner of speaking, belong to you."

"Not so fast, Black Bart," Diana replied sharply. He was getting bossy again, and she wasn't going to permit that. "It happens that I have custody of The Tiger right now. *I* decide where he goes. Maybe I have some plans of my own. Matter of fact, I've been thinking about Las Vegas. I've always wanted to see that town, and I could rig up a little act with The Tiger, and we could do a turn in one of those gambling places, and that'll pay expenses. I've got it all figured out."

"Please!" begged Eric. "Don't say things like that! Come on with us. We'll go out to that ranch and play cowboy and Indian, and I-spy, and drop-the-handkerchief, anything you want." As he pleaded with her he let his arm slide around her shoulders and then he eased her body up against his, gently, oh so gently, and he smiled down into her face, and she said oh well all right.

"Let's get downstairs," said Eric, "and cut loose from this party, and form ranks, and hitch the hosses to the ole Conny-stogies, and trek West."

Simon Horney turned and opened the door and there stood Orlando Dill.

"Uhm," he said. "Uhm-mum. I was looking for my dear sister Araminta. She seems to have vanished into thin air. Have any of you seen her . . . uh . . . on this floor?"

"Matter of fact," said Eric, "we have. She was here just a few minutes ago, standing in a dark closet trying to get out of a sand trap."

"Oh, heavens!" Dill exclaimed, passing a nervous hand across his brow. "Has dear Araminta fallen back into *that?* Did you say *sand trap?* Oh, I must get her away—get her back to Texas, back to her doctor!"

"Do I understand," spoke up Simon Horney, "that she makes a practice of shooting golf in dark closets?"

"She has spells," mumbled Dill. "She wanders into strange closets and imagines . . . Well, it's this way, Doctor Stilwell down in . . . in San Antonio . . . says it is not a common disease, but that it is beginning to crop out among women who play a lot of golf." Dill was now regaining his equilibrium; he knew he was convincing nobody, but he went ahead with the little game, a sly grin twinkling beneath his pointy mustache. "Doctor Stilwell says," he went on, "that there is a certain amount of rhyme and reason in this disease —the victims start off with the correct club. By this I mean a driver. Doctor Stilwell says, quite correctly I think, that when a woman is swinging a driver inside a closet, she can do a lot of damage to the plaster and the woodwork, and she can wake up people all over the neighborhood. For your sake, Mr. Yaeger, I'm glad that Araminta was not on drivers. The sickness progresses through twelve stages, beginning with the Number One wood club. My dear sister has been on mashie niblick for several months now, and we were beginning to hope that she might reverse the field and travel retrograde, you might say, back to the driver, and be cured. But now, alas, it appears that she has moved on to the eight iron. If she goes on from niblick to wedge to putter, she'll have had it. The putter represents the terminal stage of this frightful mental disorder. On that sorrowful day when we open a closet door and find sweet Araminta bent over a putter, her knees pressed together gracefully the way Arnold Palmer does it, the end is at hand. At that point she is likely to run amuck at any instant, trying to kill people, even her loved ones, using one golf club after another, always in the correct order or progression of numbers, and then she has to be put away. Put away, into her last earthly home, a padded cell. With no closets in it. Oh, poor Araminta! I must go find her and get her back to Texas!"

Orlando tweaked one point of his mustache, cocked his head sideways, and strolled off down the hall.

Eric looked at Diana, and Diana looked at Horney, and Horney glanced at the closet door. "Well," he observed, "as they say in West Texas, *I be a suck-aig mule!*"

"Let's go," said Eric, and as they moved toward the stairway he began a swift organization of things. "Wheels within wheels," he said, "are whirling within more wheels. I'll have the big plane ready in two hours. Simon, you drive Diana home so she can pack a bag, and you'd better stay in New York and keep an eye on things. I'll be keeping in touch with . . ." Eric stopped midway down the stairs, put his hand to his eyes, and began laughing. "Poor Araminta!" he finally muttered. "Sinking fast, toward the putter! You know, I'm beginning to find certain likeable qualities in Orlando Dill!"

They trooped into the drawing room, with The Tiger again cradled in Diana's arms, his red rag leash wadded beneath him. Diana and Simon Horney moved among the drinkers, making their excuses. Eric selected key people and told them that a small emergency had arisen at the auto plant in Michigan and that he and Diana and The Tiger and Jeremy Jenkins and Doom were flying out at once.

"That's too bad," said Judge Bippus, who had been standing with H. Allen Smith and Desmond Slattery. "Wish you could stay for this little discussion we've been having. Mr. Smith here knows just about everything there is to know about cats. Their whiskers are always of a length to match the width of their bodies, so that when they start into a hole, the whisker-spread tells them instantly if the hole is too small for the passage of their bodies. Do you . . ."

"Judge Bippus," said Eric jovially, "I do hope we're not going to inveigle you away from woodpecker holes and set you to collecting cat-whisker holes."

"Not quite, not quite," said the Judge unsmilingly. "And Mr. Yaeger, about the jog in a cat's tail. That was one of the things that had me worried. I couldn't quite see how a cat could *inherit* a bend in its tail . . . that is, a *double* bend. Mr. Smith now informs me that anything is possible in the area of heredity, that The Tiger could be a Caribbean mutation, a Puerto Rican sport, defying the ordinary laws of lineage and filiation. Now you take . . ."

"I'm sorry," Eric interrupted, "but I've got to run. Any of you seen Orlando Dill?"

"He and his charming sister left," said Judge Bippus. "Listen to this, Mr. Yaeger. Mr. Smith tells me that he is a mutation himself, that he has a double-ended nose which he inherited from his father—it doesn't show but you can feel it if you rub your fingers on it, and Mr. Smith permitted me to do so—and he has hairy ear rims which were handed down to him by a remarkable uncle named . . . let's see now . . ."

"Dicker," said H. Allen Smith. "Uncle Dicker."

"I'd like a word with you, H. Allen," said Eric. The two men withdrew to one side and Eric explained that he and the others were not going to Michigan as advertised, but to Texas, because of certain mysterious developments down in the cow country.

"I'd like for you to come along," he told Smith. "It could serve as a pleasant holiday for you and it would be reassuring to me if I had your steady hand and your cool mind close at hand. I have a feeling I'll be needing help."

Smith agreed that he might fly down a few days later; he had been tipped off that his latest book, *Quaquaversal Interaction Amongst the Faggots of Fairfield County* would be announced as winner of a Pulitzer Prize on the morrow.

"Congratulations," said Eric. "What category?"

"Poetry," said Smith. "And I must put the finishing touches on a small interim project, a book to be called *A Boy's Life of Jacqueline Susann.* After that I think I can make it. If you have no objection, I might bring these two gentlemen with me. I enjoy Desmond's little lectures on insect life, and Judge Bippus amuses me, especially with his Views on Vulgarity in Literature."

"What *are* his views on the subject?"

H. Allen Smith arched his pleasant brows. "He is a Judge, Eric," he replied, "and therefore hasn't the slightest grasp of such things."

"I see what you mean. So, we'll see you in Texas. The name of the town is Aveinte."

"Ah, yes. I know the story of Aveinte."

Diana was tugging at Eric's sleeve and now dragged him into a corner.

"I almost forgot," she said, somewhat breathlessly. "I know Araminta. I mean I know who Araminta really is. When I opened that closet door, she was bending over, and I could see down the front of her dress. Guess what I saw down there."

"I'd rather not," said Eric.

"A cigar. A cigar wrapped in foil. I saw the same kind of cigar pulled out of a girl's cleavage down in Puerto Rico. Eric, that dame is not a dame—that's a man, a man known as Mister Muff, a former international spy."

"Holy . . . uh . . . smoke! You sure about the cigar?"

"Listen, my friend. It is a psychophysiological truth that a woman can see down a cleavage better and deeper and clearer than any man alive. I saw the cigar. It's Muff. And I thought he was my friend! He's come up to New York and sold himself to Dill and that awful creature Ogden Crump. And Eric, he's a very clever man, this Muff. Dangerous."

"Don't mention his name to anybody else," said Eric. "You'd better go find your Pickwickian lawyer and get him organized if he's going with us. God! That hideous red rag!"

Behind the Banner house is a garden, and a square brick building known as a coach house, and a brick wall separating the garden from a narrow alleyway. At about the time Orlando Dill was delivering his comprehensive lecture on his sister's golf club disease in the upstairs room, two women came through the gate in the brick wall and walked across the garden to a rear door of the Banner house. They were wearing the costumes of housemaids—black dresses with little white aprons and white caps. They appeared to be in a hurry, and one of them had a large box in her arms. At the back doorstep they paused and took a quick peep inside the box to see if all was well with Shadrach.

That's who it was—Shadrach, a cat, a large, handsome, platinum-haired cat. The two women dressed as housemaids were Mrs. Maybelle Godfrey, owner of Shadrach, and Miss Clare Boothe Morse, the somewhat opinionated columnist for the *Nine Lives Journal,* who had been a witness in the recent paternity trial. Miss Morse had been, in fact, a historic witness. A leading law review had called attention to the fact that she spent twenty-three minutes on the stand and never once spoke a word that had any bearing on the case under consideration.

As these two women stand at the rear door of the Banner house, preparing to enter, let us take a moment to consider the nature of their mission and the nature of their cat. Shadrach is well known in the modeling trade as "The Platinum Pussy." A book called *This Cat Is For Hire* has been written about him. He earns something over ten thousand dollars a year for Mrs. Maybelle Godfrey by posing for advertisements fashioned to sell certain luxury products. He is shown, for example, using one delicate paw to caress a jumble of very expensive jewels spread out on a sheet of black velvet; he is shown standing on a strip of subdued purple hopsacking, gazing at one of the innest of the in sports cars. Quality stuff, good goods, always—these are the things that Shadrach is paid to sell. In the golden avenue of Madison it has been decided that a platinum pussy suggests luxury and grandeur, and appeals to people with expensive and exotic tastes. As always, however, there have been dissenters, who argue that the color of the hair-covering is not the key ingredient—it is the animal underneath that counts. Ah, if we could only be shet of all malcontents!

Mrs. Maybelle Godfrey had first been attracted to Miss Clare Boothe Morse after reading newspaper accounts of Miss Morse's singular conduct during the trial of the Tiger paternity suit. "Here," Mrs. Godfrey told herself, "is a woman who knows procedures, a woman who knows how to deal with men. Knock their nasty brains out." Mrs. Godfrey, a former chorus girl, appeared on the surface to be a winsome thing, possessed of a childlike innocence, but it ought to be specified that she had been whiggered, in her time, upside down, crossways, right to left and left to right, over a barrel, and hanging from a tree limb. It is difficult to determine why she nursed a grudge against the male sex.

So she called upon Miss Clare Boothe Morse and stated her

problem. Her platinum pussy was bringing in about twelve thousand a year but, she explained, "I have to lay out a good third of that keeping his hair dyed and groomed, buying him special costumes and accessories, and putting expensive food in front of him. He won't eat anything but imported sardines and calves' liver and pistachio ice cream—all that apcray those lah-de-dah photographers are forever feeding him in their studios. I tell you, Miss Morse, I'm being screwed right and left by the agencies. There's more money in Shad than I'm getting. I just figured that a gal with your spunk, and your cat know-how, might be able to work some angles. You have written some very nice notices about Shad in your wonderful column."

Miss Morse had a keen publicity sense and loved nothing more than working angles, so she set herself the task of finding a good one for Shadrach. Her great inspiration came a day or so later when she was playing with the platinum cat at Mrs. Godfrey's apartment. It was a matter of common knowledge that Shadrach was a male cat; he had always been "he" and "him" to Mrs. Godfrey from the moment she first acquired him from the writer Cleveland Amory, who described the cat as "all boy." But now Miss Morse noticed that the platinum cat was rolling about on the floor and crying in a peculiar voice, and this crying was quite clearly, to Miss Morse, the "calling" of a female cat. In moments Miss Morse had established beyond question that Shadrach was a female and then the Big Idea crossed her mind: a litter of kittens by the new owner of Banner Enterprises out of the Platinum Pussy! A sensation! A bigger deal than Grace Kelly and Prince Rainier! Miss Morse realized that the task would not be an easy one, that it called for shrewd maneuverings and plenty of gall. But it would be worth it!

Mrs. Godfrey began weeping hysterically when Miss Morse told her that Shadrach was a female. "Oh my God!" she wailed, "what have the bastards done to me now? When did this happen to him?"

"Look, lady," said Miss Morse, deciding to play it tough, "what are you whimpering about? What's wrong with your cat being a female? I thought you hated the male sex. And now that Shadrach's a girl cat, you've really got the world by the tail. Let me tell you the plan."

She told her. Miss Morse knew that The Tiger was to pay his

first visit to the Banner house the following day. She knew that Shadrach was rousingly in season. And here they were, on the back stoop of the Banner residence, ready for the Big Try. Miss Morse boldly opened the door and walked into the kitchen, carrying the box, and behind her came Mrs. Godfrey. Three men and one girl were still at work in the room—people from the caterer's, all darkly Latin. They turned in unison to stare at the arriving housemaids.

Miss Morse addressed them. "Erin go bragh!" she sang out. They offered nothing by way of reply.

Mrs. Godfrey addressed them: "Bejabbers to yez!"

The man wearing a tall chef's hat turned to his associates and asked a question: "Whatta kind a-craze talk is-a this?" The young woman, who had been coddling raviolas, turned snapping black eyes to the chef and responded, "Is-a must-a be Dotch pipples—gotta rocks inna head!"

The two housemaids moved on into the hallway. They could hear the bibble-babble of the guests up ahead, but at the moment no one was in sight except Willy Bodfish, who was just turning into the dining room.

"Quick, now!" whispered Miss Morse, and Shadrach was snatched from the box and placed on the carpet. "Shoo!" said Miss Morse, waving her hands at the animal, then flapping her little white apron. Shadrach began a slow and stately walk up the corridor toward the big drawing room, behaving as if she were on camera.

The Tiger lay sleepily in Diana's arms. Slowly he opened his eyes. For a moment he didn't move a muscle. Then his nose twitched, ever so slightly. He turned his head, and the nose-twitch seemed to travel along the contours of his curled-up body until it arrived at his tail. It twitched its way out to the jog in his tail, and then it seized that jog in its jaws and began shaking it like fury. Zooooooooooooooooom! The Tiger was on his way. The long red rag whipped out behind him as he skidded into the runway of the corridor. There she was, facing him, big and startled and beautiful. Shadrach, having just recently turned nubile, reacted according to the book. She turned and zizzed—zizzed for the nearest exit.

Beyond that door stood the great table spread with delicacies, decorated with the golden turkeys and the deep-red hams, and rearing up in the center that gorgeous mountain of green gelatin,

shot through with chunks of stone-crab meat. The lights in the big dining room were so disposed that the dark doorway was reflected in this glittering Alp of goo, and Shadrach must have mistaken the shadow for another exit. She leaped straight and true like a shell from a cannon, and she struck squarely in the center of the mound and her body penetrated halfway, and there she came to rest, again like a shell from a cannon, embedded deep within the aspic.

"Woooooooooops!" cried a caterer's man, and the wooden salad tools he had in his hands went flying toward the ceiling. He backed rapidly away from a situation he didn't fully understand. Immediately into the scene came two chubby ladies masquerading as housemaids, flinging their arms about and screeching authoritatively. Inside the green gelatin Shadrach executed her first wriggle looking toward escape when a yellow streak came flying across the room, trailing a long red comet-tail, and went GUHHH-LUGG into the goo just inches above the trapped Shadrach. The Tiger was on her!

Those who witnessed what happened next said it was a sort of glittering and greasy kaleidoscope. Eric and Diana had come rushing in, followed by Jeremy Jenkins and two or three others, and everyone stood aghast as the gelatin and fish bits flew about the room. It was as if a Kansas tornado had dipped down and struck the mass of quivering stuff. The two chubby ladies had now advanced toward the center-point of activity, and stood throwing pickled mushrooms and savory Gee Bow Gai in all directions. Maybelle Godfrey and Clare Boothe Morse had lost all control of themselves. It required a few moments for the onlookers to realize precisely what was going on in that wild tableau, and then it became clear—Shadrach was being ravished in aspic, and it was a ravishment of classic proportions, accompanied by crazy slitherings and slidings and, occasionally, when a cat's head broke free of the green guck, snarlings and yowlings that would have upset the patients in the middle pasturage of Hell.

The moment she caught on to the nature of things, Diana began jumping up and down and clapping her hands together like a schoolgirl, and she cried out: "Oh, goody, goody, goody! We'll get to have another paternity trial!"

This notion had not yet occurred to Eric. "Heavenly God not that!" he roared, and leaped forward, springing through the flying green gazoozlum, pausing a moment to wipe a chunk of sticky stone crab away from his eye, then plunging on and into the writhing mass on the table—the two cats were now whipping themselves back and forth, platinum alternating with smoke yellow and grubby red against the green of the aspic and the white of the crab meat, so that Eric had the sensation of a man trying to unfasten a slippery sheepshank tied in a rainbow. He stayed manfully with it, never noting that the aspic field of battle now contained additional toothsome ingredients, such as curled anchovies, black walnuts, herring in dill sauce, smoked oysters, a few baked apples, and a quart or so of sour cream. He was yelling splendid profanities as he sprawled and slithered around on top of the table, unable to get a firm grasp on the slippery Tiger, and luckily his eyes picked up an additional glitter just in time—standing wild-eyed at the edge of the table was the white-hatted Pierre Ecrevisse, both hands held above his head and grasping the biggest meat-cleaver north of Fourteenth Street. The chef was about to avenge the horrid desecration of his glorious cultural creation by mincing both cats, but he wasn't giving his aim adequate consideration, and Eric saw that his own neck was in jeopardy. Had he not rolled and jerked quickly, he would have been guillotined in gelatin. The cleaver came down with a crash, missing Eric by two inches and missing both cats, and now Eric made another great two-handed grab and got The Tiger by his hind legs. He closed his hands and gripped hard and began easing himself off the table. Shadrach struggled to her feet, shook herself a couple of times without any appreciable effect—she looked like something the dogs drug in—and she turned and gave Eric a long hard look, which may have had some enmity in it, and then she slipped off the table and disappeared.

Eric got his feet on the floor, still clutching The Tiger, and made his way back to the side of Diana. He handed her the cat without saying a word, and began trying to scrape many interesting things off of himself. As he stood, he would have been rejected by the garbage people.

"I don't know," he finally managed to say, "I really don't know if . . ."

A soft, calm, masculine voice spoke. "Don't worry. You got there in time. No tie was effected."

Both Diana and Eric turned and found that the speaker had been H. Allen Smith.

Diana looked at Eric and, shaking her head in wonderment, said: "He just knows *everything!*"

A noise somewhat on the order of "Glouuuuuuuuuuurrrrrrrk!" was heard in the room. A weird figure, a UCO—unidentified crawling object—came from under the big table. It struggled slowly to its feet and resolved itself into the person of Jeremy K. Jenkins. In the heat of the battle he had leaped forward, hit a slippery spot, and his feet had gone out from under him. As he went down a handful of savory Gee Bow Gai hit him in the face and he landed on top of a pastry bag the size of a full-grown straight-neck squash. Jeremy K. Jenkins, blinded by the Gee Bow Gai, thought the pastry bag was a spitting cat and began wrestling with it zestfully, with the consequence that he was soon decorated from head to toe with whipped cream. By the time he could work his way back to the side of Diana, the little exclamation-point tuft of white hair on top of his head had flabbed down flat, and his elegant 19th century clothing looked like something that had been cast aside after a picnic in the woods. As he cleared his face of the debris he said to Diana, "It would seem that we waste a frightful amount of food in this country."

Late that night two Cuban gentlemen were skulking through Central Park looking for Puerto Ricans to mug. The Cubans functioned on the theory that Puerto Ricans get their muggings over early, and at this hour would be loaded. Suddenly they saw a movement in the bushes, and tensed themselves, but it was an animal. They stepped closer, and the animal stopped and stared at them. It was a cat, a gray-looking cat with a half-drowned appearance, its head hanging low as if in weariness and deep despair.

"Boo!" cried one of the Cubans, frightened by this unkempt apparition though unafraid of predatory Puerto Ricans. The cat took off, vanishing swiftly, and that was the last ever seen in these precincts of the glamorous, platinum-haired creature known to the ateliers and the ad agencies as Shadrach. It seems probable that she made her way to some far place, on the order of Tibet, and that she changed her name to something more suitable—possibly Christine—and there lived out her days in loneliness . . . and trembling.

🐾 Chapter SIXTEEN

THE Tiger peered out at the big yellow bird standing on the runway at Westchester County Airport. The Tiger did not realize it, but the big bird was almost precisely the same smoky yellow as his own smoky yellow coat. Moreover, The Tiger did not at all apprehend that he was the owner of the big smoky yellow bird. One wonders if The Tiger might have felt some kind of intimate personal association with the big yellow bird if it were endowed with a jog in its big yellow tail.

But no, The Tiger was not being at all thoughtful about any of his surroundings, for he was not a happy cat. He, of all people . . . uh . . . that is, of all cats, knew what had happened, or what had not happened, with Shadrach, in that mound of green gelatin. The Tiger knew that no tie had been effected, and he was a creature with a powerful inclination toward effecting ties.

Around the corner of a nearby building lurked two men, and they too were eyeing the big yellow bird. They could see the word BANNER done in bold black lettering on the fuselage, forward of the wings, but the insignia wasn't needed to tell them that this was the flagship of the private fleet of jets maintained by Banner Enterprises.

"There they go," growled Ogden Crump. "Look at that Yaeger!

Coyotin' around, marchin' out there like he's King of the Wahl Frontier! He shore recommends hisself mighty high!"

"Diana's with him," observed Mister Muff, who was in civilian attire, meaning that he was playing himself, meaning also that he was not in drag. "She's got the cat, and now—there's Old Jenkins hop-scotching along with some other girl . . ."

"Tiddyboo," said Crump. Muff gave him an annoyed glance, then continued, ". . . and the fat guy—I suppose he's the one they call Doom. I only got a glimpse of him at the house this afternoon. Ogden, that Araminta bit came off beautifully. And Orlando was . . ."

The name of Orlando galvanized Ogden Crump. "Come on, Muff," he interrupted, seizing the Master Spy by the arm. "Le's git back to the car—Ah don't wanna leave Orlando with the señorita one extra minute. He's workin' on that sweet girl hard as he can, and Ah figure fair's fair. She belongs to me. If innybody's gonna git it, it oughta be me."

"Now, Ogden," Muff objected as they headed toward the parking area. "Señorita Tornillo is a relative of mine, I mean in a way, by marriage, and I intend to look out for her until I find out what Cousin Clyde wants done about her."

"Cousin Clyde my calloused hind end!" Crump responded. "Cousin *Petticoats*, you mean! Ah won't stand by and leave that filthy petticoat-lifter lay a dirty finger on that sweet thang."

"You don't know my cousin," Muff reminded him. "Petticoats is a very charming guy. Full of spirit, full of gay youthful spirit, got a bank full of money *without* the ranch. Suppose he does have that one little weakness . . ."

"One *little* weakness! One *little* weakness, he says! You call pushin' up a decent girl's petticoat a *little* weakness? Way Ah hear it, that chili-powder horny-handed son of a bitch is a zipperjerkin' menace to the whole State of Taixuss."

They arrived beside the car where Orlando Dill was engaged in deep conference with the beautiful Señorita Blanca Tornillo. Orlando had an arm draped around the Señorita's shoulder and was giving Spanish the old try, murmuring, "Bonita Blanca esta planty sexeee." Crump winced, and when Bonita Blanca responded in a lullaby tone, "*Ah, muchas gracias, señor . . . muy amable!*" the angry Texan began jerking his head around in a gesture of chagrin and bitter distress.

Muff left the group, went to a booth in a nearby hangar, and put in a person-to-person call for Mr. Clyde Kockamaney at Aveinte, Texas. The call went through the switchboard at Alpine, and Muff heard the New York operator sing out, "Aveinte!" The Alpine operator responded with, "Same to you, whoever you are, and the mule you rode in on!" This bit of overland exercise in Volapuk confused both Muff and the New York operator, but neither felt inclined to put forward an argument, and soon Muff had his party.

"Clyde," he said, "this is Muff. Millard Muffgainer. You all set?"

"Yawl-ud better believe it," said the Texan known as Petticoats.

"The cat and his people should hit your strip about daylight. We'll be along a couple of hours later."

"Got that Mescan bitch with yuh?"

"She's here. Now listen, coz, I want you to play it nice with her at the start. She's a lot sharper than you think. We can't let this thing get away from us. Crump's amusing himself with a plan to kill the cat, and I'm humoring him along, but we'll play it our way. And one thing more. Don't start killing and shooting and slashing people right off the bat. These are not Chivo County folks, so you and your boys keep your guns in the leather."

"Cousin Muff," drawled Petticoats, "Ah gotta idee Ah'm gonna kick you rat in the butt oncet you git out heah. You quit a givin' me awduhs! See you in th' mawnin'."

The yellow Banner jet was halfway across Jersey before Jeremy Jenkins and Diana had finished inspecting the stunning interior of the flying lounge. The exquisite taste of the celebrated decorator Nancy Van Noppenheim was reflected in every warm detail of the plane's interior. The paneling was in pecky pecan—the paint first applied and then rubbed off while wet, leaving a slight haze of citron yellow, the shade of a not-quite-ripe lemon. Karastan's custom-dyed Malaren carpeting lay wall-to-wall, a bright shade of yellowish green, darkening off to progressions of gold toward the outer edges. Built-in bookshelves stood in split pairs at each end of the cabin, their backs painted in deep gold. One of Herman Miller's Action office desks in oiled walnut, with polished stainless steel legs, stood on the right beneath one of the five picture windows. These windows were draped in Boris Kroll's Shibui silk. In the center, at the right, was Thomasville's loose pillowback sofa quilted in shades of beige, gold and green, and beside it a Heritage wing chair in an inside-outside print. Before the sofa stood a classically simple cocktail table with a Glenstone top. And beside the bookshelves on the lavatory wall was a square game table with a map of the Western Hemisphere impregnated in plastic, set into the top so that passengers might follow the course of the flight while indulging in knock rummy, chemin de fer, or klaberjass. Around this table stood Knoll chairs upholstered in a gold tweed. Across the cabin, arrayed along the wall beneath three of the picture windows, were five of Henredon's swivel-rockers in Schumacher's crushed gold velvet. Interspersed among the chairs were small accessory tables of pecky pecan from the elegant Founders line.

And then the commanding presence, the focal point, the keystone of the entire decorative scheme—a striking portrait of Rhubarb, done in smoke yellow by Leo Hershfield, the artist who from the beginning had been associated with the career of the fabulous cat. It is worth noting that in this handsome likeness, the jog in Rhubarb's tail struck the eye immediately—like a sloppy watch in a Salvadore Dali painting.

Eric suggested to Diana that she let The Tiger out of his carrier so he might roam around the lounge and get accustomed to the surroundings.

"He won't move," she said, "unless he can have his red leash on."

"Oh God!" groaned Eric, imploring Heaven's aid by lifting both his eyes and his hands in the general direction of Paradise.

So Diana let the cat out and he moved down the lounge, trailing the red rag. He sniffed at things and, reaching the far end, turned around and started back. By chance he raised his head and saw something that stopped him dead. He moved on a few steps until he was squarely in front of his Daddy's portrait. He sat down and stared steadily, without moving, at Rhubarb. The jog in his tail was tranquil and quiescent. He sat thus for six or eight minutes, staring, not moving except for a slight cocking of his head from time to time.

Eric suddenly noticed him and was both amused and astonished.

"We've got to have a picture of this," he told Diana. "You have a camera on board?"

"Nope."

"See if you can find one."

Diana made the rounds, even to the cockpit. Seven persons aboard, and not a single camera—a rank perversion of the whole institution of civilized travel.

As his sense of wonderment diminished, Eric began to worry. He summoned Doom.

"The Tiger," he said, "is likely to turn into some kind of a lunatic cat if we don't get him away from that picture—he'll wind up with a split personality, or he might turn into a manic-depressive. Better put him back in the carrier."

Doom was reaching for him when The Tiger moved. He uttered a snarl that would have done credit to a Royal Bengal tiger. He slashed at Doom's hand and missed, and Doom moved rapidly to safer ground. "My God," exclaimed the fat man, "he *has* turned into a maniac depressy!"

Eric and Diana approached their boss slowly, carefully, talking to him in soothing tones. Diana reached down and picked him up and he made no protest of any kind. A minute later he was back in the cage.

"I don't believe," observed Eric, "that in the whole history of the world there has ever been such an unusual display of filial affection."

Eric and Diana had a look at the two lavatories just aft of the card table area, and found that unlike those on most jets, these were not communal cubicles. One was for males and one for females. The deft Van Noppenheim touch was in evidence here, too. It was Miss Van Noppenheim's whim to avoid such cute designations as "Damas" and "Caballeros" or "Fillies" and "Stallions" or black silhouettes of male and female figures. In a stroke of decorative genius, she had employed simple lettering on the doors, saying "Men" and "Women." Perhaps Miss Van Noppenheim's single concession to the urge for frivolity among the better class of travelers was to be found inside the washrooms—neat metal signs purloined from French railway trains, inscribed:

> On est prié de ne pas tirer la chaine des cabinets lorsque le train est en gare.

The plane was already streaking across the Shenandoah Valley when Diana and Jenkins started back to their seats. Eric was now seated on the couch and from somewhere in outer space there had

materialized an eye-taking creature. Eric had an accumulation of telegrams and letters in his lap and a young lady at his side. The young lady was shortish, with hair the shade of polished bronze, startlingly wide blue eyes, a cleverly-made little snub nose, and just a hint of freckles surrounding it. Her body was encased in two principal garments—a yellowish green button-up shirt which was not buttoned up excessively, and tan shorts. She was stacked, this girl. Even Jeremy Jenkins permitted his patriarchal eye a rather lengthy inspection of her parts and portions, and the thought crossed his mind that she was a modern version of the Nancy Carroll whose mere appearance on the silent screen led men to whicker and whinny back in the days when sound was a tree falling unnoticed in a Zen forest. This girl, this delicious bit of Ireland, was listed in Social Security's Baltimore files as Nora

O'Neill; the people in Baltimore had no reason to record the name by which she was known to her employer: Miss Tiddyboo. She was one of his several secretaries and at the moment, high above Virginia apple orchards, she was taking dictation.

Eric was talking rapidly: ". . . you have the address, say my dear sir colon, even if I were in a position to authorize it, The Tiger capitalize The and Tiger Tiddyboo . . . The Tiger would not endorse the latest Literary Guild selection quote To Be Worried or Teased unquote period new paragraph It makes no difference that the author is a cat dash dash The Tiger is not a cat comma he is The Tiger comma and he has none of the talents of either Clifton Fadiman or Martin Levin period yours and so forth . . . Now, Tiddyboo, this to Mr. T. Cayuse Callahan, Cheyenne, Wyoming, Dear T. Cayuse I'm sorry but The Tiger won't be able to reign as King over the Cheyenne rodeo this year period apparently he inherits many traits of his father and you must remember what happened to poor Rhubarb when that square-shaped Brahma steer pawed and pummeled him half to death in your arena period I'm sure The Tiger would be leery of all cattle-critters and anyway we've gone to Texas on important business period love to the family yours and so forth and now one to Mayor Lindsay . . ."

A slightly shrill voice broke into the drone of dictation:

"Just what the bleeding hell is going on here?" It was the voice of Diana, who was standing over Eric and Miss Tiddyboo, glaring down at them—mainly at Miss Tiddyboo. "Who do you think you are?" she demanded of Eric, "taking over in *my* month. I should be making those decisions, not you."

"Now, Diana," Eric spoke patiently, and then to Miss Nora O'Neill, "Go on back and type up what you've got, Tiddyboo."

"All righty," said Miss Tiddyboo, springing off the sofa. "Okiedokie," she added with great good cheer, and then, "Yes, indeedy!" With which she went bouncing along to the walnut desk.

Diana's eyes followed her, noting all, and then she dropped into the seat beside Eric. "The young lady," she said disagreeably, "is poetic, in a revolting sort of way. She knows how to utter a strong affirmative. She says yes with great emphasis."

"I train my help well," said Eric, smiling down at her, noting the cross look she was wearing, enjoying it.

"You don't dress them well," Diana observed. "Miss Tiddyboob's costume is . . . *well!*"

"Tiddyboo, not Tiddyboob," Eric corrected her. Then his mood changed. "Hey kid," he urged, "come off it." He passed a friendly fist an inch from her chin. "Nora's a swell little gal and very efficient and you . . ."

"Oh!" Diana exclaimed. "Oh, my! We know her *real* name, too! Nora! Great heavens! Some day we may find out that she even has a last name! Tiddyboo, perhaps! Miss Nora Tiddyboo! Or Miss Nora Buttyboo! God! What is this, a flying hook shop?"

"Knock it off, Diana," Eric remonstrated. "I want to talk to you about something. Where's The Tiger?"

"Back in back," she snapped. "Why don't you just get a charter for a flying Playboy Club, get Rudi Gurnreich to pin his hair up for a day and design you a topless dress for airborne stenographers? I don't know why I should have to sail through the air with this hussy, tossing her Irish tits and her Hibernian ass all over the tonneau, or whatever the hell you call it!"

Eric flung back his head and laughed long and gratifyingly. This was great! Tremendous! Beautiful Diana was boiling with jealousy! She sat fuming until he had finished his orgy of laughter.

"And now, Miss Corset-cover," he finally said, "you'd better lay off my Miss Tiddyboo. I assure you that to me she's no more than a dictating machine, somewhat fleshed out. She's much the same as this aircraft—all modern conveniences."

"I hate to think," Diana said, her lips scarcely moving, "I really hate to think what *that* might mean."

"Please! Forget Nora. I'll let you in on a little secret. I think she's out of her skull about Captain Cogswell up front. And kindly simmer down about my handling this correspondence. I'm accustomed to it, been at it for years. I know how to brush these people off and still keep them happy. You don't need to bother your pretty head with these things." She turned and looked at him and gave him just a faint glimmer of her crinkly little grin. He put a hand gently on her arm, and her manner grew a degree or so warmer. "The thing you need to worry about," he went on, "is to avoid such a nuthouse episode as occurred this afternoon. We can't have . . ."

"What episode is that?"

"Those two dopey women throwing that platinum cat squarely in The Tiger's path, trying to get some kittens out of him . . ."

"Oh God!" cried Diana. "Less than ten minutes on this plane

and you're dragging in sex! I suppose you've got beds on board with some kind of sideways drift to compensate for hitting air pockets, and that half-naked tiddy-swinger back there . . ."

"Diana," said Eric firmly, "I want you to stop these outbursts or we'll be back in that courtroom in a week. We're snarled up together in the operation of a complicated business empire. We should be talking over the plan of action when we get to Texas. If you'll just get your mind off sex for a . . ."

"Me!" she cried. "Me! Trapped like a rat forty miles above sea level by some kind of a sex maniac! You got a set of whips on this plane?"

Eric pretended to ignore this outburst. "I've got to come back to one thing," he said firmly. "That godawful red rag. You've got to get that rag off of The Tiger. He'll be the laughing-stock of the entire financial world if . . ."

"That red rag stays," said Diana. "It stays as long as he's in my charge. And if you try to burn it when you get custody, I'll take you to court, and I'll win. You'd look pretty stupid, getting hauled into court because you want to take an old red rag away from a cat when the cat loves the old red rag. Talk about a laughing-stock! Even your precious Miss Tiddyboo back there would be laughing at you!"

"Will . . . you . . . kindly . . . get . . . your . . . dirty . . . mind . . . off . . . Nora!" Eric shouted. "She's a kid, almost a child!"

"Not out front!"

"She's the new generation, Diana! They don't care anything about sex. They've got other ways of getting their kicks. You ought to know that. My God, you can read, can't you? Sex is going out of style. Before long when kids want to have babies, they'll get it some other way—in some other form—like, say, in their pancake batter."

"Hah!" snorted Diana.

"Yes, in their pancake batter! Eat a stack of wheats and get yourself a blessed event! These young girls today are all frigid and full of . . ."

"Nuts!" proclaimed Diana. "Nuts! *Nuts!* NUTS! What kind of girls do you mess around with? You've been too fouled up by this damn corporation of yours—all this money has poisoned your mind." She was heading back into her semi-hysterical state. "You are a j-e-r-k, JERK! A pancake-batter jerk! You ought to get out of your corporate shell and put on rags like Good King Winky-sless or whoever it was in that Bing Crosby picture, go out and mix with your subjects you big horse's ass, you might get a few surprises about what kind of girls we have around today, and as for me, I'm going back there and sit down and give some thought to my future. I'm damn well tired of being told what to do by a cat power-structure. You can take it and . . ." She groped for the correct word, and came up with one that was good enough, ". . . and poke it!"

Eric made no move to stop her, but sat and stared at the coffee table a while, and then had Miss Tiddyboo, who was doubling this night as stewardess, bring him a strong bourbon highball. He was sipping it when Doom came up and sat down with him.

"Eric," he said, clasping and unclasping his fat hands, "what about this Texas? I've always bleeved in live and leave live and leave good enough alone."

"Wait a minute, Doom," Eric interrupted him. "Leave me as-similate that last sentiment. All right. I think I've got it. Proceed."

"These Texas citizens are mean, Eric. They hang a rope up in a tree and put people on a horse and slap the horse out from under and leave them floppin' around in the air like sick herrings. All they do in their taverns is fight. Least little thing, and them Texans will pick up a table and break it over your head, or throw you clean through the front winda."

"They don't have any saloons any more in Texas," Eric said.

"Same people, though," argued Doom. "So they throw you clean through the front winda of a cafeteria. I don't like it. I was gettin' along fine, writin' my book, and now this. This Texas. My God, Eric, the tracks at Laurel and Pimligo is as far Out West as I ever been, unless you count Rockingham. This Pres'dent we got, I hear he comes from Texas, *acts* like a nice man, but looka the size of 'im! Wouldn't surprise me none if he started throwin' embassadors through the front winda of the White House."

"Doom," Eric said a bit wearily, "you've got a mistaken notion about Texas and the Texans. I've been in Texas lots of times, all over Texas. The only thing that's wrong with them is that they're like people everywhere else, only a bit moreso. You take a New Yorker, he's mean, isn't he?"

"Mean as they come."

"A Texan is generally meaner. Take your New Yorker again—

he's greedy, underhanded, conniving, deceitful, heart full of larceny. Right?"

"The dirty scum!" breathed Doom. "Steal you blind in both eyes!"

"A Texan," Eric went on, "has the New Yorker outpointed. A Texan has a higher dishonesty quotient. Now, let's look once more at the New Yorker. He's a killer. It's not safe to walk the streets at night. You take your life in your hands going into the subway after dark. You know all about this, Doom. Well, it's the same way in Texas, only maybe just a little worse."

"Why do they hafta be worse about everything?"

"Because they're bigger."

"I'm bigger than most people," argued Doom, "but that don't mean I hafta be meaner and crookeder. I been hearin' talk about this Texas for a long time. Everywhere you look they got coppers they call law man. On horses, in airplanes, got black masts over their eyes. Can I pack a rod out there, Eric?"

"We'll see."

Eric gave him a hearty slap on the shoulder. "I don't think you've got a thing to worry about from the Texans," he said. Then he glanced down the lounge and saw Diana, sitting alone, her head buried in her hands, great sobs convulsing her body. He hurried down to her and took a chair beside her and put his arm around her.

"Come on now, Diana," he pleaded, and she raised her head. She had been convulsed with laughter, and her face was wet with tears.

"I just got to remembering . . ." she gasped out, "how you looked . . . sprawled out on top of that table . . . in all that mess . . . sliding around in the goo . . . yelling bloody murder! Yeeeeee—heeeeee—yeeeeeeee! How I'd love to have a movie of it!"

And Eric, remembering it, broke up along with her and they sat laughing and talking about the great sloppy events of the afternoon. Then Jeremy K. Jenkins, sitting nearby with a book, put it down and joined them and soon he too was howling with glee as Diana described his appearance as he came from under the table, the spent pastry bag clutched in his arms, all his Pickwickian dignity enveloped in a shimmering cocoon of pure whipped cream.

Before long they touched down at San Antonio's International Airport. It was around three in the morning and colorful San Antonio was asleep, oblivious to the fleeting presence of the owner of Banner Enterprises. The Tiger peered out through an aperture of his carrier and had his first look at Texas. He had no idea, of course, that he was in the Great State, and he had no inkling of the wild and woolly adventures that lay ahead for him in the cattle country. He yawned as he was carried aboard the smaller plane. A cat may looke on a King.

The airstrip outside the town of Aveinte was just long enough to accommodate the Cessna when it came in two hours later. The beginning of a bright dawn was discernible in the far sky but a blue darkness lay over the landing strip. The plane turned around and started rolling back toward a small dobe structure where two automobiles were waiting. As it trundled along, its passengers peered through the windows, hoping for a glimpse of the town of Aveinte. They didn't see it, but they saw something else.

Out of the greasewood and mesquite and cactus alongside the strip came a ghostly procession of rumbling and roaring machines, slow-moving motorcycles. One by one they came out of the sand and onto the runway and then in single file, picking up speed, they shot away, swerved into a paved road, and then onto the main artery leading to the town—the six-lane Billy Sol Estes Freeway. There must have been two dozen of them.

Once on the ground Doom took The Tiger out of his carrier and fastened on his red rag. Eric and Diana were standing staring off toward the town, toward the slowly receding noise of the motorcycles.

"Eric," Doom spoke. "The Tiger's tail is jerkin' a little."

"Good," said Eric.

✿ Chapter SEVENTEEN

THE plane which Ogden Crump and his little band of conspirators took out of Westchester County Airport was a company jet painted a dusty green, maintained by the Quality Lawn Mower Repair Service of Thornwood, New York. Crump of course could no longer use any of the Banner planes, and he certainly would not demean himself by riding in any commercial aircraft. He had been able to borrow the green plane from Dominic Vigoro, chairman of the board of Quality, who was married to one of Crump's distant cousins. It was by no means as regal as the big yellow bird of Banner, but it had a lounge (only aviational squares would keep a company plane containing orderly rows of tilt-seats). There were no built-in bookshelves, just a knockabout magazine rack stocked with publications relating to the lawn mower industry. The sofa was a mere loveseat, and the portrait above it was of Giacomo Vigoro, father to Dominic, who began life as an olive pitter in old Calabria and lived to found the Quality Lawn Mower Repair Service of Thornwood, New York.

Orlando Dill was indulging in an alcoholic sulk as the plane shot away from Westchester. He found himself a chair and a bottle of vodka and settled down with his darkling thoughts. He was unhappy over the way things were working out. For one thing, he and Muff had quarreled about the Araminta episode at the Banner house.

"You and your god damn sand trap!" the lawyer snarled at the former espionage agent after they got away from the party. "If *that* wasn't the clumsiest piece of business I've seen outside of Minsky's old burlesque houses!"

"I got away with it," Muff countered. "I thought fast and played the Texas dame to the hilt and got us off the hook."

"What you did," bawled Orlando, "was to play the part of my sister, *my* sister, as if she were bucking for mongoloid idiot. What do you suppose that does to my reputation around town?"

"Orlando, if I were you, I wouldn't speak a great deal about my reputation around town."

"Practicing your *aye-yut arn!* In a dark closet! I'll never get over it!"

Muff turned away and called out instructions to all to drag up chairs for a conference.

"Just one by-god minute!" Crump interjected. "Who put *you* in charge of this here operation? Who made *you* the commanduh-in-chief?"

"Somebody's got to be the leader," argued Muff, "and I . . ."

"Ah happen to have seniority here," said Crump, "and Ah intend to run this show. Ah want everybody to understand that rat now. If they's anybody here don't like it, they better buy theirself a through ticket to hell-and-gone and try to ketch th' next train. Now, spy boy, you tell us what you know about this Kockamaney bird."

Muff began with his own grandfather, who was a Kockamaney and who had broken with the rest of the family over a matter of business ethics. He had washed his hands of the chili powder trade just when it was beginning to prosper, just when the Kockamaney profits were going into high rise. He had taken his family off to Menard County where he finished out his life as a pecan grower on the San Saba, refusing even to visit San Antonio where the chili powder industry was centered. His daughter married Cletus Muffgainer from San Angelo and after the old man died and Oklahoma tunkworms got into the pecans, the Muffgainers moved to Lancaster, Pennsylvania, taking with them their only child, ten-year-old Millard. He hadn't lived in Texas quite long enough for the hot mush dialect to frizzle his tongue, and his father hated the Lone Star State and every Kockamaney in it. "Never tell anybody you was borned in Texas," he told little Millard. "Anybody asks you, tell 'em you're Pennsylvania Dutch. On both sides."

In the lounge of the westward-winging green jet Muff told how he had made contact with his cousin Clyde in later years, and found him to be a young man with a rough exterior, spoiled by wealth, lacking education, yet withal a man of quality and good will.

This statement brought a shrill protest from Señorita Blanca.

"He is dirty peeg!" she cried out. "He pushes up the petticoats!" Her outburst was so emotional that she pushed up her own quite a distance by way of illustrating her point. "He pushes up the petticoats!" she repeated, "and all peoples knows this, and all peoples name him Petticoats. Sawn a bitch, I no trost heem!"

"Blanca," Muff advised her, "please try to keep your emotions in check, and don't think of him as Petticoats—think of him as Clyde—that may help."

"All the same," she said, cooling off a trifle, "I would like to joke him by the neck."

Muff shrugged and glanced at Dill, who was grinning drunkenly, and pursued his exposition of Kockamaney family history. It was good for him to explore all the details again—he was not at all positive yet about the direction he would jump when jumping time came. In spying, it is advisable to stay loose and resilient. Muff knew he had a powerful weapon in his possession—the information his grandfather had gasped out just before he died—the thing the old man had found wrong with the Kockamaney chili powder business, the hateful discovery that led him to turn his back on a fortune. Muff had heard this deathbed revelation and had kept the secret down through the years. Now, if necessary, he was ready to bring it into the open. But he had to have help, the help of these people in the plane with him, and so he told them what he knew.

"If it becomes necessary," he said, "I am prepared to blow the entire chili powder complex sky high. I'll brown the Texas heavens with mushroom clouds of Kockamaney chili powder. What we have to do is cultivate Petticoats. We'll cultivate him with flattery. He's trying for a court order forestalling the sale of the ranch to Banner. He knows about the gold mine and he knows that someone tipped off Blanca about it. I think the time has come, Señorita, for you to tell us just who did give you the tip."

"I will spick," she answered, "only when we come to Aveinte."

Muff frowned, and then continued: "Let me fill you people in on the ranch itself. The entire Kockamaney chili powder business got its start there. The first batch was made right in the kitchen of the original ranch house. Back in those days all the essential ingredients were known—the ancho chilies were grown right there, the oregano came from the ranch, so did the garlic. The cumin seed, so important to the final flavor, was a Syrian importation sent out to Texas by a New York jobber. That's the way it all started. Eventually a small factory was opened in Aveinte and they began putting the stuff in jars. The operation went along on a piddling scale for thirty years and then something happened —Kockamaney chili powder began to catch on—there was a great clamor for it all over Texas. This happened while Jedediah Kockamaney was head of the firm. The story goes that Jedediah slipped a new ingredient into the powder, something that propelled it swiftly to top rank in the chili powder market. It is known that just before World War Two, the Kockamaney salesmen were traveling around Texas with a sort of whispering campaign, in which they imputed certain special powers to the new and improved product they were peddling. One of these salesmen would go into a store with a sample of the chili powder and say to the storekeeper, behind his hand, 'We got some guzzoom in it now that's good for the old yummmmmmmph!' As he spoke that last word he'd do this . . ." Muff demonstrated how the salesman would strike his right bicep with his left hand, bringing his right fist flying abruptly upward into the posture of the Arm & Hammer soda insignia, without the hammer. "Then," Muff went on, "the salesman would repeat the word bullsnortingly, 'YUMMMMMMMPH!' As you folks may know, this sort of whispering campaign on behalf of a product is common to the food business, even today, and biceps have been smacked and forearms have flown upward on behalf of clam juices, sesame seed confections, pork sausages, certain patent medicines with secret alcoholic whomp, and so on. Whether it was true that Kockamaney chili powder caused certain biological . . . uh . . . upswing, especially among middleaged people, is not at all certain, but the fact stands that the public still believes it does, and you don't fool around with public sentiment when you're in . . ."

"What is about this?" Blanca interrupted. "This I do not hear before. Is it only the chili powder that makes my hosbon push up the petticoats?"

"Precisely, my dear," gurgled Orlando Dill from his chair in the corner, "and when we get this miserable flying lawn mower onto solid Texas ground, I'm going to have a go at that secret ingredient." He waggled a masterful forefinger at Blanca and said to her, "My little road-running double-breasted bunting, you and I are going to wolf down gallons of chili loaded with Kockerninny chili powder."

"Kockamaney," Muff corrected. "And Dill, by the time we get there you won't be able to tell a bowl of chili from a barrel of molasses."

Dill turned his head slowly and closing one eye, contemplated Muff with the other, trying to achieve a satanic look. "Kocka-minny," he said with dripping scorn. "Klickamockey, Kocka-nanny, Minnykocka, Nannycockle, Kockarobin . . . bugger 'em all! . . . what I'm gonna do is put the stuff in a bottle of vodka and then sprinkle in some cumin seed and . . ." His voice trailed off, and Ogden Crump glared at him, and remarked, "Look at 'im! Already so drunk he couldn't piss through a bob-warr fence!" The lawyer now focused his eyes on Crump, and looked at him a good long time, without any sign of intense admiration.

"Ah'm beginnin' to think," added Crump, "that we might consider snubbin' Orlando to a tree stump somewhere out in the woods, oncet we git into action."

"He may be all right after a little sleep," offered Muff. "Now, let me make it clear why I've been telling you all this history of the Kockamaneys and their chili powder. There's much more to this picture than just a ranch and a gold mine. I'm sure of it."

They came in to San Antonio a few minutes later and waiting for Crump at the airport was a stoutly-built, brown-skinned man in a dark suit, string tie and curly-brimmed Texas hat. Crump introduced him as Albert Apple from Corpus Christi and the two men did a good deal of back-slapping and calling each other y'ole-pieball-summbitch back and forth.

"It'd be hahd for you folks to bleeve," said Crump, "but ole Albert and me went to school together. Show 'em your hawg-laig, Albert." Mr. Apple flipped back his coat, revealing a stubby automatic in a shoulder holster.

"Little ole thang ain't very prepossessin'," admitted Crump, "but if it was the size of a Winchester eighty-eight they still wouldn't be room enough for Albert's notches. You ole summbitch! This bassud kill his *grandma* for twenny-nine say-ents."

"Pluh-yuss say-yulls ta-yux," drawled Albert Apple, smiling.

A Beechcraft was being warmed up for the flight on to Aveinte and Crump drew his old schoolmate to one side.

"Ogg," said Albert Apple in a confidential voice, "somethin' done happen to you say-ence you went up Nawth. You losin' that nice Taixuss accent you used to have. You gittin' so you talk Yankee—you've took on a sawt of a Nawthen nasal twang. Hod-amighty, Ogg, you kin eat their black fish aigs, and their snay-yulls and their puny calf meat, but doan git to talkin' like they talk. Y'own people won't be able tuh undahstan' you."

"No mattuh whut," said Ogden Crump, reassuringly, "mah hot is a-gonna ree-main deep inna hot uh Taixuss. Albert, ole fren, thass a wuhd with a bock on it!"

The two men launched into a business discussion and if a third party had been within earshot, he might have felt that they understood the starkly sharp and clean language they employed, one to the other. It is remotely possible that they did. In part.

"Ogg," Albert Apple finally said, "Ah tell you Ah cain't do it. A cat. Ah seen that cat's picture in the *Caller-Times*. Ah couldn't shoot that little ole pussy cat."

"Then strangle 'im," pressed Ogden Crump.

"Ah jest couldn't haul off an' kill a cat," Albert Apple insisted. "A man, shuah. A woman, of co'se. But a cat? No, suh, Ogg—it's jest so sorta helpless like. Ain't they some othuh way?"

Crump thought about it.

"God dern you, Albert," he finally exploded, "Ah thought Ah could dee-pend on you. Well, it's too late for me to git me anutha fella up from Corpus. Ah mean Cawpuss. But Ah got me anutha idee. Listen careful now, Albert."

He told the Corpus gunslinger to go out and hire a large panel truck, and take it this very morning to a sign painter, and have the words "Humane Society—Chivo County" painted on it. Then he was to drive the truck to Aveinte and on to the Bowlared Ranch.

"We'll figga out some way to git aholt of that cat," Crump said, "and you can kidnap 'im and git 'im down to Cawpuss an' latuh awn Ah'll figga some way to diss-pose of 'im."

"That," said Albert Apple, "sounds more good-mannered an' gentle. But what's th' sign on th' panel truck for?"

"They's a new kinda business entaprise," exclaimed Ogden, "that maybe ain't got down to Taixuss yet. Stealin' dawgs an' cats. Sellin' dawgs an' cats tuh th' vivv-sectionists. Big profits in it now days. You got to staht out by kidnapin' th' animals an' if you got that truck with th' sign on it, nobody pays you inny mind. Now, Albert, crack yuh ass an' git that truck on th' road."

Albert cracked it.

Muff now approached Crump and said: "I heard part of that. Will you kindly explain why you want to have that cat killed? That's not the idea at all. You always seem to be going against the grain. What good would killing the golden goose do?"

"Ah got mah notions," Crump replied, and jutting his chin forward, added, "You listen to me, you snoopin' little twerp. Ah catch you spyin' on me one more time an Ah'll sick ole Albert Apple on *you!*"

Slight dissension in the enemy camp.

ɛ☿ʒ Chapter EIGHTEEN

CONSIDER the word *aroint*. Not exactly a pleasant or mellifluous seeming word at first blush . . . but, then, it was churlish old Thomas Carlyle who said that the first impression of a work of genius is usually disagreeable.

Lexicographers have traced *aroint* back to Elizabeth Barrett Browning, who took it to mean the act of driving someone away with an execration; either she, or her dog Flush, *arointed* some cats, causing them to flee. She was a sickly woman.

Earlier the word was employed by Scott, who gave it a similar meaning: Begone! Or, Avaunt! Pencils should have been kept beyond the reach of Sir Walter. He wasn't well.

The earliest employment of *aroint* is found in Shakespeare. He used it in *King Lear* and again in *Macbeth*, two of his murder stories. The First Witch in *Macbeth* asks a woman for some chestnuts which she has in her lap, and the woman responds, "Aroint thee, witch!" This woman with the chestnuts in her lap is described as a "rump-fed ronyon." A ronyon, in those silly times, was either "a mangy creature" or "the male member." Take your choice. The lexicographers suggest that Shakespeare was using *aroint* to mean what Sir Walter Scott took it to mean: Begone! Avaunt! A careful study of the evidence indicates that the lexicographers are full of stool. In the light of present-day research it would appear that Shakespeare meant something altogether different when he had that rump-fed ronyon holler, "Aroint thee, witch!" It must be admitted that, in many respects, the Varlet of Avon didn't know his arse from second base; certainly his stuff is dated, and surely we may say that it is contrived. Yet, when Shakespeare set down the word *aroint*, he knew full well what it meant. It is employed today, in the latter part of the Twentieth Century, as a euphemism for a four-letter word, which four-letter word is not often seen in print, save in current novels of a distressingly vulgar character. The euphemism *aroint* is being kept in lively circulation by certain jazz musicians. "Aroint you, Jack!" a trombone player will say to a trumpeter, and he does not mean, "Begone! Avaunt!" A lovely girl dances past the bandstand, and the piano player calls out to the drummer, "How'd you like to aroint *that* a dozen or so times?" These jazz musicians are not, as a general rule, of the progressive persuasion—they are the type of characters who indulge themselves joyously in Dixieland, and casual arointing around.

This divagation anent *aroint* is necessary for the reason that we approach a point in our narrative where the temptation is strong to use the more formidable word, the four-letter baby. There are times when a paragraph cries out, almost pitifully, for that splendidly vile vocable. But this is a proper book, and tidy. Such a word has no place in its pages. Aroint it!

In 1881 the Southern Pacific rails reached El Paso and the line was opened from New Orleans to the Pacific Coast. Two years later a locomotive on a westbound passenger train was stalled for a day and a half in the Doodah Desert section of Chivo County, Texas. Immobilized for thirty-six hours, the occupants of the stalled train tried to evade boredom by playing cards and by reading magazines and such recent book successes as *Five Little Peppers and How They Grew*, and Riley's *The Old Swimmin' Hole and 'Leven More Poems*, and *Ben-Hur*. Current literature, in fact, provoked the only real exciting diversion of the long wait. A Louisiana plantation owner and a sawmill proprietor from Beaumont engaged in an argument which culminated in their stepping off the train, divesting themselves of their coats and stiff collars, and fighting with their fists for ten minutes or so. Their disagreement had been over possession of a popular book of the period,

181

Hannah Whitall Smith's *The Christian Secret of a Happy Life.*

Early on the morning of the second day, a hairy old man arrived beside the train astride a donkey. His clothing was in tatters, his donkey was a bag of inferior bones, and he drooled a good deal from the nose. He called himself Murdo Chisum. He said he was a prospector, that he was a member of an old and respected Texas family, and he offered to show a group of passengers some of the interesting features of the countryside if they were willing to pay him in hard money. A dozen ladies and gentlemen accepted, and he escorted them across the landscape, lecturing in a lazy patois that was barely intelligible to the sophisticated travelers. He identified plants by names unknown to botany, and he called rock formations things that journeymen geologists had never heard about, but eventually he did point out a jackrabbit and identify it as a jackrabbit. Finally he arrived at a spot where there was a tremendous cleft in a mountain, which he said was Sniveling Dog Canyon.

"Oh," exclaimed one of the ladies, "I've always wanted to see a real canyon! Why do they call it Sniveling Dog Canyon?"

"Oncet a dawg sniveled in yonder," said the guide.

"I have heard," the lady went on, "that if you cry out, the words will echo back. Please give us an echo, Mr. Chisum!"

Murdo Chisum faced into Sniveling Dog Canyon, pulled a lot of hair away from his mouth, and howled:

"Aroint you!"

Back came a far-off sounding voice.

"*A veinte!*" it said.

Old Chisum grinned and turned to his little group of tourists. "That there," he said, "was a Mescan echo." He faced back into the canyon and howled:

"An' th' mule you rode in on!" No further words came back.

One of the ladies in the group stood in thought, murmuring the pretty word that came out of the canyon. "*A veinte!*" she repeated, striving for the Spanish inflection. She asked Murdo Chisum what it meant.

"Ma'am," he drawled, "it means twenny times."

"Twenty times what?"

"Twenny times back at you, an' th' mule you rode in on."

The lady didn't quite understand, but her fascination with "*A veinte!*" stayed with her. She was the wife of another sawmill owner from Beaumont, an irascible man who thought his home town was getting too god damn many sawmills in it, and so he was thinking about moving on west, even founding a town of his own. His name was Cyrus Kockamaney and a few years later he did start up his own town a few miles from the entrance to Sniveling Dog Canyon. At the urging of his wife, he named the town Aveinte.

A nice name, as Texas place names go. But please note how close the settlement came to being called Aroint.

Eric led his little band on a long walk, traversing the length of Aveinte's main street as far north as a large Baptist church, crossing over, then walking all the way back toward a restaurant where they would have breakfast. Striding along beside Eric was Morgan Heath, the big Texan who had originally brought Simon Horney to Aveinte and who was now in charge of the Bowlared Ranch. Heath was a mining engineer with a special talent for solving problems concerned with the froth flotation of ores, and he functioned as a freelance all over the Southwest and in Mexico. Of him it was said admiringly, in mining circles, "That big bassud can froth flotate innythang on earth that can be froth flotated!" Usually followed by the comment, "An' then some!" Heath was six feet five, as brown as saddle leather, as loaded with *virilidad* as Richard Burton, and as tough as tenpenny nails. Make it sixteen-penny.

Doom was carrying The Tiger, while Miss Nora O'Neill, now clad in beige stretchpants and a green blouse, walked beside him. Behind them were Diana and Jeremy K. Jenkins. There was almost no traffic at this hour but suddenly two motorcycles came slowly out of a side alley, their engines throbbing softly. They purred along the street, coming up behind the little group of pedestrians. The young men astride the machines might have been twins— each had a nautical cap pushed down over a sunburst of wild reddish hair, flaring red beards above their blue denim jackets which were cut short at the waist, tan Levis and tan cowboy boots. As they pulled in at the curb and stopped, Diana gave them a quick look and said, "Lousy color combination."

"Hey, Pussycat," said the cyclist in front, addressing Diana, "how about you and me takin' a sharr bath together?"

"Ah want this one here, with the big lung warts!" exclaimed the second set of whiskers, pointing a grubby thick finger at Nora O'Neill.

"You scoundrel!" came the shrill voice of Jeremy K. Jenkins as he leaped forward and began kicking the second cyclist in the leg. A snarl came from within The Tiger's carrier, and Eric sprang toward the other young man, hitting him a powerful belt on the side of the head and knocking him onto the pavement where his machine fell on top of him. At this point Morgan Heath seized hold of Eric, who was getting ready to leap upon the other boy.

"Back away, Mr. Jenkins!" Heath called out, at the same time dragging Eric onto the sidewalk. Then to the cyclists: "Now, listen, you boys, these men didn't know who you were—so go on about your business and let's forget it ever happened. It was a mistake."

"Mistake, hell!" howled Eric, struggling to get away from Heath. "I'll fix these cruddy punks! Let me go, Heath!"

For some mysterious reason the two whiskery boys chose to move off, though they were grumbling and casting black glances at Eric. For a few moments no word came from any of the invading Banner forces, then Doom, who had stood like a confounded statue during the proceedings, came to life.

"Sheez!" he murmured. "Drammer in everday life, happenin' to me!"

Morgan Heath, who had been nervously glancing up and down the street, now took charge. "Let's get organized, and into the restaurant," he urged, and the group went through the door of The Windmill Fixer's Cafe. Eric, Diana, Jenkins and the mining engineer got into one booth, while Doom and Nora and The Tiger occupied another. There was one additional customer in the place, a thin, dark little man in need of a shave, and wearing an old straw sombrero that looked as if it had been trod upon by six decades of stampeding buffalo. A fat man in a white apron came from back of the counter, a frown on his rubicund face.

"Mister Heath," he said, "if I was you I'd get these folks here outa town. Mister Petticoats and Mister Cottonmouth are gonna be mean raring lowdown mad. Mister Petticoats has been going around lately just looking for a dawg to stomp. Him and the Sheriff are liable to *kill* somebody."

"You're dern tootin'," came a second voice. It was the thin little man in the straw hat. He had moved in alongside the fat waiter.

"As the Mayor of Aveinte," he announced, "I welcome you to our fair city, and I also suggestink . . ." He paused, dramatically, and pointed toward the street door, ". . . I suggestink you go that-away!"

"Solly, I mean Your Honor," said the waiter, patently irritated, "get the hell out of here and let me take care of this." The Mayor gave a quiet little twist to his floppy hat brim, meant to demonstrate self-assertiveness, and obeyed, leaving the cafe.

"He's the Mayor?" Jeremy Jenkins asked.

"Figga-head Mayor," said the waiter. "Now, you folks listen . . ."

"One thing at a time," Eric interjected. "Let's hear about the Mayor."

"His name's Solly Marx," said the waiter. "Only Jewish fella we got in Aveinte. Poor Solly! He came out here years ago as a peddler, had a little old wagon hanging all over with tin pans and arn pots and eyeglasses and things. Couldn't sell a single pot. Wagon fell to pieces, mule died, his pans all got rusty. He's tried everything and failed. Solly just don't seem to have any head for business. Mister Cottonmouth, that's the Sheriff, tried to get him a political job but the only one Solly wanted was being put in charge of the Garner C'lection of Gavels over at Uvalde. Solly was just insane to get that job, be superintendent of all them gavels—they got 'em in cases and like that in the lobby of the Kincaid Hotel over there, more'n a hundred dern gavels, little ones, big ones, all give to old Garner in his time. But there was another fella had a cousin knowed Lyndon Johnson in college, so they said, and *he* got put in charge of the gavels, and it like to of killed Solly. So Mister Cottonmouth he was so mad he was . . ."

"Spittin' cotton?" suggested Jeremy Jenkins.

"Right. So he elected Solly to be Mayor. No pay. He don't do much of anything except get in the way."

"He gets a monthly check from his relatives back in New York," said Morgan Heath. "He disgraced the family by failing in business and they pay him to stay out here. He's the only remittance man in the West who gets his check from Pitkin Avenue."

"And this Sheriff?" Eric inquired.

"Cottonmouth Clarke," Heath responded. "You might say he runs things, except he don't. There's a man higher up."

"I knew it!" Diana cried. "I knew there'd be a higher-up. And it's our job to find him if we have to search till hell freezes over."

"Old Petticoats," said the waiter, grown brash in the presence of this beautiful girl. "Petticoats Kockamaney—he's the higher-up."

"What about the hoods on the motorcycles?" Eric asked of Heath. "You sure played it plenty cautious with them."

"Chili Queens," explained Heath. "Petticoats has his own private army. Forty or fifty of them. Half a dozen were borrowed from the Hell's Angels of California to get things started and the others come from different parts of Texas. Mean? Sidewinders and billy goats and heela monsters are blushing violets alongside these Chili Queens."

"So, why didn't they massacre me right on the spot?" asked Eric.

"They never throw a punch or pull a trigger till they get the nod from Petticoats."

Eric passed a hand across his forehead and then called out to Nora O'Neill: "Hey Tiddyboo—just in case I forget it, remind me to call Gloke Hooma in Michigan."

The waiter had gone back to the counter and Morgan Heath continued talking, trying to set Eric straight on the shape of affairs in Chivo County, but the more he explained, the more complex everything seemed. One thing was certain—they were on dangerous ground.

Diana got out of the booth and began wandering around the room, reading neat little signs posted here and there, and in a moment she was joined by Doom. The signs conveyed such messages as:

OUR OATMEAL'S GOOD—IT'S GOT FALLOUT IN IT.

BE REASONABLE—DO IT MY WAY!

TRY OUR SPECIALTY—A GOOD DOSE OF ROUSIN' OIL.

THREE KINDS OF PIE—OPEN-FACE, CROSS-BAR & KIVVERED.

BEES AIN'T AS BUSY AS THEY THINK THEY ARE—
THEY JUST CAIN'T BUZZ ANY SLOWER.

Diana came upon one near the cash register which said:

DON'T BE A RANCID, LEFT-HANDED OLE PARALLELOGRAM!

She beckoned Nora over and showed it to her and then said, "This one must be about me."

"Oh, no," said Nora.

"I'm sorry," said Diana, "if I was out of line. I wish you'd call me Diana."

"Sure," said Nora, "and you can call me Tidd . . . Nora."

Doom read all the signs aloud, understanding nothing, but chuckling as if he did, for he was smart enough to know that they were joke signs. Miss Tiddyboo was more intelligent about them, having once been runner-up in the contest for Miss Subways in New York. She caught the meaning of most of them.

When breakfast was over Eric announced that he and Heath and Mr. Jenkins were going to pay a call on the Sheriff, instructing the others to stick close to The Windmill Fixer's Cafe.

By this time citizens were going and coming in the street and Eric and Heath, and especially Jenkins in his old-timey getup, attracted a good deal of whispering and pointing as they walked toward a big red-and-gold sign which proclaimed:

SHERIFF'S OFFICE
Members Only

"Cottonmouth Clarke," Morgan Heath said, "has the only charter in town for a club, so he's got the only place in the county where you can go in and sit down and buy a drink. Cottonmouth won't even let other places serve beer, except the Kockamaney Motel out west of town. That's where the Chili Queens make their headquarters. Petticoats bought the whole motel for their barracks. Wild? That ain't th' word!"

"How can these people get away with this tyranny?" Jeremy Jenkins inquired.

Morgan Heath smiled his big Texas smile. "Mr. Jenkins," he said, "don't forget that we lie west of the Pecos. The Law in Chivo County is right in this building—all of the law. We've got the customary crooked sheriff, and he's in the pay of this unscrupulous rich guy, and this unscrupulous rich guy has his own private army."

"The Chili Queens," mused Eric. "Why Chili Queens? Does it mean that these shaggy bastards are all gay?"

"Gay?" Heath repeated. "Oh, they have all kinds of whoop-de-doo, in their own strange way."

"I mean," said Eric, "well—I had the feeling that they might all be fags, fairies, queers."

"Oh, no!" Morgan Heath protested. "Not that! Not at all. Well, maybe only just a little bitty bit. Petticoats named them after the Chili Queens that used to have their little stands around the Military Plaza in San Antone. Mescan women, mostly, put out for money, played the guitar, and sang suggestive songs, like, say, *After the Ball Was Over*. The name don't mean they're queer— just like I said, no more'n about thirty-three and a third per cent."

⚙️ Chapter NINETEEN

MORGAN Heath pushed his huge frame through the swinging doors ahead of his two companions. The three men stood for a couple of minutes surveying the scene.

"Eee-gad!" murmured Jeremy K. Jenkins. "It's stupendous!"

It was not quite typical of a western sheriff's office; it was a saloon, such a saloon as might have been found in the grandest hotels of New York back when it was a capital offense to goose Lillian Russell unless you were Diamond Jim Brady or one of his close kin. Here in this dusty little town was a luxurious *fin de siècle* establishment rich in its dark and somber tones, heavy with red velvet and purple satin drapings, suffused with wavering shadows cast by a series of handsome gas lamps that circled the walls. Hanging from the center of the ceiling was a chandelier that might have been salvaged from one of the public rooms in the old Waldorf-Astoria.

Back of the long polished mahogany bar, framed against the dazzling glitter of crystal, stood a robust bartender in crisp white apron and white shirt with two-toned sleeve-garters, his black hair curled in tight ringlets, his mustache also groomed into little tapering curls at the ends. His head was cocked expectantly to one side as he contemplated the three men at the entrance.

189

Standing in lonely splendor in front of the bar was another man, tall and slender and swarthy of countenance—a Latin type with almost classically handsome features and large, dark, aqueous eyes. A beautiful man, his dark magnetism accentuated by the jet black silk suit he was wearing.

"Gentlemen!" he called out. "Welcome! Welcome to Aveinte! Welcome to the Sheriff's Office! The gaming tables are in the rear, but they will not be open until this afternoon when the tourists begin arriving. Step to the bar, gentlemen. I am Cottonmouth Clarke, the Sheriff of Chivo County."

The three men moved forward and by turn shook hands with Clarke. He called each by name and told Eric he was looking forward to seeing The Tiger in the flesh.

"Alas, Mr. Jenkins," he sighed when he came to the lawyer. "It is too bad that you will not be able to remain in our lovely little city. You fit right into my decorative scheme. But we have a law against lawyers. No person in possession of a law degree is allowed within the borders of our county."

"But sir!" gasped Mr. Jenkins, "that can't be! This is still the United States of America. You cannot throw out the law. You cannot outlaw lawyers!"

"Ah, but we have, Mr. Jenkins. We have even outlawed the Texas Rangers. No Ranger ever sets foot in Chivo County. A dozen years ago I tried out for the Texas Rangers in Austin, and I busted out . . ."

"He flunked handcuffin'," came a voice from close by, and the three newcomers glanced at a man sitting at one of the tables nearby. Cottonmouth Clarke laughed heartily at the handcuffing quip, and then resumed: "They flunked me out, and though I am not a vengeful man, I decided that some day I'd get even with them. They tried to come in here for a while after I became Sheriff, but mysterious and violent things seemed to happen to them and finally they went away and they know better than to come back."

"But," persisted Mr. Jenkins, "don't you have some use for . . . well . . . just *defense* lawyers?"

"Perhaps," admitted the Sheriff, "but you bring in defense lawyers and before you know it, one of them is itching to run for Prosecuting Attorney, and that's surely one thing we don't need around here. The truth is, Mr. Jenkins, all lawyers thrive on trouble, and therefore all lawyers are troublemakers. Present company excepted. We are a peace-loving people here and we don't want trouble. So, aroint the Texas Rangers and . . . uh, the dickens with lawyers."

At this moment both Eric and Mr. Jenkins turned slowly to have a second look at the man sitting at the table. Everything about him suggested slouch. He had a mass of bushy brown hair, long and disorderly around the ears but trimmed off in back. A greasy-looking flattish cowboy hat hung between his shoulderblades, suspended from his neck by a latchet. He wore a gunbelt with two silver pistols, each with damascened barrel. His denim shirt and Levis looked as if they hadn't been washed since Broncho Billy Aronson was making cowboy pictures. Most prepossessing of all this man's accoutrements, however, were his spurs—made in Chihuahua of glittering silver, the shanks extending back a good three inches, each rowel decorated with seven long wicked points.

Over and above a certain aura of evil that seemed to surround this man were two things that attracted the attention of Eric and Mr. Jenkins. Spaced on the table before him were three telephones and a black cabinet which appeared to be a shortwave radio rig. Directly in front of him was a platter heaped with vanilla ice cream. He was eating the ice cream with the fingers of his right hand, digging into the mound, taking hold of an oozy gobbet, conveying it to his mouth and getting a part of it slopped over his chin, whence it dripped down onto his shirt. The man was paying no attention whatever to his audience. Eric stared at his slightly bizarre exhibition of table manners for a long moment, then something clicked in his mind.

"I remember now," he said aloud. "Fielding Backstage, the Blacksheep Brother, in that television sketch Bob & Ray used to do, back in the early days of TV. Hey," he called out, taking a couple of steps toward the ice-cream eater, "you got that from an old television show, didn't you?"

The man sprang to his feet and his right hand, dripping vanilla ice cream, curled at his side, inches from one of the silver guns.

"Hold it, podner!" he growled. "What's this television you talkin' about? Nuther one uh them idiot thangs you people got back in New Yawk? Ah don't know nothin' bout no television. Ah eat vanella ahs cream th' way Ah eat it because Ah'm mean. Ah'm too mean to use a spoon. Don't come no closeter, lamblicker."

"Gentlemen," Cottonmouth Clarke spoke up quickly, "let me make you acquainted with Mr. Petticoats Kockamaney. He owns this establishment. He owns the town. He owns this county. He owns *me*. Listen, Petticoats, these are new people in town—let's not make them uncomfortable. Go ahead and finish your vanilla ice cream. Want me to call out Gert?"

"Yeah," mumbled Petticoats. "Git 'er out heah."

"Now, gentlemen," said Sheriff Clarke, "I believe you are in luck. Here in Aveinte we make an effort to stay ahem abreast ahem of the times and we are now about to introduce the latest styles in ladies' wear to the Sheriff's Office—direct from San Francisco. Come on out here, Gert!"

Velvet drapes parted at the rear of the big room and a girl appeared. She stopped and posed, toe pointing.

"This," said the Sheriff, "is the latest thing for saloon fillies."

The girl had on a white pleated skirt and ballet slippers. She wore nothing above the waist.

Petticoats Kockamaney gave her a long, slack-jawed look.

"C'm heah, saloon filly!" he commanded. The girl pranced over and stood beside him, performing a fast shoulder-shimmy leading her untrammeled frontier to bob and weave provocatively. Petticoats reached out and dragged her onto his lap, then picked up a handful of vanilla ice cream and began smearing it over and between her breasts.

"Eeeeeeeeeeeeeeeeeeee!" she cried, twisting and squirming. "Don't, Mistuh Kockamaney! Pleeeeeeeeeeuz!" He responded with a gurgling laugh, then grabbed up more ice cream, and fed it into his mouth. Still again he got a squirchy handful and rubbed it upward along her inner thigh, fetching forth more squeals.

"Damn you, Gert!" he suddenly yelled. "You got no petticoat on! God damn you, you know better'n that!"

"I'll go get one, sir! Jest take a minute! Woooooooooops! Sir! Oh, sir! Oooooooooooooooo!" She bounced off his lap and went scurrying for the velvet curtains.

Jeremy Jenkins now spoke to Eric. "Does your Mr. Fielding Backstage," he asked, "do *that* with his vanilla ice cream on television?"

Petticoats half rose from his chair. "You shet you mouth, law-yuh!" he said between his teeth.

"Now," interrupted Sheriff Clarke again, turning back to the bar, "what is your pleasure? I might suggest that you try one of Elmer's specialties—a sheepherder's delight with a mule's hind foot in it."

"But we are not members of your club," Mr. Jenkins interposed. "You see, Sheriff, I even know Texas law."

"You are not a member, Mr. Jenkins, but I silently bestowed membership on Mr. Yaeger the moment he crossed the threshold. Mr. Heath has been a member for some time now. You are here, then, as a guest of members, so you may partake of a sheepherder's delight without fear of prosecution. I said *prosecution*, Mr. Jenkins."

"I heard it," nodded the New York lawyer.

"More vanella!" Petticoats Kockamaney suddenly howled from his table.

"Solly!" called out the Sheriff. "More vanilla for the boss!"

Within thirty seconds the Mayor of Aveinte came through the velvet drapes with a fresh platter of ice cream. He put it in front of Petticoats, who said, "Tuhn awn th' radio. Poo Poo's awn." Solly Marx switched on a set standing against the wall and in a short while the foghorn voice of Poo Poo Snoddy, favorite disk jockey of West Texas, was heard in the room. He was just introducing a singing group from East Texas known as Billy Bloodshot and his Beaumont Boll Weevils. They launched into a song done in a highly stylized monotone, using to great effect their inspired young voices disciplined to a range of three notes. Almost three. Not quite. Their song went:

> Some day Ah'm gonna die-hi,
> Ah'm gonna die-hi-hi,
> An' whin Ah die-hi,
> You boun' to cry-hi,
> On account Ah die-hi,
> Please gimmie some moah!

When the last notes of this tender roundelay had burst from the young and joyous hearts of the Boll Weevils, Poo Poo Snoddy's voice came lolloping in again. Of him it was often remarked that, it's not so much what he says, but the way he says it.

"Hey cats!" he shouted. "How bout that there? You cat yonda . . . you girl cat . . . c'm up heah a min. Whoss you name, pussycat?"

"Giggy."

"Real purty name, Giggy. Tell me Giggy, whuh them there lyrics mean to you? Whut you git outa th' wuds uh that cool numbuh? Whut's them wuds *con*-vey to you mine, chile?"

"Jest makes me feel weak," came the voice of Giggy. "Weak all ovuh. Rat down to mah ankle bones."

"Ah know alla that," croaked Poo Poo Snoddy. "That goes fuh *inny* uh ouah music. But whuh kinda *soul* meanin' you git? Lak Ah mean lak how you *soul* 'fected by them there wuhds?"

"Oh. Scuze me. Well, Poo Poo, uh, weh-yull Poo Poo, it plain tells me that uh . . . the *ole* people, like parents . . . they always mean rotten to us'ns . . . they outa they skulls alla tam . . . man, we onna BEAT!"

"Thassa ole Pussycat!" cried Poo Poo Snoddy approvingly, and the Boll Weevils swang into another swirling tone poem about yew-tole-uh-tole-uh-mee-hee-you-tole-uh-tole-uh-mee-hee-but-Ah-dint-hee-uh-yew-Ah-dint-hee-uh-yew-hoo."

"Seems to me," Eric addressed the Sheriff, "that you people out here are right on top of all the cultural advances that we have inaugurated back East."

"We keep up," smiled Cottonmouth.

Jeremy Jenkins, of an older generation, was not so favorably impressed. "How," he said, "do you prevent that sort of thing from scaring the livestock?"

The Sheriff frowned and shook his head, nodding ominously in the direction of Petticoats, who was following the beat of the Weevils by jerking his neck muscles, making pecking motions in the manner of an assiduous hen picking up cracked corn.

But Petticoats heard. He stood up suddenly and started toward the street door, then leaped abruptly off the floor as if a covey of crotch-crickets had taken hold of him, whirling in the air to land on his feet, facing Jeremy K. Jenkins. His arms were curved at his sides, and he went into a fearsome performance known throughout the territory as Kockamaney's Spur Dance. He first moved his left foot forward, tilting it so the rowel of his spur would strike the floor and whirl; then the right foot, and the right rowel whirled. It was said that when Petticoats performed his Spur Dance, he was sufficiently aroused to kill. To Eric's eye, however, the act was more ludicrous than frightening; in order to whirl the rowels, it was necessary for Petticoats to lean his body slightly backward, and he had the appearance of a ninety-year-old man with fierce rheumatism striving earnestly to execute a few simple dance kicks. Yet people said that the Spur Dance had its terrifying side, that Petticoats had been known to get a man on the ground and grind the long silver points into him. More than that, people said he always refused to take off his boots and spurs when bedding down with a woman, it being his whim to make ribbons of sheets, blankets and mattresses during the act of love.

Jeremy K. Jenkins knew nothing of the potential violence involved in the Spur Dance, and so he stood with a slight smile, as Petticoats glared at him. Suddenly Petticoats leaped forward, seized the lawyer by his mid-Victorian lapels, raised him off his feet, shook him a couple of times, and snarled: "Lawyuh, you makin' funna Poo Poo?"

Mr. Jenkins was struggling, his square derby hat cocked sidewise over one eye, and he was screeching words that poorly behooved a man of his age, aspect and seeming gentility—words that must have been acquired during a golden boyhood spent in Kentucky poolrooms or out behind Ohio barns.

Morgan Heath took a long minute to debate with himself, then stepped in and stopped it. "That's enough," he said quietly to Petticoats. "You want to shake somebody, try me." Petticoats whirled and his hands dropped again to his guns. He started to go into his Spur Dance again. Heath's eyes narrowed. He spoke slowly, in the manner of a man with a determined mind:

"You . . . want . . . me . . . to . . . break . . . open . . . Mama's . . . Hat . . . Room?"

Petticoats Kockamaney turned white. As the color drained from his face his eyes bulged and he stared in disbelief at the mining engineer.

"You wouldn't day-yuh!" he said, and his voice was almost pleading.

"I'll do 'er," proclaimed Morgan Heath. "And while I'm at it, I'll . . . break . . . the . . . magic . . . chain!"

Petticoats stood aghast. "God damn you!" he suddenly howled. "You bin in there! You bin in that room! You vi'lated th' awduh of th' co't! You busted inta Mama's Hat Room!"

"Hold it!" ordered Heath, raising his big hand to command silence. "I've violated nothing. I've not been in the room!"

"Ah'll kill you quicker'n you can spit an' holler howdy!" fumed

Petticoats. He was clearly in a state of deep mental distress, and sorely embarrassed over his own lack of control. Then an alien voice broke the tension.

"Mist' Petticoats, sir! You want me lak this heah, rat now, befoah all th' tew-riss comes?"

Standing in the velvet doorway was Gert, the saloon filly. She was now bottomless as well as topless. She posed gracefully, toe pointed, one shy hand covering a breast.

"Ah tole you, *petticoat!*" roared Petticoats. "Beat it!" The naked saloon filly backed through the velvet and her master stood glaring at the floor a moment. A telephone rang and he walked quickly to his table, listened for a second ring, then picked up one of the three instruments, a mauve Princess model.

"Kockamaney," he said sharply. "Yeh. Yeh. Yep. That's good. Lemmy see now . . . this's Mondy, Ah'll fly you in a fresh crock . . ." He stopped, and glanced at the men at the bar, then resumed, ". . . Ah mean fresh supply . . . by Wensdy noon. That soon enough? Right. Rodjuh. Ovuh. Able. Bake-uh. Boom Boom. Undeh. Out. An' up yore ass with a three-prong hay hook!" He put the phone down and dropped back into his chair, and sat thinking. Then he reached over and flicked a switch on the radio, went through a few rodjuhs and bake-uhs and boom booms, made contact with someone, and barked, "Git t' wuk!"

Eric felt that things were moving rapidly enough, but he wasn't at all sure about directions. Morgan Heath was comfortably swigging away at his sheepherder's delight and chatting with Cottonmouth Clarke.

"Of course I'm crooked," Sheriff Clarke assured him. "You ever hear of an honest sheriff anywhere? Wouldn't be stylish. But one thing I can tell you, Mr. Heath. You surely know that there is a season in a Texan's life known as *Mama-Promisin'-Time.* The moment comes when . . ."

"Cottonmouth," came sternly from Petticoats, "don't you say one wud bout mah Mama, bout innybody's Mama. Sept you own."

Sheriff Clarke nodded. "When I was a little boy," he went on, "my sainted Mama called me to her knee and made me promise that I would never steal any money, never take a dishonest dollar, never finagle even a red cent from my fellow man. I have kept that promise, Mr. Heath. I'm sure my Mama meant cash money. So I only take negotiable securities and land and livestock and chattels and the like of that."

"Very honorable of you," observed Heath with a wry grin.

"I believe in democracy," Sheriff Clarke continued. "Majority rules. The majority stays honest, maybe, when it comes to cash money, and concentrates on taking property. This is a town that has always believed in majority rule and pure democracy. Years ago there was a rough saloon and gambling hell down the street called The Yeller Dog. One day a dude drummer from the East walked in and ordered a beer. He was enjoying his drink when a dozen ranch hands came whooping into town and rode their horses into The Yeller Dog and began milling around and shooting through the ceiling. The dude drummer stood his ground but when one of the horses jostled him real roughlike, he summoned the bartender and ordered him to clear the premises of those disorderly people. That bartender, Mr. Heath, was a true democrat. He said, 'Listen, drummer, whatta you mean comin' in heah *unmounted!*'"

At this moment the swinging doors flew open. Framed in the doorway was a grim-lipped old lady with celluloid grapes on her hat, a bulging reticule lifted above her head, and blue tennis slippers on her feet. Her little darting eyes took in the scene and then she scampered like a gray chipmunk straight for the table where Petticoats Kockamaney was sitting. She swung the reticule, but he caught the blow with his right forearm and grabbed the old woman around the waist and pulled her onto his lap. She was wrenching and struggling and now Petticoats began to bellow with laughter.

"Godamighty!" he roared, "this heah little ole tew-riss lady tried to bus' mah haid open! Little ole lady, Ah'm gonna spank you ass!"

Still laughing, he whirled her over, backside up. Deftly, as if from long practice, he whisked up her skirt.

"W'y, Ma'am!" he cried out in mock wonderment, "you ain't got no petticoat awn! You vi'latin' th' rules! Ah'm gonna spank you ass real hahd!"

He seized hold of her white underpants and gave them a quick downward jerk. Then he froze, staring down at her.

"W'y, Ma'am!" he stammered. "W'y . . . W'y . . . Lan' sakes!" And he began flailing away at the bare buttocks of the little old lady.

"Stop it!" she cried, but her voice was the voice of a man. "Stop it, Clyde! I'm your cousin, for Christ's sake!"

Petticoats dumped Mister Muff, international spy, roughly onto the floor.

"Whut the hell kinda way is that to come bustin' in heah?" he demanded. Then he turned to the men at the bar. "Evehbody out!" he ordered. "That means evehbody!"

They all departed, except the Sheriff. Walking back toward the restaurant, Eric said to Morgan Heath, "Mr. Heath, I had come to believe that the affairs of a vast worldwide industrial complex, the intricacies of a global corporate structure, could become most baffling and accumulate difficulty on top of difficulty. Yet this situation here has got anything beat for unexpected angles that I've ever seen or heard of."

"Let's pile into the cars," suggested Heath, "and get on out to the ranch. I'll straighten out as much as I can for you, but I'm afraid it won't be much."

In the cafe Doom had fallen asleep in the booth, the cat-carrier grasped in his arms. Nora O'Neill was looking at an astrology magazine, for she believed in the art of the horoscope. Diana . . . well, Diana was fuming.

"Where in God's name have you been all this time?" she demanded.

"Meeting important people," said Eric, and then continued with a twinkle, "including a lovely saloon filly named Gert, who appeared before us first wearing a topless costume, and later on took off the rest. This is a fascinating little community with fascinating people. Oh—your friend Muff the spy seems to be here."

"Wait'll I get my hands on that crummy bastard!" Diana said in a tone tremulous with anger. "I'll cream 'im!"

Eric rode beside Morgan Heath during the journey out to the Bowlared Ranch. Heath drove and talked, and Eric learned quite a few things he hadn't known before. For example, something about the Lost Nigger Mine—that *ignis fatuus* that had lured them into the wilds of West Texas just a few hours ago.

There are "lost" gold mines scattered all over the Southwestern States. The most famous are in Southern California, probably because the population explosion in that area has a greater filbert content than other regions. The Lost Peg-Leg Mine, the Lost Dutch Oven Mine, and the Lost Arch Mine, are all located within a triangle drawn from Indio up to Needles and down to Yuma. They are located within that triangle, although they are not.

They are located nowhere, at least they are located nowhere that anybody knows about. For certain, that is. In fact, to discuss the location of a "lost" mine is as nebulous a proposition as trying to discuss one of Judge Ambrose Bippus's woodpecker holes caught without any wood around it. The celebrated Lost Dutchman Mine is in the Superstition Mountains east of Phoenix and Scottsdale, an area which also boasts of its high yield of human cashews. But the Lost Nigger Mine belongs to Texas. Or maybe Mexico.

Again we venture onto touchy ground, made dangerous by atrabilious pressure groups, who hold that the Lost Nigger Mine should be called by some other name. The people in the region where it is, or isn't, who inhabit the rugged landscape where it is located, although they cannot locate it, and nobody knows if it's around there, or anywhere else for that matter . . . these people, Texans, refuse to call it anything other than the name by which it has been known since the 1880s, when it first got itself lost. That is, if it ever was capable of getting lost, tangible enough to.

It is not even known, in fact, whether it acquired its name from the fact of the mine being lost, or the nigger being lost. Both were. Or are. There are some who say that Nigger Bill Kelly was not a Negro at all, but a Seminole Indian, or half one. There is even argument over the size of the nuggets he is said to have brought out of the mountains; some say he displayed a nugget the size of a cow's liver while others insist that if he had any nuggets at all, they were no bigger than the droppings of pronghorned antelope.

Nuggets to one side, it is known that Nigger Bill worked for a cattle outfit owned by four brothers named Reagan back in 1887, running beef in the border area to the east of the present Big Bend National Park. One day Nigger Bill and Lee Reagan were out looking for some stray horses and Nigger Bill began talking, as he often did, about the gold mine he had discovered in these parts. He said that the gold mine was "over yander" and pointed to a ridge. Soon after that Nigger Bill vanished, and along came a railroad conductor named Lock Campbell, from San Antonio, with some gold nuggets he said Nigger Bill had left in his care. This Lock Campbell was the one who talked it around that he had the rock assayed, and that it came out eighty thousand dollars to the ton. Nigger Bill was gone, for good as it turned out, and old

199

Lee Reagan spent the rest of his life wandering around the mountains, stopping now and then to try to remember which direction Nigger Bill had been pointing when he said "over yander," and then scratching his dumb, hoary, forgetful head and moving on, still searching, as hundreds have searched down to this very day.

"So now," Morgan Heath told Eric, "there's a report going around that somebody has turned up with a paper locating the mine right in this general neighborhood. Some say that Petticoats Kockamaney's divorced Mexican wife got the paper from a Kickapoo Indian and . . ."

"You mean to sit there with a straight face and tell me," said Eric, "that there really are Indians named Kickapoo?"

"Certainly. They live in a town named Nacimiento about a hundred miles south of Eagle Pass. Real queer bunch. They got shoved all over the map in this country and so they moved to Mexico. They seem to have citizenship in both countries and go back and forth without being bothered. We see them around here now and then, just one or two at a time. Maybe *they do* know something about the Lost Nigger Mine."

The main house of the Bowlared Ranch was no sprawling Spanish structure, but a big rectangular three-storied mansion that might have been lifted, white pillars and railed galleries and all, right out of the Mississippi delta country. Glistening white against the drab backdrop of the brown land, it was truly a sight to behold, but Eric wasted no time admiring its substantial beauty. He hurried inside and got on the phone. In minutes he had Gloke Hooma on the wire.

"Slobbla ooo eeeyok!" he greeted Gloke. "How you, boy? Listen. You got any of the Fer-de-lances ready? Wonderful! Now, get this—I want fifty of them to . . ."

When he finished with the conversation he sat for a moment, then turned to Morgan Heath.

"That," he said, gesturing toward the phone, "was the greatest sports car designer-engineer living today. He's a Cow Fulani."

"Say that again," suggested Heath.

"Comes from a nomadic group of Fulani people in West Africa. I ran into him one evening in the bar of a North African fonduk. The Lamborghini people had him backed into a corner and were about to sign him on to design a Lamborghini Fulani. I doubled the fee and bought him for Banner Motors. His first car,

the Fer-de-lance, is just coming off the assembly lines at Bannerville. It'll be the sensation of the automotive world, and you'll
get to look at one shortly. One, hell. You'll get to look at fifty."

"Excuse me," said Morgan Heath, "but where did a Cow
Fleelonny learn to design sports cars?"

"Good question," said Eric.

⸉⸊ Chapter **TWENTY**

A tourist named Sam Rogers, manufacturer of marbles in North Carolina, stood on the main street of Aveinte squinting through his viewfinder at a telephone pole rising out of the sidewalk.

"Vanishing America," he murmured, screwing his face into an expression that would have frightened little children half to death. "Part of ole Vanishing America!" Click. He had his closeup of an old-fashioned wooden step, one of a dozen fastened to the pole for the convenience of telephone linesmen. Mr. Rogers would take his film back to North Carolina, have it developed, order an enlargement of this nostalgic bit of Vanishing America, look at it, and then put it in a box where it would vanish from America, possibly forever.

"Name's Lunsford Scruggs," sounded a voice, and Mr. Rogers turned around and faced a stranger. "Got a herd uh Herefords out south uh town. Know what a double-ett is? A two-foot stop on a French pipe organ. On your way to Big Bend?"

"No, I . . . that is, my wife is . . ."

"That's the Baptis' church up the fur enda this street," said Lunsford Scruggs. "Got another Baptis' church down yonder, the other end. Both closed down now. Petticoats Kockamaney run both preachers outa town. You ever eat Kockamaney chili powder, mister? Well, speaking of colleges, when Petticoats was a mere kid of a boy his Daddy tried to get him a college education. Sent 'im to Southern Baptis' over to Fort Worth. Boy got canned outa there. Sent 'im to Dallas Baptis' College where they advertise they got Quality Education in a Christian Context and all. Boy got canned outa there. Sent 'im to Southwestern Baptis'. Boy flunked at the front gate. Tried East Texas Baptis'. No go. Pulled some po-litical strings and got 'im entered in Baylor, biggest by-god Baptis' school in the country, he was ex-pelled in one week fer peein' in a English professor's coffee pot. Houston Baptis' College said they'd heard about 'im and kindly get him clean outa Harris County and outa Texas if possible. So then they tried to . . ."

"Excuse me," Sam Rogers interrupted with a weak smile, "but my wife is . . ."

"Certainly," said Lunsford Scruggs, nodding vigorously. "They tried to swing it for Petticoats at Southern Baptis' Thee-logical, under some kinda special diss-pensation, but it wouldn't work, so his Daddy—in case you didn't know it, his Daddy was a good Baptis', believed strong in the Baptis' church—his Daddy, as I say, thought a little while, thought maybe he'd fly in the face of Almighty God and give it a whirl at Southern Methodis' up to Dallas, but then ole Jed Kockamaney said no, by god, he'd wither on the vine first and so he went clean the hell to Crockett and got Petticoats entered at Mary Allen Baptis' and the boy lasted there . . . what did you say your name was, Mister?"

"I didn't say, but . . ."

"That's fine. I can spare you another couple minutes, but then I gotta hurry along, sposed to meet a fella up at the Sheriff's Office, so Petticoats he lasted two weeks at Mary Allen, they called him on the carpet and says he's givin' the school a bad name. He was goin' downtown to an ice cream parlor there in Crockett and orderin' vanilla ice cream a half a gallon at a time and settin' there and eatin' it with his hands. That's ole Petticoats! The school people asked him to use a spoon when he was eatin' his ice cream and he told them to go fart up a flagpole, just like that, and they bein' a little scairt of his Daddy, him the chili powder king of Texas and all, so they said they would buy him a solid silver spoon with a picture of Davey Crockett on the handle if he'd use it in the ice cream parlor, and you know what he . . ."

"Really, sir," said Sam Rogers from North Carolina, "I'm going to be late for . . ."

"He said the way he et ice cream was his way of bein' lowdown mean, and the school people told him it didn't suggest meanness so much as it suggested a real slow noggin, and that boy told the head people he was goin' down and buy two quarts of *strawberry* ice cream and bring it back and ram it clean up their . . . well, they *run* him all the way to the front gate and down the road three mile, the way I heard it. His Daddy didn't give up—he hadn't run outa Baptis' colleges by a long shot, so he tried the Texas Baptis' Institute at Henderson and they said they'd close up shop and move to Idaho first, and so he made a personal trip to the University of Corpus Christi, which is solid Baptis', and they said they wasn't in, and to try later, and so ole Jed come on home, sorta discouraged, and died. He was a man always wore seersuck suits. He wasn't cold in the ground till Petticoats got back at the whole Baptis' church, north and south and every other which way, and run both Baptis' preachers outa Aveinte and nailed up the doors, front and back. Maybe it's all fer the good, because they's some folks say that the whole State of Texas is over-Baptissed, but I don't . . ."

"Sir," said Sam Rogers firmly, "goodbye and thank you." He turned quickly and hurried off down the street.

"Well!" exclaimed Lunsford Scruggs. "Damn Eastern people got no manners. Whatta you suppose makes them so abrupt like? Man acted like he had a possum in his pants." He glanced around, but found that no one was listening, so he strolled on his way toward the Sheriff's Office.

He didn't appear to notice it, but most citizens of Aveinte who saw him approaching lit out on urgent errands that took them across the street or up side alleys. Mr. Scruggs spent most of his time on his dairy ranch. He was a bachelor and had no friends and always seemed to be lonely. He employed nine men, eight of them handling the stock, and it was said in town that all of his hands ran from him when they saw him coming. Among the jokes told about Lunsford was one in which it was said he once cornered one of his Mexican hands under a cliff and talked him to death, standing up. His ninth employee was a Chinese cook named Dang. Lunsford often invaded the kitchen and rambled on for hours but it was all right—Dang understood no English. In the Aveinte barbership somebody remarked one day that Dang was a most *on*-usual style of Chinese ranch cook—he'd never had a man.

The lonely rancher entered the Sheriff's Office, where he held an associate membership, and went to the bar.

"Heard about a fella the other day," he said to Elmer the bartender, "had a real smart horse, so smart he could almost talk Mescan, lived over beyonst Presidio, this horse could . . ."

"Mist' Scruggs," said the bartender, "tell me what you want in the way of a drink and then don't talk to me none, please, just don't say nothing whatever to me, as I am in bad shape. Last night my wife hit me alongside the head with her arn spider, the middle-size one, and I got a headache today that . . ."

"One rye," said Lunsford Scruggs abruptly, "and I wouldn't talk to you Elmer if they was holdin' you in solitary confinement up the state pen and you hadn't seen . . ." He whirled around and made a wild grab with both hands and if ever extrasensory perception existed on this earth, this was its finest hour, because Lunsford's claws fastened firmly and accurately on the person of a frail creature who had been slipping along behind him.

"Mistuh Mayor!" Lunsford cried out. "Very man I was lookin' for. You bothered any by deer? Deer come up to your house and eat all the shrubbery up, and kick your vegetables all over the county, and ruin every flower on the place? Don't worry. I got the cure for it. Listen to this. Friend of mine clean out in California . . ."

"Misteh Scruggs," pleaded Solly Marx, "please leave go my arms! Please excuse me, I got to go velcome the Greyhond tourists!"

"Only take a minute, Mistuh Mayor. This friend of mine, deer was eatin' up everything, gnawin' the corners offa his hay barn, so he writes to the Department of Agriculture, they send him this little bottle of stuff. It says put a couple of drops on a piece of cotton and hang it on the bushes and flowers and no deer will come in ten mile uh the place. It says on the bottle . . ."

"I got no deer!" protested the Mayor. "I got no shrobbery! You know I live at the boarding house alonksite the depot!"

"Oh," said Lunsford Scruggs apologetically. "I had you mixed up with . . . I ever tell you about the time . . ."

Sheriff Cottonmouth Clarke appeared suddenly at Lunsford's elbow. Gently he unfastened the rancher's hand from Solly Marx's arm.

"Mr. Lunsford," he said, "will you do me a favor? We are having an important business conference over at that table where Mr. Kockamaney is sitting with those other people. Would you please not talk any more until the business conference is over?"

"Wasn't sayin' a word, Sheriff," Lunsford responded. "Just happened to mention to my friend the Mayor here about the damn deer takin' his plants, and he could get a bottle of what they call cougar urine, but what is only plain ole panther piss, for three dollars and twenny-five cents, and it . . ."

"I know," smiled Cottonmouth Clarke, "but if I hear one more word out of you I'm going to cancel your membership. Understand?"

"Of course." The rancher returned to his drink, glancing a couple of times at the table where Petticoats was sitting with three men and a beautiful girl. Lunsford recognized the girl—it was the Mescan lady Petticoats had married. The Sheriff had rejoined the group and all five were examining a raggedy, rumpled piece of brown butcher's paper.

Millard Muffgainer had returned to mufti, having divested himself of his grandma costume. During the violent episode with his cousin he had undergone a few moments of apprehension, but as it turned out Cousin Clyde had eventually seen some humor in the affair and they had enjoyed a good laugh together.

Now all was dead serious.

Ogden Crump was present, and beside him Orlando Dill, somewhat haggard but surprisingly alive. Blanca Tornillo sat as far from Petticoats as she could get, and kept her eyes away from him.

The heir to the Kockamaney chili powder fortune had a grim and stony look on his face. He wasn't talking. He sat motionless in his chair, staring at the untidy brown paper, on which appeared some lettering. It looked this way:

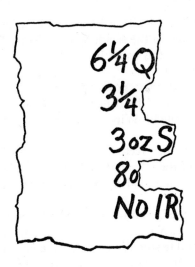

Petticoats knew what it was—but not what it meant. It was a part of the formula for the secret ingredient—it had nothing to do with the Lost Nigger Mine, or any other mine. It was a part of the formula. The paper had been torn in half, probably on purpose. Petticoats was the sole surviving member of the Kockamaney family, yet he didn't know the secret. No Kockamaney had ever known it. It belonged to the Kickapoo Indians down in Mexico, and they had never been willing to hand it over to any white person.

Petticoats was boiling inside, but he did his best to hide his emotions. Someone had given his divorced wife this paper with *half* the secret on it. Where was the other half? The dirty Kickapoos were mixed up in this. He thought now, as he had thought before, of taking his boys on a raid into Mexico, maybe wiping out the whole village. But he knew that wouldn't work, because he was dependent upon them for something other than the formula. Something they brought with them each time they came up to Aveinte. Mama's Hat Room was mixed up in it. It was the Indians who had told him how disaster would follow on the breaking of the chain of hats.

His cousin Muff was speaking. "Now, Blanca," he urged, "see if you can remember just one or two more details. Medium height. Bushy black eyebrows. Brown skin, not black. Wore an old hat. Try to remember something else."

"I have told all I can," the Mexican girl said. "He was handsome man. He come to the ranch house. At first I don't trost. But he sayze I must have this paper because is important. Is gold mine. I do not understand it."

Petticoats Kockamaney now slapped his hand on the table. "Whirr bouts was Ah!" he demanded, "when this sneak of a Indinn come to the ranch? Why wasn't Ah there, you peppuhbelly ho?"

Blanca leaped to her feet, Latin fire flashing in her eyes. She reached for one of the telephones, clearly intending to clobber her ex-husband. He now stood up and fairly shrieked at her: "Ah said peppuhbelly ho!"

In this moment of confusion Lunsford Scruggs walked past, glanced at the brown paper on the table, and went on into the men's wash room. He stood in there for a couple of minutes, playing the flute and speaking absently to the wall: "Six and a fourth que. Three and a fourth. Three ounces five. Eight oh. No ear . . . No ire." He repeated the thing several times and then returned to the big room just in time to hear Petticoats Kockamaney tell Sheriff Clarke, "C'm awn, Cottonmouth. Ah wanna go see th' min ovuh to th' mo-tel."

As they walked to the street Lunsford fell in behind them, ready to ask them if they would finance him in a project which he believed would make millions. They either didn't see him at first, or paid no heed to him, for Petticoats was talking earnestly.

"Gold mine mah hind end!" he said to the Sheriff. "What Ah want back is Snivelin' Dawg Canyon, and you know dern well why. An' Ah want th' ranch—Ah was borned there, an' so was mah Daddy, and mah Daddy an' mah Mama they died there, an' Mama's Hat Room is there. Now some lowdown sodwinder has got in that room an' like as not broke th' chain. Spose it coulda been that god dam cat, Cottonmouth? Spose that cat got in that room an' kicked them hats all outa place? Ah'll boil that son of a bitch cat alive, Ah lay hands on 'im. C'm awn!"

Lunsford Scruggs walked off down the street, heading for his car.

At the Bowlared Ranch Eric Yaeger and Diana Fowler were sitting on the big veranda quarreling about The Tiger. That distinguished crook-tailed leader of American industry was on his mouldy red leash which Diana had tied to the leg of her rocking chair. The cat was nibbling at an uncooked frankfurter.

"We've still got Ernie von Flugel on the payroll," Eric said. "You persist in treating The Tiger as if he were some ordinary alley cat."

"He eats like one," said Diana, "and he sleeps like one."

"That's not the point, Diana. He's got to be taught things. He's got to be trained into the role he must play. I've been through this whole thing before. He's *big!* Once again I've got to tell you—we have to cultivate an image to match his importance, and we've got to stay with that image. Let me have von Flugel go back to work as The Tiger's personal chef."

"Ha!" Diana snorted. "I'll not stand for such stupid foolishness."

"Suppose," Eric suggested, "we put Ernie to work just for show. He can serve up the same frankfurters, but we can heat them up in a handsome chafing dish, maybe trim them into little curley-cue designs. Listen, Diana. Ernie was chef to Rhubarb for five years. He knows how to shop for cat food, and he knows how to cook for an aristocratic cat."

"God in heaven!" breathed Diana. "You're really out of your mind. This is *not* an aristocrat. This is a cat—a cat out of the alleys of Old San Juan. He doesn't *want* his frankfurters with curleycues on the end. I was beginning to think you were a man with a slight amount of intelligence. I was wrong."

But Eric wasn't giving in. He began describing a cookbook for cats that had been published in the last few years and as he talked, Diana quietly unfastened The Tiger's collar and he strolled over to the edge of the veranda and popped down into the yard. By the time Eric noticed him he was out sniffing at the base of a salt cedar.

"He's loose!" Eric exploded, jumping out of his chair.

"Hold the phone!" cried Diana. "Sit down, you big creep! I *turned* him loose!"

"Again? You turned him loose *again?* After I distinctly ordered you *not* to do it again?"

"When *you* . . . ordered . . . *me?* Can't you get it through that numb, wisdom-clogged skull that *I* am in charge of this cat? Damn your hide, Eric, I've got a good mind to light out right now for Vegas."

Eric sank back into his chair. "Please," he moaned.

"Now," she said, "watch this." She called out, "Tiger! Come to Mama!"

The cat looked up, glanced back at the tree trunk where he had just enjoyed his first sniff of armadillo odor. Then he came trotting back onto the veranda and jumped lightly into Diana's lap. She picked him up and dropped him into the yard again, and he wandered back toward the tree.

"Call him," said Diana. Eric winced, but sang out, "Tiger! Come to Papa!" The Tiger came.

"Now, Señor Wise Guy," said Diana, "I'll make a deal with you. It's ridiculous to have a high-bracket chef for a cat, no matter how rich the cat. A cat enjoys a piece of fish, and he enjoys the piece of fish more if it's been dredged around in a mixture of sand, seasoning salt and cow manure. It is also ridiculous to keep a cat penned up. The Tiger needs to spend a little time outdoors. By himself. Away from his people. I've got him trained so he'll come on the trot when I yell for him. He'll do it for you, too. So . . . you agree to a little freedom for him, I'll go along with the nut idea of the chef."

"You'll also go along with the nut idea of not referring to *my* ideas as nut ideas," Eric responded. He was usually a good loser, but he'd never lose good to this girl. It needs to be added, however, that in his own mind he was ready to admit that he cared more for Diana Fowler than he cared about keeping a cat in top corporate trim.

"It looks," Diana observed suddenly, "as if we are about to have company."

ᏚᏚ Chapter TWENTY-ONE

THE automobile came up through a double line of ponderosa pine trees, each a hundred and forty feet tall. The car pulled in at the front of the house and a man got out and came smilingly onto the veranda.

"Name's Scruggs," he said. "Lunsford Scruggs. Got a small place on down the road a trifle. You folks must be the Banner people. That the cat? Well, bless my jinglebobs! Looks just like any ordinary kinda cat, don't he? Know what a ox pecker is? It's a . . ."

"Pardon me," Eric interrupted him gruffly. "Who the hell are you and what do you . . ."

"A ox pecker," Lunsford rumbled on, "is a little ole bird they got in Africa, rides around on the back of critters and picks the ticks offa them. Mostly oxes, I guess. They don't like to eat nothin' but ticks. He . . ."

"We got a man works for us," put in Diana spiritedly, "who can put little curleycues on frankfurters and I bet he could put little curleycues on ticks for the ox peckers."

"Damn you," said Eric, routinely. "Now look, Mister . . ."

"I know some Kickapoo Indinns," Lunsford continued, "that knows how to make dolls with beads all over 'em. I got an idea, make us millions. Need some financin' from somebody's got a lot of money, like you folks. Big thing nowadays is the talkin' doll. Seen some over at a store in Fort Stockton last Christmastime. Dern little ole doll just sets there and talks. Talks! Says ten different things. Only trouble is, a man cain't rightly understand a word that doll says. It's got a machine inside of it and when it says these things, it talks Nawthen talk. Wouldn't give you a nickel for it that way. What I wanna do is set up a fact'ry with these Kickapoos and make dolls that talk like people talk. I figger maybe I could get ole Petticoats Kockamaney to do the talkin' on a little record or however they do it and it would be old Petticoats's voice you hear so you'd have the doll sayin' something like, 'Ah lak mah li'l ole calico dray-yuss awn account it's gotta big ole ray-yud ribbon onna back uv ut.' That way a man'd be able to figger out . . . you folks ever hear ole Petticoats talk? I seen him bout an hour ago up in Aveinte and he . . ."

"I think," said Diana, as if she were sensing intellectual bloat, "that it's time for us to go inside for something, like maybe a stack of wheats."

"Never mind," said Eric sharply, "and try not to be vulgar." He was now leaning toward their visitor, displaying a sudden interest in his conversation.

"I think," continued Lunsford, "that ole Petticoats is superstitious about somethin' you got right here in this ole house. He calls it Mama's Hat Room. It's up on the top floor and it's all sealed up with sealin' wax and got four different locks on it and a arn bar acrost the door, and nobody's sposed to know what's in that room sept Petticoats. His Mama's bed that she died in is in there, and she put a circle of her husband's hats all around the bed, touchin' each other, and they say that if somebody moves one of them hats so they don't touch, then The Chain is broke, and The Secret is out—I spose you people know about The Secret . . ."

"No," said Eric, hiding his eagerness. "Tell us."

"Petticoats," went on Lunsford, "says he ain't superstitious and neither am I but I got beliefs like everbody else. If a lady eats a chicken neck it will make her purty. That's a fact. If you got a toothache and bite down on a nail, it'll stop. If a man has a mustache a different color from his hair, he's gonna make trouble. When you got a fresh package of gum, always pull out the middle stick first because if you don't all your teeth are gonna fall out. Things like that. Beliefs. Not superstitions. A stingy man always wears his heels out on the inside. Ever know that? I've seen it work. You got the hives? I know how to cure 'em. Walk backwards blindfolded three times around a persimmon tree without thinkin' about a possum. I told that one to Sheriff Clarke, but he's some kind of a commanuss and he said it wouldn't work. He said that in order for a man to not think about a possum, he's gotta think about a possum so's *not* to think about it and that cancels out the whole deal, but he's some kinda atheiss. Now, let me tell you about ox peckers. No, I already did. But I . . ."

"Mr. Scruggs," Eric spoke up in a respectful tone, "do you think there might be something in that room upstairs that might be important to me? I mean to the Banner company?"

"Might be," said Lunsford with a meaningful glance. "That room's sposed to be sealed up by court order, but it's my guess ole Petticoats and the Sheriff faked that court order. Little while ago I seen a piece uh brown paper they was all mighty innarested in, but they got only half of it—they's a message of some kind on it, but somebody ripped it right down the middle, looks as if. Me, I cain't understand what all the fummadiddlin's about. Anybody wanned to get in that room, anybody with any ingineerin' sense, all you gotta do is loosen up a winder and lift 'er out and have a look, and then put 'er back."

"Will you excuse us?" Eric said, quickly rising. "Just make yourself at home and I'll send our friend Mr. Doom out—he'll enjoy some of your fascinating stories. Come on, Diana. Call the cat."

For a few minutes Lunsford Scruggs sat contentedly alone. He was thinking about the anomalistic feel of the Bowlared—julepy plantation rather than cattle ranch—when he saw a girl walk into view from the side of the house. She was a looker, with golden hair and a figure that fairly burbled within brownish tight-fitting slacks and a green blouse. She had the cat on its red leash and she sauntered along toward a grouping of black willows four or five hundred feet from the house. Must be the girl secretary, Lunsford mused, as he watched the way her bottom rolled. Then his eye jumped ahead to the black willows and he saw a man, and pretty soon the girl joined the man and they stood quite close together, almost as if they were embracing—and that, Lunsford thought, in spite of the fact that the man was an Indian, a Kickapoo.

Doom came out of the house, where he had been having a nap. He nodded sleepily and eased himself into a chair. Lunsford Scruggs spoke not a word for a full minute and eight seconds. Apparently he was gathering his strength, collecting his thoughts, assembling his ammunition. Then he set sail:

"You like giblets, Mistuh Doom? This is a big turkey state, Texas. Grow more turkeys than Loozyanna grows muskeetahs. You can take turkeys and prove there is order in the universe. Ever know that? You probly don't care about eatin' grasshoppers but you eat 'em just the same. A turkey eats grasshoppers by the bushel and then you eat the turkey and so you get your grasshoppers in your diet. That's the way it goes. Order in the universe. Clockwork, run by a supreme bein'. Now, you take a horsefly. He eats horse, or he'll even eat people, then a frog eats the fly, and a raddlesnake he eats the frog, and a goat comes along and stomps the raddlesnake to death and takes a few bites, and a Mescan eats the goat—no, wait a minute, ain't anybody gonna eat a Mescan—a panther eats the goat, and then a mountain lion eats the panther, and along comes a bear and he eats the mountain lion, and a cowboy kills the bear and eats him, and then a gunslinger knocks off the cowboy, and a buzzard eats what's left of *him*, so now what happens? A horsefly comes along and eats the buzzard. You see how it works. All these god damn dirty atheiss, they ain't able to reckonize the beautiful order we got in the universe. They tell me that raddlesnake meat is now bringin' a dollar seventy a pound and that's higher'n good lean bacon. I ever tell you about the . . ."

"You mean to say," Doom interrupted, "that people around here eat rattlesnakes?"

"These two old people," Lunsford gubbled on, "name of John and Hanner Billings, they the ones owned my ranch till I bought it. They both took down sick and they called a doctor and he said they had the dip'theria and to stay in bed four-five days, but along come a vet to look at a saddle horse jumped up in the air and come down on a sharp post, damn near went clean through him, and when he found the Billingses both laid up he looked them over. He said Miz Billings had bovine mastitis which is a fancy way of sayin' caked udder, and he had bovine farcy, and that's a kind of glanders. John and Hanner Billings decided to believe the vet and get the hell away from cows and that's why they sold me the place and moved to El Paso. They had this Chineyman name of Dang for a cook and I kep' him on. He's a funny one. He thinks ever

214

time I leave the place I'm goin' to town to get laid and so when I come home he grins like a Chinese hyena and says, 'Boss go pushy-pushy?' That's what he calls it, pushy-pushy. I tell you! One day he comes to me real serious and frownin' and says, 'Boss, pushy-pushy one time, nice, *good!* Pushy-pushy too many time, no good, *make sick!*' Ain't that a howl? What the hell would a Chineyman know about a thing like that?"

"When they cook rattlesnakes," Doom spoke up, trailing far behind, "do they . . ."

"Nobody in Texas," said Lunsford with an authoritative air, "far as I been able to find out, nobody in the whole State knows what the 'O.N.T.' means on a spool uh Clark thread. You ever see 'O.N.T.' on a spool uh Clark thread? Always there. Ask somebody what it means. I don't think the Clark people themselves know. I set around sometimes and think . . ."

Eric and Morgan Heath came onto the veranda. Eric had a piece of brown paper in his hand, and remarked in an aside to Lunsford: "The window was unlocked—we just opened it up and crawled in." Lunsford looked as if he'd enjoy examining the paper, but Eric didn't offer it to him.

"Better get it put in a safe place," Heath was saying. "That gang'll find out it's gone from the room—they got ways of findin' things out. You get it hid, and we'll try to figger a way to get ahold of the other piece."

Eric sat down and gave some thought to this suggestion. "I got it," he said. "Last place they'd ever think of. Doom, let me have your wallet."

Doom derricked his hulk out of the chair, unfastened a button on a hip pocket, and took out a folding leather pocketbook that looked as if it might have a thousand dollars in greasy one-dollar bills wadded inside.

"Don't see how you would ever be able to sit down with this monster on your hip," Eric observed, turning it over in his hands. "What you got in it?"

"Oh," said Doom, "peddy cash, but mostly credit cards."

Eric unfolded the wallet and began plucking out cards.

"You've got credit cards from every gasoline company on earth," he said, "and that's nice goin' for a guy who doesn't even know how to drive a car."

"Emoigencies sometimes arise," Doom said pontifically.

"Now watch," ordered Eric. He folded the piece of brown paper until he had it in a three-inch square, bunched credit cards around it, and put it into the wallet. "Keep it in your pocket, and keep that pocket buttoned," Eric instructed him, "and at night lie on top of it—that way they won't get it."

Lunsford Scruggs watched Doom put the wallet in his pocket and they sat for a few moments. Then Lunsford spoke to the fat man.

"Mistuh Doom," he said, "they got a new machine here, delivered a few days ago, call it the Instant Roundup. The hands got it set up back by the main corral. Le's mosey over there and have a look."

They left the veranda and strolled around the house and out past an assortment of barns and sheds and pens, and as they ambled along Lunsford was strangely silent, and appeared to be in deep thought. Now and then he threw a surreptitious glance at Doom's hip pocket. He was, without question, interested in that wallet.

At the corral they found the new machine all set up—a huge black boxlike structure made of heavy metal, open at the top, with steel gates at either end, wires running off to a nearby powerline, a four-inch water pipe coming in from the other side. The box itself was about twenty feet long and six or seven feet wide. A couple of cowboys were busy tightening bolts and stringing wire out to a steel table set under a mesquite tree. On the table was a control box of some kind. Lunsford called one of the cowboys over, a young man with a bent nose, and started asking questions.

"This here thang," said the cowboy, "is a new kinda Argentine corral doo-dad. It'll do more fer critters than critters can do for theirselfs. We gettin' her ready fer her first job tomorra, gonna run two dozen young bulls through. All kindsa clamps will grab aholt of the bull and twist him into different positions, and he'll be soaked with spray fer ever insect this side uh Montanny— sprays a-shootin' at 'im from both sides and from over and under. Wholl this is goin' awn, they's some steel arms that'll begin stabbin' needles in the critter, head to foot, 'noculatin' him foah ways t' breakfast. More clamps come out up front and grab him by the head, and then these two steel arms move in with curved saws on 'em, and zuzz-zuzz-zuzz-zuzz, off comes his hawns. An' wholl *that's* takin' place, a chunka arn that's white hot comes out in back and presses into his hind end, and he'll squeal like a baby with th' whipworm colic. Lawdy! It's gonna be better'n a rodeo!"

He took them over to the steel table and showed them the control box, which had a row of levers and buttons on it, each governing a single function inside the big chamber of horrors. One lever was red.

"This un," grinned the young cowboy, adhering to the laconic manner of the typical Texan, "is the best un of all. By the time that bull goes through what I jist described, he's gonna be tard of it all, and he's gonna maybe say to hisself that it is all over now, but it ain't. Down goes this red lever. Out comes another steel arm. Swizz-swizz-swizzzzzz! Off comes his dornicks as neat as if it was done with a 'lectric carvin' knife. Out comes another arm. Slop-slop-slub-slub. Medsin goin' on. Then this button over here, bang, and all the clamps come off and the saws and hypuhdemmicks and nut knife and all ree-tracks, and the front door opens, and the bull goes rollin' out onto God's green earth—you'll be able to smell 'im alla way to Amarilluh—he's all ready for the party, but he ain't goin' to none. Man! I cain't wait!"

"You people out here," Doom observed, "lead a different kinda life than us back in New York."

He and Lunsford started back toward the house but at the rancher's suggestion they skirted out toward some distant hills, moving through desert land, mostly sand and boulders and various forms of cactus. Lunsford appeared to be so preoccupied with his thoughts that he wasn't wagging his tongue as tirelessly as usual. He was reduced to a little lecture about desert plants, with special reference to a growth called sotol which has served Indians and prospectors and cowboys for long ages, furnishing fuel for campfires and passable food for both man and beast. Doom was a man with no interest whatever in the flora of the desert, but he listened attentively, because Lunsford was being real friendlylike, even dropping his arm around the big man's shoulders.

Arriving back at the ranch house Lunsford announced that he had to get on home, but that he'd be back tomorrow.

"I wanna see them bulls go through that machine," he told Doom. "You wanna watch th' show with me?"

Doom had his doubts, but he nodded his head.

Far out beyond that part of the desert where Doom and Lunsford had walked, another man was wandering and his thoughts were on bulls too. He was lost, and he was bitter. Albert Apple had driven US 90 all the way out from San Antonio, through Uvalde and Del Rio and Sanderson. His panel truck had been fired upon several times when he was passing through hilly sections. On either side the white lettering was clearly legible: HUMANE SOCIETY—CHIVO COUNTY. Still, the bullets rattled against the steel truck and when he asked a gas station man in Sanderson about it, the man said, "They mus' think you one uh them dawg-nappuhs, been a lot on the teevee about. Texas people is kindly tode animals."

Mr. Apple bore south from Aveinte, searching for a back road that would take him into the ranch, and he found one, and headed into a forbidding wilderness. He got bogged in the sand a couple of times but managed to work his way out, then it came on dark and he decided to wait till morning to finish his journey. He left his truck in the middle of the narrow gravel road, drank half a pint of whisky, ate a couple of cheese sandwiches and a can of beans, and then tried to listen to his radio for a while. All he could get was a disk jockey named Poo Poo Snoddy who seemed to possess the gift of tongues and who played recordings apparently waxed just before and during bloody penitentiary riots.

"These heah people out heah in Wes' Taixuss," mused Albert Apple, "ain't even got theirself civ-lized yet." He turned off Poo Poo Snoddy, got into the back of his truck, adjusted his shoulder gun and went to sleep on a pile of blankets.

He was awakened at daybreak by a tremendous crash. Something, possibly a trailer truck, or a railway train, had collided with the Humane Society car. Albert Apple lifted himself up on his elbows, alarm showing in his face, and there came a second crash, shaking the panel truck down to its very brake linings.

The well-mannered killer from Corpus was not exactly frightened, but he was uneasy. He crawled to the rear and unfastened the doors and pushed one of them slowly open. He was about to ease himself down onto the roadway when, CRASSSSSSSSSSSH! He slammed the doors shut and crawled up to the front and got into the cab where he could see out. Three black animals, looking to be as big and as hardy as tank cars, were standing beside the road, contemplating the truck. Then a fourth came into view—obviously the one that had just whammed into the steel side. Now it was another bull's turn. He slowly lowered his head, pawed the

218

ground gracefully as if he were the greatest *toro* in all Spain, and shot forward, hitting the truck such a lick that it almost overturned.

Albert Apple tried desperately to get his engine started, but the mighty blows had dislodged things, might even have knocked the motor completely loose from its moorings. By this time the bulls apparently had noticed signs of life inside the truck. They looked at one another, quizzically at first, then in a knowing manner; Albert Apple swore later that he saw one of them grin. And now they ceased taking turns, and came at the truck in pairs, and three at a time, and it wasn't long until HUMANE SOCIETY—CHIVO COUNTY was lying on its side in the sand. One bull rammed away at a wheel, snapping it off as if it had been on a doll buggy; another animal stood off and cocked his head, studying the situation with a kind of scientific detachment, then he turned and backed up and began clobbering the hood with both his hind hooves, a procedure that might have been heard in New Mexico. Albert Apple was now permitting himself to howl for help. Eventually he was able to get his gun out, and pull himself into an up-right position, and then he fired a few shots at the foe. The attackers didn't seem to notice the bullets, but continued banging away for another five minutes. Then all four of them reached an agreement that they'd had enough of this sport, and they wandered away.

Albert Apple was speaking profanely when he got a door open and crawled cautiously out of the truck. His gun was still in his hand, but the hand was shaking, for he had never gone up against four bulls before. He had an earnest desire to be at home in his little cottage on Staples Street in Corpus. He inspected the damage briefly, got out his sack of food, bottle of whisky, and one blanket, and started walking—hoping that his course would take him to the Bowlared Ranch and hoping also that he would see no black bulls, either today, tomorrow, or during the whole of his remaining days on earth.

✦ Chapter TWENTY-TWO

FIFTY strange-looking automobiles were standing on the infield turf of the Banner Motor Company testing grounds at Bannerville, Michigan. They were ranged in orderly lines of ten, each had two occupants, and the occupants wore bright yellow crash helmets. The cars were pencil-lean and had a rocket look, with glittering wire wheels, the bodies a mottled brownish green. Somehow they had the semblance of living creatures. Snakes.

A dark-skinned man in a white shirt and brown slacks, with a yellow sash at his waist, stood on a wooden platform facing the cars. He had been talking to the drivers, and the men who were riding shotgun, through an amplifying system. During his lecture a helicopter landed close by, a man in a yellow crash helmet got out, climbed into an extra car identical with all the others, and moved to a position at the front of the lines.

The man on the platform raised his arms and called out:

"Slobbla ooo eeeyok! Dilate!"

Each driver reached forward and seized a white knob and gave it a pull. From either side of each car a mottled brown apronlike steel wing moved quickly outward and locked into place, and the cars now looked as if they might be huge and quite horrible brown stingrays.

"Retract dilation!" shouted the man on the platform, and the wings moved back into the bodies. The dark-skinned man was Gloke Hooma, engineering sensation of the sports car world, and the models on the field were Fer-de-lances, his first cars for an American manufacturer.

Gloke Hooma dreamed his masterpiece for the rich teen-age market. The Fer-de-lance had the customary forward fender-cannon, retractable of course, and firing black eight-balls made especially for the car by a large billiard table company. Gloke Hooma was a man well-versed in the gentle lore of the reptile world, and he knew that there are certain snakes known as venom-spitters; they point their fangs at the eyes of their enemies and spit a jet of blinding poison straight and true. The Cow Fulani from West Africa, who often thanked God for not having be-stowed this gift on humankind, had nevertheless adapted it for use on the Fer-de-lance, installing venom-jets in the four hubcaps where they served a double purpose. The driver could, by pressing a green button, spray a poisonous mist a distance of fifteen feet from each hubcap; on the other hand the mechanism would activate automatically if a fun-loving hobbledehoy so much as laid a lar-cenous hand on one of the hubcaps. Within three days the thief's head would shrivel into the shape of a prune.

A radar speed-trap-jammer worked off the headlamps. A low-slung fake luggage rack on the rear could send up a smoke screen, or a semipoisonous fog, or it could spray the highway with one of two chemical mixtures—a thin coating of sassatate diluted in quinine water, to raise blisters the size of baseballs on the tires of any pursuing vehicles, said blisters then being exploded in concert by target-finding gamma rays, causing the pursuing vehicle to be thrown through the air and hideously wrecked; or, a spray of sassatate, diatomaceous earth and radioactive sawdust, designed to rot the feet off of persons or animals or space goblins pursuing on foot. It should be noted that the latter chemical is a slight variation of the alkahestic powder made exclusively by Banner and used to sore up the feet of the nation's cockroaches—just one more praise-worthy instance of industrial diversification coupled with know-how.

In designing the Fer-de-lance, Gloke Hooma added little grace notes here and there to illustrate his Cow Fulani sense of humor. For the teen-agers of Southern California he dreamed up an amusing anti-smog device which stores up exhaust fumes and neutralizes them in an expanding tank while the car is being driven in traffic. The purified fumes are released into the air when the car is stopped at a traffic light—the comic touch being the noise made in the process, a loud slowly diminishing flutterblast like an elephant fart. A sure thing to tickle the fancy of the California kids as well as their elders, warranted to send surrounding motorists as well as pedestrians into gales of laughter.

There were so many innovations in the new car. Under the dashboard was an unobtrusive shoe-dirtier. Then too, a flick of a small lever brought a zither-styled guitar sliding out from the dash, positioning itself at the driver's right elbow so that he might strum it while chanting "God Damn Your Black Soul I Love You," or "The Nondescript Mud Turtle's Lament." Gloke Hooma had been worried about the installation of a workable guitar, until he found it was not necessary to have mechanical fingers pressing the strings to produce the chords; juvenile-oriented engineers advised him that one single chord was sufficient—a brand new one called J-flat.

These clever little comedy touches should not be allowed to detract from the one major revolutionary feature of the Fer-de-lance: the Gloke Hooma improvement on the Hovercraft principle. The spreading of the steel wings made it possible for the car to leave the ground, scoot along for a few feet without touching the pavement, then suddenly arch into the air in a giant leap which made it, in a sense, a flying machine. This development would have a tremendous appeal to teen-agers, permitting them to leap over rivers and thus avoid toll bridges, carry them over rotten rat-fink traffic cops, and allow them to avoid hazards that commonly confront young drivers, such as houses, stores, picnics, banks, baseball games, police stations, political conventions, and so on.

After the flight principle had been tested and refined, Gloke Hooma tacked on a mechanism that would permit the car, in the middle of a rainbow leap or while hovering overhead, to open its hood like a pit viper's jaws, revealing a pair of giant red steel fangs, and then dive downward and bite other automobiles, or people. While Hooma was working out this piece of equipment (optional) one of his assistants came up with the superlatex rape belt, which would flop back the righthand bucket seat, spreadeagle a teen-age miss, slap pancake makeup on her acne, and hoist her

223

skirts all in one deft operation, performed with such swiftness that she would not even have a chance to holler, "Give it tuh me cat!"

During the period in which the Fer-de-lance was on the drawing board, there were several emotional upheavals among the directors of Banner Motors concerning the way the car was shaping up. It was not so much a matter of moral sense as it was the fear that the law would crack down, once the car hit the showrooms. The arguments grew so heated that Eric Yaeger was summoned and a major policy conference was held at the factory in Bannerville.

"All these weapons," said a director named Alexander Moon, "are too dangerous for our teen-age children. This car is going to be running around the country shooting pool balls out of its fenders, spitting venom out of its hubcaps, rotting the feet off of folks who are guilty of nothing more than walking across the road, destroying property right and left, jumping into the air and coming down to bite big chunks out of innocent bystanders . . . gentlemen, I tell you, I don't think the law is going to like this. I haven't even mentioned the rape belt, but I have three daughters and it is my firm belief that Mr. Hooma's rape belt is simply uncalled-for."

Eric lowered his head and smiled behind his hand. "I don't think," he said, "that we need to worry about the law. This car is for teen-agers. We have been in steady consultation with the most settled and sensible teen-agers in the land all during the building of the Fer-de-lance. The consensus says go man go. The kids want it, and the kids get what they want. Their parents have nothing to say about it—they simply close their eyes, swallow hard, open their checkbooks and then go somewhere and get majestically stoned. The law? Gentlemen, the law doesn't dare cross the teen-agers. The law is afraid of them. The communications industries are in thrall to their spending habits. The United States Congress is frightened of them. I think we can go ahead with anything Gloke devises for the kids, including the rape belts."

"Okay," agreed Mr. Moon, "but just remember that I put in a word of dissent. You may see the day when a fleet of Fer-de-lances roars along Pennsylvania Avenue, jumps into the sky, and chews up the whole god damn Congress, and then spits venom all over J. Edgar Hoover. And one other thing. Don't for Christ's sake let it get out what I said here today—my girls, bless their hearts, will drench my Prince Albert pipe tobacco with 2,4-dichlorophenoxy-acetic sassatate weed-killer."

Thus the Fer-de-lance. Keen. Cool. Groovy. Out yonder.

From his platform Gloke Hooma reminded the drivers that they were the very first outsiders to have the honor of taking the new car to the open road. They were to proceed swiftly, in groups of ten, each group by a different route, all cars to be spaced at least five miles apart to attract as little public attention as possible. They were not to use the eight-ball cannon, except in case of road blocks, until they arrived at the scene of battle. They were not to use the venom-spitters unless motorcycle cops tried to interfere with them. They were not to dilate their wings unless expressly ordered to do so by their Commander.

"Slobbla ooo eeeyok!" Gloke Hooma cried again, using the stirring, triumphant motto of the Cow Fulani tribe, which in loose translation means, "Them that has, gits."

The cry came echoing back from a hundred and one throats and the Commander, in the front Fer-de-lance, raised his helmet and gave it a vigorous wave. He had the look of an outsized chipmunk with its cheeks full of unhulled walnuts, and there was a smile of intense eagerness on his face. So it seemed. He was Hickey Dolbier, famous corporation counsel, off on perhaps the greatest adventure of a life that had been, up to now, a bit on the sedentary side.

His little army was comprised of boys who were, for the most part, high school seniors or college freshmen recruited out of the Midwestern States. They had been selected months ago for trial runs of the Fer-de-lance, with no thought in mind of an expedition to West Texas. Beneath the yellow helmets, each boy had a head of hair resembling the most frightful of all fright wigs. There were no beards because of the intricate control mechanisms on the car, and many boys had refused to join the Banner task force when the restriction against whiskers was made known. As for their clothing, they looked as if they had suited up for the Newport Jazz Festival, or got together their wardrobe for Easter in Fort Lauderdale. The style was Midwestern Booger because most of the lads, being Midwestern, were chary not only of the styles being imported from England and France, but of the New York and Ivy League sartorial splendors. These boys had their own folklorical battle cries, such as "Muck th' Mods!" and "Bugger th' Brolly Male!" They wore turtleneck sweaters, pants that strangled what little manhood they might have possessed, and boots of various styles. Their insignia was stamped on the front of their yellow helmets—a snarling head of The Tiger as he may have looked when he slaughtered the black dog in serene Old San Juan.

Hickey Dolbier had on one of the season's gutzier sports coats.

"Twangers out!" he cried, and fifty hands struck fifty small levers, and fifty flat guitars slid out of their nests, and a mighty unified twang sounded, and the beginning of a song—"Scatty wah ... whamp whamp ... git muh to th' scene on time ...."—lyrics adapted from the public utterances of Ringo Fox.

Tuh-wang!

Now a gigantic throbbing sound rose into the Michigan heavens and the Command Fer-de-lance moved slowly toward the exit giving on the road to the south, and the fifty deadly steel vipers wheeled out in sections of ten, their powerful motors pulsating, and over the inter-fleet radio came the voice of Hickey Dolbier:

"Roll your arointing wheels!"

TUH-WANG! TUH-WANG! TUH-WANNNNNG!

At the Kockamaney Motel—no longer a haven for tired motorists but a barracks and a bawdy house—a hairy-faced young man strode to a pole standing in the wide courtyard, pressed a button, and a police siren wailed mournfully over the compound. It was the call to assembly.

Within a few minutes Kockamaney's Chili Queens stood before their leader—a dirty, hirsute, slouching, disorderly, scurvy group of young men, meaner than any band of rustlers or road agents ever to terrorize the decent citizens of an older West.

Petticoats, who wanted them that way, surveyed his army with his nasty piggish eyes. Cottonmouth Clarke stood beside him.

"Min!" Petticoats addressed them. "Ah finely got good news for you. We gonna have us some action. Min! Lookit them purty hawgs uh yourn over theah!" He waved a hand toward the Harley-Davidsons standing or leaning in various parts of the court. "It takes guts," Petticoats said, "it takes real guts to straddle a hawg th' way you fellas straddle 'em."

"Guts!" echoed Cottonmouth Clarke, dramatically raising an index finger into the sky.

"Min!" shouted Petticoats, "we got us some innamies! Rattlesnakes outa th' Nawth. Eastuhn people. *Nawth* Eastuhn people! We'll send them bastuhds a-zizzin' for the tules like th' heel flies was nippin' at they butts!" He went into his awkward Spur Dance,

226

kicking his legs forward, whirring the rowels. "That," he added, "er we'll kill 'em! Ain't that rat, Sheriff?"

"Right as rain!" hollered Cottonmouth.

"Min!" cried Petticoats, getting into full billygraham stride, "Ah want you to know that th' sacred onnuh of mah dead mutha is *in*-volved now. An' th' reppatation uh mah ole Daddy! We gotta fight faw Kockamaney chili powder, min! Let all them others have they dumb cattle and they dumb all wells. Cattle stinks! All wells stinks! But min! Chili powder smay-yulls good! They ain't no smay-yull on this earth as nice to th' nose as good ole Kockamaney chili powder! You min, some uh you, you the sons of min that've gone fur in chili powder, min that have bin with Kockamaney all they grown lives. Ah want you to go into trainin' as of rat now. By tuhmarr mawnin' Ah want all th' fillies outa you rooms here. No poon uh inny kine! No hahd licka to be drunk faw the nex' fo-five days. Innybody got inny questions?"

"Yeh!" came insolently from one of the Chili Queens in the front rank, a husky fellow with a dirty yellow beard. "Ah wanna know what we doin' all this faw, beside pay an' booze an' fillies. What's th' *motive* behine alla this scraggy-whaggy?"

"Dobie!" said Petticoats, a snarl in his voice, "you wanna wake up tuhmarr with you own pussonal prairie-oystuhs missin'? Huh? Slassed off with a ole rusty razuh blade? Dobie, you gonna git it you don't watch you big slobby mouth!"

The Queen called Dobie faded back into the group. Another one, with a flaring red beard, took a step forward.

"How soon," he asked, "we gonna git to kill th' innamy?"

"Purty soon, Chigguh," said Petticoats.

"How minny we git ta kill?"

"Maybe eight, maybe tin."

"Well, that ain't minny. Guess it'll hafta do."

" 'Membuh now," Petticoats called out in peroration, "fillies all out by mawnin'."

"Shore boss!" came the cry of assent from four dozen loyal throats.

No fillies would leave.

෯෯ Chapter TWENTY-THREE

A strapping cowboy with brown curly hair showing beneath his tilted John B. rode slowly along a trail leading in from one of the far corners of the Bowlared Ranch. He was about thirty and there was a craggy handsomeness about his face, tanned a deep russet. His name was Chip Lassiter and he had the appearance and the manner of a citizen who knows his way about. He was ramrod of the Bowlared. At this moment there was a pensive expression on his face, as if he were savoring the sweetness of the morning.

Lassiter was savoring no sweetness. He had no eye for the tiny desert flowers blooming across the undulating stretches of sand and chaparral; he had no nose for the clean smell of the Texas air. A slow bubble of anger was working inside of him.

There had been a time, not too long ago, when Chip Lassiter had been a cheerful, boyish, fun-loving man. He had loved rough-housing it with the boys, playing practical jokes, sitting around a campfire at night and singing the time-tested ballads of the range, the sad songs that cowboys have been crooning down through the decades. It used to be that Lassiter felt a pleasurable tingling in his backbone when his cronies asked him to sing his own favorite, "Ah'm Nailin' Up Fences Ag'in Cattle Drives, That Never Come Thoo Inny Moah."

These days he wouldn't have sung that dirty management song for a month's wages. All those old ballads celebrated the sanctity of the Vested Interests and where Lassiter had once loved them, without ever realizing the evil of the messages they carried, they were now as wormwood and gall to him. In short, this man cut in the classic mould of the heroic westerner, was a member in good standing of Americans for Democratic Action, and his affectionate name for his horse was Hubert Horatio. He had seen the vision one afternoon in the barber shop in Aveinte when, by chance, he had picked up a copy of *Time* magazine. Something he read in that magazine changed him from an easy-going rider of the purple sage to a cantankerous and dedicated enemy of The System. In actuality, he didn't quite know what The System was, and for the life of him he could never remember what that dang article in *Time* was about. In other words, he enjoyed a better-than-average grasp of all that is going on in the world around him.

On this sunny Texas morning he was mad at a machine, a machine now installed on the Bowlared Ranch, a machine which the hands called the Instant Roundup. Chip Lassiter saw it clearly for what it was, what it represented: automation. Displacement of men. He could remember back when the milking machines first came in—but they hadn't bothered him. He hadn't given a thought to the automation aspect of those mechanical udder-pumps. But today he was a disturbed cowboy, and things were different. He wanted to do something to get rid of that hideous black box, and the thought of dynamite had crossed his mind, but he dismissed it; he hadn't come that far in liberalism yet. The exasperating thing, at the moment, was the utter absence of any individual to blame, and to cuss out. The ownership of the ranch was in a state of flux and confusion, and the only people Chip Lassiter could denounce were The Interests, and up to this point in his development as a political animal, there was something vaporous and intangible about The Interests. They were like skim milk, the Holy Ghost, and cuckoo spit—a man couldn't get a good holt on 'em with his hands, couldn't take a hammer and nail 'em down. "God dang!" said Chip Lassiter as Hubert Horatio brought him over a rise where he could see the hated black monster. The crowning, crushing ignominy—the greatest irony of all—lay in the fact that Lassiter had been delegated by Morgan Heath to the operation of the machine's remote control box. He had come up from the line camp this morning to fiddle around with the buttons and levers, and to study the book that came with the Instant Roundup.

He climbed onto the stool at the control table and sat staring at the big box, fifty feet away. He was in that posture when a vagrant idea flicked across his mind. His face brightened. Suppose, he said to himself, just suppose a *man* got into that thing by mistake, and some switches got thrown by accident, and the machine half-killed the man, and maybe even neutered him—maybe then they'd get rid of it, say it was too dangerous to have around. But what man?

Doom came walking around a corner of the stable and ambled out past the machine and came up to the control table.

"Hey, Mac," he said to Lassiter, "you see a big yella cat with a jernt in his tail come out this way?"

"Nawp," said Lassiter.

"Well," said Doom, "I ain't been able to find him anywheres. He's the cat owns this place and half the rest of the country. Eric and Diana," he went on, as if the cowboy knew them, "are up the wrench house fightin' like married people. She bleeves in lettin' the cat out to do his doody and get his exercise, he bleeves the cat's too important to turn loose out here where even the damn rabbits is killers. So she let The Tiger out three-four hours ago and he ain't been seen."

"Ah jus' got here muhself," said Lassiter and returned to his work. Doom went over and sat down on a flat rock the size of a bass drum. A full-grown mesquite tree cast its shade over the fat man and he had just succeeded in dispelling all worry from his mind, when he heard a scurrying, scrabbling noise behind him, accompanied by a wild scream such as might be uttered by a sinner being given the hot-prod on arrival in Hell.

An animal came whanging out of the bushes, leaped for the trunk of the mesquite tree, delivered itself of another soul-shriveling scream, and scrambled for the upper branches. Behind it came The Tiger.

The owner of the Bowlared Ranch went up the tree with a speed that was astonishing. The other animal, some kind of a cat critter, bigger than The Tiger, was making its way out on a limb that was beginning to bend, and in a second his pursuer was right behind him. Then both cats stopped for a moment, each gauging the sway of the limb.

"I be double dawg gone!" exclaimed Chip Lassiter. "Yonda's yer cat and look what he's a-doin'! That's a Texas wahl cat he's after, we call 'em a bobcat. And sure as Ah live and breathe, it's a female bobcat. Man, this is one for the books! That yella cat uh yourn is aimin' to rapefy that bobcat and it begins to look to me like as if he'll do 'er, too!"

Zoooooooosh! The bobcat leaped for the ground and when she hit a small cloud of dust arose, and she stood there a moment till it settled. She was a chestnut brown, grizzled with black spots, and Doom was surprised to note that her truncated tail was twitching in a convulsive manner. Up in the tree The Tiger was tensing himself, preparing for his leap, and the jog in his long yellow tail was jerking so rapidly that Doom imagined he could hear the little bony parts rattling inside.

As The Tiger leaped, the bobcat took off like a scatback, and shot straight into the open gateway of the black machine. She seemed to sense her mistake and turned to come out, but The Tiger was on her in two leaps and she shrieked a wildcat shriek that surely was heard the yon side of Aveinte. And now across the dusty ground lumbered big Doom, the utterly fearless ex-bookie from Times Square. He knew nothing at all about the potential of the Texas wildcat, which is capable of converting itself into a hurricane with fur on it; he knew only that The Tiger was about to indulge in a pastime that was forbidden to him. Doom went through the door and started for the wildly writhing cats, and out at the table the splendid anarchist Chip Lassiter reached out and delicately flipped a switch for the Common Man, and then another, and his forefinger tapped a lever down, and he grinned as he shoved a thumb against a button. Things happened.

The steel doors swung shut with a clang and Doom didn't even have time to express surprise. Things came at him from all directions, grabbing him, wrestling him around, whirling him over, twisting him back. He bellowed louder than any bull, but the Instant Roundup clanked and banged along, shuddering from end to end with all its multiple activity, and doing its job. Both cats were now screaming in what may have been rage, or ecstasy—Doom was too occupied to render a judgment about it. Vile liquids were shooting out of holes and drenching him—he didn't know it but five or six different types of spray were aimed at his slowly rotating body, and the one that had the odor of triple-strength creosote possessed the dominant fragrance, and now a couple of glittering curved saws began moving out from the walls toward his head, but they must have recognized the fact that he had no horns, for they suddenly stopped, looked around, and then retracted. Doom was howling and sputtering but he was still dimly aware of the presence of the cats, snarling and slithering in the floodtide of insecticides beneath him, and then all of a sudden he felt frightful stabbing pains in various portions of his expansive hide—piercing jabs that elicited such cries as might emanate from a man being eaten alive by sabre-toothed tigers.

Out at the control table Chip Lassiter saw a dark object rocket out of the top of the black box. It hit the dirt and materialized itself into the wildcat. It was a sorry-looking wildcat, for it too had been drenched with creosote and other sprays, alien to its nature, and its fur had been ripped and tormented and violently teased. It stood there a moment and glanced around and then shuddered all over, and Chip Lassiter swore later that it looked cross-eyed at him and then *smiled*, following which it lit out for the hills. The Black Hills, probably. Or Beverly.

Now The Tiger came in view, perched on the top of the machine's black wall. The clanking and jangling went right along, and the bellowing of Doom had not diminished by any noticeable degree. The Tiger glanced down at the proceedings within, then looked off toward the horizon. He may or may not have caught a glimpse of the fleeing bobcat. In any case he stood there, licking his chops and inspecting the damage that had been done to his body. He looked tired. He had been through an act of love never duplicated in the entire centuries-long history of feline friendliness, and he seemed fully cognizant of the fact that it had been a special thing, and had taken a good deal of the zip out of him. If he had been a rationalizing creature, he might have thought back to the adventure in the green gelatin, and then considered *this* romantic interlude just ended, and putting the two together, he could easily have decided that there were other things in life. Be that as it may, The Tiger took one more glance down at the howling fat man, then leaped to the ground and disappeared into the cactus.

Chip Lassiter shifted his attention to a pair of levers he had not yet touched, the white one marked "Brand" and the red one labeled "Cut." He debated with himself a moment, then made his decision. He'd brand the fat man, but spare him the cutting. He hit the white lever and a few extra clanks sounded and Lassiter set himself for the shriek of shrieks. For some reason it didn't come—the yowling had, in fact, begun to slacken off; apparently Doom had about exhausted his strength. So Lassiter pressed a button labeled "Fait Accompli" and the rear steel doors of the machine swung open, and long steel rods with heavy pads on the ends, similar to the padded poles used in water-jousting, began jabbing and pushing and rolling Doom out of the box and, having got him clear of the exit, the rods withdrew and the doors closed and the big man lay on the ground panting and aching and burning and smelling like a city dump. "Igggggg-ggg-ggghhhhhh!" he remarked, and his eyes closed and he seemed to be asleep.

Another man now came out from behind the stable, skulking along by the main corral fencing, then ducked in back of the machine where Chip Lassiter could not see him. He bent down and rolled Doom's inert mass over a few inches so he could get at the hip pocket. He unbuttoned the pocket and quickly snaffled out the leather wallet, and it was in his hand when Eric and Morgan Heath came running up and grabbed him.

The wallet thief was Lunsford Scruggs.

Eric flipped open the leather to make certain that the piece of brown paper was inside, and Heath kept a firm grip on Lunsford.

"Hot wallet," said Eric with a grin, extending it toward Heath, who put a finger on it to feel the heat. "Look," Eric said, turning it over. The Bowlared brand had been scorched into the leather—the hot iron had never touched Doom's blimplike butt. This is the brand:

It represents a bowl of chili. When a man walks into a restaurant almost anywhere in Texas, and certainly anywhere in San Antonio, and says, "Bowl uh red," they know what he means. An altogether appropriate brand for the Kockamaney ranch, birthplace of the famous chili powder. In future times Doom would be offered large sums of money for his wallet, because tycoons in the great chili and chili powder industry knew it to be a fine collector's item—a fragment out of chili history. But Doom would never part with it, and cherished possession of it the rest of his life, and often rubbed an affectionate fat paw over the scarred leather, saying, "Kep' me from gettin' sizzled a inch deep right on my big ole ass."

Eric bent over and asked Doom how he felt, and Doom was too depleted to respond.

"Stay right here and rest a few minutes," Eric said to him, "till we get this conniving bastard up to the house, and then Morgan'll come back with a jeep and pick you up. Take it easy, now."

Doom opened his mouth and succeeded in gasping out a single quavering sentence: "Run f' y' life."

"Now," said Lunsford Scruggs, almost defiantly, as they escorted him toward the ranch house, "let's not get high and mighty about this thing. So I lost. I'm willing to be reasonable about it. I wanted that scrap of paper a lot more than you do."

"You are a scurvy, sleazy crook," Eric retorted.

"I am no such thing," Lunsford protested. "I've only been sort of crooked. Business crooked. I happen to represent a syndicate of other people involved in the chili powder trade."

"Oh," said Eric, surprised. "That makes it a bit different."

"I'm an actor," said Lunsford, "hired as a kind of spy. I set myself up as a likeable, garrulous, entertaining, middle-aged ninny. I had to fool that egregious ass Petticoats Kockamaney, and that posturing idiot Cottonmouth Clarke. I've been ten years at it and I'm sorry it's over, because I've had a hell of a lot of fun, especially dreaming up my little stories. I've got a thousand of them."

"And your job was to . . ."

"Find the secret ingredient. My people manufacture the competing brands of chili powder. Every one of them has a good product, but none of them has ever been able to find out what Kockamaney has that they don't have. They've put chemists on it, but the labs failed to find the secret. They have known that something of a most delicate and esoteric nature has been used by Kockamaney down through the years, and they have always referred to that something as 'the tumescence-factor.' "

"Hmmmmm," came from Eric. "You think it really works, this tumescence-factor?"

"Of course. Else why would I risk getting shot full of holes by this cruddy Kockamaney crowd? It works, and the secret lies, at least in part, in the prescriptive lines on those two pieces of brown paper."

By this time they were on the veranda with Diana, and she wanted to know immediately what was meant by the term "tumescence-factor."

"Let it go," said Eric, irritation in his voice. "It's no concern of yours."

"The hell it's not," she replied in a vibrant voice. "Mr. Heath, tell me what it is."

"Well," said Lunsford Scruggs with just a slight hesitancy, for Texans are straightforward people, "when my employers first became interested in it, they called it the 'hard-factor.' "

"Oh," said Diana.

"Now," said Lunsford, "I'm willing to tell you what I know. I saw the lettering on the other half of that paper down in the Sheriff's Office. I memorized that lettering. The paper contains the formula as set down by a Kickapoo Indian named Frankie Deadbird. We've got to go back to . . ."

"Morgan," Eric spoke suddenly to Heath, "I almost forgot— run up there and get Doom." Morgan Heath left the veranda and departed in a jeep.

"The original powder," Lunsford Scruggs continued, "which we have been calling the tumescence-factor, was discovered by the Kickapoos. They used it straight, like a medicine, an aphrodisiac. They had been mixing it and using it for God knows how many hundreds of years. Then along came the Kockamaneys, and it was old Jedediah, father of Petticoats, who got wind of the stuff when he was on a hunting trip in Mexico near a town called Muzquiz. He and his companion wandered into this Kickapoo village of Nacimiento, and Jedediah found out about the powder, and tried some. They had to drag him off of every squaw in the village, and the legend goes that he was shagging nanny goats through the cactus before the effects wore off. At that time the Kockamaney chili powder business was dying on the vine, but old Jedediah made a deal with the village chief and gave him a carload of fine rifles and shotguns in exchange for the secret, or access to the secret."

"You mean those dumb Indians gave away *that* for a shipment of guns?" Eric demanded.

"The Kickapoos have always been great hunters," Lunsford said. "They probably enjoy hunting deer and other game as much or more than they enjoy . . . uh . . . women. They went ape for those beautiful guns. But they didn't really give the formula to the Kockamaneys. They just farmed it out. The tumescence-factor is a white powder and the Kickapoos are still the only people who know how to produce it. Periodically they send two or three of their men across the border and up to Aveinte. These men always bring several gunnysacks full of some kind of vegetation that goes into the powder. It must be something that isn't available in this area. For several years now the Indian in charge of the Kickapoo end of things has been this Frankie Deadbird. I might advise you that he has already been tomcattin' around with your cute little Irish secretary."

"No!" Eric protested. "Mr. Scruggs, my cute little Irish secretary is as loyal as they come."

"I didn't say she was being disloyal. Frankie Deadbird is somewhat older but he's a good-looking Indian and I've seen them together."

"I'll have to look into it," said Eric. "Tell me, now, what the hell happens when the Indians get up here with their gunnysacks?"

"Petticoats has a hideaway somewhere," Lunsford explained, "and much as I've tried, I haven't been able to find it. I'm sure the secret ingredient is mixed at that hideout, and I'm also pretty sure that Petticoats himself couldn't do the job alone, without the Indians."

"But what's all this gogga-ma-goggle about Mama's Hat Room and breaking the chain, and where does the brown paper fit in?"

"Frankie Deadbird is a clever guy for a Kickapoo," said Lunsford. "He has found out that there is a strong superstitious streak in Petticoats. And Frankie Deadbird knows something else. He has found out that Petticoats has been plotting against the Kickapoos, even planning on hijacking the boys with the gunnysacks. So Frankie Deadbird has been working on Petticoats and his superstitious nature, and getting him so confused that Petticoats doesn't know which end is up. The idea is, that chain of hats in the bedroom is never to be broken. To break the chain would mean that Kockamaney's business rivals would surely get the formula. Now, we come to an important element in the story. Frankie Deadbird tore the paper in half and gave part of it to Señorita Tornillo. Why? Because he believes Petticoats will keep on with his plotting and scheming and some day very likely will get his chance at the formula. The Indian has been trying to outfox him by giving half the formula to his divorced wife, and planting the other half in that room of superstition. Frankie Deadbird reasons that if anyone is to get the formula, he'd prefer to have it be the Mexican girl, and he has been trying to rig the thing in her favor."

"So," said Eric, "what's in the gunnysacks?"

"I haven't any idea. But if you'll let me have that paper, I think I can reconstruct the formula."

In short order Lunsford had worked out this:

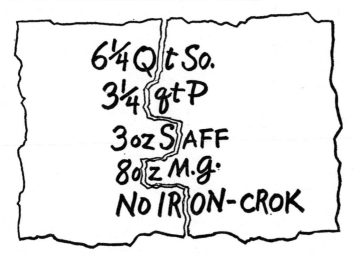

They sat and studied it.

"It's beginning to make a little sense," Lunsford finally muttered. "Just a little. Those two top lines . . . I don't know. The thing we've got to find is that hideout where they mix it." He paused in thought for a few moments. "Mr. Yaeger," he finally resumed, "I think I see a little light. I want to work along with you, but where do I stand? I've been at this job ten long years—don't you think my people ought to get something out of this in the end?"

"Let's take that up when we get to it," suggested Eric. "Right at this moment, I can say I'm favorably inclined toward you."

"Good enough," nodded Lunsford.

When Morgan Heath drove the jeep up to the big black box, the machinery inside was grumbling and clanking again, and howls were emerging, and there was no sign of Doom. Heath hurried over to the control table where Chip Lassiter was gayly playing the levers the way a man plays the vibes. A western hat, battered almost beyond recognition, came flying out of the box, followed by fragments of cloth and some bits of leather.

"You put the fat guy back in there?" Heath wanted to know.

"Nawp," said Lassiter. "He finely got up and wandered off yonda—walkin' nawth."

"You got a bull in the machine now?"

"Nawp. Sassy fella come up ovuh the rise and acted snot-mean, wanted to know if I'd seen that cat, th' yella one that jazzed th' wahl cat, and I tol' him to mind his mannuhs, and he called me a sissified nussmaid to a buncha cow crittuhs, and so I told him th' cat had went inside that big black box, and that's him you're a-hearin' in there. God dang, I'm givin' it to 'im good!"

"Let him out," ordered Heath. "I want to see him."

The doors swung open and a forlorn Albert Apple was prodded and pushed out of the box. He lay in tatters, soaked with insecticides, bruised and battered, and great groans came out of deep recesses within him.

"Ah woosh," he mumbled, "a panther had got me when Ah was young."

Heath said, "Who the hell are you, stranger?"

"Oh, God! Ohhhhhhhhh God!"

Lassiter came up beside Morgan Heath. "Hey, Mistuh," he spoke cheerily to the man on the ground, "you mind a lot if I go back now and nussmaid my buncha cow crittuhs?"

"Ohhhhhhhhhh God! Please, gentlemen. This here's been the wuss day Ah evuh had in mah whole bawn life! Ohhhhhh Jesus! You lookin' at a ruint man! *Ruint!* Goin' along mindin' mah own business, up comes foah big black bulls, biggern baddleships, staht rammin' inta mah truck, knocked it ovuh like it was . . ."

"I think," said Heath, "that the poor guy's out of his mind. I'll take him up and put him to bed. And listen to me, Lassiter. Don't be sendin' any more humans through that box."

While Lassiter helped get Albert Apple off the ground and into the jeep, Morgan Heath asked him if he'd seen the yellow cat.

"Yep," said Lassiter. "Went off east."

"Why didn't you grab him? You know he owns the ranch, don't you?"

"Yep. That's why I left 'im go. To be honest about it, I don't aim to punch no cattle fer no cat."

"Ohhhhhhh God!" came again from Albert Apple. "Gentlemen, that fee-rocious thing come within a eighth of a inch uh takin' off mah diddledywhacker!"

The jeep moved off toward the ranch house.

⚙ Chapter TWENTY-FOUR

THE desert philosopher Frederick Beck once remarked that when
he was a small boy his ambition was to grow up and track people,
but that now he doesn't know anybody much worth tracking. Had
he been on the great sprawl of the Bowlared Ranch this day he
would have seen tracks of a most peculiar character and if he had
ever learned to read sign, he would have deduced that a sozzled
rhinoceros was wandering over the sands, and he would have
tracked it. It was the spoor of Doom.

The big man, still in a state of shock and confusion, moved un-
certainly through the desert brush, driven by some piping inner
voice that told him to find The Tiger at any cost. The sun beat
down on his uncovered head and he was thirsty. He had some
vague notion that a liquid could be extracted from cactus, and
there was cactus aplenty as far as his eye could see, but every
piece of vegetation he approached seemed to reach out and slash
at him with its claws. Doom was a sick man—sick from the horrific
walloping and goosing and stabbing and sloshing the black machine
had given him, sick from worry over the cat, and sick from the
certainty that he would soon be dead of thirst, starvation, and sun-
stroke. The deeply troubled state of his mind was apparent in the
continuing thought that at any moment the big black box would

come trundling over the sand, snatch him back into its steel jaws, and give him another going over.

Luck was with him in one respect; he found a land tank where water was stored for the livestock. It had something of the taste of hot Elliman's Universal Embrocation, but he gulped it down, and decided to stay close beside it. Maybe a cow would come along to get a drink and he could ride it back to civilization. He lay down to rest for a while and fell asleep, and when he awoke he was thirsty again, and hungry. He drank some more of the hot liniment and then he remembered Lunsford Scruggs's description of a plant called sotol, which was good to eat. He strolled around and finally came upon a shriveled little cactus-type growth that he thought must be sotol. It had a round head about two inches in diameter, set with little buttons. Doom located a piece of mesquite wood and dug in the sand and finally brought up the root, which was the shape of a sickly carrot. He washed it off in the tank, scrubbing the top with sand, then rinsing it, and finally he sat down to give it a try. Bland. Meaty but tough. Still, he sensed that it would furnish a little nourishment till that damn cow came along. It was not sotol he was eating. It was a small cactus called peyote.

A bit later he was gnawing on the cactus and staring at the metallic glisten of the water tank when a head rose slowly from its brassy surface. A Medusa-head of writhing serpents, all purples and pinks. The head began to expand, and grew as big as Doom's own body, and then twice that big, and then there was a puff of vapor engulfing the head and when it lifted, the snakes had turned to a luminescent red. After his ordeal in the Instant Roundup, one might assume that Doom would now arrive at a quick determination—an acknowledgment that he had had it up to here, that this was a God's plenty for one day. Not so. He sat as though in a trance, fascinated, staring hypnotically at the head as it continued changing color. A swirling mist arose again and the head was gone, but Doom was aware of bright movement in another direction— two beautiful maidens wearing filmy skirts came tripping across the sand, scattering flower petals on cactus and greasewood; they appeared to be singing, yet the music he heard was that of a pipe organ playing the stately and ever-lovely canticle, *When the Bell in the Lighthouse Rings Ding Dong.*

The music was almost unbearably beautiful, and then Doom began to feel a strange sensation in his toes. He glanced down at his feet and saw that his toes were beginning to explode, just like popcorn, and as each toe popped and flew into the air, big and white and fluffy, tickling sensations ran up his legs. Then the two girls came slithering up, and caressed him, kissing him on the ears and nose and forehead and lips, and after that they began fastening great luscious strawberries onto his feet in place of the toes, and he found that he could wiggle them, and felt like bending over and consuming them. Meanwhile the popcorn, formerly his true toes, drifted upward one by one and exploded into bubbling sunbursts. Hallucinogens can be hell on toes.

Both his sensory consciousness and his cellular consciousness were now blending in a riot of color. A bowl of wonton soup appeared before his eyes, sparkling as if big diamonds were afloat in it, and suddenly he saw beyond the wonton soup a grouping of bright green icicles, bigger than ball bats. Through the icicles strode a man, straight at Doom. It was Marshal Dillon, without his big hat, without Miss Kitty, without Doc. Ropes and rainbows of color swirled between the long legs of Matt Dillon, and then above his head Doom saw the big cement ditch in Los Angeles and the cement walls and one of the holes like a cave. Marshal Dillon turned and pointed, and he spoke in a voice that seemed to rumble out of a deep echo chamber, and what he intoned was: "Go – Find – Yon – Gold – Mine! Bite – the – Black – Knob!"

Everything vanished. Doom stood up and started walking. He walked straight and true, impervious to the stabbing of thorns and spikes as he moved through the brush. Soon he came to the entrance of a canyon, and he turned in, and marched on as if he had the strength of ten. His course took him upward in the canyon and after a while the stone walls widened and he looked upon a bosky dell, with green grass and pleasant little trees and a gurgling brook. Above this tiny park he saw the entrance to his gold mine—a dark cave in the side of a cliff. A path led up to it and Doom didn't hesitate. A few moments later he strode into the cavern and came to the bright green icicles, which actually were crystalline calcium carbonate. Doom put his hand on one of them, a stalagmite, and exclaimed, "Rock-sickels!" He moved through the rock-sickels and came to a large illuminated chamber where a long wooden worktable stood against one of the walls. On the table were mortars and pestles of various sizes, fashioned from volcanic stone, and mottled gray enamel cups and small pots and spoons, and a household scale with a capacity of twenty-five pounds. Piled elsewhere on the table, and on shelving across the chamber, were chunks of a white substance with the look of peeled turnips. Doom moved up to the table and noticed, at once, other little mounds of the cactus plant he had been eating just before the visions came to him. There were large bowls containing seed, and some kind of crushed herb. Standing in a corner of the room were several three-gallon stone crocks, and Doom had just started toward them when he heard voices.

Out of a rocky corridor came an Indian, then another Indian, and behind them a tall white man. Doom froze in his tracks.

"Stand whirr you are!" the white man commanded, and two large silver pistols appeared in his hands. He had on a greasy old cowboy hat and Doom noticed the big glistening spurs on his boots.

"One move and you a gawn goose!" the man said.

"Listen, Mac," said Doom with surprising boldness, "I been a gone goose so many times since I got up this morning that it ain't gonna make much difference I get myself gone again."

"Grab 'im," said Petticoats Kockamaney to the Indians. They stepped forward and seized Doom by the arms. Petticoats put one of his guns down and moved over to a low ledge cut in the rock wall. A small radio cabinet was set into this shelf and after twitching a knob, Petticoats spoke to it.

"Cottonmouth," he said, "git ovah to the mo-tel and git the Queens ready. Thangs is beginnin' to pop at Command Post Kickapoo. Move it!"

"Roger," came the Sheriff's response.

"Ovah," barked Petticoats, "undah, out, in, acrost, aroun' and thoo!"

"Now, stranger," he said, gesturing with his gun at Doom, "mosey."

"Huh?"

"Ah said mosey!"

"Mosey to you," said Doom, who had never moseyed.

Petticoats pointed the gun at the floor and fired a shot that struck within two inches of the toes that had just recently been large luscious strawberries.

If the fact has not been discernible up to now, let it be clearly understood that Petticoats Kockamaney was a man of deep senti-mentality, with strong currents of familial reverence, encompass-ing both Mother-love and Daddy-worship, plus an intense af-fection for the soil of Texas (he was one of those patriots de-scribed as being so proud of Texas that they cain't sleep at night) and this is why he decided to butcher Doom like a pig.

Butchering a man like a pig isn't such a frightful affair when analyzed; it's the telling him about it in advance that hurts.

"We gonna hang you filthy cockuss up by the heels," Petticoats said to Doom, who now lay trussed on the floor of the cavern. "We gonna strip you down, and then we gonna butcha you like a Kansas City hawg." His eyes glittered as he went into his famous Spur Dance.

Doom stared at him speechless, his eyes wide and imploring.

"Ah, pussonly," continued Petticoats, "aim to cut off yore meat in big ole strips, and we gonna git us a big arn pot, and we gonna boil you up and make lahd outta you. Man, you gonna render down inta a heap uh lahd!"

Words now burst from Doom's lips, reflecting the fact that he had spent many hours luxuriating before television sets. "Please," he begged, "grant me the boom of death before a firin' squad. Please don't berl my meat!"

Petticoats sneered, then turned to the Indians and said, "C'm awn, boys, le's go git them gunnysacks and git along with the work." The three men left the cave and Doom lay for a while, sick at heart, unable to think straight. Then he remembered Matt Dillon in the vision. He turned his head and found that he was lying within a few feet of the radio. Slowly he began wiggling his body, scooching along the stony floor. Once within reach, he lay resting, staring at the black panel. Then he struggled up to a point where he could reach it, and he bit – the – black – knob. He waited a minute, then spoke in a voice of great desperation:

"Help! Police! Eric! Somebody! This is Doom. They got me in this cave. It's out in this big rock valley by a little park with a stream runnin' through it. This dirty Protisan son of a bitch is gonna berl me up in a big iron pot and make lard outa me. Eric! Fuh Chri' sake!"

He dropped back onto the floor, and rolled over, and in a brief while, out of sheer exhaustion, even in the face of this awful prospect of being rendered into shortening . . . he dropped off to sleep.

Down at Aveinte, in the Sheriff's Office, only one man had
heard the cry for help. He was the Mayor of the town, Solly
Marx. Doom's appeal did something to him. He took off his hat
and smoothed his hair and stared at the shortwave set. Something
was wrong, extremely wrong. Nobody should put a man into a
pot and boil him and make lard out of him. Solly Marx made his
decision. He scurried out of the saloon and lit for the Bowlared
Ranch.

During all this time what has happened to the magnificent
motorized legion commanded by the valiant Hickey Dolbier? A
remnant of that group was, at this very moment, roaring down
the Billy Sol Estes Freeway toward Aveinte.

The expedition had been away from its Michigan base no more
than three hours when Hickey Dolbier began to suspect that
something was amiss. The boys in the cars didn't seem to like
the idea of spacing themselves out—they were a gregarious lot,
with many common interests and the urge to socialize. They
were beginning to bunch up in their groupings of ten, so that
they could enjoy little races, and play chicken, and indulge in
other youthful pursuits. After a while one squad, traveling between Indianapolis and Terre Haute, began playing with the wing-
spread controls. This group was led by an All-American boy of
seventeen, Foxworth Foxhall, son of a wealthy and permissive professor at Ann Arbor. Foxworth had always been mechanical, with

a creative and inquisitive mind, and so he was the first to bang the white knob. Out came the steel flaps, there was a flutter of jet force, and Foxworth's Fer-de-lance left the pavement. It scooted along smoothly, then took off in a graceful arc. A great tuh-wangetty-tuh-wang of boyish enthusiasm came from the nine cars behind him. Other eager young hands whacked the white control and several more of Gloke Hooma's beauties began a progress down the highway like frightened giant grasshoppers. A lad out of Evanston, Illinois, took the chance with the Fang button. He was sailing along fifteen feet above the pavement when the jaws of his car opened, exposing the red steel fangs. He eased in just above the car ahead of him, which was still traveling on the ground, came down to an altitude of seven feet, leaned his head around the windshield and yelled: "Hey, Forsythe!" Forsythe turned and looked straight into the hideous jaws; he screamed in terror and swerving his Fer-de-lance, shot off the road, crashing through a rail fence and into a pasture where his car began leaping about crazily in the manner of a big steel flea. The terrorized driver had lost all control of it. Foxworth Foxhall, who had been enjoying himself up front doing little dips and wing-waggles, heard the guitar-twangs employed as a distress signal, banked sharply, waved to the others to follow him, and headed over the cow pasture. In the distance two men in overalls were running toward the scene and at the other end of the field eighteen cows were trying to hide behind a single elm tree. The jaws of the flying cars were groaning open and the two farmers stopped running, made certain what was happening, then turned and raced like gazelles in the direction of South Chicago. The boy named Forsythe was making a manly try at getting his idiot snake-car under control, and he did manage to slow down the leaping action, but then a car just above him went into a loop, a burst of smoke came from its jet pipes, it shot forward on its side, and hit the turf in that position. The driver leaped out and in spite of the fact that flying cars were clanging together and falling to earth, pointed upward and cried: "Man! Lookit that cat go!" Those who had time to look saw Foxworth Foxhall's car shooting straight up—its jaws wide open and its driver's personal insignia, a handsome foxtail, flying bravely from its snout. When Foxworth finally came back to earth with a mighty crash, all cars under his command were out of action, some smashed, some smoking, and the ambulances were already on their way from nearby towns.

Another group of ten Fer-de-lances, carrying boys from junior colleges, stopped for a rest beside a cluster of cottonwoods below Grand Tower, Illinois. They were looking at their maps when one of their number wandered off through the trees and soon came back with news.

"Hey cats," he said, "there's a whole big mother-arointin' river right the other side of these trees. Good spot to cool the clavicle."

They sprawled themselves out on a hillside overlooking the river where, many years before, another boy near their age traveled on a crude raft—but he was a boy different from them, without the advantages.

"Spring loose the pot," ordered the squadron leader, and out came a manila bag, and soon the young heroes were placidly puffing away at their marijuana and discussing various philosophical matters, such as whether wearin' neckties gives ya a pinched head. Ah youth.

Unscheduled things happened to the others. One squadron drove into a Southern Missouri town after dark, looking for beer, and got a bit out of hand after the police chief told them the place was bone dry by local option. These lads found out that a Parent-Teachers organization was holding its regular monthly meeting in the Forty Gallon Baptist Church and so, forgetting the great work that lay ahead of them in Texas, they lay siege to the church, throwing rocks and bricks, and kept the people penned up the whole night. They got away the next morning and made it as far as a Texas community near the Oklahoma border. There they made the acquaintance of some teen-age sky divers who were trying to work out a new angle to their sport—parachuting animals to earth. These ebullient kids had already tried a stunt with a Texas mule. They rigged a parachute harness for the animal and took him up to twenty thousand feet. Then they shoved him out of the plane, saw that his chute opened, then two boys leaped and rode the wind, trying to maneuver so that one or the other would end up astride the mule. They hadn't made it on the first try and they were now debating about a second. The mule had fortunately landed in a fresh-plowed field else there probably would have been a fragmented jackass, followed by mule fricassee. The Fer-de-lance lads were so fascinated by the experiment that they decided to hang around a few days, maybe ride a few mules down themselves. One of their number, in fact, came up with a suggestion for making the sport of mule-diving even more spectacular, by fastening smoke bombs to each of the mule's hooves.

There was one other group that got into difficulty in an Arkansas town, simply because they felt their rape belts needed some test runs. The details are somewhat squalid, and exhilarating, and can be passed by—such a communal outburst of feeling was characteristic of their age group, all ten being high school seniors; it may be that they caused a good deal of future trouble for two dozen high school girls in the town, but they were good girls from solid families, young and impulsive and no doubt attracted by the experimental nature of what they were doing. Friend reader, please pardon an old timer's moment of editorial reflection: these exuberant young people were questing for methods of creating their own joyous worlds, adventuring out in a search for new horizons and golden sunsets, creating new behavior patterns for themselves, such as jumping out of an airplane with a mule under each arm. Bear with these wonderful youngsters—one day they will rule our world. Beezarp!

And so, as stated, we find the final remnant of the Gloke Hooma panzerdivision speeding along the superhighway, hurrying toward the Bowlared Ranch, this final remnant consisting of one Fer-de-lance occupied by Hickey Dolbier, still wearing his gutsy sports coat and his yellow helmet, and sorely bewildered by his inability to make radio contact with a single one of the other cars.

But he, Hickey Dolbier, was not to be sidetracked by pot, by games of chicken, by skydiving mules, by high school girls. He was not to be stopped.

The police siren sounded at the Kockamaney Motel and the stalwarts of the Chili Queens brigade tumbled off their chicks, climbed into their battle dress, slouched blinkingly into the bright daylight, and straddled their Harley-Davidson hawgs. A proud and picturesque lot, these men. Errol Flynn, in all his long career, never led such doughty warriors.

"We move, men!" cried Sheriff Cottonmouth Clarke. "Our leader is in peril. The enemy is about to capture the secret of Kockamaney Chili Powder."

The voice of the Queen called Chigger was heard.

"This heah the time we gonna git tuh killum?" he asked.

"Yuh damn right!" shouted Ogden Crump, stepping quickly forward and jostling Sheriff Clarke out of position. The Sheriff turned and, using both hands, gave Crump a hard shove in return.

"Don't push me!" said Cottonmouth. Crump pushed him.

"Now, men," spoke up Muff Muffgainer. "For Lord sake, is this any way to set an example to the Chili Queens?"

"You keep out of this," snapped Cottonmouth. "I've had about enough of your high-and-mighty spy crap. Go put on your dress and funny hat!"

Muff was in a fury. He stepped quickly forward and brought a hard karate chop down on Cottonmouth's right shoulder, striking near the neck. The Sheriff didn't flinch. Muff gave him a harder chop, this one on the left shoulder. Nothing. The Sheriff reached out and seized Muff by the hair and drew his hand back with the clear intention of administering one of those demeaning slappings seen only in films—rapid back and forth blows, alternating back of the hand with palm of the hand.

The sound of a motor interrupted everything. All eyes turned toward the driveway leading onto the main road. A Land Rover was departing in a great hurry. Driving it was Orlando Dill, and at his side, clutching him out of affection, was Señorita Tornillo, the former Mrs. Petticoats Kockamaney.

"Now where the hell do they think they're going?" asked Sheriff Clarke, his hand suspended in midair.

"Don't ask me," said Muff, staring at the departing vehicle. "Why don't we follow them and find out?"

"Follow them my hind tit," said Cottonmouth. "We're heading out for Sniveling Dog Canyon. On the double!"

The Sheriff drove and Muff and Ogden Crump were in the jeep with him. The Chili Queens apparently had been hitting the jug quite energetically—they were having trouble getting into formation and a few fell off their machines, and these matters delayed the departure for three or four minutes. Then the cavalcade moved down the highway and passed through Aveinte, and bore southward in the direction of the Bowlared Ranch and the canyon.

Orlando Dill and his Mescan chick were traveling in the same direction, but they were far out ahead of the Chili Queens.

"Blanca, my pretty bobolink," said the famous lawyer, "we have in this world a type of person who stands superior to his own kind. We speak of a man being a lawyer's lawyer, a ballplayer's ballplayer, a novelist's novelist. I have been much in the presence lately of a horse's ass's horse's ass. Ogden Crump. And I do believe the designation will apply equally well to Mister Muff, and to all those we have just left behind."

"I do not understand," said Blanca, squeezing Orlando's arm.

"You don't need to," he answered. "We're changing sides."

৪৩ Chapter TWENTY-FIVE

AS she swung along the sandy trail Miss Nora O'Neill's thoughts were on the supernal splendor of the world. She was not concerned with the harsh beauties of nature surrounding her on every side. She was thinking rather of the gorgeous treatment she was getting from life. "Look at me," she said to herself, shifting the upside-down shotgun under her arm. "Just look at me—three years ago a nothing in New Rochelle. Then all of a sudden runner-up in the Miss Subways contest, and after that private secretary to that beautiful hunk Eric Yaeger, and all the fun that went with it, even when he gave me those little gooses, and riding around in de luxe planes and cruise ships that were I mean outathis-world, and now . . . love! Love at first sight! In love with an Indian! W'y, up to this week I never even *saw* a real live Indian!"

She stopped from time to time and looked at the paper she had in her hand, a roughly-drawn sketch telling her the trail to follow to Sniveling Dog Canyon. She had never in her life been able to read a map, couldn't have located Florida or even Ireland if they gave her an entire day with an atlas. But this map she could understand; her Frankie had drawn it for her, and true love makes maps clear.

She arrived at the entrance to the canyon, at the very spot where old Murdo Chisum once bellowed through his whiskers to fetch forth a vulgar echo, checked the map again, and strode quickly up the path that led into the craggy fastness.

She knew very little about Frankie Deadbird. That didn't matter. She knew that she loved him and in her own way of putting it, she'd go with him to the ends of the earth. It would have made no difference to her if she had been told that Frankie was a Kickapoo Casanova. He had traveled some in the West and once on a ranch in Nevada a mildewed movie actress told him he bore a striking resemblance to Rudolph Valentino. From that moment forward Frankie Deadbird looked upon himself as a Great Lover, and all but wore out his lap trying to prove it. He developed a predilection for paleface ladies, or at least for ladies outside his own tribe. Thus Lunsford Scruggs had been slightly inaccurate in his estimate of Frankie; the Indian had given Señorita Tornillo half of that formula because he had a rage in his pants for her, and hoped to carry her off to the wilds of Coahuila with him. Then along came Miss Tiddyboo, and Frankie Deadbird altered course. Miss Tiddyboo had it. All of it.

Frankie had told her that he would probably be in grave danger this day, and asked her to get a rifle from the gun rack at the ranch house and bring it to him in the canyon. Wherefore, the heavy double-barreled shotgun she was carrying butt-forward under her arm.

As she approached the little oasis on the floor of the canyon she heard voices somewhere above and she moved into the bushes and soon saw her lover, and his cousin Paul Moves-the-Tail, each with a burlap sack over his shoulder and accompanied by a tall white man. She crept along in the brush and fell in behind them and watched them go into the cave. She stood outside the entrance and heard:

"Yes suh! We gonna boil you in a pot, soze Ah can fry mah aigs in you grease foh two anna half yeahs."

Then she heard Doom's familiar voice cry out:

"You'll pay with your life in the hot squat, you daster!"

Miss Tiddyboo glanced down at the shotgun, turned it around, and strode into the cavern. She pointed the weapon straight at the white man and announced:

"This is a stickup!"

"Miss Nora!" cried Doom from the floor. Petticoats Kocka-maney put his hands above his head and turned to look back over his shoulder. He gave her a long appraising glance, down then up, up then down, and he smacked his lips.

"You mus' be th' one," he said silkily, "they call Tiddyboo. Ah tell you somethin' Miss Tiddyboo. When Ah git this thang all straightened out, Ah'm gonna scrozzle you tell you teeth rattle in you haid. You might as well git yourseff readied. You gonna git it. Hooooo-weeeeeee!"

Frankie Deadbird quickly stepped forward and kicked Petti-coats just as hard as he could, right in the britches. Petticoats was so surprised that he couldn't speak. Miss Tiddyboo rushed across the room and handed Frankie Deadbird the shotgun, and then flung her arms around the Indian and began kissing him ener-getically on the lips.

"Oh, Frankie darlin'!" she cried. "Are you all right?"

"Climb offa me!" the Indian barked at her. "Save it for later. You got my arms pinned, gal, and this son of a bitch might get ideas."

"Miss Nora," spoke up Doom, "what's goin . . . would you . . . I don't . . . have that Indian get me outa these ropes. You hear what this Texas fella said? You was a witness. Gonna berl up my meat and fry eggs in me!"

Doom was cut free of his bonds and Frankie Deadbird, assuming command, ordered everyone out of the cave. He walked behind Petticoats, advising that scowling creature to keep his hands in the air.

"What in God's name's with you and this Indian fella?" Doom asked Nora O'Neill as they moved toward the opening.

"Love, Doom," breathed Nora, her eyes feasting on her heroic Kickapoo. "I knew it the first minute he spoke to me. He told me that among his people a girl with gold in her hair is the absolute most. He said that if he could return back to his tribe down in Mexico, with me as his squaw, he would be the chief inside of six months and we could have the loveliest wickiup in the village."

"Well I'll be," nodded Doom. "Sure sounds like love."

The little group had yet to emerge from the cave when a pleasant-mannered jackrabbit came into the green clearing that lay below it—the flowering oasis with its gurgling brook and its tall pines. The jackrabbit sat for a few moments, inspecting the calm

253

prospect, then made his way slowly across the grass. At the far side he paused, glanced around, and then seemed to say, "Too quiet. What I need is a little action." And he hippity-hopped on his way, disappearing from view. Oh, foolish rabbit! Oh, short-sighted cuniculus!

Hands still aloft, Petticoats Kockamaney stepped out of the cave and into the sunlight, followed by the others. Frankie Deadbird took one look and the shotgun slipped from his hands, and the others gasped in surprise. Standing before them were Sheriff Clarke, Ogden Crump and Muff Muffgainer, pistols leveled.

"Reach!" proclaimed Ogden Crump, "Reach, afore Ah make a lead mine outa yore guts!"

All reached. And in the distance could be heard a crazy clat-tering and banging and the roar and sputter of engines.

"What kep' yuh so long?" Petticoats demanded, taking charge. He turned quickly and planted a fist squarely on the brown nose of Frankie Deadbird, and Frankie hit the dirt. Whereupon Miss Tiddyboo delivered herself of shrill banshee noises and flung her-self at the heir to the chili powder fortune. Petticoats laughed uproariously as she tried to reach his face with her nails, and he contrived, in spite of her frenzied activity, to run a hand back and forth across the delectable mounds whence came her sobri-quet. "Ah tole you!" he roared, "Ah tole you Ah was a-gonna aroint you. An' Ah'm a-gonna!"

He glanced down the canyon. "That mah boys?" he asked.

"That's them," Cottonmouth Clarke answered. "Petticoats, you should have got them some kind of dune-buggies or Tote Gotes for this kind of country. Listen to them bang around down there!"

"They didn't want anything but hawgs," said Petticoats, "and hawgs is what they got. And speakin' of hawgs . . ." He turned and looked at Doom, who shuddered first and then whimpered, "Oh Gord here it comes again!" Kockamaney's attention was dis-tracted, however, by the appearance down canyon of the first of the Chili Queens. Three of them had come in sight. They were moving along slowly, for the way was stony and blocked by clumps of cactus. One machine struck a boulder and fell over, pinning its rider to the ground. Others were being pushed along by their owners. They were just coming into the clearing, and Petticoats was giving them a wave of welcome, when . . .

"Everybody stand still!" sounded a voice close by, and four men came striding around a huge rock near the cave entrance. Morgan Heath was in the lead, carrying two big revolvers; behind him was Eric, armed with a rifle, Lunsford Scruggs with a six-shooter, and Jeremy K. Jenkins, pointing a shotgun.

Muff Muffgainer chose the course of escape. He yelled something that sounded like "Texas Rangers!" and the abruptness of it distracted everyone as he took off down the slope toward the approaching Chili Queens. Morgan Heath casually brought him to earth with a single shot.

"Creased his shoulder, is all," said Heath. "Anybody else wanna try for a flesh wound?"

Nora O'Neill took a step forward. "Mr. Heath," she said, "these Indians are not bad men. This one is Frankie. I'm going to marry him."

"You're gonna what?"

"Marry him, and go live in Mexico with him."

"Well," mused Morgan Heath, "if *that* don't rip the rag off the bush!" A rattle of gunfire came from below and the Chili Queens could be observed moving forward.

"Can we get out of this gully at the upper end?" Eric asked.

"Don't call this a gully!" snapped Heath. "Sniveling Dog is a box canyon. We'll have to . . . Hold it! What in God's name is that?"

A strange-looking object, a vehicle of some kind, of a brownish mottled coloration, was coming up the canyon. A man in a yellow helmet was at the controls. As it moved closer everyone heard, first, the steady pulsations of its motor, and then a second sound . . .

Tuh-wang.

Tuh-wang!

TUH-WANG!

TUH-WANG!

As that fourth mighty dissonant sound rolled up the canyon, the vehicle was seen to spread a pair of narrow wings, and then leave the ground.

"It's the Fer-der-lance!" cried Eric. "But where . . . where is . . ."

The flying snake-car came through the air, straight at the

Chili Queens, who had halted their advance and gone into a huddle, clutching at one another in sheer terror. The Fer-de-lance dipped toward them once, veered off, sideswiped a large tree but continued airborne, and now it began to open a pair of huge jaws, revealing the fangs of a hideous serpent. At the same time a fusillade of black pool balls began ricocheting around the canyon, and spurts of vapor came from the hubcaps of the car. The whiskered Chili Queens, cravens all, cowered in fright, and then began spreading out, seeking some place to hide from the flying monster, but it now began an encircling maneuver, dipping downward to drive each man back into the herd, behaving much in the manner of an Enzedder sheepdog.

Suddenly something went wrong with the Fer-de-lance. It began to sputter, and then backfire. It came down and hit a rock, then rose in the air again, higher than before, and sheared the top branches off a pine tree, then wobbled crazily in the air, a dozen feet up, and finally banged against the wall of the canyon and dropped to earth like a dead thing. Factory defect, probably.

Now a roar of rage came from the throats of the Chili Queens, maddened by this crazy unexpected attack from the air. They surged toward the fallen Fer-de-lance, then changed direction and started up the slope again, bent upon liberating their chieftain, and Sheriff Clarke, and slaughtering the dirty Easterners and raping their womenfolks.

Jeremy K. Jenkins, his square derby hat in place, his abbreviated frock coat looking as if it had just come from the valet, stepped to the forefront of the group at the cave entrance, shotgun in hand.

"Mr. Scruggs," he said to Lunsford, "you and the Indians keep these prisoners covered. And keep them exposed. Mr. Heath, you and Mr. Yaeger stand behind these rocks with me."

The clamor of the approaching thugs grew louder and Jeremy K. Jenkins turned slowly, raised his scatter gun, and fired. The roar was like that of a cannon. Two Chili Queens stumbled and sank to the ground. Half a dozen others went running off into the bushes. The remaining group, comprising about two dozen, halted for just a few moments, then renewed their frenzied yelling and started slowly forward again.

"They'll get us in the end," said Jeremy K. Jenkins, "but they'll pay a heavy price." He reached in his coat pocket and pulled out a shotgun shell and looked at it. "Where do I put this thing?" he asked, and Morgan Heath showed him.

"When I give the order," he now spoke calmly, "fire straight into their ranks."

The Chili Queens halted their cautious advance for a consultation.

"If we start a-shootin'," said one of the shaggier of the lot, "we gonna knock off old Petticoats an' ole Cottonmouth an' ole Crump."

"Whoss wrong with that?" demanded the bloodthirsty Chigger. "Le's go! Le's kill 'em all! Ah want me some good rape!"

"Evuhbody agreed?" asked the original speaker.

"Yay!"

Outlined against a blue-gray October sky, high on the lip of the canyon, a lone horseman suddenly came in view. He sat tall in the saddle, and motionless. Then another rider came up beside him, a girl with swirling, shoulder-length, corn-yellow hair.

The surviving force of Chili Queens stared up at the tableau, openmouthed. So did the people at the top of the slope in front of the cave.

The cowboy looked back over his shoulder, raised his hat in signal, and then the sound of his voice came rollicking down the canyon, "*Adelante, mis amigos!*" Chip Lassiter steered his horse onto a trail angling down the canyon wall, and the yellow-haired girl fell in behind him, and then horseman after horseman—at least twenty cowboys, threading their way downward.

It was all so impressive, so dramatic, that no one seemed to note the incongruity presented by the appearance of the final rider. He was a little man in a big straw hat, riding a mule, and as he came in view he raised *his* hat in salutation, and cried out:

"Call off the war! Solly Marx is here!"

It was the figurehead Mayor of Aveinte.

Jeremy K. Jenkins uttered an exclamation and pointed to something that was happening below. The Chili Queens had been taken. They stood now, hands elevated, facing a single gunman who had crept up and made the capture. It was Albert Apple, the killer from Corpus, and he was holding two revolvers. The last anyone had seen of him, he had been in bed, trying to recover

257

from his ordeal in the big black box. Nobody could say where he came from now, how he got to the canyon, or why he had jumped Kockamaney's private army.

Chip Lassiter and Diana rode into view and with them was another girl, Señorita Blanca, riding beside a smiling Orlando Dill.

Eric walked up to Diana's horse, a look of ineffable wonder on his face.

"You never told me you could ride a horse," he said.

"I can't," she said. "I never have, till today."

She scrambled out of the saddle and Eric promptly wrapped his arms about her and kissed her.

"Any sign of The Tiger?" he then asked.

"No. I'm so worried—I guess you were right. Maybe."

"You've been real heroic," Eric assured her. "For a while there the forces of right and justice were getting real cluttered up. Morgan, please get somebody down below to relieve that man who's captured the motorcycle boys."

Diana, climbing uneasily off her horse, noticed Petticoats glowering at her. "Howdy, higher-up," she said to him. Then to Eric: "Don't overlook Orlando Dill here and his Mexican sweetie. Orlando finally decided he'd had enough of this shabby crowd, and headed for the ranch to tip us off to things that were going on."

"Orlando," said Eric, "if you expect to get involved in the affairs of Banner Enterprises, which is entirely possible, you'd better ride down and see if Hickey Dolbier is . . ."

"He is here!" sounded Dolbier's voice as he came around the big rock, his gutsy sports coat in gutsy tatters.

"Where in hell are the other cars?" Eric demanded, grabbing Dolbier by the shoulder in a gesture of appreciation and affection.

"All fell by the wayside. Apparently they're scattered all over the map. I suspect that they were just slightly lacking in the mature point of view that was needed here."

Now a deep droning sound smote the warm Texas air. All eyes were lifted to the sky as a sleekly beautiful aircraft came barreling over the canyon.

"It's H. Allen Smith!" shouted Eric. The custom-built jet, colored a masculine shade of lavender, swooped and dipped and then vanished in the direction of Aveinte's airstrip.

"By the way, Hickey," Eric resumed, "what on earth ever happened to Simon Horney?"

"Simon went back to the party at the town house," said Dolbier, "and later went out in the back yard to see some fireworks, and fell in the well and was drowned. A short while afterwards, that fellow Desmond Slattery went out in the back yard to look at a nose cone going over, and *he* fell in the well and was drowned. Slattery had a can of his worm-painters with him when he fell in, so you'd better have the well drained when you get home."

"Anybody else fall in the well and drown besides those two?"

"Not to my knowledge."

"At least," observed Eric, "it's a sound technique—Mark Twain used it to good effect and cleared the atmosphere of five or six different characters that he couldn't otherwise get rid of. I'll order the well cleaned out, and perhaps it can be used to good effect at some future date."

Eric now spoke to Morgan Heath and Lunsford Scruggs and had them go with him into the cave, to look into the matter of the secret ingredient, the troublemaking tumescence-factor. As they disappeared, Solly Marx stepped up to Jeremy K. Jenkins.

"Mr. Jenkins," he said, "how would you like to be the new judge of Chivo County? I saw what you did. A veri-tibble Wyatt Yurp. We will at last bringing law and order to Aveinte. As the Mayor, and no more figgahead, I appoint you judge if you want it should be."

"I want it should be," smiled Mr. Jenkins, "if Miss Fowler will release me as her attorney."

"Take charge of the prisoners," said Diana.

"Now," said Mayor Marx, "you are the Law that is quite a ways West of the Law that is West of the Pecos."

"I am honored," said Judge Jenkins. "Mr. Lassiter, please have your men herd all these scamps back to the ranch. That goes for Kockamaney, too, and the *former* Sheriff. Put them all in the big corral for the time being."

And shortly thereafter Chip Lassiter, back in the saddle, had returned to his old self, and was singing, advising the little dogies that they should git along.

Chapter TWENTY-SIX

IN the main living room of the ranch house the roots and seeds and crocks and metates and scales from Petticoats Kockamaney's grubby lab in the cave had been assembled, and Eric was puzzling over the formula as reconstructed by Lunsford Scruggs.

Scruggs himself, now comfortably rid of his role as the garrulous dairy rancher, was doing his best to help. Miss Tiddyboo O'Neill was on a couch gazing rapturously into the eyes of Frankie Deadbird, her Kickapoo Valentino. Orlando Dill and Señorita Tornillo were behaving themselves quite properly—at least the Señorita was keeping her hands to herself—and scattered elsewhere around the big room were most of the others: Hickey Dolbier, flushed with his triumph in getting his Fer-de-lance to the Western Front; Chivo County Judge Jeremy K. Jenkins and Mayor Solly Marx and big Morgan Heath. Diana was sitting off to one side, still deeply concerned over what had happened to The Tiger.

Morgan Heath had just moved up to the long refectory table where Eric and Lunsford were mumbling over their hieroglyphical puzzle, when a man came striding into the room, bare of head, a graceful and attractive man with supple muscles, shirt open at the neck giving him a striking Byronic appearance.

"Eric," he called out in his vibrant voice, "you need another three and a half feet on the town's airstrip. I didn't make it on the first pass."

"H. Allen!" Eric exclaimed. "Sorry you didn't get here a few hours earlier—we had a bit of excitement."

"Clash of arms, eh?" smiled H. Allen Coeur de Lion. "I was delayed in New York. The way people *do* impinge upon a fellow's time! There was that Pulitzer prize affair. Then I had to do some last minute designing on the jackets of my two most recent books."

"Oh? What books are those?"

"One is called *Priscilla of Old Levittown.* A novel of a man's quest for the meaning of life. I knew I'd have to tackle that difficult *leitmotif* some day. The other is a book concerned with spiritual redemption, called *I Was Public Relations Director for a House of Ill Fame.* In this one I think I've achieved what Louie Auchincloss has been striving to get his teeth into."

"I'm sure they'll both be great hits," said Eric.

"Oh, they'll sell like hot cakes, but as you must know, hot cakes futures are depressed at the moment and the market is sluggish. But enough talk of my pamphleteering. I stayed on long enough to accept the Blue Belt of the Mensa group, the so-called High IQ Frat, and gave them a little speech of encouragement. An extremely pleasant lot, Eric, but the poor things don't know quite what to do with themselves."

"Did you fly in alone?"

"Judge Bippus came with me. He's out somewhere, probably searching for charred balsams. I suppose you heard of your man Horney and my old friend Desmond Slattery falling into your well. The papers said that Desmond was looking at astronauts, but I know better; he was out there catching lightning bugs and putting them in a Mason jar."

"He didn't have his worms with him when he splashed down?"

"No. Just the lightning bugs."

Eric now gave H. Allen Smith a quick summary of all that had happened, and explained the presence of the equipment that had been brought down from the cave.

"Let me have a look at this stuff," suggested H. Allen, pushing a wavy brown lock of silky hair back from his tanned brow. "I've had a bit of experience, y'know, in the Black Chamber as well as in the chemical lab."

He spent the next few minutes puzzling over the formula, sifting the seeds about and sniffing at them, then examining the two groups of root vegetation with a magnifying glass, often referring back to the lettering on the paper. At last he straightened up.

"Here it is, Eric," he said. "These fibrous chunks are from the sotol and should be dried and then ground fine in the larger *metate*. They must not touch metal, ever. Nothing in this formula is to be brought in contact with metal. These buttons—they are from the peyote plant, the precursor of LSD, the hallucinogenic growth used by certain tribes of Indians in both Mexico and our own Southwest."

"The little ones," spoke up Doom excitedly, "is the ones I et, Mr. Smith, and man oh man, did I have a dream. These two broads come at me throwin' flars around and ..."

"Doom!" from Eric.

"Six and one-fourth quarts of sotol and three and one-fourth quarts of peyote, all ground to a powder, are put into one of these three-gallon crocks. Next comes three ounces of the safflower heads, or florets, pulverized in a smaller *metate* and added to the crock. Finally, eight ounces of morning glory seed, again pulverized into a fine powder but in a separate *metate*. There it is ..."

Frankie Deadbird detached himself from the loving clutch of Tiddyboo O'Neill and moved up to the table. "Hell's pecker, fellas," he said, "I could have told you all that."

"Well, why the hell didn't you?"

"Because I was working for that fathead Kockamaney, and because I didn't know that such a gorgeous creature as Miss Tiddy-boo O'Neill existed on this earth. Just keep one thing in mind—like this dude here said—grind the stuff in *metates* and don't let it touch metal. Kockamaney tried to work it out for himself, wanted to double-cross us, used a couple of old coffee-grinders to speed up the work. The dumb bastard didn't get nowhere."

"Mr. Deadbird," H. Allen Smith interjected, never offended by the reference to himself as a dude, "that's a most interesting speech pattern. Could it be Kickapoo?"

"Kee-rect!" said Frankie.

"With an overlay of West Texas?"

"You dang tootin'!"

"Tell me, Mr. Deadbird . . . I detect a suggestion of . . . have you ever been associated with jazz musicians?"

"Yay man! Back about ten years ago I worked a while on a ranch up near Elko in Nevaddy, ranch run by ole Bing Crosby, all the hands was trombone players. One uv 'em by the name of Teagarden talked like nobody I ever heard before. Or sence."

"Interesting combination," mused Smith. "And this powder is a very interesting combination. A potent mixture, or I miss my guess. I would say that it induces a feeling of distant serenity, accompanied by some kind of dynamic arousement."

"We've been given to understand," said Eric, "that the dynamic arousement is the thing. In the chili powder game they refer to it as the tumescence-factor."

"Hmmmmmmm," came from H. Allen Smith.

"Eric," put in Tiddyboo, "could my Frankie boy go back to the cave and grind up one of those big crocks full so we can take it and go on down to Mexico and get into that wickiup and have a lot of arousements?"

"Wait a sec," said Frankie Deadbird, grinning, and then, lapsing into store-bought Indian talk, "Kickapoo no more need powder. Kickapoo need only golden blonde squaw with *teta grande*."

"Big tits," H. Allen Smith translated, speaking behind his hand.

Into the room now came the picaresque ramrod of the Bowlared, Chip Lassiter.

"Half mah boys are out on the range," he reported to Eric, "lookin' fuh some trace uh the cat. They grumblin', but Ah don't aim to eat 'em out about it. They accustomed to pursuin' Braymer bulls and squawlin' calfs and ole muley cows. They argy it is

263

onseemly and degradin' to be sent out lookin' for a dang cat. Know what they threatened to do? Th'ow a strike again me. A strike! Make cahdboard signs and picket this very house! Signs sayin' the Bowlared is OnFair to Bronc Stompers and Heel Squatters."

"How'd you finally get them to go?" asked Eric.

"All I done was disscribe how that cat uh yourn banged that bobcat twicet his size, arointed 'er in the big black machine with all the insterments goin' *and* Mistuh Doom in there with 'em, squealin' like a stuck pig. That made it all right. Cowhands a-strikin'! Slap mah war-sack if Ah evuh heard of such a thang!"

"And the prisoners?" asked Eric.

"All in the corral. Some uh mah boys havin' a little spote with Petticoats and that slick ole Cottonmouth Clarke. Hittin' 'em in the jaw, bangin' 'em in the teeth, flattenin' out their ears, little thangs like that. Them two sidewinders been high-and-mighty tords mah boys too long. What you want done with 'em?"

"You got Albert Apple out there?"

"Yup. He's injoyin' hisself, cloutin' that Mistuh Crump in the nose a little. He says Mistuh Crump is a traituh to the sacred land uh his birth, meanin' Corpus Ah reckon."

"We'll head out there shortly," said Eric, just as Judge Ambrose Bippus walked into the room, accompanied by Doom. The Judge was in a holiday mood, happy to be shorn of his weighty tribulations back in New York, and his nose appeared to have lengthened by about half an inch.

"So this is Texas!" the Judge exclaimed, waving a bony hand in a wide arc. "From all I'd heard, I thought it'd be much bigger."

Mayor Solly Marx leaped patriotically to the support of his chosen State's chief quality, inordinate extensiveness. "This here," he said, "ain't all of it. There's a lot more of it, attached onto the sides of this part."

"Find any trace of woodpecker borings, Judge?" asked H. Allen Smith, and his voice had grown even more magnetic. Diana stared at him. So did Tiddyboo. Señorita Tornillo forgot Orlando Dill for the nonce and fastened her eyes on the celebrated writer.

"He's just so superb charisma-wise!" Diana whispered to Tiddyboo.

"You can say *that* again," agreed Miss O'Neill. "He's certainly it, whatever it is."

"Oooooooooooooooooo!" murmured Señorita Tornillo in her soft ecstatic Latin voice. She clasped her face in her hands, afraid to look at this man further.

"No," said Judge Bippus.

"No what?" asked Eric, having somehow lost the thread of things.

"No woodpeckers," explained Judge Bippus. "But they have been telling me about the Texas roadrunner. I saw one, trotting about in the sagebrush. Scrawny, mean-looking bird—reminded me of that rather noisy old cat-journal editor who caused so much trouble at the trial. Tell me, does this roadrunner peck holes in anything?"

"Only in snakes," said Morgan Heath, "and lizards."

The Judge turned his attention to Orlando Dill. "They tell me, counselor," he said pleasantly, "that you've found a gold mine down here."

"Quite true, Judge," smiled the lawyer. "She's right here at my side. Ever see anything this choice in all your life?"

"Not outside of a charred balsam," replied the Judge.

"By the way, Blanca," Orlando said to his companion, "you seem to be the one who started all this gold mine stuff. You said that Frankie Kickapoo here . . ."

The Señorita turned her dark sexy eyes toward the Indian. "When he gave me that tore paper," she said, "he told me it was for the Lost Nigger Gold Mine."

"I did no such thing," responded Frankie. "I told you in plain West Texas overlay that it was something much more valuable than the Lost Nigger Mine."

Hickey Dolbier now got into the conversation. "It begins to sound," he said, "as if you've made a double discovery—the secret ingredient *and*, perhaps, deeper in that cave, the lost gold mine."

"Couldn't be," Morgan Heath observed. "I've had a strong hunch about that gold mine. Got my notions. That Lost Nigger Mine is down in Mexico, about twenty-five mile south of La Linda in the State of Coahuila. Right smack on the side of the mountain they call Pico Entero—as purty a mountain peak as a man ever looked at. Let's get us up a syndicate and go down there and . . ."

"Morgan," said Eric, "why don't we just forget the gold mine. It's as Frankie Deadbird says—what we've got is worth more than all the gold in Fort Knox. I propose that Hickey and Orlando put

265

their heads together and see if we can retain control of the tumescence-factor. We can start turning it out by the trainload."

"Put it in toothpaste," spoke up Diana eagerly. "Put it in drinking water instead of those fluorides. Put it in cigarettes, let people die happy. Put it in Hershey bars and beer and Campbell's soup, marinate steaks in it, sprinkle it on fried chicken, shoot it into watermelons . . ."

"Now, Diana," cautioned Eric, "let's not go overboard—though I must say you're beginning to sound like a person with sound business instincts. Maybe we ought to indulge in a grand gesture and present the secret ingredient to all mankind. Let everybody have it. Let Lunsford's chili powder companies in on it—God knows he worked long enough and hard enough trying to steal it for them."

"Acquire it," Lunsford corrected him, "not steal it. And don't forget that I had to spend those ten years acting the part of a Texas bore—hit plumb woah me out, doan see how these heah Taixuss folks kin keep at it foh a hull dang lafftime."

"That, suh!" came the voice of Chip Lassiter, "is insultin' tuh th' State uh Taixuss an' ain't th' way we'uns talk a-tall."

"Eric," Doom whispered, "I'm sure glad Willy Bodfish ain't down here, exposed to all this ignernt kinda langwidge—my God we'd never be able to learn him nothing."

"Doom," said Eric, "you so dang co-reckt!" He turned to the others. "I foresee the time," he told them, "when we can convert this ranch and a large part of Chivo County into one huge plantation for the production of the tumescence-factor, cultivating . . ."

Frankie Deadbird interrupted. "One thing you may have overlooked," he said, "is that the peyote in Texas is no good any more. What there is of it, has lost all its charisma. The only peyote that'll work is the kind we grow down around Nacimiento. Years ago the stuff was all right around here, but it caught some kind of a sweet potato blight and never was worth a damn after that. Tell you what I could do—I could bring the Kickapoo plants up here, and get 'em started, and I'd be happy to run that end of the business."

"What . . . about . . . that . . . wickiup!" rose the voice of Miss Tiddyboo.

"You can have wickiups all over Texas," said Eric. "We'll cultivate sotol, and bring back strong and healthy peyote to the soil of Texas, and produce vast acres of lovely shining safflowers, and we'll have morning glory vines climbing all over the walls of Sniveling Dog Canyon, and . . ."

"What I'd like to know," Tiddyboo interposed, "is what does a safflower look like?"

"Oily, I imagine," Diana answered.

"Meanwhile," Eric continued, "we've got to do something about that corral full of prisoners."

Doom leaned toward Eric again.

"Boss," he said, "I found that cave for you, didn't I? I suffered and darn near died in this nuthouse Texas on behalf the compn'y, didn' I? I et that stuff that gimme th' technicolored DTs. I got a request to make."

"You did good, Doom," Eric agreed. "Make it."

"That big black box out there by the horse barns. I wanna take this cowboy guy . . ." he motioned toward Chip Lassiter, ". . . and I wanna th'ow th' switch and run him through that box the way he run me through it. Then I wanna run that Petticoats through it oncet, an' then I wanna run him through it again, in case the foist time didn' take."

"Mistuh Doom," said Chip Lassiter, "Ah wanna assuah you that they was nothin' pussonal to it. It was *po*-litical. Ah was in a crazy rage agin th' machine—you jus' happen to come along when Ah was in a tempuh."

"Let's hold it," spoke up Judge Jeremy K. Jenkins. "Judge Bippus, I am about to sit for the first time as County Judge. Would you do me the honor of occupying the bench with me in my first important trial?"

"My pleasure," Judge Bippus responded. "And if you feel so inclined, Judge Jenkins, you may flip your coattails at me from time to time."

"Thank you, your honor," Judge Jenkins responded with a slight bow. "You are indeed a paragon of virtue and wisdom in this somewhat implausible world we inhabit—an ornament to the American bar."

Judge Bippus lowered his head and some of those present thought they detected a single tear trickling down his cheek. The only sound that came from him was a scarcely audible, "Cruck-crick, crick-cruck."

🂠 Chapter TWENTY-SEVEN

BENEATH a shimmering sky on the tough and gritty soil of Texas—God's own footstool—court was summoned to order. The two judges perched side by side on the large flat rock in the shade of the mesquite tree. A Madame Defarge on the sidelines, flashing her needles in the sun, would not have been out of place.

"This is the way we do things in Texas," declared Judge Jeremy K. Jenkins, as if he had been resident in the Lone Star State since the days when the boy Stephen F. Austin was playing at chaw-raw-beef along the creeks of Washington County, Missouri. "Mr. Lassiter," he commanded, "please take your seat at the controls."

"Wait a minute, Judge," called out Doom, almost in a whimper. "He whanged them switches on me. He whanged 'em and he kept whangin' 'em till I thought that awful machine was gonna cut me up into scallopini. Then this other feen outa hell was gonna butcha me like a pig and cook me inta lard and fry his eggs in me. Judge, I ain't been trut right in Texas."

"Just remain calm, Mr. Doom," urged Judge Jenkins. "The lard-rendering matter will be taken care of in due course. As for Mr. Lassiter, he came through when the chips were down. Now, bring out those motorcycle scoundrels, one by one."

There was no taking of testimony. "I, myself, was a witness," observed Judge Jenkins, "and that is sufficient." Each member of the Kockamaney Chili Queens was put through the black box a single time, with three levers thrown. In addition to the overall punching and pummeling and hurling about, they were sprayed for horn flies and ticks, and then inoculated against shipping fever, foot rot, pink eye, malignant edema, anaplasmosis, red water disease and female hormone swarm. This depleted them somewhat, but even greater pleasures were to come.

"Adjust for that hog bristle remover that you told me about, Mr. Lassiter," came the order. Lassiter went to the machine and threw a couple of levers. "Fix it," said Jeremy K. Jenkins, "so that it will only affect them from the neck up." It was so fixed, and the unhappy Chili Queens were sent through again. They came out with their heads and faces covered with a thick coating of a green plaster-of-paris composition, which had been dried instantly by blowers. This gave them a most peculiar aspect, as if they had just arrived by flying saucer. Waiting at the machine's exit gates were two cowboys with ball-peen hammers, which were employed to knock the green masks off, and lo! each Chili Queen was now totally destitute of whiskers, not to mention head hair. Possibly because of the loss of their beards, they were now wailing or weeping or cursing, and some fell to the turf and beat the ground with their fists. One covering phrase could now be used for them —pooped beyond all estimate. Judge Jenkins ordered that they be flown forthwith to Southern California, all transportation costs to be met by the Kockamaney Chili Powder Company.

Albert Apple, a technical defendant, now appeared before the two judges and spoke a heart-rending appeal for clemency. He pointed out that he had already made one trip through the big black box.

"Yonnuh," he said, "that god dang machine tried tuh take off muh oysters. Wore me to a frazzle. To . . . uh . . . frazz . . . *zull!* Judge, Ah nevah kilt nobody except for money. Innybody would do that, Judge, if it was their line uh work."

"Sounds real sensible," Judge Bippus whispered. "I'd like to suggest that these people shouldn't be judged by their own moral standards. Give them the benefit of New York standards. Let him off."

"Mr. Apple," said Judge Jenkins pleasantly, "I witnessed your

269

single-handed capture of those ruffians out in Sniggering Dog Canyon. It was a brave and manly bit of work. If we let you go, will you promise that you will hang up your roscoe and shoot no more people for the rest of your life?"

"Only one, Judge. Don't tell me Ah cain't shoot that polecat ovuh yonda, Ogden Crump. He's th' one got me in this, got me run thoo that god dang machine. Ah jes' *gotta* kill ole Ogg!"

"We'll take care of Ogden Crump," Judge Jenkins promised him. "You go on back to Corpus Christi and spend the waning golden years in some quiet cove, fishing and reading Thoreau and observing the wonders of Nature. No more shooting."

"Oh God!" groaned Albert Apple. "Mah whole life is a dern flop an' a dang failure! But Ah'll do 'er, Judge." He turned and sought out his enemy, still in the corral. "Ogg Crump!" he shouted. "Ah sin-silly hope they th'ow you in this machine an' cut off your tossel clean up to your belly-button. Ah sin-silly do hope it!"

Thus departed from the public arena the greatest Texas gun-slinger of modern times. Thus did the cold-eyed killer of Corpus Christi vanish from the scene. There still were Instant Roundup notches all over him, but there would be no more on his guns.

"Fetch Crump before the bar," Judge Jenkins called out, and the scowling Texan was hustled up from the corral. Eric Yaeger moved over to the rock and held a brief whispered conference with the judges.

"Mr. Crump," said Judge Jenkins, "I think we shall spare you the discomfort of a trip through the machine. Mr. Yaeger has just informed me that your punishment lies ahead. You have always been an ambitious and grasping man, eager to reach the highest peaks in American industry. Now, according to Mr. Yaeger, you could not get a job as a fry cook in an outlying Chock Full o' Nuts."

Ogden Crump snorted disdainfully. "Says Puddin'head Yaeger!" he exclaimed. "Ah'm goin' to work and put him and his whole smelly crowd outa business. As fer that machine yonda, Ah wouldn' be caught daid in it! You know why? Go look at that little ole brass plate on the bottom uh the gate. Know what it says on that little ole brass plate? It says, 'Product uh the Banner Computer Corp-ration.' That means it's no good—it'll break down."

"Watch your tongue, Mr. Crump," warned Judge Jenkins, "or I'll give you a taste of the red lever."

"And you!" Crump said, addressing Eric and ignoring the Judge, "Ah outsmotted mah own Mama on Mama-Promisin'-Time. Ah reckon Ah could outsmott yew, yew po' *ex*-cuse foh a prickelly-paiuh!"

"Ogden," Eric replied, laughing, "don't look now but your Texas accent is feeblin' off."

Crump glared at Eric a moment, then stamped his foot in the manner of a frustrated girl-child, and turned and walked away.

"Where's Muff the Master Spy?" called out Eric.

"He's in the hospital," said Chip Lassiter. "It's his nerves more'n anything else, they tell me. Got 'im on loddinum soze he can sleep. Nuss told me that when he wakes up he allus hollers th' same thing. He hollers, 'Peyote! Oh Lord, and poor grandpa was sartin it was Spanish fly!' Want me to go git 'im?"

"We'll deal with him later," said the Judge. "Bring out the defendant Kockamaney."

Four cowboys hauled Petticoats before the rock bench and he struggled and fought them every inch of the way.

"Just for the purpose of calming the defendant down," the Judge ordered, "run him through just one time. Three levers."

They flung him into the Instant Roundup, the steel doors swung shut, and the machinery began to clank and whirr and swish and clack and slosh. Before long the howls of the chili powder heir were coming from the black box.

"Bran' th' son of a bitch!" came a cry from one of the cowboys, caught up in the general enthusiasm.

"You call *him* a son of a bitch?" demanded another rider of the far range. "W'y, hell's farr, you'd be able to pick him outa a field of twenny-five thousan' sons a bitches withouten no trouble a-tall!"

"This man doesn't appear to be well-liked," Judge Bippus remarked to Judge Jenkins.

Petticoats was a sad spectacle as they led him, walking rubber-legged, back before the court.

"Now, young man," said Judge Jenkins, "you are going to agree to certain procedures that we have worked out for you. We'll have the papers for you to sign later in the day. Firstly . . ."

271

"Ah ain't a-signin' nothin'!" growled Petticoats. "You cain't break th' speerit of uh Kockamaney, you pair uh aig-suckin' ole billy goats!"

"Did you include me in that statement?" demanded Judge Bippus.

"You god dern tootin' Ah did, you long-laiged, pointy-nosed piece uh pig dirdy!"

Judge Bippus, splendid ornament of the American bar, turned quickly to his colleague.

"Judge Jenkins," he said, "I understand that we are close to the home country of the celebrated Judge Roy Bean. I have heard tales about him. He made a great name for himself in the law and in our country's folklore. It is my feeling that you, Judge Jenkins, should get off on the right Beanian foot. Throw the hooks into this lad!"

Judge Jeremy K. Jenkins nodded vigorously, and his round face appeared to glow with anticipation as he faced the prisoner.

"Kockamaney, you dirty dog," he said, "I want to give you a little lecture on how they classify mentally deficient people under the procedures of psychology. The moron stands highest in the ranks. Below him comes the imbecile. A few notches down from the imbecile we have the idiot. That's as far down the ladder as they have gone. You, you sideburn-suckin' low-grade syphilitic son of a bitch, they have not yet got down low enough to give *you* a classification!"

"Capital!" exclaimed Judge Bippus. "What an excellent upbringing you must have had, Judge Jenkins. Sentence the son of a bitch!"

"Back in the box!" Judge Jenkins commanded. "Levers four and five. Hold six in abeyance."

Now they were giving Petticoats the hot sprays warranted to kill all known parasites by chemical action, if not by scalding. Great clouds of steam arose out of the black box but the heavy vapors did not modulate the wild shrieks and howls of the man inside.

"Dump him out," the court finally ordered, and this time they had to drag Petticoats to the bar of justice.

"*Por favor,*" came the voice of Señorita Tornillo, entranced by the sight of her former husband brought to such a condition.

"Will the nice Jodge send heem through one more time jus' for me? Give heem, *por favor*, the cut-off?" Then to Petticoats: "*Nada mas* push up the petticoats!"

Judge Jenkins ruled the Señorita's request to be slightly out of order, and then addressed the prisoner: "You ready to agree?"

"Aroint you!" howled Petticoats from the dust. "Aroint you, and the mule you rode in awn!" He licked his dry lips, thought for a moment, then added, "What you want Ah should agree to?"

"The court," said Judge Jenkins, "will award the Kockamaney Motel to Mayor Marx and he will have the privilege of operating it as a legitimate enterprise—I'm sure he'll be able to make a paying proposition out of it. Then, if Mr. Heath will accept appointment as Sheriff of Chivo County, he will take title to the bar and gambling casino now known as the Sheriff's Office."

"Nevuh!" gasped Petticoats.

"Back to the box!" ordered the Judge. "And bring out the former Sheriff, the one they call Cottonface, the sworn enemy of the legal profession. Put the two of them in together. Mr. Lassiter, kindly give them first the icy spray, then flood them with hot bug-killer, followed by the Bowlared brand, and after that . . ."

"Off with them thangs?" asked Chip Lassiter eagerly.

"Off with them thangs!" echoed Judge Jenkins.

"Wait!" cried Cottonmouth Clarke as they dragged him toward the mechanized oubliette. "Don't do this to me! I have a story to tell about this scurvy dog Kockamaney, a story involving his . . ."

"Ah'll sign!" yelled Petticoats. "Git th' papuhs ready! Ah'll sign 'em! Hesh up, Cottonmouth!"

"Sign the papers," Cottonmouth told him. "Sign the papers and agree to everything they say, or I'll tell the truth about your Mama and all those hats . . . I'll tell who the hats belonged to and . . ."

"Git th' papuhs ready!" Petticoats screamed.

"Both of you," said Judge Jenkins, "will be compelled to surrender anything and everything you own in this county, and you'll be exiled from the county, forever and a day."

"To run consecutively," put in Judge Bippus.

"And now," Judge Jenkins addressed the assembled company, "I would suggest that we organize a party to celebrate the coming of law and order to Chivo County—a good old square dance, with fiddles and mandolins, and maybe some hard cider and . . ."

"Bobbbbbb-cat a-comin'!"

The cry sounded near the stable and the words were still rolling across the desert sands when a Texas wildcat came skidding into view, a look of terror on its face. It hit the open space in front of the improvised judges' bench, sprawled to a halt, took a quick look backward over its shoulder, and then shot like a bullet into the bushes. At the same instant another animal came flying onto the scene.

"Tiger!" cried Diana.

The smoke-yellow son of Rhubarb spied the big black box and came to an abrupt stop. One glance was sufficient. He remembered. He turned his handsome head and looked appealingly at Diana. But instead of leaping into her arms, he whirled and sped back around the corner of the stable, racing toward the ranch house.

"Get that hoe-down organized!" Eric yelled, and taking Diana's hand, went in pursuit of The Tiger.

There was no sign of him up ahead, but within a few minutes they found him. He was in Diana's room, pawing gently at the ragged strip of red leash that had come from a dressmaker's shop on Calle Fortaleza in Old San Juan.

"I told you he'd come back to me," said Diana. Eric was tempted. He could have said that The Tiger came back to the crummy red rag. He put his arm around her. "Of course you did," he said. "You were right all along. You'll always be right."

She kissed him.

"That lovely, shimmering, beautiful red rag," he said, "makes me think of Puerto Rico. Tell you what. Let me order the *Thaddeus* down from New York, and we'll pick her up at Galveston, and go to San Juan and . . ."

"Oh, excuse me!" came a voice and they both turned. It was Judge Bippus. "Just wanted to let you know," he said, "that there's one more adjudication to be made before we adjourn court. You two don't need any further test period. I hereby ordain that the custody of the cat known as The Tiger, son of the cat Rhubarb, deceased, be given jointly to Miss Diana Fowler and Mr. Eric Yaeger."

"Thanks, Judge," said Eric. "Would you care to join us on a cruise to Puerto Rico?"

"Can't make it, sorry to say. Back to the New York salt mines."

When he was gone, Diana squeezed Eric's arm and gave him her crinkly little girlish grin.

"I will," she said, "on one consideration."

"You will what?"

"Uh . . . uh . . . I'll be happy to join you in . . . in a stack of wheats."

"And what's the one consideration?"

"That when we dock in Old San Juan, we take The Tiger off the ship and carry him over to The Street of Cats, and turn him loose—just for one night. He's entitled to a real quiet sort of . . ."

"You're not serious?"

"Remember, dear," she said, "he always comes back to Diana— or at least to the shimmering ole red rag."

"You win," he said, and put both arms around her, and they looked over at their multimillionaire cat. He had fallen asleep on the old red rag and if anyone had bothered to look at him closely —which nobody did—it would have been discovered that he was sleeping with a grin on his face. They was sho wearin' on a body, them Taixuss wahl cats, but they was fun!